CW00833224

Good Girls Don't Drink Vodka

C.A. Larmer is a journalist, editor, indie publisher and the author of multiple crime series, two stand-alone novels and a non-fiction book about pioneering surveyors in Papua New Guinea. Christina grew up in that country, was educated in Australia, and spent many years working in London, Los Angeles and New York. She now lives with her musician husband, two sons and cheeky Blue Heeler on the east coast of Australia.

Sign up to her newsletter: www.calarmer.com

ALSO BY C.A. LARMER

The Sleuths of Last Resort
Blind Men Don't Dial Zero (Book 1)
Smart Girls Don't Trust Strangers (Book 2)

The Murder Mystery Book Club
The Murder Mystery Book Club (Book 1)
Danger on the SS Orient (Book 2)
Death Under the Stars (Book 3)
When There Were 9 (Book 4)

The Ghostwriter Mystery Series
Killer Twist (Book 1)
A Plot to Die For (Book 2)
Last Writes (Book 3)
Dying Words (Book 4)
Words Can Kill (Book 5)
A Note Before Dying (Book 6)
Without a Word (Book 7)

The Posthumous Mystery Series
Do Not Go Gentle
Do Not Go Alone

Plus:
After the Ferry: A Gripping Psychological Thriller

An Island Lost

A Measure of Papua New Guinea:
The Arman Larmer Surveys Story (Focus; 2008)

C.A. LARMER

Good Girls Don't Drink Vodka

Sleuths of Last Resort
(Book 3)

LARMER MEDIA

Copyright © 2022 Larmer Media

All rights reserved, including the right to reproduce this book, or portions thereof, in any form without written permission except for the use of brief quotations embodied in critical articles and reviews.

This is a work of fiction. Names, characters, places and incidents are either the product of the author's imagination or are used fictitiously, and any resemblance to actual persons, living or dead, business establishments, events or locales is entirely coincidental.

Published by Larmer Media
Northern Rivers, NSW 2482
Australia

www.calarmer.com

Paperback ISBN: 978-0-6452835-6-3

Cover design by Nimo Pyle
Cover photography by uatp2 from iStock

Edited by The Editing Pen
& Elaine Rivers, with thanks

For good girls, and bad
And the freedom to be whomever you wish to be

A NOTE FROM THE AUTHOR

I first conjured up this series after a delightful conversation with an agent in the UK who loved my *Murder Mystery Book Club* (formerly the *Agatha Christie Book Club*) but wanted to know—as agents often do—what else I had in my kit bag. Could I create something similar but anew? As my thinking cap went on, my two sons, then still in their teens, were mad about the *Marvel* movies, and that really sparked my "leetle grey cells".

Why not create a team of "supersleuths"?

I didn't want my amateur detectives to have *actual* superpowers, because it's so much harder for real people with real bodies, fears and foibles to triumph, don't you think? But I did want them each to bring something special to the group, and it all started with my bumbling, seemingly clueless Clue/do champ Merry (no points for guessing my favourite boardgame).

I've enjoyed creating this eclectic team and lobbing impossible mysteries—and personal obstacles—at them and seeing how well they fare. It won't be the final in the series but it does resolve a trilogy of mysteries that I set in place from the very first sentence.

Which is why I recommend reading this series in order. While each book can be enjoyed as a stand-alone *whodunit*, this third story contains spoilers for the first two—*Blind Men Don't Dial Zero* (Book 1) and *Smart Girls Don't Trust Strangers* (Book 2). If you have picked this one up inadvertently, might I suggest you pop it aside and check those out first? Not only do they introduce the characters, but each book contains glittering nuggets that will help you solve the mystery at the heart of this one—if you've got your hardhat handy and know how to mine for clues, that is!

Happy reading everyone, and thanks for embracing my supersleuths, flaws and all.

xo Christina

PROLOGUE

The woman's body was a kite, let loose in the breeze, her hair its flapping tail as she swooped towards the sea. Above her the moon was just a sliver, the night air brisk, but she didn't feel a thing.

All that lovely vodka made sure of that.

She giggled as she tripped along the sand, sniggered as she peeled off her faux-fur jacket and everything underneath, gasped as she plunged into the dark, swirling surf.

Then she gasped again as someone slipped in beside her.

"Thought I'd scared you off," she said, her words tumbling into each other like the waves. "Thought you still hated me after what I done."

"Not a chance," came the smooth reply, one hand reaching out to fondle that hair. "But you were very naughty, weren't you?"

She giggled like a schoolgirl, yet her old friend wasn't smiling.

"I don't hate you. You need to know that. This is not personal."

"Hmm?" she said, splashing about, not understanding.

"I mean, if you'd just shut those luscious lips of yours, none of this would be happening."

A snort now. "What are you on ab—"

She didn't get to finish that sentence. The woman's hair was now being pulled down and under, her mouth fast filling with water. Too shocked to comprehend at first—*this was a joke, right? Surely it was a joke?*—she tried to play cool, tried to be patient, but her lungs were exploding.

Then the panic took hold.

First she tried to scramble to her feet, but the sea floor had mysteriously vanished. Then she tried reaching out, scratching and clawing, grappling for something, *anything*, to pull herself back up, and she *did* pull herself up for one gloriously brief—*oh too brief!*—moment before she was yanked back down and under.

Her body was now an anchor. Her hair was its chain, and

1

she could not cut it free.

If she hadn't consumed quite so much booze she might have been able to fight back, but she was beyond fighting, and they both knew it.

Her fate had been sealed with too many free shots of Russia's finest.

It didn't take long for the woman's struggle to be over. Just another minute of desperate clawing before she let out a final, acquiescent bubble. Another minute or so before the chain was released and she returned to the surface.

Her body was a kite again, waterlogged and floating out to sea...

CHAPTER 1 ~
AN ARRESTING FUNERAL

The old man's funeral should not have presented any surprises. Or detectives wielding handcuffs for that matter.

Sir George Burlington was just shy of ninety, after all, and had been fading fast for months. Ever since his family had successfully obliterated themselves in a night of blood-soaked horror, the mining magnate had all but given up.

Or so people thought.

"Who'd want to live after everything he's been through?" said some.

"Who could blame him for holding up the white flag?" added others.

But one detective decided there had been no white flag, someone was to blame, and it wasn't the mining magnate himself. Or his psychotic family.

And so, as the funeral procession wound its way towards him down the mossy-green hillside away from Mr Burlington's overpriced coffin with its underweight corpse and staggering collection of roses that had been tossed in behind it like final exclamation marks, the detective knew it wasn't the final word at all.

There were more exclamations to come.

Holding his breath and his place on the path, Detective Inspector Andrew Morgan locked eyes with his old adversary, Earle Fitzgerald. The one-time head of the homicide division was trailing the official party, his fellow sleuths like a superhero cape around him. More like the lunatic fringe, Morgan thought, as he watched Earle's eyes kick-start with surprise upon seeing him. Then something else— was that anxiety? Fear, perhaps?

The retired copper *should* be fearful, Morgan decided, befriending a murderer like they were kin.

3

It was only as the official mourning party approached—what few of them remained—that Morgan allowed himself a smile. He would enjoy taking down Earle as much as the suspect.

Then he relaxed his lips—no need to be unprofessional—and furrowed his brow and prepared to say what needed to be said before the evidence was concealed beneath the worm-infested earth up yonder.

Calling out the suspect's name first, Morgan watched as the entire procession stopped and looked towards him, the suspect with a blasé *What on earth are you doing here?* smile.

The smile would be fleeting.

"I'd like to inform you," Morgan continued, "that you are under arrest for suspicion of the murder of George Thomas Burlington." Then, pausing for the inevitable gasps, he added, "I must caution that you are not obliged to say or do anything unless you wish to do so, but whatever you say or do may be used as evidence against you..."

He recited the caution while the suspect stood blinking back at him, speechless with surprise. What wasn't surprising was how quickly those blinking eyes turned Earle's way and how quickly Earle and his loonies stepped forward to envelope her in their cape.

But DI Morgan knew this was one case the so-called Sleuths of Last Resort could not derail. *He* was the head of Homicide now, his evidence was all lined up, and there was only so much a bunch of motley amateurs could do to keep a guilty woman from her fate.

Even one as lovely as Verity Vine, Sir George's proficient personal assistant.

Deadly proficient, as it turns out.

CHAPTER 2 ~
ONE WEEK EARLIER:
A SAD INVITATION

Kila Morea wanted nothing more than to reach across the table and smack the serene smile from the younger man's face. But he couldn't do that.

At least, not yet.

He was there to get answers from the monster who had slaughtered his sister four years ago, and not even his constantly beeping phone would distract him. Verity and her boss could bloody well wait.

"You want to get that?" someone said. Dragon Malone. Like he was calling the shots.

Kila ignored him—resetting the scales—and dragged a seat out noisily, never losing contact with the monster's eyes. Because he was a monster, no doubt about that. He might look benign, all freshly scrubbed in his prison greens, sitting like a shiny bauble in the middle of the private visitors room, but Dragon Malone was still a fire-breathing monster.

Had still torched Chili's life one horrendous night. And Kila's along with it.

The prickly private eye sat down slowly, crossed his legs over, then his arms.

It was not a defensive pose, and Dragon knew it. He met Kila's blazing stare from across the table and said, "Thanks for finally agreeing to see me."

"I'm not here for you, Dragon. I'm here for my sister."

He nodded once and said, "It's Deaglan."

"What?"

"It's Deaglan Malone now. I don't use Dragon anymore."

Kila twitched. "Don't give a shit, *Dragon*. Get on with it."

The man exchanged a look with the two guards by the door, and that's when Kila realised one of them wasn't a guard at all. He was in civilian clothing and was clutching something in his hand. Was it a *bible*?

Dragon cleared his throat. Swallowed. Said, "I need to tell you the truth about what happened to—"

"Don't you say her name," Kila growled, arms unfolding, reaching for the desk. "Don't you bloody dare."

The guard stepped forward, and Kila folded his arms again, lowered his voice. "You don't get to say her name. Not after what you did to her. And why should I believe a word that comes out of your lying mouth anyway?"

Dragon looked almost impatient then. "Believe what you want, Kila. But I'm speaking my truth to you today."

"Your *truth*?" Kila glanced back at the civilian by the door. Shook his head, incredulous. "So *that's* what this is about. Turned spiritual in here have you? Found God? Spent time with a priest or hippy psychotherapist that my taxes pay for?" He blew a puff of air up towards his black, tangled fringe and went to stand. "Haven't got time for this shit."

"I let her go."

And there they were again. Those four little words that had shaken his life to the core three months earlier and brought him to this cretin's door. He hated himself for being here—had organised then canned the visit multiple times before—but he could no longer ignore those words:

I let her go.

Until recently, Kila was convinced Dragon Malone had taken Chili's life. The cretin had never admitted guilt in any shape or form. Never even admitted meeting his sister. Said they'd flirted online over Tinder and then she'd stood him up on their date.

Now he was changing his story. Or trying to.

Dragon leaned back in his chair. He knew the gravity of his words, but he had a mantra to repeat. "I need to speak my truth today. I need to accept my part in the story. It's my only chance of redemption."

"*Redemption?*" Kila roared suddenly, leaning forward at the same moment as the guard. This time he drew a few deep breaths before holding up a placatory palm, eyes locked to the man at the table.

Dragon Malone. Deaglan. A name change wasn't going to change the fact he was a vicious reptile.

"Yes," the man said. "I did..." A gulp. "I did meet your sister that night."

"*Meet?* Is that what they call rape in here?" Kila's voice was a deep, low rumble.

Dragon closed his eyes. "Okay... I... I hurt her. I admit that." Eyes flitting open, he quickly glanced at the man by the door, then leaned back like the PI might rip out his throat.

And Kila would have, too, if it wasn't for the aforementioned guard and the man beside him and the other one behind the door. The extra security was not for Dragon, and everybody knew it.

Kila swallowed his fury like he was swallowing razors and said, "Go on."

"I didn't mean to hurt—"

"Nope. You don't get to make excuses either. There are none. Get on with it."

Dragon nodded. "Yes, okay. Do you want me to tell you what I did—?"

Another stop sign with his palm. Four years ago, Kila thought he wanted to know. *Needed* to know. Now he knew it would send him over the edge. Ignorance, it turns out, was bliss. That and a shit ton of lager.

"Just get to the point, dickhead. So you hurt her and then, what, you just let her waltz away?"

"She wasn't waltzing, but... yes, Kila. I promise you. She was alive when she left me. I dropped her back exactly where I found her, just before midnight. And she was *alive.*"

"So how'd she end up in a laneway not breathing?"

As always, Kila could never use the word *dead* in relation to his sister, and he never would. She was still alive to him in every photo he'd framed and every dream he had and every time he placed an order at a bar and added a lemon squash that remained untouched beside it.

And now this bastard was saying she was still breathing after everything he'd done to her?

Dragon leaned forward. "I don't know how it happened. See? That's what I'm trying to tell you. I need to own up to what I done, yeah? Speak my truth, Kila. I didn't kill her, and I didn't put anything

7

in her drink. The truth is I like them sober."

Kila's eyes turned thunderous. There was so much to hate about that comment, but it didn't make any sense. Somehow he managed to hold himself back. "You're still lying, fuckhead. My sister was tanked. Loaded to the eyeballs with vodka. She didn't drink alcohol, never touched the stuff. You forced it down her throat."

The inmate shook his head. "Didn't come from me. I'm telling you my truth now. That's all I can speak. Now you need to find *her* truth. I promise you this, it had nothing to do with me."

"Nothing?" Kila was on his feet again, reaching across the table. "You started this nightmare, you fucker!"

And now he did try to smash that smug smile into oblivion as the guards scrambled to pull Kila away. But as he railed and thrust and smashed and roared, deep down, Kila knew the monster was telling the truth.

He had come here for closure, but instead, his sister's case had been cracked wide open, and the wound was once again alive.

And killing him.

~

Meredith Kean was clinging onto an oversized cushion, trying not to look at Dougie's closed right-hand fist, when she heard the first beep. She leapt upon her mobile phone like it was an emergency beacon.

"Everything okay?" This was Dougie, and he was not referring to the text message she was now reading from her screen.

Merry's boyfriend could see how tightly she was clutching that cushion, how she held it like a plate of armour in front of her belly. It made him frown behind his round Harry Potter-style glasses.

"It's Verity," Merry said quickly, scrolling through the incoming message from a woman she had come to know well in the previous nine months. "You know, Sir George's personal assistant? Could be another case—" She stopped short. Blinked. Scrolled rapidly down. "Oh no. Oh dear. How sad."

Dougie didn't ask anything else, just sat back and waited. He was patient like that. Behind her own pink spectacles, Merry's eyes morphed from relief to something else entirely. Angst perhaps?

"Poor Sir George," she said eventually, finally meeting his gaze. Then when he didn't appear to comprehend, she added, "Verity's boss. The wealthy old guy who brought us sleuths together."

"That's right," he said as she nodded sadly, her eyes now two shimmering puddles.

"The darling man has just passed away. Verity says his heart finally gave up, and who can blame him, hey? After the tragedies he's endured."

Then the tears began to plop onto her plump cheeks and her lower lip began to quiver, and Dougie moved closer to console her, wrapping his left arm around her protectively while he thrust his right fist deep into his jacket pocket, dropping the tiny velvet box safely back inside.

She had bigger things on her mind now. His proposal would have to wait.

~

Martin Chase was trying very hard to keep an open mind, but the moment he set eyes on his father, perched at the bar of O'Reilly's Hotel, he wanted to bolt. Once he wanted to punch him, then he wanted to question him, now he knew he was not up to either task, even a man old enough to be his grandfather. So fleeing seemed like a smarter option, especially after just reading Verity's text message, and he was nothing if not smart.

Except, was he so smart? Really? Martin had spent his whole life thinking of Glenn Wicks as a violent monster, an antagonist at best, and only recently been told by his mother he had that terribly wrong. In fact, according to Olivia, his father was a hero. Had saved *her* from a life of violence. Turns out *Glenn* was the protagonist.

The world-famous crime writer had not seen that one coming. Nor was he able to picture it as he watched him now from behind a dusty plastic frond on one side of the bistro.

His dad was clearly with an old mate. They were chugging back schooners of something, barely conversing, comfortable in each other's company. What did that feel like? Martin wondered. He'd never felt that kind of comfort with anybody, certainly not his parents.

His dad had aged considerably since the last time Martin saw him on that rusty boat, the day he'd accused him of assaulting his mother who was just sixteen when she fell pregnant—the day he got two black eyes and a broken nose for that comment—but then he would be old. He was old when Martin was born. Just turned forty. Must be into his mid-eighties now.

Glenn was skinny, sinewy, with the plop of a beer belly, receding grey hair and a smattering of tattoos. Hardly a heroic-looking figure. Hardly worthy of a book, let alone as the central figure. Even with Martin's vivid imagination, it was a step too far.

And so he fiercely stroked his reconstructed nose and stepped away—from his ageing father and this dingy pub and a life he could not face—and returned to his car to reply to Verity and immerse himself in somebody else's life again.

~

Frankie Jo finished reading Verity's text, then dropped her phone back on its charger. Yes, it was terribly sad and all, but there was nothing particularly surprising about Sir George's passing, and she didn't have time to process it anyway. She was on a stakeout, felt a little like Kila as she sat slumped in her car seat. Except she was ten years younger, half his size, a damn site prettier (thank you very much) and encased in a conspicuous blood-red Audi.

Might as well have been waving a flare.

All it would take was one glance across the road for her target to spot her. She almost wished Jan would. It had taken some time to track down her nemesis, some courage to watch her, even from this distance. But as she watched Jan sweeping between shops, long, frizzy hair flowing, bulging calico bag slung over one shoulder, Frankie's courage suddenly evaporated.

Jesus, woman! she told herself. Get a grip! You were once Australia's top crime reporter. You've interviewed drug lords and gang leaders, serial killers and rapists! Jan is your oldest friend. Just speak to her.

And yet Frankie couldn't even reach for her door handle.

It felt safer to keep the distance she had enforced last summer. The distance that Jan had found so intolerable, so worthy of punishing, that she had destroyed Frankie's life in response—stalking her for months, then detonating her career. But that would be nothing if Jan released the real dirt on Frankie. Broadcast the fact that the great crime crusader had really committed a crime of her own, breaking her journalistic code and pushing a man to suicide. She'd scored Australia's highest media accolade for that behaviour, but it would all be gone if the truth ever came out.

Frankie didn't want the truth to come out.

She just wanted to ask Jan for a ceasefire.

If only she could find the courage to get out of her car.

When Jan vanished into a deli, Frankie swept blond locks from her pretty face and conceded defeat. Perhaps another day. If she could find her spine. She buckled herself back in, resparked the engine, and began to drive away, but as she did so, she noticed another message come through from Verity.

Hang on a minute... that wasn't Verity's number. Snatching glances at her phone as she steered through traffic, Frankie could see the number was unfamiliar, but she could read the full text, and it sent a shot of fresh adrenaline down her spine.

"Gutless as always, Frankie," came the message, followed by a laughing emoji and signed "The Boss".

Turns out Jan had noticed Frankie's flare and set off one of her own.

The war was still raging.

~

Earle Fitzgerald leaned back in his seat, stroking his Santa Claus-style beard, also in stakeout mode. Sort of. He was watching a man keenly, a man who was so lost in his own world Earle could have let off a series of flares right beside him, and he probably wouldn't have noticed.

He was mumbling to himself as he rifled through a dripping garbage bin just outside Wynyard train station, his baggy clothes a dark, oily brown. You could almost smell him from across the street.

Earle felt his heart drop. Not so much for the man he'd never met, although he always had a soft spot for the homeless, but for Fiona, his daughter's partner. Or ex-partner, he should say, because Tess and Fiona had not spoken more than a few sentences since their own daughter was born.

No, since *before* that, when Fiona realised this old street bum was actually her dad, a man she hadn't seen since she was a teenager. It had caused the rift between them. Fiona refusing to have anything to do with her father, Tess unable to comprehend life with a woman who could be so "heartless and unforgiving".

But Earle knew it was more complex than that. Told Tess it didn't matter, she needed to let it go, be a little less "heartless and unforgiving" herself. As you can imagine, that went down like a lump of cement, especially with the missus.

But they had a kid together now, Tess and Fiona, and it was probably the last kid Tess would have. She was in her forties, after all. It was time to patch things up. And so here he was, scoping out the old guy, seeing if there might be a way through.

A way for two stubborn women to come back to each other.

Truth was, Earle couldn't understand his daughter's relationship— it was beyond an old-timer like him—but he knew there was genuine love there and now a gorgeous daughter. Little Saffron Fitzgerald-Mottson. They needed to shake it off, for Saffie.

The problem was, he could not. So here he was, staking out a stranger, wondering how to approach. He was just opening his car door when his mobile phone sang out.

Glancing down at it, he could see it was a text message from Verity. A very long one. He sat back and slowly read the words, felt a stab of sympathy for old Sir George—a man with so many homes it was obscene yet as miserable as a derelict and equally lonely.

"I'm organising the funeral now," Verity had typed towards the end of the text, "and would love you all to be there. George had such a soft spot for you supersleuths, and I could also do with your support."

Oh, how prophetic those words would become.

CHAPTER 3 ~
ONE WEEK LATER:
AN AWKWARD WAKE

Sir George Burlington's funeral was not at all how Verity had planned it. She wasn't there for a start—that dastardly detective Morgan!—and her absence was like the maid of honour missing from the wedding. Oh, who was Merry kidding? It was like the entire bridal party had gone AWOL, such was Verity's presence in the old man's life. Or at least that's how it felt to the middle-aged mum, who couldn't perceive of the mineral baron's wake without his formidable personal assistant present and pulling it off with aplomb.

Verity Vine had been so much more to Sir George than his personal assistant. She had been his chief cook and nursemaid in those final months, as busy taking memos as she was overseeing his medication. Was with him every day from dawn to dusk, pushing him forward, keeping him on track. Keeping his heart pumping.

And now she was being accused of stilling that heart? Not a chance, Merry thought. Just could not believe it.

The rest of the mourners seemed lost in disbelief as well.

No sooner had Detective Inspector Morgan cuffed Verity's wrists so ceremoniously in front of all of them, then hauled her away happily—because he had looked inappropriately delighted—the crowd stood around, aghast. Mute and immobile.

Until the priest, bless him, had clapped them all to their senses and insisted they celebrate the old man's life regardless of the "melodrama" and ushered them on to the wake, which was being held at George's final home, Seagrave.

A gaudy mega-mansion perched at the top of a rugged cliff, it made for a dramatic last setting for a man whose life had been equally dramatic.

Born into enormous wealth, his father a successful mining

13

prospector, George had proven even more adept, especially at the business end, and quickly turned an impressive fortune into a multi-billion-dollar enterprise. But as the wealth built up, the family began to crumble. George lost his first wife to an even richer Greek tycoon and then his second wife to a fall from a cliff just two years after moving in to Seagrave. But nothing compared to the drama a year and a half ago when George's daughter, Susan, now in her forties, turned postal.

But that didn't bear thinking about…

And so here they were, a motley crew of mourners, sixty in all, scattered around the mansion's Yellow Room, each clutching whisky tumblers or cups of tea and staring at one another blankly, some whispering through clenched teeth, others stunned into silence, biding their time until they could politely escape the drama.

All except for the sleuths, of course, who were revelling in it.

"I can't believe the old guy was murdered," said Martin, stroking his nose softly as they perched on matching leather stools around the living room bar (they were all in the whisky camp). "And by her trusty personal assistant, no less. That's a plot twist even I couldn't have conjured up."

"That's because it didn't happen." Merry hissed at the author, her pink spectacles slipping down her nose. "Verity didn't kill Sir George. That's ridiculous. We need to prove her innocence. Clear the poor woman's name."

"I think we should talk to her first," said Frankie, adjusting her Hermès scarf. "In case, in fact, she *did* kill old George."

"You cannot truly believe that!" said Merry.

"Still, it's an important question to ask," agreed Earle.

And the ex-copper had a point.

Soon after being slapped into the cuffs, they had expected Verity to scream out and beg the team to save her, just as she had implored them to help twice before. Instead, she'd given them a look that still sent shudders through Merry's body. Verity had seemed, well, *resigned* to her fate. Guilty almost. And Earle had obviously clocked it too.

"I want to hear Verity tell me she didn't do this thing, and then we can take it from there," he said. "But that's not going to happen in a hurry. They've only just arrested her, so first she'll be questioned, then they have to formally charge her, if indeed they do, and after all that, they may refuse her bail, in which case she could be held in custody for some time. If she's a smart cookie, she'll demand a lawyer first, and that will slow it all down further."

"Oh, she's a smart cookie," said Frankie.

He nodded, scratched his shaggy white beard. "DI Morgan is supposed to interview her in a reasonable amount of time, but if I know Morgan, and you know I do, he'll string it out for as long as he can. I really need to get down to homicide headquarters before they all knock off for the weekend." He looked around the room. "I'll do a respectable stint here, then I'll mosey on over."

"Say hi from me," said Kila, or slurred it really, as he leaned against the bar, only half listening as he stared through tangled curls at his whisky.

Merry noticed the gumshoe's dark curls were particularly unruly today, his shirt especially creased, and he had what looked like a fresh drink in one hand. Decided it wasn't such a bad day to get drunk and held her half-empty glass out to the barman to refill.

"I don't care what Morgan has to say, Verity didn't do it," Merry said. "I know that in my bones."

"Are these the same bones that once accused Verity of bumping off half her boss's family in the name of loyalty?" said Martin.

Merry stared back at him. There was nothing unruly or uncreased about Martin. His dyed brown hair was neatly slicked back, a stiff grey dinner shirt replacing his usual statement T-shirt, and thank goodness for that! After all, what could it possibly say at a time like this? LIFE'S A BITCH! Or maybe: THAT'S ALL, FOLKS?

"That was *before*," said Merry, and they all knew what she meant.

Before they had got to know Verity.

Before they had come to like her. Trust her. Want her to be innocent.

"I'm all for helping Verity," said Frankie, tapping manicured nails against her crystal tumbler, "but can we really afford to? I hate to sound like the devil's advocate here—"

"*Bullshit*," Kila mumbled, pretending to cough at the same time.

For her part, Frankie pretended she hadn't heard that. "But can she afford to hire us at the moment? That is the question."

"She must've been on a decent salary, working for Sir George," said Merry.

"Yes, and she'll need every cent of it to pay for a decent defence. What we need right now is a paying client. Our first priority has to be the agency, and you know how desperate we are."

"You guys are desperate?" said Martin, sipping his Scotch.

The sleuths had set up their own detective agency three months earlier, and Martin had not joined them, nor had Kila. This left Merry, Frankie and Earle, who were now swapping worried glances amongst each other.

"The Sleuths of Last Resort are not desperate, no," said Earle. "We just haven't got any future work lined up as of yet."

"But we will!" said Merry. "I can feel it in my—"

"Don't say *bones*," said Frankie. "Your bones cannot be trusted! Listen, put Verity on the back burner for now. I think I have a client for us." She glanced around and then leaned in. "Remember the Kings Cross laneway murder I was working on before I stepped down from the *Herald*?"

"*Stepped down?*" scoffed Kila. "Is that what we're calling it?" Then he coughed/cursed again.

This time Frankie offered him a scowl.

"Yeah, I remember the story," said Earle. "Dodgy ex-con knifed while out on parole by his equally dodgy mate for no good reason."

"The ex-con's name was Phillip Weaver, and there were five thousand good reasons," said Frankie. She waved a hand in the air like it did not matter. "Look, Weaver's sister approached me. Loved my articles." Another scowl towards Kila. "She believes there's more to her brother's murder. Thinks the cops have the wrong guy in jail. She wants to hire us to investigate it further."

Merry's nose crinkled as she chewed on one thumbnail. "It doesn't really fit the protocol though, does it? We only take on cases of the truly needy, remember? That's what we said."

"She is needy. Her brother's been murdered, and an innocent guy's been locked away."

"Innocent?" said Earle. "They always say that."

"Well, I, for one, believe him. Or for two, because Weaver's sister, Tiffany, does as well. Look, I've been thinking, and perhaps we need to broaden our business plan. We have to take this case. We really need the cash flow."

"But Verity needs us now," said Merry.

"Verity could very well be guilty, Merry. And who knows if she can afford us? Tiffany is offering to pay us up front. Immediately. We have to think of our new business."

"But we wouldn't have the business if it wasn't for Verity," Merry persisted. "She introduced us all, remember? She's the one who brought us together."

"Not strictly speaking she didn't," said Martin, signalling for a food tray. "Sir George did that. Verity was just following his orders. We'd be betraying him if we defended Verity. Besides, she could be guilty."

"Shhh!" hissed Merry as a waitress appeared with a platter of fig and prosciutto crostinis. "These look delish!" she told the young woman. "You guys are doing such a stellar job."

The waitress smiled like she needed to hear that and moved away, so Merry turned back to Martin, her voice low. "Guys, can we discuss all of this later? It's not really the time or place. Besides, if Verity did want to... well, you know? She'd pull it off without anyone ever finding out. She's that good. But she wouldn't do it in the first place."

"Well, somebody did it," said Martin. "There must be a few people in this room with a motive to kill. You don't make that kind of wealth without breaking a few friendships."

Then his gaze flitted around the room, the others' following.

Most of the mourners here were elderly, all overdressed in black couture, designer watches, receding hairstyles... All except for a stressed-out twenty-something in an ill-fitting maroon skirt suit and a bright young spark in a dainty red dress who was holding court in the centre of the room.

"Or we could just focus on the obvious suspect," said Frankie, her eyes now settling on the spark in red.

It was Charlotte Burlington-Brown. Sir George's teenage granddaughter. The sleuths had met Charlotte—Charlie—nine months ago, during their first investigation, and knew she adored her "Gramps", but they also knew she would have motive aplenty. Several billion dollars' worth in fact. After all, she was his only surviving heir (because you couldn't count Sir George's daughter Susan, who was currently serving fifteen to twenty years in a federal penitentiary).

"Oh, don't be so silly!" squeaked Merry again. "She was 16,000 kilometres away in London! She's only just back for the funeral. She has an ironclad alibi!"

"If it's anything like her last alibi," said Frankie, "it's not worth the cost of that cheap, high-street dress she's wearing."

Frankie's eyes narrowed as she studied the now seventeen-year-old across the room. Why was the heir to a billion smackeroos wearing such a cheap frock at such an important event? It was straight from the racks of a fast-fashion label; she'd almost bought the same dress herself (oh they really needed to make more money!). Had Gramps cut off the purse strings? Was that why she'd killed him? Because Frankie wasn't crossing young Charlie off the suspect list, not yet. Unlike Merry, she wasn't sentimental when it came to true crime.

"I think we need to slow down here, folks," said Earle. "There may be no mystery. Let me get the facts straight first before we start running in half-cocked. We did that the first time and it got us nowhere, remember?"

They all thought back then to the first mystery that brought them together last summer—Susan's shocking crimes. Her niece, Charlie, then sixteen, had survived thanks to being locked away in boarding school. Or so they had thought...

"You seriously think Morgan will even talk to you?" asked Martin. "Hasn't he banned you from homicide HQ since you crashed his last case?"

Earle's eyes twinkled behind his steel spectacles. "That is true, but he's not my only source." He drained his glass. "I'm going to head off, folks. If we're all free, might I suggest we continue this conversation tomorrow? Merry's right. This is not the time or place. We can also debate the merits of taking on the Phillip Weaver case then too."

"Hang on, tomorrow's Saturday," said Martin. "You guys work weekends?"

"No, we barely work at all," said Frankie, "hence the need to take on Weaver." A pointed look at Merry.

"Can we at least meet at the café?" Merry pouted. "My Archie's eaten me out of house and home, and I'm not sure I'll get to the supermarket before then. You see, Dougie's cooking his famous pot roast tonight and—"

"Okay, thanks Mez, we don't need all the details," said Frankie. "Let's make it ten."

Earle turned to Martin and Kila. "I know you gentlemen aren't part of the agency, but if we do take Verity's case, we could really use

18

your help. What do you say, Martin?" The author half shrugged like he didn't really care, but Frankie could tell he was champing at the bit. "How about you, Mad Dog?"

Kila had eyes only for the barman, was waving his glass about, like he couldn't believe it was empty. Earle and Merry flashed worried looks at Frankie, and she offered them a serene smile in return, like it wasn't a big deal.

They all thought Kila was blue over the death of Sir George.

Oh, how little they knew…

CHAPTER 4 ~

OLD FRIENDS AND NEW

Merry was the last sleuth to leave the wake. She felt obliged to hang in until the bitter end, if only for Verity's sake. Still couldn't get over the fact that the most influential person in Sir George's life was not there for its conclusion. It felt so dreadfully wrong.

"Are you all right?" came a voice beside her as she sat alone now at the bar, and Merry glanced around to see a face that looked vaguely familiar. It took her a moment and then she broke into a smile.

"Angus! How are you?"

It was Angus Johnson, the manager of the Burlington family's winter ski lodge in the Snowy Mountains, and a man she had interrogated all by herself during their first case. Verity had driven her up to see him and, while Angus was an innocent player, his throwaway comments to Merry had proven crucial in the end—*not* that Frankie had even bothered to mention them in the articles she'd produced soon after the murders!

"I'm good," he replied. "You, however, look maudlin."

She tried to conjure up a smile. "I'm just worried about Verity."

"You and me alike." He rubbed his fuzzy red beard and shook his head. "It's bollocks, you do know that? No one would ever hurt George deliberately. We all owe him so much, but no one more so than Verity. She adored the old guy; wouldn't hurt a hair on his head. They must have it wrong. Must have!"

Merry couldn't quite nod along. "You came down for the funeral? All the way from Jindabyne?" It was at least a six-hour drive.

"I'm just here to pay my respects. I owe George and his family so much."

Angus's eyes drifted to a couch where Charlie was seated, and

Merry instantly recognised the two women seated on either side who were now looking towards her. They were Prue Chambers and her daughter Chanel, past clients of the sleuths, and before she knew it they were jumping up and smothering her with hugs. When Merry looked around again, Angus was leaving, but he offered her a small, sad smile at the door, and she felt her heart drop all over again.

Angus was so much like Verity, she realised, one of Sir George's many loyal hounds. She wondered what he would do now and just hoped he, too, would be okay.

~

Who knew when he retired, several years ago now, that ex-Detective Inspector Earle Fitzgerald would be spending so much time back at his old stomping ground—or in this case, close enough to it. His first visits back to homicide headquarters in Sydney's west had been met with such warmth. Now it was like a spaghetti western every time he showed his face—a whoosh of strained silence, then guns at fifty paces. Which was why he'd saved them all the aggro and arranged to meet his only true ally, Detective Odetta Soderbergh, at the pub around the corner. She headed the Missing Persons Unit, and they had bonded on his last case. He hoped the bond still held.

It was not yet four p.m. The police day would still be in full swing, so he had a hunch he wouldn't cross paths with Morgan or his cronies here.

He was right.

The Wobbler's Arms hotel was empty except for two old drunks (retired coppers by the look of their haunted expressions) and Odetta nursing a soft drink at the bar. She was in a plain black suit, and her arctic-white hair was now a little longer, a little softer. It suited her, Earle thought.

"I'm sorry to drag you away," he said as he took the stool beside her and ordered a beer.

"No, you're not, and neither am I. Only thing on my plate these days is missing cold cases. And I mean well and truly frosted over."

"Ah, I wondered if they'd punish you after we helped you last time. I'm sorry."

"Okay, I believe that one, but I think you got it the wrong way round. I helped you; you guys were the ones running the show. I didn't have a problem with that. Pity my bosses do. I'm in your

21

camp—as long as we catch the baddy, who cares who gets the credit?"

"Been hard?"

"Nah, just dull. But I'll claw my way back to the heat soon enough." Then she smiled wider and added, "Morgan departs with his fake gold watch next month. Did you know that? Free at last. Can. Not. Wait."

Neither could Earle. "How are those pooches of yours doing?"

Odetta owned not one but six French bulldogs.

She grinned. "I've got seven now!" She laughed. "But you didn't drag me here to talk about my social life. You want the goss on Ms Vine, I'm guessing."

He nodded enthusiastically, but Odetta's gossip was fairly limited. She knew Morgan had just charged Verity with suspicion of murder, that he was opposing bail, and already had a team searching through her property and all of Sir George's.

"What they're searching for I do not know."

She did know that Morgan was first alerted to the suspected homicide, not by the doctor who attended Sir George's death and saw nothing untoward, happily signing the death certificate, but via a tip-off that came in the night before the burial.

"*Last night?* That's cutting it fine," said Earle. "So that's why Morgan disrupted the proceedings, made it all so damn dramatic."

She gave him a sympathetic look. "I think it had more to do with showing you lot up in front of a rapt audience, but if you want to be kind, sure."

"So who was behind the tip-off? Do you know? And what did they say?"

She shook her head. "Morgan's team turns all whispery when I enter the room."

"He's gotta have more than hearsay to disrupt a funeral, slap a woman in handcuffs and make an official arrest. Morgan must have something concrete."

"Give it a few days and the pathology will tell the story."

But Earle wasn't feeling so patient. "Who first found the deceased? Who called it in?"

"Verity. She didn't tell you?"

"Been pretty busy organising the funeral."

"Right, well, nothing untoward there from what I hear.

Verity found Mr Burlington deceased in his wheelchair at the Seagrave premises. Usual procedures were followed, a doctor attended, declared death by natural causes, and that was that. Now they suspect it wasn't quite so natural, hence the fresh autopsy." She sipped her drink.

"What are they looking for, do we know?"

"My guess? Signs of asphyxiation. But don't quote me on that. Like I said, it all goes hush-hush when I appear. In fact, knowing Morgan, he's feeding me red herrings. As tasty as they are."

She sniggered at her joke. Then straightened her smile. Turned to face Earle head-on. "It's nice you want to help, Earle. It's real gallant and all. But I'm not so sure about this one. I got to know Verity a bit last time, and I like her. It's not personal. But I have a terrible feeling you could be backing the wrong horse this time."

"She needs us, Odetta."

Odetta dropped her head to one side. "No, what she really needs is a bloody good criminal lawyer. The best Queen's Counsel money can buy."

"Well, that's not going to happen. Sir George might've been loaded, but Verity was just his overworked PA. I doubt she can afford a QC."

"Really?" Odetta blinked as she sat back. "Are you sure about that?"

He waited.

She said, "Another reason Morgan's so sure Ms Vine *done it*. The old guy left her a very tidy sum in his Last Will and Testament. She didn't mention it?"

No, he thought idly, she did not. "She do all right in the end, did she?" *Good for her.*

Odetta's enormous green eyes sparkled. "More than *all right*, Earle. Sir George left Verity half of everything."

Earle nearly choked on his ale.

"Oh yes, my friend," Odetta continued, "the *overworked PA* never has to work another day in her life. Verity Vine is now one of the wealthiest women in the country."

CHAPTER 5 ~
THE GAMES ROOM CAFÉ

The dollar notes were grubby and creased at the corners, but Merry happily placed them in their allotted spot as she prepared the Monopoly board for the group's arrival.

She was ensconced at her favourite eatery, the Games Room Café, at a table she had never chosen to sit at before. Cluedo was her passion, and she was exceptionally good at it. Had won several global championships, in fact.

But Monopoly seemed more Sir George's style, and it was not lost on the sleuths as they took their seats around the board.

"How very appropriate," said Martin, plucking up one of the silver tokens, a miniature top hat. "I quite like this game. Not bad at it either."

"That'd be right," said Frankie, who wasn't into board games, period.

"Where's Kila?" Merry asked hopefully. "Don't tell me he's late again."

"Can't make it," was all Frankie said, lips pursing enough for them to know to drop it. She fondled some tiny, plastic houses on the board. "I wonder who wanted to have a monopoly on the old guy's dosh? Other than the obvious of course."

"Launching straight in, are we?" said Earle, shaking his head as he waved the waitress over. "Can we at least order our breakfast first?"

"Charlie couldn't have done it!" said Merry, ignoring Earle. "She was in London, remember."

"About that…" Frankie held a finger up briefly as she stopped to give her order. "I've just checked out Charlie's socials." She then pulled out her phone, tapped on her Instagram app and scrolled for a bit. "Ah, here it is. A very pretty selfie of @ChaChaBurlyBrown flying in over the Sydney Harbour Bridge. In business class no less."

"So? Charlie flew in for the funeral."

"Look at the date, Mez. She flew in *three weeks ago*. That's two weeks before the murder. Her alibi's wide open."

Merry looked crestfallen. She had managed a quick chat with George's granddaughter after greeting the Chambers, and Charlie acted like they were virtual strangers, giving Merry just five minutes of her time before disappearing with the flustered young woman in the ill-fitting suit. And Merry didn't blame her. She was probably still in shock. But guilty? Of her grandpa's death? She just couldn't see it.

Martin could. And he liked the view. "We're gonna wrap this case up quickly then. She got tired of waiting for Gramps to cark it, came over, knocked him off for his billions."

"Half his billions, to be precise," said Earle.

Frankie's eyes narrowed. Merry went to say something, but Frankie held up a finger. Pointed it at Earle.

"Tell us what you know," she ordered, and so he repeated what Odetta had told him—how Verity Vine had just inherited half the Burlington estate.

"I did some cyber-sleuthing of my own," he told them. "According to *Forbes* magazine, that's half of more than three billion dollars, folks."

Then he sat back and slurped the tea he'd just been handed, giving them all a chance to stomach that whopper. Because it really was a whopper.

Martin digested it first. "Whoa. This thickens the plot considerably."

"Poor Verity," said Merry. "I mean, I know she's now rich and all, but this does not help her case one bit!"

"It helps *us* though," was Frankie's take. "Now she can afford to hire us."

She earned a groan for that comment.

"We still don't know if she wants to hire us," said Earle. "She might plead guilty for all we know. I have it on good authority that Verity's applying for bail first thing on Monday, so provided she gets it, I suggest we approach her after that and see how she's feeling."

"Hang on. Verity is *still* in custody?" Merry was aghast. "She's going to be there *all weekend*?"

"At the metropolitan remand centre, yes. Morgan questioned her just long enough yesterday to ensure the bail courts closed for the weekend so she couldn't apply. He's opposed bail, says her newfound wealth makes her a flight risk."

"That's ridiculous," said Merry. "As if."

Frankie plucked up an orange card and pretended to read from it: "Verity Vine, go directly to jail. Do not pass go. Do not collect one and a half billion dollars."

Now they were all groaning again.

"I'm sure a sympathetic magistrate will grant her bail," said Earle. "I'm hoping she'll be home by lunchtime on Monday. I think it's best we adjourn this discussion until we see her in person. I know Martin's in. What about your other half, Frankie?" Then, when she stared at him blankly, he added, "Kila? Your boyfriend?"

"Oh." She shook her head firmly. "Forget about Kila for this one."

As plates of cooked eggs arrived, Earle said, "Okay, that's settled. Now let's move on to the second order of business, and then we can enjoy our breaky and get back to our lives." He picked up the salt shaker and began covering his food. "Frankie, you mentioned something yesterday about that Kings Cross murder victim. Do you still want us to meet with his sister?"

Merry started to frown at both the salt and the client, but Frankie was already waving them off.

"I'm passing that one on to Mad Dog," she said. "It's more Kila's style."

And not just his style. It had all the elements that Kila lapped up, including a few surprises too.

Frankie just hoped Kila said yes to the pretty blonde who'd be knocking on his door that very minute…

~

Pretty was not a word that Kila Morea would associate with Phillip Weaver's sister. Not that Tiffany wasn't attractive—big blue eyes, blow-dried blond hair, gym-perfect figure—but she had a hardened look about her. Like she hadn't just seen the worst life had to offer, she'd absorbed it, too, in every pore of her being.

It had left its mark in her hoarse smoker's voice and her cold, steely gaze and the way she held her chin just slightly upwards, like she was ready for a beating.

"Thanks for agreeing to see me on your weekend," she said when he opened the door to her at his small inner-city bedsit.

He shrugged and waved her in. "I'm doing this as a favour to Frankie." He'd do anything to get back in her good books. "She said you were desperate, but I don't get why. Your brother's dead. His killer's behind bars. Nothing's bringing him back."

Tiffany gave him a sly look. "Yeah because that sentiment works well for you, right?"

Kila frowned, then offered her the tiny sofa. "So she told you."

"Said we had a lot in common."

He pulled out a kitchen stool but remained standing. "Sorry, Tiffany, but the way I see it, we have nothing in common. My sister was an innocent victim. Your brother was a con man and a thief. No offence to you, but he brought this upon himself."

Tiffany's expression was deadpan, like she'd heard that all before. "I'm not talking about Phillip. The thing we have in common is Dragon Malone."

Just hearing the monster's name made Kila flinch.

She gave him a smug smile. It was fleeting. "Your sister died at Dragon's hands. I know all about it, and I offer my condolences. But I think my brother was killed by Dragon too. Just indirectly. I know he's in jail, but I think Dragon ordered the hit or is somehow responsible." Now she looked angry. "That scumbag gets out in twelve years, could be less with good behaviour, and I hear he's been a very good boy. Found God apparently, and my brother's the con man?" She made a pft sound and sat forward. "Don't you want to put him away for even longer? If we can prove Dragon was involved in my brother's murder, that would do it."

Now Kila was interested, as she knew he would be, and he offered her a drink, then sat down and waved her on.

"I know Phill was what you'd call a loser," she said. "But he didn't seem like a loser when he first got out of jail. He acted like a winner, like he was turning his life around. Said he was onto something positive. Said it was all thanks to some guy called Dragon."

"He said that?"

She nodded. "I had no idea who this Dragon bloke was, right? Not at first. But I figured he was decent. Thought he'd given Phill a job tip or something. Then ten days later Phill's dead and his best

27

mate is being charged with his murder."

"Jakab Kovacevic. I read about the case. It's yet to go before the court."

"But it will if I don't do something to stop it. JayJay didn't kill my brother. Those two were like brothers themselves, thick since high school. No way JayJay did this. So I talk to JayJay, right? He's as flipped out as I am."

"There was the five thousand dollars cash he had on him. They said he shanked your brother for it."

"Bullshit. He was just holding it for Phill. That's what he told me, and I believe him. The real question is, where did Phill get that kind of dough? He was fresh out of the clink, only had the few hundred I'd given him. JayJay didn't have a clue, but he did know two things. He knew there was more coming—that's what Phill told him—and he knew it had something to do with Phill's cellmate, a guy called Deaglan Malone."

"Dragon."

A knowing nod. "Reckons my brother wouldn't tell him any more than that. Said it was for his own safety. So I try to talk to Dragon, right? Maybe he knows where this mysterious money originated, but he won't have a bar of me. Refuses all requests for a visit. Why? What's he hiding?"

She stared at Kila like he had the answers, and Kila just stared back blankly.

"Here's what I think," she said. "I think my brother was doing Dragon's dirty work and that's what got him killed. I want to find out what that dirty work entailed. Could be drugs, could be—"

"I don't help drug dealers."

"And neither did Phill! Even he had standards. Which is why I'm flippin'. All I know is, it had something to do with Dragon Malone. I want to swing it back to the man who's really responsible."

Kila must have looked unconvinced again because she quickly added, "Look, Phill's all I had in the world. We had a rough upbringing, Mum shot through early, Dad was a deadbeat—"

"I don't need to hear the sob story." Frankie must have told her to go heavy on the heartstrings too. Needy women had always been Kila's kryptonite.

"Well, maybe I do," she shot back. "You might call my brother a con man, but to me he was a saint. He looked after me, and that took some doing. I wasn't exactly an angel myself, but he pulled me through school, insisted I finish, made sure I had what I needed because Dad sure didn't. Look, I won't bore you with the lurid details of our neglected childhood. Suffice to say the only way I ever got anything was thanks to Phill and his crafty ways. He'd nick cash from Dad's wallet and risk a beating or con it out of a neighbour or a teacher, pinch it from somewhere."

"Okay, I get it."

"No, I don't think you do. Everything Phill did back then, every cent he conned and stole he gave to me. He was looking out for me, making sure I did not go without. Eventually, when he was old enough to get a job, he realised conning it from others was easier, or maybe he just didn't know any different. Perhaps he figured the world owed us everything he took. Any case, I smartened up, but he didn't or couldn't or something. I tried to repay the favour, begged him to go straight, and when that didn't happen, I scored a scholarship and studied law so I could help him, as I inevitably knew I would. And so I have, on multiple occasions, until that last charge, until that last stint in a cell with Dragon. If it wasn't for him, Phill would still be alive. And so would your sister."

Kila shook his tangled curls. Whatever his hardships, whatever his fate, Phillip Weaver did not belong on the same song sheet as Chili.

She nodded like she got it. "Phill was no saint, but he wasn't Dragon. That prick ripped my only family from me. One way or another, I just know Dragon is behind Phill's murder. And I'm willing to pay someone to investigate."

"Can you afford me?" he asked, hoping Frankie hadn't mentioned the fact that money didn't motivate this gumshoe.

"Told you I was a lawyer, didn't I?" Then she smiled, properly this time. "So I'm even more of a con man and a thief than my brother. But at least I have the law on my side."

CHAPTER 6 ~

CATCHING UP WITH THE ACCUSED

It was two o'clock, Monday afternoon, a week since Sir George had been murdered, three days since his funeral, and two hours since Verity Vine had been released from police custody on conditional bail.

And the sleuths did not want to waste another minute.

So there they were, standing outside Verity's house, staring across the patchy dirt lawn to the drab brick exterior. There was a leaning carport to one side with barely enough room to hold Verity's small black hatchback inside, and in front of that, on the driveway, stood a muddy white Nissan Patrol with an impressive-looking bull bar and ski racks on the roof.

It was not at all what they had pictured.

"I thought she'd live in something cosy and cottagey," said Earle.

"I was picturing a minimalist apartment," said Frankie. "All shiny and crisp with hospital corners."

"I've never been able to picture her outside of Seagrave," said Martin. "She seemed to be part of the furniture."

"Now she can't go within five hundred metres," said Earle.

It was one of the bail conditions and the reason they were all there. Well, except for Merry, who had been summoned to a meeting with her youngest son's school principal (that had her in a spin), and Kila who, Frankie reiterated—one more time for the dummies!— would *absolutely* not be joining them.

"Shall we?" she said, pushing the gate open and leading the way up the mouldy cement pathway to the front door.

The security grill was open, and she pressed the doorbell but was met with silence. Was about to knock when the front door burst open and a short, stocky man with a trimmed ginger beard came bounding out, nearly cleaning Frankie up in the process.

"Oh, apologies, ma'am. I didn't see you there," he said, managing to take a bounce back before they both fell over. He pulled some wraparound sunglasses down from his balding head, then simply called out, "Verity! You have guests!" before stepping around her and across the lawn towards the SUV, ignoring the others entirely.

They stared after him even more surprised.

"Ma'am?" said Frankie. "Did he just call me ma'am?"

"I didn't know Verity had a flatmate," said Earle.

"Could be her boyfriend?" suggested Martin. "Or brother? He looks familiar."

"He looks like Dougie, that's why," said Frankie, thinking of Merry's new partner. "Come on. Let's go in."

She squinted into the shadowy hallway. "Verity?" she called out, then took a step inside.

They found the PA in the kitchen, at the end of the hall, leaning against a bench top, staring into an empty cup, lost in her thoughts. She was yet one more surprise. Unlike her usual attire—a neatly ironed, no-nonsense business suit—Verity was in a baggy tracksuit, her red curls limp against her head, not a lick of makeup on her freckled features.

"Verity?" said Earle, making the woman jump.

She threw a hand to her heart. "Jesus, Mary and Joseph!" she said, her Irish accent surprisingly heavy. "You scared me! What are you doing here?" Then, eyes turning furtive: "How did you get in?"

"Your boyfriend was heading out," Earle said, and she frowned as she dumped the cup and swept back down the hallway, the sleuths following.

"Oh, Gus is just a friend. Did you lock the door?"

"It's okay, Verity," said Frankie, watching as she glanced up and down the street. "The paparazzi haven't worked out your address yet. Took us long enough. Why aren't you returning our calls?"

Verity secured the grill, then locked the front door and swept back towards the kitchen. "I have been rather detained, Frankie." She did not smile at her pun.

The gang swapped concerned looks, then followed her back, Frankie glancing into the lounge room as they passed, noticing a simple couch, a bare coffee table, a few prints leaning against one wall.

"Nice place you got here," she said even though it wasn't nice,

31

and Verity frowned again.

Her eyes danced around the kitchen, like she was seeing it clearly for the first time. "I'm never normally here on a weekday," she said as though that explained it. "I was just making coffee. You want some?"

The kitchen was livelier than the lounge room but only just. A ceramic fruit bowl stood on the counter, two brown onions and some garlic inside, while the large fridge door was void of happysnaps and clipped recipes and other everyday mementos. Beyond that was a doorway that appeared to lead into a bathroom. Frankie could just make out the edge of a ceramic vanity top, the corner of a shaggy bathmat.

They watched as Verity plucked four mismatched cups from a high cupboard, then searched a surprisingly well-stocked pantry for some instant coffee, also surprising considering the many plungers of freshly roasted coffee she used to make for them.

Reaching into the fridge, she pulled out a carton of milk, smelt it and winced, before turning back. "Haven't had a chance to get fresh supplies. Sorry, are you guys okay with it black? I think I'm all out of sugar too."

Now Frankie was frowning. No, she did not like black, unsweetened coffee, and certainly not instant, but she nodded along with the others as Verity slowly made four cups.

None of this—the yard, the house, the sour milk—married with her efficient facade. Because now it did feel like a facade to Frankie. How could the PA who ran a mining magnate's world so brilliantly live like she'd only just moved out of home?

As though reading her mind—all their minds—Verity said, "Like I said, I'm not usually here during the day. It's really just a place to refuel and rest my head. And help my friends when they need a bed." She nodded her head back towards the front door and the sound of the departing four-wheel drive.

Frankie was going to ask about the driver, but Verity looked so damn skittish she just took her coffee cup and tried not to scowl. Earle was sipping his happily enough while Martin stared into his warily, and Verity held her cup to her breast like it was a defibrillator.

Martin gave up the pretence first, dropping the cup to the kitchen bench. "So, how was lock-up?" he said. "Harrowing?"

"No, no, not so bad. At least I made bail." She offered them a grim smile. "There's something I never thought I'd hear myself say."

"Yes, that was very lucky," said Frankie, "considering bail was set at half a million dollars."

Frankie's right eyebrow hitched up, and Verity glanced across at her and then the others.

She understood the premise and placed her own cup aside. "You heard about the inheritance." It wasn't a question. They were as efficient at their job as she was.

"Why didn't you tell us?" said Frankie. "When we spoke before the funeral? You never said a word."

"Because it's not important!" she barked before scraping a hand through her oily hair and offering an apologetic smile. "Or maybe I didn't believe it. Maybe I still don't. Any case the judge does because it's thanks to that, that my lawyer was able to secure bail. The irony." She stared into her murky brew. "If it wasn't for the inheritance, I'd still be in there."

Earle cleared his throat. "If it wasn't for the inheritance, you might never have been detained under suspicion of murdering your boss, Verity."

She glanced at him, smiled weakly. "So they say."

"Do you know what's behind this murder charge?" he asked. "What did DI Morgan say to you during questioning? On what basis does he suspect homicide? Did he present any evidence?"

"No!" she replied. "I mean... he asked me lots of very odd questions, mostly about our routine together, what I did for George, how I handled his business affairs, domestic duties, that kind of thing. What time I did this, what time I did that. It was all so *vague*."

"*Okay.*" Earle swapped a look with Frankie. They both knew that wasn't good. "But your lawyer must have asked for a brief of evidence, yes? To find out what they've got? That's your right."

She stared at him like he was speaking in tongues. "I'm meeting with her later this week. I guess I'll learn more then."

"And how will you be pleading?" Earle asked.

Verity looked even more confused now. "Not guilty, of course."

"So you didn't do it?"

"Isn't that what I said?"

"Not exactly."

The PA's cheeks burned red; her eyes turned hard. "I know you have to ask that, Earle, but it breaks my heart."

"It's not personal, Verity. It's an important first question. And you still haven't answered it."

"*Earle*," said Frankie, sensing he'd gone too far.

"It's okay, Frankie. I want to answer it." Verity's eyes never budged from Earle's. "Of course I didn't do it. You have to know that."

"I make no assumptions in a case. I've always told you that. I have more questions if you're up to them."

Verity breathed in, shoulders back as though steeling herself.

He said, "Until we know what the police have got, we need to get some basics, starting with what I can only assume is their suspected motive. Did you know about the inheritance? Before George died?"

This time she didn't hesitate. "No, I did not. I learned about it at the same time Charlie did, at the reading of the will, the week before the burial." She gave them a sad smile as she corrected herself. "*Attempted* burial. Poor George. To be lying in a morgue in cold storage…"

A tear slid down one cheek. Followed by another.

As they watched her reach for a tissue in her tracksuit pants, the tears chastened them all, but they did not surprise Frankie. Earle might have indirectly accused her of murder, but they all knew how close Verity had been with Sir George. By the end she was signing cheques on his behalf after all.

Verity said, "I assumed I was asked to the reading of the will to take notes, to be honest." She smiled sadly like she wished that was all it was. "Poor Charlie was so shocked when she heard I was getting a third."

"A *third?*" said Martin. "So, a third to Charlie, a third to you. Who gets the other third?"

"Susan, of course."

"Susan!"

"Ah yes," said Frankie, internally kicking herself. That's right. The old guy never did turn against his daughter after she was arrested for killing her own brother and most of his family. In fact, he had gone out of his way to buy Susan the best legal representation he could muster.

Verity nodded. "George split his inheritance three ways—a third to me, a third to Charlie, and a third to Susan."

"But Susan's in jail," said Martin. "I can't believe he left that confessed murderer anything. And didn't his will have some provision for scandal? I thought she'd be disinherited."

"Then you never really knew George. He removed that provision soon after Susan was charged. I told you all before. Family was everything to my boss. Even wicked family, it appears. He would not give up on her even after everything that happened. Which is why I never assumed I was a beneficiary and I'm as surprised as everyone else. I suspect Charlie will challenge it, as well she should."

"You worked your arse off for that man," said Martin. "Don't concede one cent."

"And I was paid an annual salary for my arse, Martin," she shot back. "I did not expect anything more." Then her face crumbled. "Even if I had known... I would never hurt George! Never! You know me. You know I was trying to keep him healthy. Looking in on him, feeding him—" Her eyes turned furtive. She stared at her phone. "I keep waiting for them to call, tell me it was all a gross misunderstanding... I'm sure the autopsy will prove it's just one big mistake and everything will be... fine."

The sleuths had a varying mixture of pity and disbelief etched across their faces, none more so than Earle. He knew how stubborn DI Morgan could be. They all did. And none of them liked her chances, but they weren't about to tell *her* that.

Verity looked as though hope was the only thing keeping her from slumping to the kitchen floor.

"You may well be right," Earle said instead. "But we want to help. We want to do what we do best—take an independent look at the case and see if we can't find another solution that does not end up with you behind bars. We've cleared the decks—"

"Well, you shouldn't have!" she said suddenly, vehemently. "I didn't ask you to help me. After everything you've done for this family..."

"We *want* to help," Martin repeated.

"I can't afford you," she said even more brashly.

"You just inherited a billion dollars, Verity," Frankie replied, adding quickly, "Not that we're doing it for the money."

Martin made a scoffing sound, but Verity was shaking her head.

"The inheritance might have secured my bail, but I may never see one cent of it and not just because it might get challenged by Charlie. The prosecutor is now freezing George's estate, pending this investigation, and if I lose my case, my share will be considered proceeds of crime." She sniffed, blew her nose. "Look, I know you guys want to do the right thing, and I appreciate that. But I also know you've just started your new agency and Merry already mentioned you were struggling a bit. You need clients who can pay up front, not clients who may never give you a dime, especially if they get found guilty."

"We better make sure they find you innocent then," Frankie replied, dumping her own untouched cup into the sink. "Come on. We haven't got time for this martyr act. You know we're going to investigate whether you want us to or not. Can't help ourselves. It's in our DNA." She winked. "It's why you and George hired us in the first place. So let's just get on with it, shall we?"

Then she stepped across to the side door and pushed it open to reveal that it was, indeed, a bathroom, freshly renovated by the look of the compact shower and modern toilet/sink combo. She said, "How about you take a long, hot shower, put on something a little more... uplifting... and we'll meet you at our office in an hour? Merry should be back by then."

Verity looked wary again. "Can't we just talk here?"

Frankie shook her head. "You have nothing to hide, Verity, so stop acting like it. Besides, we have fresh milk at our digs. And some decent bloody coffee."

~

The tea was lovely, the chair comfy, the spring sunshine dappling in through the open window, but they did nothing to calm Merry's nerves as she sat in front of the school principal, the Year Eight advisor beside her.

Merry should not have been nervous, had sat here many times before (her seventeen-year-old, Lola, was no saint). But she honestly never thought she'd be dragged in to "discuss" her youngest. He was her good one!

"I'm sorry to report, Ms Kean," said Principal Rogers, "but we're having a few *issues* with Archie."

She swapped a look with Mrs Delhunty, and Merry's stomach tightened. "What's happened? What's he done?"

"Nothing too dramatic. Please don't panic yourself," said the principal. "But we can see the trajectory and we would like to put some speed bumps in place."

Trajectory? Speed bumps? She made Archie sound like an out-of-control vehicle. Last time Merry looked, he was a sweet and harmless fourteen-year-old.

"He's been giving a bit of lip to the teachers," explained the advisor. "Acting out. We caught him vaping in the toilets at lunchtime."

"Vaping?" Since when did her son vape? But that wasn't her biggest concern. "Giving lip to his teachers? What's he been saying?" That was so unlike Archie.

"Nothing too shocking, I assure you. Just snide comments. A little bit huffy whenever his phone is taken from him. Oh, and he walked out during home economics this morning. For no apparent reason he dumped his pasta in the bin and stormed away. That's when we found him vaping."

Merry was thunderstruck. Cooking was Archie's favourite subject! If there was food involved, Archie was your guy.

The principal tried for a comforting smile, but it was too late for that. She leaned forward. "As I say, it's early days. If we can get on top of it now, we could bring him back."

Back? Like he was headed for the abyss. Or an ice den!

"Is something going on with Archie?" Mrs Delhunty asked. "Is there anything we need to know? Any *issues* at home?"

"No!" Merry said, knowing she said it too fast. "I mean, I broke up with his father a few years ago. I… I thought he was over it."

"Some children react to things more slowly than others," said Principal Rogers. "Perhaps it's only just hitting him now."

"And his older brother moved down to Melbourne a few months ago. I know he misses him."

"That could also be a factor," said Mrs Delhunty. "Or maybe something more recent? Did anything specific happen last week or over the weekend, perhaps?"

Merry gulped. "No." In fact, she hardly saw Archie over the weekend. First she had breaky with the sleuths, then she was hanging with Dougie while Archie seemed perfectly fine, chilling with his friends. Maybe *they* were a bad influence!

She suggested as much, but Mrs Delhunty was having none of it. Those boys were still angels apparently. Butter wouldn't melt and all that. Nope, it was just her Archie.

"So… what do I do?" Merry cried. "What do you suggest?"

The principal sat forward and gave her a warm smile. "I suggest you do the hardest thing the mother of a teenage boy can do." Her smile deflated. "Get him to open up."

Merry stared back at her, stunned, like she'd just been asked to split the atom.

~

It was the beer coaster that finally swung it for Kila. Or for Tiffany, really.

He hadn't given her brother's case a moment's thought since she left his bedsit on Saturday, and he'd made no promises other than assuring her he would flick through Phill's notebook, which she handed to him, along with a recent photo, as she departed.

It wasn't the mugshot or the little blue book that changed his mind today or anything scribbled inside it—just a bunch of random names on page one: *Kiara, Lars, Jill, Jerry, Henrietta, Bertha*. It was the coaster that fell out of the middle.

Reaching for it, he'd stared at it for some time, then turned it over to see a simple date scribbled on the back.

Kila dropped the coaster like it had ignited.

He blinked. Picked it up slowly. Stared at the date again: 20/09/2018. Then felt his heart go rigid.

There was nothing simple about September 20, 2018. That was the date his sister was taken from him. The day his life imploded.

Why that date was written in red biro on the back of the coaster, Kila didn't know, but he did know the name of the bar printed on the front. It was an ad for Taboo Wine Bar on Victoria Street, Potts Point, his regular drinking hole and the place where Chili's nightmare had started. Or close enough to it.

Tapping the coaster against his stubbled chin, Kila began to spiral backwards to the night Chili had… Well, *that night*. Kila had been exceptionally close to his much-younger half sister; they adored each other, in fact. And yet that Thursday night, September 20, he had headed out on a date with a woman he barely knew and ignored the phone messages coming in from a woman he would have died for, if only he hadn't been so selfish, as he often was back then.

According to the police report—because she had mentioned none of this to Kila beforehand—Chili had a blind date with a man called

Deaglan Malone. Aka Dragon. He hadn't used that nickname of course. His Tinder profile looked and sounded soft and sweet and benign. Too benign. It would have raised red flags for Kila, but he'd been around the block too many times. Chili was just nineteen and had barely left the house.

She'd arranged to meet Deaglan on the street outside Taboo Bar at eight o'clock that night. The police never really considered why she'd chosen that particular bar. She never went in, according to reports, so they didn't think it was important, but in retrospect, it was as clear as the vodka they later found in Chili's stomach.

Or at least it was clear to Kila.

Even though his sister lived with an aunty, suburbs away, and never drank, rarely went to Taboo Bar, she knew it was her brother's new favourite hang and she was hoping he'd be there to give her blind date the once-over.

But that night, of all nights, he was absent.

While he was meeting his own needs, young Chili was meeting a murderer.

The last time Chili was seen alive was when she was getting into a car with Dragon. Twelve hours later, Kila got the door knock. The cops. The news that his sister was lying lifeless in an alley many blocks from the bar. And that's when everything went to shit.

Kila was never the same again, never quite as cheerful or carefree. Or selfish. Became a bit of a crusader instead, trying to rebuild his life and heart daily by helping desperate women with deadbeat partners, and pitching himself at Taboo where he could rescue future Chilis from potential predators, and themselves.

And now Taboo was being linked to another murder.

Kila vaguely recalled Frankie mentioning something about the bar in relation to Weaver when the case first hit the news, back when she was still writing for the *Herald*. Just couldn't remember the details. Hadn't thought any of it important. Considered calling her now, but something stopped him. He'd have to work this case alone.

So he stared at the coaster some more. What secrets did that bar contain? Was there really a connection to both murders? Or was he as delusional as Tiffany, seeing coincidences as clues?

Glancing at his watch, he saw it was early afternoon. Taboo wouldn't be opening for hours yet, and his old mate Trevor, the barman, was probably still sleeping off his late shift. So Kila busied himself with his other clients: a woman seeking vengeance for her philandering husband—"Sorry, lady," he told her. "I'm not in the seafood business anymore"—and a man trying to find his long-lost twin—"Thirty-five years is a long time, mate. I think you're throwing good money after bad."

But he kept coming back to Phillip Weaver.

It was scratching at his insides, like a hookworm, frantic to get out. Just couldn't think of anything else. So eventually he gave up trying and picked up his mobile, searched for the number, then pressed Dial. When it answered, he said simply, "I'll do it."

At the other end of the phone, Tiffany Weaver squealed like she'd just been told her brother was still alive and thieving.

CHAPTER 7 ~
GETTING THE STORY STRAIGHT

In contrast to Verity's sparse digs, the sleuths' headquarters looked like it had been occupied for years even though they had only recently moved in. Just down the road from the Games Room Café (yes, Merry had chosen the location), it comprised a large communal workspace, a separate kitchen, and a tiny, terraced area out the back. There was a comfy sofa set, a circular conference table and three sets of desks and chairs.

It didn't take a detective to work out who sat where. Merry's desk was cluttered with happysnaps of her kids, as well as two giant Cluedo trophies. Earle's featured a photo of his granddaughter sleeping soundly on the belly of his old dog Gruff, as well as a framed copy of his newly minted PI licence. Earle was the agency's principal; he had the transferrable law enforcement experience after all, while the other two had completed a fast-track training course and were now trying to get their surveillance hours up.

There were no photos or personal items on Frankie's desk, but her presence was obvious in the quality furnishings and freshly painted white walls and the kitchen's gleaming espresso machine, towards which she was now striding.

As she began to whip up "decent lattes", Merry loped in, waving off Earle's questions about Archie and insisting it was nothing compared to what Verity was going through. Except he could tell it was important to her by the way she fell into the sofa and reached for a cushion.

They had just got her up to speed with Verity's news when the PA herself arrived, and it took some time to pry Merry from the poor woman, who was used to Merry's bear hugs but looked today like they might just polish her off.

She had done as Frankie instructed and dressed in a neat jacket

41

and jeans, but it was going to take more than a costume change to resurrect her spark.

"I'm fine, Merry, please, you mustn't fuss," Verity said as she extricated herself.

And yet fuss Merry did. First she led Verity to the sofa, then she produced a plastic container of coconut muffins.

"Baked fresh over the weekend," she told them. "Had to hide them so my Archie didn't scoff the lot." Her brow crinkled as she handed them out.

"Thank you, Merry," said Verity. "I'm not sure when I last ate. How are your kids?"

Before she could answer, Frankie had a hand up. "No time for niceties please. We're working." She glanced at Earle. "Do you want to start?"

He nodded but said, "There's always time for niceties, Frankie. We're not machines. Or Sir George for that matter." He smiled at Verity. "He never was one for small talk."

She smiled back, sadly. "All efficiency, no tea, I used to say. But Frankie's right. We should launch in. I'm beat, and I know you have busy lives."

Then she dropped her uneaten muffin to the table, dusted off her fingers and said, "To be honest, I still feel like this is a giant waste of time. I mean, surely they'll come to their senses soon."

Not Detective Inspector Morgan, thought Earle once more. If Morgan believed George had been murdered and the culprit was Verity, nothing short of a miracle would dissuade him.

So it was time to find themselves a miracle.

"Let's just fill in a few blanks this arvo," he said, "and see if we can't make some sense of it all, hey? We won't try to overthink it." That comment was directed at his colleagues. "We'll just lay out the facts, and we can meet again tomorrow when you're feeling more bushytailed."

She agreed and accepted the coffee Frankie was now offering with a look that said *This is more like it.*

"Let's start with George's death," said Earle. "Can you tell us a little bit about the morning you found him?"

After a fortifying sip, Verity said, "Okay, so that was what? A week ago now? Ten days?" She shook her red curls, wet from her recent shower. "It feels like a lifetime. Um... so I arrived at Seagrave

42

for my morning meeting and knew something was up almost immediately. George wasn't at his usual perch."

"Which is?"

"On the Juliette balcony just outside the Yellow Room. There's enough space for his wheelchair and a lovely splash of sunshine that he soaked up every morning. I usually found him there with a cup of coffee and the papers. But not that day."

"What time did you get there?"

"Just on six thirty, like I do every day."

"That's early," said Martin.

Verity shrugged. "George has always been an early bird, but more so as he got older. I liked to be there in time to check on him. Make sure he hasn't burned the house down trying to make his coffee, get the business of the day started..."

Her voice cracked, and Merry leaned over and squeezed her hand. "You're going to miss him so badly."

"Already do. But it's not just that... It's the job. I loved the job too. And Seagrave. I grew to love that crazy pile of bricks." She wiped a finger under one eye. "So, um, yes, he wasn't on the balcony so I assumed the kitchen, the bathroom... I looked everywhere. I began to panic, wondering if he'd taken a turn in the night and called an ambulance? Was at hospital and no one had told me. I remember thinking how sad that would be... not realising that the truth was far, far worse." Her voice cracked again.

"Where did you find him?" asked Earle.

Verity waited a beat, then said, "The ballroom."

"Are you serious?" said Merry. "I didn't even think he liked the ballroom."

"He doesn't. That's why I didn't initially look there."

Merry squinted behind her cat's-eye glasses. "But hang on, that's down a sweeping staircase. I didn't realise he could get down there."

"He can't! At least, not easily. I had been begging him to put a chairlift in ever since he began to rely on a walking stick and then of course the wheelchair, but he... Well, he just wouldn't. Said it would destroy the grandeur of the place. And it's not like he ever used the space or the pool on that level, even when his son lived there."

"So how...?"

"There is a way, but it wouldn't have been easy. He must have wheeled himself down the exterior pathway and used the lower entrance, the one near the pool. Those sliding doors were wide open. I have no idea what he was doing down there, but I assumed the exertion must have been the final straw for his dear old heart, or perhaps he had another stroke. I never knew that he'd been *murdered...*"

"How did he appear?" asked Earle. "Did you see any signs of a struggle, strange bruising around the neck? Dishevelled clothing?"

"You think he was *strangled?*" Verity looked horrified.

"It's one theory floating around, but we won't know until the autopsy is complete."

She nodded. Gulped her coffee again. "Well, I didn't notice anything like that. As for dishevelled clothing? Sure. I mean, you guys saw George not so long ago. He'd given up on making an effort, didn't really care about himself or the property. But to be honest, that morning, he looked peaceful. I thought he was asleep at first. I..." Another pause, another tear trickled down her cheek. "I remember laughing, calling out to him, telling him he was an *eejit*. But he didn't respond, and he should have. He wasn't a deep sleeper. He should have responded."

Merry squeezed her hand again, and this time Verity squeezed it back, gave her a teary smile. "I reached him, touched him. That's when I knew. He was so cold. He'd been there, we think, all night."

"All night?" repeated Merry.

"Who's *we?*" asked Frankie, who never missed a beat. "Was Charlie at Seagrave when it happened?"

"No, thank goodness. His granddaughter *had* been staying at Seagrave since she returned from London, but she was staying with a friend that night, and I'm so grateful for that. It would have been horrendous if Charlie had found him, especially after everything she's been through. No, I was on my own initially. I called his doctor straightaway then Charlie and told her to come home, then I called Shannon." To their confused expressions, she added, "You know? My assistant, Shannon Smith? She came quickly. It was a relief as I didn't want to do all that alone."

"Oh yes," said Merry. "I forgot about your assistant. The PA's PA."

"And not a very good one," said Verity. "But I'm glad Shannon was there. It was a dreadful, dreadful day."

As Verity shivered anew at that, Frankie watched her closely, her mind racing ahead, tangling in all directions. None of which she was prepared to voice just now. Like Earle, she wanted to get all the facts lined up first. It was the journalist in her. *Ex-journalist...*

She shook the unbearable thought away.

"Tell us about this inheritance," she said instead. "When did you first find out?"

"I told you this," Verity replied, her tone weary, almost sulky. "At the reading of the will." She took some calming breaths. "We met with the family's long-time solicitor a few days after George died, at his rooms in the city. I was asked to attend, and like I said, I foolishly assumed I was there to take notes or provide support for Charlie. I honestly didn't..." She let that trail away. "Anyway, you can imagine my surprise when I was named as a beneficiary."

"And not just a beneficiary," said Frankie. "A bloody big one."

Verity's eyes narrowed as Frankie stared back at her.

"So who else benefits?" asked Merry, her tone chirpy. "Give us some suspects to work with."

"Well, as I said, a third to Charlie, a third to me, and a third to Susan. God knows what use it will be to her in prison."

"Her lawyers cut her a pretty good deal," said Frankie. "She could be out in less than fifteen years, plenty of life left to enjoy it."

Verity nodded. "Apart from that, there were some smaller gifts."

"Such as?" prodded Earle.

"What? Um..." Another sigh. "A hundred grand, I think, to the couple who had been looking after Charlie in London."

"Who are they?" asked Martin now.

"James and Gillian Duxton-Worthy. Distant relatives," said Verity. "I've never met them in person, but we did speak over the phone several times."

"They didn't come out for the funeral?" asked Martin.

She shook her head. "George left similar amounts to various charities and not-for-profits, twelve in all I believe; some business associates got a slice. I can give you those details if you want. But as far as I know, they're all fairly wealthy, so I can't see them killing for such a paltry amount."

"Of course a hundred grand would seem paltry now you have a cool billion," said Frankie, making Verity's eyes squint again.

"What else?" said Earle, flashing Frankie a frown. He knew what she was thinking, didn't like it one bit.

Verity pulled her gaze from the petite blonde. "Um... so there were some paintings left to family friends in Paris—the Rousells. They're quite elderly so also didn't make it for the funeral. The book collection, the one at Seagrave, went to another family friend, Persephone someone or other."

Frankie was now squinting. "Persephone? How do I know that name?"

"It's from Greek mythology," said Martin. "Daughter of Zeus. Abducted by Hades, king of the underworld."

"Sounds sinister," said Merry.

"And totally irrelevant," said Earle, bringing them back to reality. "Keep going. Any other gifts worth mentioning?"

"That's it, as far as I recall."

"What about Lia Segeyaro's family?" asked Frankie.

Lia had been the family housekeeper and one of Susan's victims, but Verity was shaking her head.

"George paid the Segeyaros a very handsome compensation settlement soon after Susan confessed. They were both surprised and disinterested. I believe they donated the money to a childrens charity in Papua New Guinea."

"That rules them out as suspects," said Frankie glumly. "And I can't see anyone killing for a few paintings and some old books. Tell us about your inheritance then, Verity. What exactly does it entail? A third of what? The murder mansion, George's city penthouse, what else?"

Verity blanched. "Um, okay, so apart from the penthouse and *Seagrave*"—she flashed Frankie a look, clearly not happy with the term *murder mansion*—"there's a house in Perth, another in Barbados, an apartment in Paris, a yacht moored up near the Great Barrier Reef, a rather staggering share portfolio that I can't even wrap my head around..."

While Verity continued rattling off the extensive inheritance, Merry was surprised by one omission now.

"What about the old ski lodge?" she said. "You know, the family holiday home you drove me to in the Snowy Mountains? Who gets that?"

Merry had spent a night at the lodge during their first case and knew it would have been worth a bomb, perched as it was right on the edge of one of Australia's premier ski resorts. It was old and outdated, but the location had million-dollar views across Perisher's ski slopes and down towards the neighbouring village of Jindabyne.

Verity frowned. "Oh, George sold that a few months back."

"Really?" Merry chewed her lower lip.

She should not have been surprised. It was the diving point for the family's latest tragedy—the place that triggered Susan's murder spree. It's little wonder George had disposed of it, and quickly.

"So what about Angus Johnson?" Merry asked. "The lodge manager? What happens to him?"

She recalled the sad man she had just seen at the funeral. Knew how devoted he had been to George and how worried he was for Verity.

Yet Verity seemed more worried about *him*, and she offered Merry a sad smile of her own before glancing at the others. "I've been helping him out a bit, but he's gone for another lodge job up in the mountains. So fingers crossed he gets that and gets to move on with his life."

Merry crossed her fingers and held them high while Earle cleared his throat.

"So that's the full list then, Verity? Of inheritance and bequeathments?"

"Isn't that enough?" she replied, her voice thin.

"Don't you fret," said Merry. "We're going to get you off this charge if it's the last thing we do!"

Martin watched as Merry consoled Verity, but he knew it wasn't just the murder charge that was making Verity anxious. He knew a little of going from rags to riches and the headaches that came with it. *Not* that his best-selling crime fiction had ever earned that kind of fortune.

"You don't know how you're going to go with all that dosh, do you, Verity?" he said. "How it will change you and everyone around you?"

Because it had changed him. And not in a good way.

She placed a trembling hand to her lips. "I'm not complaining. I would never complain, but..." She nodded. "It does feel like a curse. Especially now... because Earle is absolutely right. If it wasn't for this inheritance…"

She let that sentence dangle, but Martin was now sitting forward, brow furrowed.

"You know I don't think this is about the inheritance at all," he said. "At least not directly."

"How do you mean?" asked Frankie.

"If you think about it logically, none of this adds up. Because even if the police think you did it for the money, Verity, or we can prove that someone else did—one of those beneficiaries you mentioned—it doesn't explain the timing. Why kill him *now*? The guy was pushing ninety, right? Had all but given up? So why take the risk of murdering a man for an inheritance you were due to get very soon anyway?"

He leaned back and slapped them all with a smug smile. "I don't think George's murder had anything to do with the inheritance. I think there's something more sinister going on." Then he glanced at Frankie and added, "Something that would give Hades a run for his money."

~

Across town, Kila was pulling some cash out of his wallet as Trevor placed a pint of lager on the bar, followed by a glass of lemon squash. By the time the barman had processed the change, Kila had polished off half the beer.

"Everything okay, mate?" said Trevor, eyes shifting from Kila's to the glass and back. "Go easy, hey? Bar hasn't even opened yet. This rate you'll be on the floor before you get to save your first damsel."

Kila frowned. "Oh, I'm sorry, should I be sitting here reading a book?"

Trevor held his palms out. "Just worried about you, that's all. Antoine said you went in hard over the weekend, couldn't keep up with your orders. What's going on?"

Why are you sinking so much? was what Trevor was implying, and he wasn't talking about beer this time. Kila knew they were all concerned about him. But it was none of their goddamn business, and he would have told Trevor that if he didn't owe him a favour. It was late afternoon, and the barman had agreed to meet him here early "for a chat", and so Kila watched as first he tapped the keg and then began to pull clean glasses from the dishwasher.

"You remember the Phillip Weaver case Frankie was working on before she got the boot from the newspaper?" Trevor looked up from the dishwasher, bemused, so Kila added, "Bloke's body was found stabbed nearby in Kings Cross, but she did some prodding and learned he'd come in here before he was murdered. This would've all been about three months ago."

"Yeah, okay, now it rings a bell. Frankie popped in and asked me a bunch of questions, but I wasn't much help. What of it?"

Kila produced the white beer coaster. "Weaver had this amongst his stuff."

Trevor blinked, then closed the dishwasher door and stepped towards Kila. Took it from him. His smile lit up. "That's an oldie but a goodie. We've rejigged the look since then."

He nodded towards a fresh stack of coasters near the cash register.

Kila said, "So how old is that? Do you think?"

"A few years now. You think he hung around here back then?"

He shrugged. "Check out the other side."

Trevor turned it over and glanced at it, then back to Kila. "It's a date."

"Not just any date. Look at it properly."

Trevor looked again, still seemed confused, then must have started calculating. "Oh shit. That's not the night your sister...?"

"Yeah, it is. Why would this Weaver loser have that particular date written on an old Taboo coaster? It happened four years ago."

"Could it be a coincidence?" Then to Kila's sidelong look he added, "You saying Weaver might have had something to do with... with Chili?"

Kila went to nod, then shook his head. "Not really. I don't know. But I do know Weaver shared a cell with Dragon. Maybe Dragon gave that to him. Maybe he told him something, something that got him murdered."

"Jesus."

"Yep. That's why I'm trying to go over it all in my head. Do you remember what Frankie said about Weaver? Why he came into Taboo the night he was murdered?"

"He didn't come in the night he was murdered. I remember that. She said he came in about a week earlier. I couldn't see the connection, frankly. I mean Weaver was fresh out of jail. Must've gone to a lot of bars, probably trying to hook up."

"Yeah, probably," said Kila. "So why's he got my sister's date written on this bar's coaster? Feels like a connection to me."

Trevor shrugged and returned to unpacking glasses.

Kila stared at the coaster for a long while, then back at Trevor. "Okay, let's forget about Weaver for a minute. Who *was* here on September 20, back in 2018? Who was working the bar the night that Chili…?"

Now Trevor was looking at him sideways. "You really want to hash all that out again?"

"Just answer the question, mate. You weren't here, right?"

Trevor frowned. "You know I wasn't. You sent me a bunch of text messages the next morning, frantic remember? I was up the coast with my girlfriend. Geraldine."

"That's right. Geraldine the geriatric nurse. Can't remember her. Whatever happened to Geraldine?"

"Took a job out west." The barman smiled sadly. "I'm almost as big a loser in love as you are." He rubbed a hand through his closely cropped ginger hair. "You don't think I've agonised over this every day since? That if I had been on duty that night, maybe I would have seen something?"

He knew, as Kila did, that young Chili had hooked up with Dragon outside Taboo.

"If I'd seen that bastard hanging about on the street, I might have stopped her from ever getting into his car. For your sake."

"And Chili's."

"Of course, that goes without saying." He shook his head. "Why do you reckon I put up with all your shit, Kila? Why I let you sit here night after night, wrecking perfectly innocent hookups? Why I step up for you when you're not here and put girls in cabs myself. I feel as bad as you do." Then he quickly added, "Well, maybe not quite as bad. But you know what I mean."

Kila nodded. Trevor was a good mate. A good person. "So who *was* working here that night? Can you remember?"

The barman rubbed his jaw, giving it some thought. "I should know. I had just made manager, remember? That's why I took some days off, was having some R&R before the shit hit the fan. Little did I know the shit was already happening…" Gave Kila another sympathetic look. "It was a full-on time. Maybe I blocked it out."

Kila wished he could do the same. "Do any of these sound familiar?" He pulled Phillip's little blue book out of his jacket. Turned to the only page with anything written on it and read out the names: *Kiara, Lars, Jill, Jerry, Henrietta, Bertha.*

Trevor looked at him blankly. "Who are these people?"

"That's what I'm asking you. Their names were listed in Weaver's notebook, and I'm trying to work out why. They could just be random friends, right? People who were gonna help Weaver with a bed or a job or drugs or something. And if it wasn't for the coaster, for that date jotted on the back, I wouldn't have thought any more of it. But now I think it's all linked to Dragon and Chili and this bar. I just want to know if you know any of them."

Trevor leaned forward. "Read them again."

Kila did, adding, "Were they regulars in here maybe?"

"Don't know half of them, but Kiara sounds familiar," said Trevor. "So does Jill and Henrietta. That has to be Henny. Jill and Henny worked the bar back then. Left ages ago though."

Kila frowned. "I barely remember them. I was drinking here in those days. Why can't I remember anybody?"

"The operative word there is *drinking*. You did a lot of it back then." He stared pointedly into Kila's glass, probably wanting to add "Even more so now" but was too polite. Too much of a friend.

Instead, Trevor said, "Don't beat yourself up. We used to go through a lot of staff, still do. The job's so transitory. Some are just here for a few weeks before they find a better offer."

"Yeah but which weeks? I want to know exactly who was rostered on that night. You were open between, what? Five p.m. and one a.m. as usual, right?"

"I s'pose. But why does it matter? I don't understand why you're heading down this path. I think you're seeing connections that don't add up. I mean, Chili never even came *into* Taboo. That's what the witnesses said, and the pigs. She met Dragon out on the street and later... Well, she was found miles from here." His eyes clouded over like he hated discussing this with Kila and knew how much it took from both of them.

Kila pushed on. "Dragon told me he dropped her back here. After."

"Here?"

"Said he dropped her where he found her, just before midnight, and that she was still alive."

"You believe that shit?"

"No, I fucking don't," Kila growled. "Until now, until this…" He held up the coaster. "Just humour me, mate, is that so hard? You're the manager. You must have access to the old rosters, payment slips? Something?"

"Maybe. Probably, in the basement. Jesus, man, have you seen the state of that basement? It's like a festival of mould down there."

"Come on, Trevor, take a look, it could be helpful."

He sighed. "Course, mate, you know I'll do anything for you." Then he nodded up at the television clock. "But not right now. I have got to push on if I'm going to open up in time for happy hour—"

"Yeah. Yeah. Wouldn't want your book readers to be miserable."

Then he waved Trevor on as his eyes turned back to the coaster.

CHAPTER 8 ~
FILLING IN THE BLANKS

Darkness descended quickly outside, and the sleuths moved from coconut muffins to Thai takeaway, which had just arrived in steaming plastic containers from the eatery around the corner. While loading up their bowls, Earle phoned his wife, Beryl, to apologise for missing dinner, then watched as Merry finished up a call to her kids, instructing Lola to heat up last night's leftovers and "keep a firm eye on Archie! He's not to go anywhere. And make sure he stays off that PlayStation!"

After pocketing the phone, she offered Earle a bright smile, but he wasn't buying it. There was trouble afoot, and he would find out what. For now though, they needed to focus. Verity was slumped in her seat, picking at her pad thai like she didn't have the strength to raise the rice noodles to her lips. Perhaps they should have given her a few days to recuperate.

Frankie was more interested in the contents of the fridge. "We should really stock up on some decent plonk," she said, returning from the kitchen. "We haven't got so much as a beer in the house."

"This isn't a *house*, Frankie, it's an office," Earle told her, "and detecting is better done with a clear head, in my experience. No time for that."

"Oh, but there is time for niceties? I know which one I'd prefer."

"Still," said Earle, giving her a pointed look, then flicking his gaze towards Verity, who now looked like she was about to slip into a coma on the sofa. "Let's try to wrap up for the evening, hey? We still haven't answered Martin's question, and it's a very good one. I should have thought of it myself. Why speed up a death that's imminent?"

"But *was* it imminent?" said Frankie, ever the fact-checker.

53

"Sure, he'd lost his *joie de vire*, but how was his health? Generally? I know he was eighty-nine, but could he have lived another decade, Verity?"

Verity stared at Frankie for a moment like she didn't understand the question. Gave her body a shake, then her head. "Maybe another year or two if he was lucky. His doctors and I were worried. He'd had that small stroke a while back, hence the wheelchair, and some bouts of dizziness lately, some stomach pain. His blood pressure wasn't terrific, and I had to nag him to take his blood-thinning meds. He certainly wasn't helping himself—didn't eat well, unless I was doing the cooking, never drank enough water. The last few weeks, especially, he seemed to lose all his energy." She looked pale. "To be honest, I wasn't surprised when I found him in his chair. His doctor wasn't either."

"Which brings us back to Martin's question—why now?" said Earle. "Why kill a man who was not long of this earth?"

"Impatience?" suggested Merry, dabbing at some curry sauce that had dropped onto her blouse. "Someone might have known they were in the will and wouldn't—or couldn't—wait a year or two to inherit. Maybe someone with a gambling debt or a drug habit? Creditors at their door?"

Earle nodded. *Not a bad theory.*

"Or maybe it wasn't planned!" Merry continued. "Maybe someone dropped by to see George and a fight broke out, or maybe a random stranger broke in…"

Okay, now she was over-reaching. He turned to Verity. "Seagrave still locked up like Fort Knox? Still need access codes to get anywhere near the joint?"

She nodded. "And George had no patience for random visitors— strange or otherwise. I sincerely doubt his death was the result of a break-in. I certainly didn't see any signs of that. Nothing had been taken or disturbed, at least not that I noticed."

"There are plenty of other motives," said Martin, thinking back to his books. "Loftier motives, like passion, power, revenge."

Verity looked startled by all of them, and Earle felt a little weary himself. Knew it was time to hold up the white flag on her behalf (and his own if he was being honest). He glanced at the large clock he'd hung above his desk, then pushed his bowl away and stood up.

"It's getting late, and Verity could do with an early one. I suggest we call it a day and reconvene in the morning. If you're up to it, Verity."

She looked at him vaguely, then dropped her untouched bowl to the table.

"It's going to be okay," he told her, helping her to her feet. "Tomorrow is a new day, and perhaps we'll have the pathology report and a clearer idea of what we're working with."

"And if we don't?" she asked, her voice just a whisper.

"Then we push on anyway, because that's what we do, right sleuths?"

Earle turned to the others, and they all nodded, Merry holding two thumbs up and making Verity smile properly for the first time in days.

~

The house was silent when Merry walked in, and it made her frown. The kitchen looked like a bomb had hit it, and Lola was nowhere to be seen.

Damn it, thought Merry. She was supposed to be here supervising Archie's detention!

"Helloooo? Anyone home?" she sang out, but only silence replied.

Then she heard it, the gentle squeak of a mattress. Coming from Archie's room.

She placed her handbag aside, then steeled herself and walked slowly towards it.

The door was closed, of course it was closed, it was always closed these days, so she raised a hand and tapped.

"Munchkin?" she called out. "I know you're in there. Can I come in? Please?"

Again, nothing.

She slowly turned the knob, slowly pushed it open. Archie was lying on his bed, earbuds in place, eyes closed. She felt herself exhale, then almost giggled. What had she been expecting?

"Archie?" she said, this time louder.

His eyes flew open and he sat up with a start. "What's up?"

"I... well, nothing. I was just wondering how you are?"

He shrugged. "How's your new case going?"

"Oh, forget about that. I want to know how *you* are!"

He shrugged again and looked away, and she felt her heart plunge.

Archie's eyes used to light up when she entered the room. Now he could barely look at her straight.

"Did you get some of the spag bol Lola heated up? It's your fave."

"Yeah, but it's not my fave. Not anymore."

"Really? You've changed your *favourite meal?* And you haven't *told* me?"

She was joking, but he didn't look amused.

His eyes flew back at her. "You're not the only one who gets to change. I'm allowed to change too."

"Of course you are," she said, although changing into a brat wasn't ideal. Then, "You think I've changed."

Is that what this was about?

"I prefer lasagne now," was his reply.

"Okay, well, I'll see if I can find time to make it on the weekend. How does that sound?"

But he didn't hear that bit. He'd reapplied his earbuds and was already turning away.

~

Earle's house was also strangely silent when he got back, and he felt a burst of relief. There was no blaring TV or yapping dog or crying, screeching baby.

Beryl was missing, but he could see his daughter slumped on the couch, and for a moment he thought she was sleeping, dropped his things as quietly as he could as he tried to tiptoe past her.

"She's wheeling Saffie around the block," came Tess's voice, and he glanced down to see her blinking up at him. Lovingly. "She refused to settle."

He smiled, sat down beside her. "You never were a very good sleeper yourself."

"So it's karmic then?"

"Nah, it's just parenting. Anyone who tells you their baby is a perfect sleeper better watch out. In my experience perfect babies make appalling teenagers."

Tess sat up and stretched her arms out. "In that case, Saffron will be an angelic fifteen-year-old."

He laughed. "Can I get you something? Cold drink? Tea."

"Water will be good. I might need to feed when they get back."

He went to the kitchen and poured her a glass, then steeled

himself as he returned. Now was as good a time as any.

"We need to talk, honey," he said. "It's about a homeless man."

~

"You're home at last," came a cheerful voice as Martin pushed open the front door to his beachside apartment building.

Rachelle Easterly was standing just outside her ground floor unit, a book in her hand, a smile on her ruddy face. "I wanted to give you this. It's the first in that Hilary Mantel trilogy I was telling you about. Thomas Cromwell's scheming will give your baddies a run for their money!"

She handed the well-thumbed paperback across, and he thanked her.

"Although I've got a new case, so I might not get a chance to read it for a while."

"Not another missing woman I hope," she said, and he shook his head. "Phew." Then she nodded at the book, causing her fire-engine red hair to flop down over one eye. "Take as long as you need, Martin. If I require it back, I know where to find you."

Then she grinned mischievously and closed her door behind her.

Martin was grinning, too, as he made his way up three flights of stairs. He had gone ahead and bought the Balmoral apartment that had caused so much consternation during their last case. The wild-haired owner, Rachelle, had eventually agreed he'd be a good match and not just for the building. Martin had a hunch she was eyeing him off too, and he wasn't sure how he felt about that and not just because his last girlfriend had perfect blond hair and was a stunner.

He'd sworn off women for a while. Well, women who weren't his mother.

Still, it didn't hurt to make a friend. He'd never really had one of those before...

~

Frankie's heart almost stopped as she stepped out of the elevator and glanced across the corridor to see her oldest friend leaning against her apartment door.

"Haven't moved in with your bit of rough then?" said the woman, retrieving her large calico bag from the carpet.

"J-Jan," Frankie managed.

"Oh, I'm sorry, did I scare you?"

Before Frankie could respond, Jan reached into her bag and pulled out a cake tin. An old-fashioned one, the metal kind, with a floral pattern stencilled around the side. "Just wanted to leave this with you. Thought you might need sustenance after all the hard work you've been doing for Verity."

"How do you know about that?"

Jan chuckled. "When are you going to get it, honeybun? I know everything. Although…" She dropped her head to one side, her ample chin wobbling. "I don't quite know what you were doing the other week, spying on me from your lovely Audi. Do you miss me? Or was it just curiosity?"

"No… I…" Frankie wasn't sure how to respond.

"Well, I think it's sweet you miss me. Perhaps we can go back to how things ought to be. Wouldn't that be a relief? For *everybody*!"

Then she smiled innocently, twirled clumsily, and headed for the elevator, which pinged open upon her call.

Frankie watched mutely as the elevator took a beaming Jan away, then grappled for her keys, let herself in, and pushed the door secure behind her. Leaning up against it, she tried to get her ragged breathing back in check. Tried to remember her latest mantra— "I willingly release the past; I am exactly where I need to be"—before giving up on that and dropping to the floor.

It took Frankie two hours, four episodes of *Emily in Paris*, and a bottle of pinot grigio to return to the cake tin that had been abandoned by the front door. She picked it up, slowly opened the lid, not sure what she was expecting. A dog turd? A bomb? Anthrax?

It was so much worse.

Peering inside, Frankie could see a carrot-and-walnut cake with thick lemon frosting. It looked utterly delicious.

She exhaled loudly, scooped the cake out with both hands, then lifted it above her head and hurled it at the door.

CHAPTER 9 ~
A TIME TO SPECULATE

Tuesday morning's sky was a fluffy ball of grey, not unlike Merry, who was dressed in a smoky-coloured cardigan and pouting into the empty muffin jar. If only she'd had more energy last night, she would have baked something fresh for today's nine-o'clock meeting. She thought back to Archie and how hard she'd tried to talk to him. How quickly he'd shut her out, insisting he wanted to get on with his homework when they both knew homework was the last thing he wanted to do. Or at least it used to be. Now, it seemed, having a conversation with his mother was even lower down Archie's dreaded to-do list.

It made her heart break into a thousand pieces.

"Penny for your thoughts?" said Earle, strolling into the office kitchen.

Merry looked up with a start. "What? Oh, just wishing I'd baked some fresh treats." She discreetly brushed a tear from one eye.

"You know, we brought you into this agency for your mind, not your muffins," said Earle, leaning past her to fetch a fresh cup from the cupboard in the kitchen before flicking on the kettle.

"I know, but I can't help myself. I'm a feeder, like Verity."

Or at least, like Verity used to be. No one was expecting Verity to show up today with a platter of treats.

"And we appreciate it. But I'm not sure I need any more feeding." He patted his ample belly and chuckled. "You're making my Beryl jealous."

"Morning!" sang out Frankie as she strolled in, Martin close behind her. "Verity not here yet? Home still, counting her money?"

Earle gave her a stern look. "She's on her way," he said. "But while it's just the four of us, I wanted to have a quiet word with you, Frankie."

The young woman batted her thick black lashes innocently. "*Moi?* Why?"

"I know what you're doing," he said, "and I don't like it one bit."

"Doing? What am I doing? Exactly?"

He gave her a weary look just as another voice sang out from the interior office.

"Hello!"

Earle held up a finger. "We'll talk about this later, but please remember Verity is our client, so be polite."

"I'm always polite," she said as he left the kitchen.

Verity was standing at the front door, a white cardboard box in one hand, a laptop bag over one shoulder. Her hair was bouncier and her clothes fresh, but she still had the haunted look in her eyes, and her Irish-white skin looked even whiter. Like an egg about to crack. Then she opened the box and it felt like the old Verity was back. Inside was a delectable mix of chocolate eclairs, jam donuts and one particularly tasty-looking strawberry tart.

"I couldn't let Merry do all the heavy lifting," she explained as she placed them on the conference table. "Of course they're not home baked, but—"

"They're perfect," said Earle. "Did you get any sleep?"

She smiled. "I'm okay, thanks, Earle. I... I just can't stop thinking of poor George, still at the morgue..."

Then her smile flickered out and her eyes filled with tears.

"Come, sit," he replied. She was fooling nobody. "I'll get Frankie to fire up the espresso machine."

Twenty minutes later, after the requisite small talk and slurps of replenishing coffee, Frankie decided it was time to get down to business.

"I gather nobody's heard anything from the pathologist," she said, and both Verity and Earle shook their heads.

"My solicitor hasn't received the autopsy results yet," said Verity. "She... Well, she is rather concerned that we're doing this. She advises me to lie low and say nothing to anybody."

"Except we're not just *anybody*, are we?" said Merry. "We're your friends. We're here to help."

"But how far can we get without the pathology results?" she asked. "I mean, what do we do now?"

"We do what Earle despises, honey, and we speculate!" said Frankie as she picked up the box of treats on the table. "I want to get back to Martin's question from last night. Why kill a man who was already dying? Merry mentioned impatience—somebody wanting to get ahold of the money sooner rather than later—but I have to wonder whether it had more to do with selfishness. Maybe somebody didn't want to share."

Then she scooped up the lovely tart Earle had been eyeing off and plonked it on her plate, causing the old man to frown.

"Share? How do you mean?" asked Merry.

"I don't know a lot about inheritances—never been quite so lucky." Another loaded look at Verity. "But it seems to me that George really spread his wealth about—gifts here, there and everywhere. And a *third* of everything to his lowly secretary? Extraordinary."

Now Verity was frowning. "What are you saying, Frankie?"

"I'm saying there's one person who needs to be right at the top of our suspect list. Charlie Burlington."

Earle looked relieved as Frankie nodded at the shiny new whiteboard that was standing to attention on one side of the office. This was another Merry addition and was currently decorated with random doodles and smiley faces, also thanks to Merry, of course.

Not that Merry was smiling now. She still refused to consider young Charlie a suspect and sat back in her seat, her arms crossed.

"I won't be writing her name up there," she said. "It's ridiculous."

"Is it? Really?" said Frankie. "Think about it logically, Merry, without your Mother Hen hat on if that's possible. Charlotte is supposed to be George's one and only remaining heir—we all assumed as much, right? And yet he's splashed his wealth about. Perhaps Charlie got wind of what was happening and came back from London to confront her grandfather. Or maybe he told her of his plans when she returned three weeks ago. No offence Verity, but 'surprised' would be an understatement. She must have been furious to find she had to share her inheritance equally with the person who'd slaughtered half her family—Aunty Susan—as well as some lowly secretary."

"I really wish you would not use that word," Verity said sullenly.

"What? Lowly or secretary?"

"It still doesn't explain why Charlie would go on and kill George *before* she'd convinced him to change his will back," said Earle.

"It does if he refused to change it and was even considering giving away *more* of the family silver," said Frankie. "Think about it. Young Charlotte arrived home *two weeks* before his death. Very suspicious timing. And yet she wasn't at Seagrave the night her granddad died? That's even more suspicious! I know she told you she was at a friend's place, Verity, but how do we really know that? Hm? Anyone check her alibi? Little Miss Butter Wouldn't Melt? Maybe Charlie *was* at home and she popped a pillow over Gramps's face to stop him from giving away more of what was rightfully hers, then cleared out and pretended to be staying with a friend."

"Oh, Frankie!" said Merry. "That's a terrible thing to say! She wouldn't do that to her beloved Gramps!"

Frankie rolled her eyes at Merry. "You are far too soft for this business. I'm not even sure what you're doing here."

"Better than being an ice queen!" Merry retorted while Frankie just bit into her tart.

Martin watched the exchange with disinterest. None of this was where his mind had been heading. He wanted to get back to the big-ticket motives he'd mentioned last night.

"There is another reason George might have been killed prematurely," he said. "It doesn't always come down to money, you know. I keep telling you, the inheritance is such an *obvious* motive, but it doesn't make it the only one. If this were a Flynn Bold adventure"—now they were rolling their eyes his way as they always did when he brought up his best-selling fictional detective—"the inheritance would be a massive red herring. What if we're looking at this all wrong?"

"Oh, for the love of God!" said Frankie, chewing. "Cut to the chase, smug author man. We haven't got a commercial break to get to!"

"What if it's all about revenge?" He looked very pleased with himself as he brushed some crumbs from his statement T-shirt—this one read LET'S FIND A CURE FOR STUPID. "He might have been frail in the end," he continued, "but Sir George was an indomitable force in his prime. Must have made countless enemies."

Verity did not seem convinced. "George was a hard task master, sure, but he never received any death threats if that's what you're referring to. There's certainly no one I can think of offhand."

"What about closer to home?"

Martin jumped up and grabbed a non-permanent marker pen from the lip of the whiteboard, gave them all another smug grin, then scribbled down the name Susan LeDoux. Sir George's incarcerated daughter. The woman they had all helped put away.

There was silence for a few minutes, then Merry scowled. "That doesn't even make sense. She's locked behind bars."

"Doesn't mean she can't organise it from within," said Frankie, grappling for her smartphone. "You might be onto something, Marty babe! Susan must despise daddy dearest for how it all turned out. If he hadn't hired us, she'd still be swanning about, sipping champagne poolside. She's the perfect suspect. I love it!"

A glance at Verity now. "She's at Long Bay Correctional Centre, yes?" The PA nodded warily as Frankie checked her watch. "Okay, I've missed the morning slots, but there's visiting hours between two and three this afternoon, so I'll give the women's deputy warden a buzz and see if she can squeeze me in with late notice."

"You're going to see Susan in person?" said Merry, dumbfounded.

"You know the deputy warden *and* the visiting hours?" was more Earle's concern.

She ignored them both as she scrolled through her phone, looking for a number. "Of course Susan may refuse my visit"—she pressed Dial—"but I can only... Oh, hello, yes, it's Frankie Jo here. Could you put me through to Rosetta Testino's office, thanks."

Then she winked before stepping away to take the call.

Martin turned back to Verity. "I have one more reason to kill a man prematurely, if you're up for it." Verity didn't look up for it at all, was already hitching her shoulders defensively, as he said the word: "Power."

Verity's shoulders dropped. "I'm not following."

"We're forgetting about the biggest asset of all, Sir George's mining company. Burlington Holdings. What happens to that now? With the old guy dead? His son and grandson also gone. Who's taking over the reins?"

"Don't be so sexist!" called out Frankie, still on hold, one palm over the receiver. "It'll go to Charlie of course." Then she shot a look at Merry and added, "Her name should definitely be up on that board. She's got a few crosses against it now."

"No, no," said Verity as Martin went to write. "Charlie's only young; she's not ready and nor is she interested in the family business. Besides, George had already set up his succession plan, his CEO has taken over. Graham Fergerson. A lovely chap, very loyal, very good at what he does."

"Could he be a suspect?" asked Martin. "Maybe he felt George was running the company into the ground and needed to get the old guy out of the equation before the share price plummeted."

"That's a very long bow to draw, Martin," said Earle.

"And very unlikely," added Verity. "Like I said, it's a family business and lately, a poisoned chalice. I know for a fact that Mr Fergerson had his work cut out for him trying to learn the ropes from George. I doubt he'd try to speed that process up. He's been thrown in the deep end, and he certainly looked shell-shocked when we met before the funeral."

"Still worth looking into," said Earle, indicating for Martin to jot down the name.

"I'll speak to Fergerson," Martin said as he scribbled away. "I know my way around that office."

Martin had been to Burlington Holdings' swanky headquarters last summer when he interrogated Susan's French husband Clem LeDoux. Clem had worked for Sir George before it all imploded. He'd played a large part in the implosion, and the last Martin heard, he'd been sacked and banished from the fold.

"Fabuloso," said Merry. "In fact, shall we split up the chores like last time? According to our skill sets?"

"Hang on just a sec there, Merry," said Earle. "It's good to chew this all over, but we don't even know what we're dealing with yet. Perhaps it'd be best if we wait until we speak to Verity's lawyer, see what evidence they have against her. We still need to wait for the pathology report and—"

"Oh, for goodness' sake, Earle," said Frankie, returning to the table. "You promised when we set up this agency that you were going to stop being a handbrake. It's a bore!" His lips smudged downwards as he heard her out. "You know as well as I do that those reports can take days, even weeks, and we've always worked best to a deadline, a very tight one, so let's not mess with the template now. I suggest we hit the ground running. Lovely Rosetta has just added my name to

Susan's visitor's list, so provided she agrees to see me, I can firm her up or tick her off before the afternoon is out. And the rest of you should pick a suspect too."

"Yes, but—"

"And forget about our so-called skill sets," Frankie rattled on. "I think this case is more about our established contacts. Mine is Susan. God knows she flirted with me hard enough last time. And yours, Earle, is your old buddy Detective Soderbergh. Talk about flirting!" She smirked as Earle's lips went even further south. "See if you can't charm more info out of her. And Verity, it won't hurt you to go back through your boss's business affairs and see if he had any clients who wished him dead."

"I'm not permitted anywhere near the office, Frankie. It's a condition of my bail. I'm to avoid his homes, his workplaces…"

"That's where I come in," said Martin. "Can you set up the meeting with Fergerson for me, Verity? I could also ask the CEO about threats while trying to work out if he was a threat to George himself."

Verity nodded, and Frankie glanced across at Merry. "What about you, Festive? Who did you bond with last time? I can't recall…"

"I could talk to George's old lodge manager, Angus? He might have some clues again," she suggested but Earle was shaking his head.

"He's miles away, and wouldn't have had access to Fort Knox anyway, right?"

This question was directed at Verity, who agreed. "He'd never been to Seagrave before the funeral, nor did he have the access codes," she said. "Only three people had them—myself, Charlie and Shannon."

"What about Charlie then?" said Merry. "I spoke to her last time. I could have another whirl?"

"Hmmm…" Frankie clearly remembered how badly that first interview went.

"I'll get more out of her this time, I promise!" Merry countered.

Frankie darted a look at Earle, and he just shrugged. "Fine. But don't let her play games with you this time."

Merry beamed. "Actually, games are *exactly* what I have in mind."

CHAPTER 10 ~
A TIME TO PLAY

It was COLONEL MUSTARD in the CONSERVATORY with the ROPE. Merry knew that for certain. Had done her calculations and was now staring at the Cluedo board, unwilling to give the game away just yet.

Not only was she having fun, but her opponent, young Charlotte, seemed so desperate to "whoop Merry's arse"—Charlie's own words as the game began—that Merry simply didn't have the heart to tell her she hadn't even come close. Not after the year Charlie had had.

It was a miracle the young woman had even agreed to see her so quickly, but she had a hunch it had less to do with Merry's company and more to do with the choice of location—the Games Room Café—where they were currently hunched over a Cluedo board. Of course.

"This is going to be my new favourite hang!" Charlie declared as she moved her bright red figurine into the LIBRARY.

Charlie had chosen to be Miss Scarlet—who else?—and that suited Merry just fine. Mrs White had always been Merry's character of choice, right from the start.

Merry recalled her first game of Cluedo back when she was a child, on the sandy floor of her cousins' tent. They were older and bolder and had raided the characters, choosing the "coolest" and "sexiest", and so she was left with "dumpy" Mrs White.

Yet Mrs White had won her the game, and so she had stuck to her ever since. A good luck omen, if you will. At one point, her ex-husband told her she had "turned into dumpy Mrs White"—this was not long before he found his own Miss Scarlet to replace her—and she recalled thinking she should be offended but really couldn't manage it.

And so here they were, enjoying cups of hot chocolate and

melting macadamia brownies while the younger woman's eyes shifted from her cards to the back of Merry's.

Like she had X-ray vision.

"How about this then," George's granddaughter said, scooping up the yellow figurine and the tiny knife and plonking them in the room beside Miss Scarlet. "I think it's Colonel Mustard, with the dagger, in the library."

She gave Merry a smarmy look, and Merry made a show of checking her cards.

One out of three wasn't bad, but it wasn't nearly good enough. Merry reached for the dagger card she was holding and showed her.

"Damn it," said Charlie, her perfect little forehead wrinkling as she crossed it off her list.

"So how are you going?" Merry ventured, deciding it was time to get serious. The way Charlie was going, they'd be here all day.

"I'll work it out," she replied.

"No, honey, I mean, after your grandfather's death."

"His *murder* you mean. Can you believe it? Verity! A dark horse all along!"

Just as she had bluffed her way through the trauma of her parents' passing, Charlie was acting apathetic again, like it was as trivial as the game they were playing.

But it wasn't a game, and perhaps it was time for Merry to show her that.

She rolled a seven, picked up Mrs White and marched her to the pool room in the middle of the board where the waitress had earlier placed a small orange envelope.

"Colonel Mustard, in the Conservatory, with the rope," said Merry, omitting the question mark, bringing the game to its conclusion.

Charlie frowned and rifled through her cards. Rifled through them again.

"You're bluffing," she said. "You know I don't have any of them because you have one. Maybe two."

"That is a tactic, yes. But not this time. Sorry."

Then she reached for the envelope and pulled out three cards to reveal the killer, the room and the weapon.

It was indeed COLONEL MUSTARD in the CONSERVATORY with the ROPE.

"Damn it," said Charlie again, but there was admiration in her tone this time. "You are good."

"I don't win championships for my looks, sweetie," Merry replied and then quickly added, "But you put up a good fight. Come on, let's replenish our drinks. We need to talk."

Charlie had managed to distract her long enough. She called the waitress over, and they ordered another pot of hot chocolate, then she asked, "So what will you do now? Will you stay on at Seagrave?"

"Not allowed! It's all locked up behind police tape now, and I'm not staying at the penthouse! I mean, it's close to Town Hall station, which is handy and stuff since I don't drive, but it's so large and empty and... *cold*." She shuddered just thinking about it.

Merry couldn't help shuddering along. She'd been to the city pad once, back when she first met Sir George, not long after the initial tragedies occurred. Merry had never warmed to the place either. There was far too much steel and chrome.

"If I wanted cold I'd go back to London," Charlie was saying. "No, I'm going to finish school by correspondence, then do some voluntary work with an animal rescue shelter in Ecuador."

"Ecuador? In South America?"

She nodded proudly. "I'm going to give back. I'm not the spoiled little princess you all think I am."

"Oh, I've never thought that," said Merry. *Poor little rich girl, perhaps...*

"I'm going to make something of my life," Charlie was saying. "I'm not letting that gold-digging traitor ruin it for me."

Merry pushed her glasses into place. "You really think Verity did it? Why?"

"For the money *obviously*. She's probably been plotting it for years... manipulating her way into my poor grandpa's heart."

"You think your grandfather loved Verity?"

"Well, not like *that*! But yeah. For sure. She was the only one who could boss him about. Everyone else was scared of him. But not Verity. She was running everything in the end. You know that, right? I don't know why she didn't just, like, move into Seagrave. She was there all the time. You know she was doing all his banking for him? That's sus! Maybe she forged her way into the will. Or maybe she just bossed him into it."

Merry dropped her head to the side. Perhaps Frankie's hunch was right. Choosing her words carefully, she asked, "When did you first learn about the contents of your grandad's will?"

"How do you mean?"

"I mean, did you have any inkling that he was giving so much to Verity?"

"Hell no! I was, like, whoa!"

"He never mentioned it?"

"To me? Not a word, but then he wouldn't. We didn't talk about money. It's disgusting to talk about money. Obscene."

Merry nodded. She agreed, but they needed to keep talking about it if they were going to solve this thing. She thanked the waitress for the fresh pot of hot chocolate, then topped Charlie's cup up and said, "How did you feel about your grandad giving away so much of the family wealth to an outsider?"

Charlie grabbed a brownie and began chewing. She half shrugged, speaking with her mouth full. "I wasn't thrilled, *obviously*, but, like, who would be?"

"Do you mind if I ask where you were the night your grandfather died? You weren't staying with him. You were with a friend?"

Charlie licked her lips and shook her glossy blond hair from her face. "That's right."

"Which friend?"

Charlie looked annoyed. "Nobody you'd know. Just a girlfriend. Penelope Cromer if you must know." Then she dropped her lower lip and gasped. "Oh my God, that's what all this is about? You're helping *Verity*! You don't think she did it. You're going to interfere again!"

"Hey, it's not interfering if she's innocent. We're just exploring the case further. Like we did with your brother's murder."

"Oh dope, because that all turned out brilliantly."

Merry was gobsmacked, although she got it. By clearing Heath's name, they had all but detonated the final bomb in the young girl's life, outing her Uncle Clem as a pervert and locking away her murderous Aunty Susan.

Charlie shook herself out. "Sorry. I know you were trying to help, but..."

Merry nodded. "The truth hurts. It was hard. I do know that."

The sleuths' revelations had left Charlie more alone than before, and now with her grandfather gone, she had no one.

"So you were at this friend Penelope's house when Verity called you? Yes?"

"Just said that, didn't I?" Then she blew some air through her lips as though trying to calm herself down. When she finally spoke again, her voice was softer, gentler, more wounded. "It was such a shock when Verity called. We've never been tight or anything, so I figured something was up. She said, 'Do you think you could come back to Seagrave?'" Charlotte attempted an Irish accent but didn't quite pull it off. "I told her to sod off, that I was busy. But it wasn't that."

Charlie's eyes welled with tears. "I just knew." Then she flicked Merry a pointed look, making a tear dislodge. "I've had enough experience to know when someone's about to give me bad news."

"Oh honey," began Merry, reaching a hand towards her, but Charlie stiffened and pulled back.

"Anyway, I refused to budge until she told me exactly what was going on. That's when she said that Gramps had passed, like he had some kind of 'use by' date!" Charlie swiped at a tear that was now trickling down her cheek. "So that's when I got Penelope to drop me back. She's... Well, she's been awesome."

Merry handed her a serviette, and she took it, wiping below her eyes. "I'm glad you've got your friends then. Do you still see Igor?"

"Iggy? God no! That tattooed loser. What was I thinking?"

"I thought you were in love." Merry was mocking her a little, but she didn't seem to notice.

Charlie dumped her serviette in her half-finished chocolate and said, "I've grown up a lot since I've been in London."

"I can see that. Which is why I know you won't be offended when I ask this next question. Why *did* you come back to Sydney when you did, Charlie?"

"Sorry?"

"You came home two weeks before your grandfather died, right? It just feels so fortuitous that you'd made it back just in the nick of time."

Charlie stared at her for a moment, then it clicked. "Oh, so murder runs in my veins, does it? You think I came back to kill him for the fun of it?"

"No, I'm not saying—"

"Verity told me to come home, if you must know. *She* said he wasn't well and didn't have long to live." She gave Merry a pointed look. "How did she know that? Hmmm? It's like she's been calling the shots from the start, like she was giving me a chance to say goodbye before she… before she…"

Then she buckled over her cup, sobbing into the hot chocolate. Merry reached over and patted her back, then smiled kindly at the waitress who was handing her some fresh serviettes.

"I'm sorry, Charlie, I really am," she said, placing the serviettes beside her. "I really liked your grandfather, and I'm so sorry it had to end like this. But you can't honestly believe that Verity is capable of that."

Charlie looked up, mascara running below her eyes. "Oh, but *I* am?"

"You know I don't believe that either."

She snatched up a serviette. Dabbed below her eyes angrily. "What I can't believe is that you lot would really think Verity is innocent, even knowing she conned Gramps out of his money! I'll have to sell everything now, you know? Including Seagrave. I have to hand a third of it to her and a third of it to creepy Clem!"

"Clem?" Now Merry looked angry. "Why does Susan's ex-husband get a third of Seagrave?"

Charlie's uncle, Clem LeDoux, had been busted watching her in the shower at the ski lodge one winter holiday. It was all he was busted for in the end, but it had been enough to turn his name to mud and his wife to murder. It was that one criminal act—because it was criminal to Merry—that set off a spark that ignited the family tragedy.

"Ex-husband?" echoed Charlie. Then she almost smiled. "You're not as cluey as you think you are, Merry. You didn't know?"

"Know what? Why would your grandfather leave that pervert anything?"

"He didn't. He left it to Aunty Sue. She can't use it in prison, and she's still married to Clem. His lawyer's already been in touch with mine. He wants to start selling everything. Claim their share, apparently."

"They're still *married*? Susan and Clem? After everything that happened?"

"Yaha! And so they should be. Susan is only in jail because she tried to defend Clem, so how rude would it have been for him to dump her?"

She made a valid point, thought Merry, especially if he still gets access to her bank account. And to all those multi-million-dollar properties that he seemed in an awful hurry to sell off. Her anger dissolved as the prospect of a fresh suspect—a *more deserving* suspect—materialised before her.

"Is he still at the house they shared?"

"Oh no, Aunty Sue sold that before trial. I can't believe my aunty. I mean, the guy was perving at me and she's still *married* to him? Now *that's* obscene! I guess if you want to look for suspects, well..." She glanced down at the Cluedo board and said, "The Paedo Frenchman, in the ballroom, with the..." Her hand hovered over the tiny weapons before she plucked out the tiny round vial and said, "poison."

Then she offered Merry a knowing look as she took another bite of her brownie.

~

The last time the sleuths had seen Sir George's only daughter in person, Susan LeDoux was hyperventilating as the police dragged her from her father's clifftop mansion, under arrest for the murder of half her family.

Except for Frankie that is.

The one-time reporter had attended the court hearing and watched a far more controlled Susan sit placidly throughout, making notes and chatting to her lawyers. It was just a sentencing hearing—Susan had readily pleaded guilty to the manslaughter of her brother, Roman Burlington, and to the second-degree murders of Roman's wife Tawny Burlington-Brown and their son Heathcliff. Then guilty again for the subsequent murder of Tawny's loyal housekeeper Lia Segeyaro.

The early guilty plea was not given to end the trauma and misery she had wreaked but to secure herself a lighter sentence, and it worked. Susan got just twenty years, thanks in large part to the red carpet of well-heeled references that George managed to roll out, including several esteemed psychiatrists who pointed the blame at everyone but Susan (her "estranged" mother, her "errant" husband, her "neglectful" father...).

To Frankie, it was insulting, a slap on the wrist. Four innocent people murdered, and yet with good behaviour, the remorseless killer could be out in fifteen.

Susan did not even flinch when the sentence was handed down. The only time the calm veneer cracked was when Frankie had looked up from her typing to catch Susan staring at her across the courtroom with such savagery, Frankie knew she would never be forgiven. Nor would Susan agree to see her, which she never did even as Frankie wrote a series of exclusive articles on the murders. It had all been from Sir George's perspective.

Yet here Susan was, sitting across from Frankie in the visitors' rooms at Long Bay Correctional Centre, not just agreeing to see her but back to her flirty self. She looked gaunt though, her once glossy auburn hair now flat and going grey at the roots, her flowing silks swapped for baggie prison greens, but she had a familiar glint in her eye as she gave Frankie the once-over.

"The fearless Frankie Jo in person," she said. "This must be my lucky day."

Frankie smiled back. "Thanks for agreeing to this. I wasn't sure if you were talking to me."

"I haven't forgiven you, if that's what you mean." Her eyes turned flinty. "You're just lucky it's dreadfully dull in here and I'm gagging for visitors. My so-called besties all dropped me as quickly as your... Well, your editor I believe." She stopped to let that sink in. "I heard you were sacked and after all those award-winning stories you wrote about me!"

She grinned as Frankie shifted uncomfortably in her seat and added, "I might be locked away, but I still have my Clem, remember? He's good for a bit of gossip."

Unlike Merry, Frankie wasn't surprised by this news. She'd seen Clem sitting in the pews of the court, not far from Susan's barristers. He hadn't missed the hearings either, even though he was being blamed for her "spiral downwards". Had been the person she first turned to when the sentence was handed down.

"You know, I always wondered why you stayed married to a paedophile," said Frankie, trying to regain the upper hand.

"Be careful there, Frankie," she shot back. "My husband was never charged with anything. Besides, he's still married to me, so I'm pretty sure he's got the short end of the stick." Frankie was not so sure, but she let her continue. "Clemmie is such a faithful hound. He's stuck by me through it all. And he's my eyes and ears out there,

tells me everything, including what the interfering sleuths are up to."
She winked at Frankie before her expression turned snarly. "Not to
mention that money-hungry bitch."

"You're referring to Verity?"

"Is there another money-hungry bitch I should be worrying
about?" Her lip curled further. "Can you believe Father left her a *third*
of everything? A third! She was just the hired help for goodness' sake.
She must have been screwing him."

Frankie had wondered the same thing. "Was she? Do you know?"

She chuckled. "Ask her yourself! I can only assume you're here
doing her bidding. Trying to find someone else to point the finger
at."

"You are a very good suspect though," said Frankie, smiling, and
Susan smiled back.

"I'll take that as a compliment. Those are few and far between in
here as well." Then her smile vanished.

"When did you first learn about your father's will? Did he tell
you?"

"Hardly. We weren't exactly speaking in the end. I mean,
Father was generous to a fault, but he wasn't very forgiving.
We communicated through his solicitor. I nearly fell off my chair
when old Fogerty told me about Verity. It was bad enough that dotty
Persephone had got her claws into the book collection, but—"

"Persephone?" There was that name again...

"Yes," said Susan impatiently, "Persephone Dupont, old family
friend. Do keep up. But when I heard *Verity's* name listed as a
primary beneficiary, I almost screamed. She did not deserve any of it.
So yes, I might have wanted to wring Father's neck for giving that
witch a third of everything, but it couldn't have been me could it?
I am locked up in here, so you'll have to flick your gorgeous almond
eyes elsewhere."

"Ah but you're forgetting *your* 'eyes' out there—Clem. How do we
know he didn't do it all on your behalf for revenge against your
father? After all, you saved him once. Maybe he was repaying the
favour."

That made Susan chuckle. "Oh, I love the symmetry, that is good!
But why would I want to avenge my father?" Her tone was earnest
now. "He was already in his own quiet purgatory. You lot did him no
favours. Nor did Verity. If only she had talked some sense into him

and never brought you together in the first place."

"You're seriously going to blame Verity for...?" Frankie waved a hand around the bustling visitors' room.

"Why not? The way I see it, Verity is the *only one* who has profited from all this. Charlie was banished to dreary England, Father lost his will to live, and you lot aren't exactly kicking goals even though he handed you far too much money for effectively detonating his life. Only one person came out on top after all that—the interfering PA."

"How about this then," said Frankie. "You knew your dad was dying, so you got Clem to bump him off and planted it on the interfering PA. Hoping you'd meet her in here one day."

Susan laughed her deep throaty chuckle, catching a guard's eye. She smothered the laughter down and said, "That is a better theory. Definitely stick to that one." Then she straightened her smile. "Don't think I haven't thought of grisly ways to torture the smug secretary who caused all this in the first place. But Clemmie? Bumping someone off. Hardly. He doesn't have the ticker. He's a lover, not a fighter, certainly not a doer. Hence the reason he liked to look at young girls but never touched. The very reason he's still free as a bird despite your best efforts."

Frankie frowned. Yes, speaking of regrets, Earle had never got over the fact that Clem was not charged with anything, never even fined. No one would speak out against him. Not Susan, not Charlie, not even Angus, who knew all about Clem's prying up at the ski lodge. They had circled the wagons, but it wasn't Clem they were protecting. It was Sir George. Like the indignity of having a paedophile son-in-law was worse than a murdering daughter.

"You were wrong about my husband, Frankie. He's harmless. Spineless even. But he's not a murderer."

"Even if that's true, you must have forged some pretty seedy contacts in here. Perhaps someone on the outside did you a favour, knowing you were coming into millions. And like you said, you can't use it. Why not throw some to an assassin to assuage your quest for revenge?"

"Assassin!" She snorted loudly now, and the guard approached. She waved a hand, not needing to be told, and lowered her voice, hissing. "You're not writing for that dirt rag anymore, Frankie, so you can forget the salacious storylines. And if that was even half true, then surely my *quest for revenge* wouldn't stop at Verity. I would also have five nosy little sleuths on my hit list."

She wasn't laughing as she said that, and Frankie tried not to squirm. An officer approached, and she wondered if he'd overheard her threat, but Susan was now nodding towards him.

"They're calling last drinks. Was there anything else, my darling?"

Susan was back to her flirtatious self, and Frankie felt creeped out by it but also frustrated.

"Another suspect would be good," she said.

"Why don't you start with Persephone Dupont?"

There was that name again. "Isn't Persephone the one who inherited Seagrave's library collection?" Frankie asked. "Why would she kill for some old books?"

"Not just *old books*, darling. It was a staggering collection! There's a very rare Shakespeare in there, might fetch millions! Last I heard, Persephone had been dumped by her third husband, or was it her fourth? Perhaps she needed some spending money."

~

Back at Sleuth headquarters, Earle was staring miserably at his phone. Odetta had promised to call as soon as she got a sniff of the autopsy results, but the afternoon was wearing on and still radio silence.

Martin, too, was angsty. He'd gotten exactly nowhere with George's replacement, Graham Fergerson, or more specifically, Fergerson's personal assistant. She'd been polite enough, had promised to pass on his message, but that was as far as the promises went.

And so they had spent the day helping Verity sift through George's files, his *online* files that is, the ones she still had cluttering her laptop.

And there were a lot of them.

They were looking for anything that sounded even vaguely aggressive or threatening. He didn't mince his words, old George, but apart from a few blunt-sounding exchanges, nothing seemed inflammatory enough to lead to murder.

By early afternoon, they were tired and bored and ready to give up. So it was with some relief when first Merry and then Frankie returned, both strolling in with matching jubilant expressions.

"Somebody's made some progress," said Martin. "Come on then, give us the goss."

And so they did, both women revealing how surprised Charlie and Susan were to learn of the PA's inheritance.

"Charlie says she only found out as you did Verity, at the reading of the will."

Martin stroked his nose. "She could be lying."

"So, too, could Susan," said Frankie. "She makes the same claim. I guess it's their word against ours."

"Not necessarily," said Martin, glancing back at his phone. "Maybe I should forget the CEO and call George's lawyer. Maybe he'll have more to say."

"Good luck with that," said Verity. "I reached out to Mr Fogerty after I was arrested, and he wouldn't have a bar of me. His assistant said it would be a conflict of interest. So I guess he's in DI Morgan's camp."

"Pity," said Earle.

"But that's not even my exciting news," said Merry. "Charlie told me that Susan and her creepy hubby Clem are still *married!*"

"Oh, that's old news," said Frankie, stealing Merry's thunder and then repeating everything Susan had told her.

"Did you know?" Merry asked Verity.

"Yes. I'm sorry, I probably should have mentioned it." Verity frowned. "I haven't slept properly since George passed… My head is all over the place."

"Oh honey," said Merry. She gave her a moment, then asked, "Why would Sir George leave his money to Susan, knowing Clem was still on the scene?"

"Well, I'm not sure that's a fair assessment," said Verity. "I mean, Clem's not really *on the scene*. Susan is locked away. But I think Susan is right. Sir George's heart broke that day you guys revealed what a monster his daughter was. I don't think he ever got over it. That's probably why he kept Susan in the will. I often wondered if he regretted involving you."

"Even after what she did to his family?"

"The operative word being *family*. He really did not expect you to point the finger at his only remaining child. Look, he was a pragmatist. He wanted to know the truth, but it left him gutted. It's the reason he had all but given up, because nothing had worked out as he had hoped or expected. Which is why when I found him that morning, the way it was staged made an awful kind of sense. I… I figured it was his final salute to them all, his—"

Earle's phone suddenly rang out, and he glanced at it annoyed, then his expression lightened. "Hold that thought. It's Odetta. Finally. Excuse me folks."

Earle strode to the other side of the office, and they used the time to replenish their coffees. When he returned, his lightness had evaporated. Merry felt a prickle run down her spine.

"What's happened?" she demanded.

"Pathology results are back," he said. "They've confirmed foul play. Found thirty grams of brodifacoum in Mr Burlington's stomach. That's the active ingredient in rat poison."

"He was *poisoned?*" said Merry. "How positively *Cluedoesque!*" That reminded her of what Charlie had declared earlier over the Cluedo board: "The Paedo Frenchman, in the ballroom, with the poison."

Did she know? Or was it just a very lucky guess?

Martin wasn't buying it. "That doesn't make any sense. I know poisons, have used them in several of my books. Thirty grams of brodifacoum might hurt a child but not a grown man, even one as frail as George."

"It will when that man's on blood-thinners," said Earle.

Verity gasped. "I was the one who insisted he take his stroke medication!"

"You can't blame yourself—" began Merry.

Earle spoke over her, eyes firmly on Verity. "That's not all. You said he'd been dizzy lately, Verity? Some stomach pain?" She nodded slowly. "The pathologist has consulted with his doctors and believes that more than one dose was administered. They found traces of it in his blood, liver, brain, spleen… All of that is highly consistent with having been poisoned over a period of time, perhaps several weeks."

"Several weeks?" repeated Verity now. She reached a shaky hand to her heart. "How could that happen? I mean… he lived alone at Seagrave. I was virtually the only one with access! I would have noticed if someone was in there poisoning him! How… how did they manage it?"

Earle gave Verity a sympathetic look, then turned to the others.

"Pathologist found traces of the rodenticide amongst the remnants of George's last meal."

"Okay, so what was his last meal?" asked Frankie.

"Something with beef, potato, carrots…" Earle turned his gaze back to Verity and said, "They believe he was poisoned through his Irish stew."

CHAPTER 11 ~

WHEN IRISH EYES AREN'T SMILING

The Dublin-born secretary stared hard at the sleuths, her eyes ablaze, her skin mottled pink. She knew what they were all thinking because she was thinking it too—there was only one person who cooked George his favourite stew, and that was Verity. And she had cooked a lot of it in his final months. Had admitted as much to everyone.

"But... but that's ridiculous!" she said. "I didn't poison George's food! I would never do such a thing!"

"Of course you wouldn't," said Merry, jumping to her defence again.

"But you did cook the stew?" said Frankie. "At Seagrave, right?"

Verity was now lost in her thoughts, her eyes zigzagging around the room like she was trying to work it all out. Or find a quick exit.

"Hello! Earth to Verity!" said Frankie, making the woman snap out of it. "We need to uncover how the poison got into *your* stew. It can't have been by osmosis."

Merry gasped at that, and Earle slapped Frankie with a scowl while Verity just looked wounded.

She closed her eyes and moaned. "Oh Lordy, I'm doomed!"

"Okay, let's all ease up a bit and try to think this through logically," said Earle. "Verity, are you okay? Do you need a drink? Anything?"

She shook her head, but Merry jumped up anyway and fetched her water from the kitchen, then pressed the glass gently into her hands, forcing her eyes open. She blinked at Merry. Thanked her.

Earle continued. "Right, so I'm guessing George didn't do his own grocery shopping or cooking?"

Verity shook her head firmly now. No.

"So who else provided George's meals? Did he have a housekeeper, a caterer? Order home delivery regularly? Maybe it got administered that way."

Verity's head was shaking again on each score. "He did have a cook for years and a regular housekeeper at the penthouse, but when he moved back into Seagrave, after Susan…" She didn't finish that sentence. "Well, he didn't want any strangers around after that. Didn't like having other people about. In the final months it was just me…"

Her hand began to tremble as she held the water glass, and so Merry took it off her and placed it on the table, then swapped a worried look with Earle.

"So you provided *all* his meals?" said Earle. *Talk about going above and beyond.*

Verity nodded, looking up. "He… Well, he only ever had a coffee and some grapefruit for breakfast. I usually managed to get a sandwich into him at lunchtime between meetings, and then… well… then I'd heat up some tinned soup for his dinner or cook him a quick egg on toast. But it never felt like enough, you know? He was wasting away, wasn't at all interested in cooking for himself. That's when I suggested my stew. He'd had that before, loved it. I think his mother used to make it." She gulped. "Oh God, no wonder they arrested me!"

Then she dropped her head back into her hands. When she next spoke, her voice was barely audible, just a wretched squeak. "I… I'd heat it up for him before I left each night. He didn't even eat it half the time."

"Well, he ate enough of it to kill him," said Frankie, making them all flinch now.

Earle almost growled at her. She was not helping. "So how did it work? You cooked the stew in a giant pot and, what? Stored the pot in the kitchen fridge? He helped himself or…?"

"Um…" She looked up, seemed confused. "No. Most of the time I put some in a small bowl and I'd zap it in the microwave for him. Leave it on the kitchen bench as I left for the evening."

"Okay, that's good!" said Merry. "Somebody could have wandered in and added the poison to the bowl after that."

"Except who?" she replied. "I was usually the only one there, always the last to leave."

"That's not strictly true," said Frankie. "What about Charlie? She was staying at the house during this period. She could have added it."

"She could have been poisoned too!" said Merry, shifting in a different direction.

Verity shook her head again. "No... she... she never ate any."

"Well, that's suspicious," said Martin.

"No, no," insisted Verity. "Charlie's a vegetarian. I always made beef or lamb stew. George needed the protein..."

She broke down again, head in her lap, and Martin looked disappointed, but Frankie wasn't buying it.

"Maybe Charlie just *told* you she was a veggo, Verity. Maybe that was to avoid getting poisoned by her own hand."

"So now you think it's Charlie again?" said Merry.

"Just keeping an open mind, as should you."

Merry's eyes were back on Verity. "I know the place was Fort Knox, but surely *other* people must have had access to the kitchen, to the stew. George must have had visitors at the house from time to time? Business associates? That CEO you were talking about?"

"Yes, of course," said Verity, looking up, wiping a hand across her face. "Mr Fergerson_was a regular at Seagrave, so too the CFO. George had various meetings set up over those last months and weeks, but I was always there, taking notes, making tea, seeing them in and out. I would have *known* if they were wandering off to the kitchen, tampering with my stew."

"Not necessarily," said Merry. "I remember the Seagrave layout perfectly. George worked out of the study, yes? Well that's on the same side of the house as the kitchen, just a few doors down. So anyone who was there for a meeting could've said they were using the loo but slipped into the kitchen, found the stew in the fridge and plopped some poison in it while no one was looking."

"Except he was poisoned gradually, over time," said Earle. "Several weeks, they think, judging by its presence throughout his organs."

"*Yes*," said Merry. "But is it possible it was all added in one dose, and it was *George* who consumed it slowly over time? Didn't you say he was barely eating, Verity?"

"That is true," she conceded. "I could never get him interested in more than a small bowl each evening, but if there was any left over after a week, I always discarded it and made him a fresh batch. Usually with a few different ingredients to liven it up."

"Okay, so someone who visited him weekly. They could've added it in several large doses, right, Earle?"

Earle scratched his white beard. "I guess that's a possibility."

Merry beamed like she'd been given a gold star, but Martin just looked deflated.

"That leaves the suspect list wide open again," he said.

"What about your assistant?" asked Earle. "Shannon wasn't it? How often was she at Seagrave?"

Verity looked stunned by the suggestion. "Shannon? Rarely, certainly never on her own. She worked out of headquarters, running my office while I ran Seagrave. The only times she would be at the house was when I called her in."

"But she had the codes? To Fort Knox?" asked Martin.

"Yes, but... but there's no reason she'd *want* to hurt George. Like I said, he was the one who insisted I employ her. She adored the man. What possible motive could she have?"

"She's not in the will?" Martin prodded. Verity shook her head this time. "So what will happen to her now?"

Verity shrugged like she hadn't given it a moment's thought. "We were both so busy after George passed, organising the funeral, sorting out George's business affairs. I never really considered what would happen to either of us to be honest. In fact, I haven't given her much thought since all of this... That sounds cruel. She's still young. I should check in on her. See if she's okay."

"You're the one going through the ringer, Verity," said Martin. "Has she called you since this exploded?"

"No, but she's probably very confused. Not sure who to believe. You can't honestly think she's involved? I just can't see it."

"You're too close to her," said Frankie dismissively. "I agree with Martin. It's bizarre she hasn't called you. You are her boss, after all. I'd like to meet her. See what she's got to say for herself. Can you set it up for me?"

"I guess so." Verity glanced worriedly at her phone.

"Good, make it happen. I think she's our best bet. She had access to the house and more importantly the kitchen, and there may be a motive somewhere that we just haven't come across yet."

"Perhaps they were having an affair, Shannon and Sir George," said Martin, and Verity nearly choked on the water she was now sipping.

"That's… that's ridiculous!" she said. "The girl's all of twenty."

"That never stopped a randy old bugger," said Frankie, swapping a conspiratorial smile with Martin.

~

Tiffany Weaver gave Kila a look that bordered on flirtatious as she stepped through the door and into his office, a waft of something sweet and musky emanating from her.

The grumpy gumshoe hoped she didn't have the wrong idea. He was keen to talk the Weaver murder over with somebody, and barman Trevor still hadn't called with any news. Knew he couldn't call Frankie, so he'd asked Tiffany to drop by instead.

And here she was, perfumed up, lips extra glossy, a slinky strapless number on. He dampened down his smile and offered her a tea, pretending his own cup was full of something similar. She accepted and then crossed her legs provocatively, glancing around.

"Nice office you've got here," she said.

"Thanks." He produced the blue notebook. "Your brother had a bunch of names written in here. Any of them mean anything to you?"

She smiled. "Not much for small talk then?"

"Not my cup of tea."

Her smile dropped. She nodded at the book. "I would've told you if they meant anything."

"Fair enough." He pulled out the coaster now. "What about this?"

She took it and glanced at both sides, another shake of the head. "This was in my brother's notebook."

"Was he a regular at Taboo? Before his last jail stint?"

"Hardly. I checked it out myself when I found that coaster. Not seedy enough for Phill." She smiled again. "Not *his* cup of tea."

He smiled back. He liked Tiffany. Maybe at another time, in another life… "The date on the back is the date my sister was taken."

No one was smiling now. "Aw, shit."

"To say the least. I think you're right. I think your brother's murder is linked back to Dragon, but it's not drugs. I think it might be linked to Chili and to that bar on the front of the coaster, Taboo. It's *my* regular hang. Somehow, some way, they're all connected."

She placed her cup down and sat back. "Talk me through it."

And he did. The way Kila saw it, Dragon and Weaver shared a cell together, so they had a lot of time to talk, a lot of time for confessions. Dragon no doubt told Weaver what he'd told Kila—that Chili was still alive when he'd finished with her, and he dumped her outside Taboo.

"Dragon said that to you?" said Tiffany, breaking through. "That he didn't kill her?"

"Regretted saying it, but yeah, that's what he insists. And if that's the truth—if she really was left outside Taboo and she was hurting…" Kila's jaw tensed, and he took a moment. Swallowed hard. "Then there's only one logical place she would have gone next."

"Into your regular hang, looking for you."

He nodded. "She didn't go to the police; we know that. Didn't come to my house. I know that too." More tightening of the jaw. "So she went into Taboo. I'm sure of it. Whether Dragon actually saw her go in or your brother put two and two together and worked it all out on his lonesome, the fact is, Taboo could hold the key. I think *that's* why your brother went there the minute he got out of jail. I reckon he was in there asking questions about Chili."

She sat forward suddenly. "You think Phill was helping to clear Dragon's name or maybe try to find out what really happened to your sister?"

Kila tried not to scoff. "Sorry, Tiffany, but I don't reckon your brother gave a flying toss what happened to my sister. And he probably didn't care too much about clearing Dragon's name either. If we just go on past behaviour—and as a PI that's all I can trust— then I'd say Phill was doing it for the money."

She sat back, shrugged, like he hadn't just insulted her brother again. "The five grand."

"Exactly. I think your brother believed Dragon's story about Chili and realised there was someone out there who'd got away with murder. And he wanted to hunt that person down and extort some cash from him."

"Blackmail," she said.

"If the shoe fits…"

She nodded. Irritably. "Oh, it fits. Far too snugly. Go on."

He looked down at the notebook and the coaster, both now

sitting on the desk in front of him. "I figure Dragon gave Phill the old coaster and your brother wrote down the date so he'd remember it. Then he went into Taboo and started asking questions about September 20, 2018. Who was there back then? Who might have seen something? Who might be a witness?"

"Or a killer," she added, and he nodded.

"He must have found his answer pretty fast because a week after he went into Taboo, he had all that cash. Well, you have to ask yourself, Tiffany, who would pay a stranger five quid out of the blue? With the promise of more to come?"

"Someone who needed to keep something quiet."

"I think your brother discovered who killed my sister. And that's what got him killed."

"Aw shit," she said again. "So if you find out who killed my bro, you might also find out who killed your sis."

He nodded. Was glad she'd articulated that because he was struggling to wrap his head around it.

"But who is this person? Were they in it with Dragon, do you think?"

"Maybe, maybe not."

Another thing that didn't bear thinking about.

"So why don't we go back and talk to JayJay? He might know more than he realises."

"You're welcome to," he said. "I'm banned from going anywhere near Her Majesty's Correctional Centres for a while."

She sniggered. "Something to do with your aforementioned conversation with Dragon Malone?"

He scraped a tousled black curl from one eye and sniggered along. Then pointed at the notebook. "I think your brother's already done the hard yards. Those names must tell us something. I've just got to work out what."

And he just had to hope Trevor found some answers soon in that mouldy basement of Taboo.

CHAPTER 12 ~
DUTCH COURAGE

Verity Vine looked like a woman reborn—her mottled cheeks had settled and her hands were no longer shaking as she sat on the couch in the centre of the sleuths' office.

And they had Frankie to thank for that, conceded Earle.

The ex-journo had brought in a bottle of whisky that morning, insisting that no office was complete without something strong stashed away, and she'd just proven its worth by handing Verity a shot of single malt. And then another.

The difference was extraordinary. Perhaps it was also the drink that gave Verity the courage to say what he hadn't been expecting; it had come right out of left field.

"There is another solution," she said as they began to finish up for the day. Then she placed a hand at her breast and added, "I can't believe I'm saying this. It's going to sound like I'm trying to deflect the blame…"

"That is what we're trying to do here," said Frankie. "In case you hadn't worked it out."

Still Verity wavered.

She closed her eyes briefly, then flung them open and said, "What if it was suicide?"

There was a mixed reaction to that comment, and Earle, for one, did not look convinced, so she quickly added, "It's only that there was something so staged about his death… I just can't help wondering…" She put the glass to her lips. "I can't tell you how relieved I was when the doctor said it was probably a stroke. Especially for Charlie." She gulped. "I didn't want her to think her beloved grandfather had abandoned her."

"Had Mr Burlington ever given any indication of wanting to end his life?" asked Earle.

"No, not directly. But like I told you, since Susan got put away, it seemed like he'd given up. Perhaps I should have been more worried. Perhaps I should have sought help."

"You can't blame yourself," said Merry.

Verity shook her off. "George Burlington was a man who liked to be in control. Demanded it in fact—hence the reason he hired you guys in the first place. Maybe he felt helpless and decided to take back control of his life? Perhaps he waited until I left each night and then added the dose himself. Explains why he was in the ballroom that final night. He knew he was close and wanted to be where his family had been happiest. Like I said, it had felt so creepy, so staged…"

"Staged, yes, you said that before," said Frankie. "How so?"

"The way I found him. The lights, the music—"

"What lights and music?"

"I didn't mention this earlier? Sorry, I'm a basket case at the moment. Can't seem to keep my thoughts straight."

Verity took another sip of her whisky, like that would make the difference. "It was Shannon who first pointed it out, after I'd found George, after I'd called her in… We were waiting for the doctor to officially declare it and…" She swallowed hard. "Shannon said something like, 'Isn't it creepy?' I didn't really know what she meant at first, but then… she's right. It was creepy. George wasn't just in the middle of the ballroom, but the chandeliers were all on—blazing bright, and I know I hadn't switched them on. But that's not the really creepy part. The record player had been set up, and there was a record on it. It wasn't playing, but it was so… *odd*."

Martin's eyes narrowed. "What was the record, Verity?"

It was a good question, and all eyes turned back to her, but she looked baffled. "That was the creepiest part of all. It was Nina Simone."

"What's so creepy about Nina Simone?" he asked.

"She was Pookie's favourite artist."

"Pookie? Who's Pookie again?" asked Merry.

"George's second wife," explained Verity patiently. "You know? She died soon after moving into Seagrave. A terrible, terrible accident."

"That was no accident," scoffed Frankie. "According to my sources, Pookie threw herself from a rugged cliff, just outside the…

Wait for it, people... *ballroom*."

Then she slapped them all with a suggestive smile as she refilled Verity's glass.

~

The bourbon was cheap, but it was doing the job, and Kila splashed another shot into his teacup as he thought about Weaver and then Tiffany, her musky, woody scent still lingering long after she'd left his office. That got him thinking about mould— *sorry Tiffany*—and it suddenly occurred to him that he might not need Trevor and his files after all.

He had some files of his own to look through.

Grabbing the cup, he strode to an old filing cabinet that was gathering dust between the kitchenette and the toilet. He pulled out a drawer he had not looked in for some time, then a file he had never wanted to look into again.

It was marked SIS and contained a photocopy of the police report.

Kila had managed to convince a pretty clerk to steal it for him but had only ever looked at it through smudged, soggy eyes, and even then only briefly. Thank God. In the end they'd got lucky and caught Dragon quickly, so Kila never spent much time perusing the files, punishing himself. But flipping through it now, his eyes wide and dry, he could see that the police had questioned a bunch of people in relation to the bar where Chili had last been seen—people from neighbouring businesses, residences, passers-by, and bartenders from Taboo.

Two names in particular stood out like dog's balls. Two names that matched up with the names in Weaver's book: Jill Berring and Lars Karlsson.

Lars and Jill.

Reenergised, Kila dumped his cup and started wading through their statements, but neither had anything of any interest to tell. Both said they were working at the bar from five p.m. that fateful night, and both saw and heard nothing. Neither was looking out on the street around eight when Chili met that fate.

Kila faded fast, reached for the bourbon, then saw that there were home addresses and phone numbers listed for both bartenders, landlines by the look of them. Emboldened, he returned to his desk and tried the first number, the one for Lars. It was disconnected.

"Bugger it," he said, then tried the number listed for Jill.

"Hello?" came a croaky female voice on the other end.

"Hello, Kila Morea's my name. I'm looking for Jill Berring."

"Yeah, darls, aren't we all?"

"Sorry?"

A small cackle. "What are you? An old boyfriend or something?"

"Something like that. I just wanted to have a quick word."

"Then get on a plane to London, love. She's backpacking somewhere in Europe. Free as a bird. She didn't mention it?"

"No." *Bugger, bugger, bugger.* "Do you have a mobile number for her?"

The woman made a scoffing sound. "But if you do manage to get ahold of Jill, do me a favour will you, love? Tell her to call her mother."

She wasn't cackling anymore as she hung up, and Kila wasn't laughing either. Nor was he giving up. He had one more chance to find Lars. He jotted down a copy of the address he had given the police, polished off the last of the drink, then grabbed his jacket and headed out.

~

"That *was* creepy," said Merry after Verity had departed in a taxi.

It was just on dusk, and the PA looked wiped out as she left, a little drunk too, but it would do her no harm. Perhaps she'd finally get some sleep.

The sleuths, however, were feeling pumped. Or at least Merry was.

She wasn't in any hurry to head home to her sullen son and had an hour to kill before catching up with Dougie for their weekly date night.

Coordinating schedules was difficult for the couple. Dougie had a bookshop to run, a teenage daughter of his own and a bossy ex-wife, and so they reserved each Tuesday night for dinner—just the two of them—at the small Italian restaurant next door to his shop in Balmoral, a hop, skip and a jump from Martin's new place, as it turns out. Merry's daughter was happy enough to get dinner ready for herself and Archie those nights (it was the weekends she fiercely defended), and until recently, Archie had never shown the slightest problem with the arrangement.

Now Merry wondered if she should be heading straight home.

"Which part was creepy?" asked Martin, dragging her from her reverie.

They were still seated at the conference table, several of them now with their own tumblers of whisky. Not Merry. She wasn't much of a drinker.

"The fact that George might have been poisoning his own food?" said Martin. "Or the fact he was sitting in the middle of a room he hated, with the lights blazing? Or the part where he was listening to his dead wife's music?"

"All the above," she replied, trying not to giggle at the absurdity of it all. "I guess that's why Verity thinks it was suicide. He was sending a message—I'm going the way my beloved wife went. But you know, if he did do it, it's a pity he didn't leave a note or something. I mean he wouldn't want his faithful assistant to get the blame, would he?"

"Less than a third of suicides leave notes," said Earle. "Which is a pity because it would be helpful, I agree. I want to know how George got his mittens on the drug. He was housebound in the end. And I know for a fact that the rat poison located in his system was the toxic variety—a non-coagulant rodenticide, they call it." Then, to their confused expressions, he explained: "It requires stringent accreditation to access. They don't sell it willy-nilly in this country."

"Oh, you can get anything over the internet these days," said Frankie dismissively.

"Don't tell me that!" said Merry, thinking of Archie, home alone now with his devices. *Oh dear, perhaps she should be heading back…*

"He could have ordered it from a less stringent country," Frankie continued, "or accessed it via the dark web, although I can't see George doing *that*."

Still, Merry looked faint and Martin chuckled. "I don't think Mez wants to hear about the dark web, Frankie."

Earle felt like stuffing his fingers in his ears too. Was glad he was no longer in the Force. How could you possibly police something like that? And what would the world look like when his granddaughter was old enough to trawl the internet? It didn't bear thinking about.

He quickly changed the subject, pointing towards the whiteboard and the suspect list.

The way he saw it, despite the new evidence and Verity's accusation, there were only four viable names worth investigating:

Susan LeDoux—George's jailed daughter
Clem LeDoux—George's disgraced son-in-law
Shannon Smith—Verity's assistant
Charlie Burlington-Brown—George's granddaughter

Merry had reluctantly agreed to add Charlie's name to the list, but they'd both nixed the idea of adding George's. For Earle it wasn't about being soft. As a homicide investigator, the rule had always been to prove a suicide, assume homicide and work backwards.

Still, it was worth thrashing out. If only to eliminate the idea entirely.

Earle said, "Okay, we know where George—or anyone for that matter—might have got the poison, but what about the ballroom? If it was suicide, how did George get down there? We really think he could have wheeled himself down via the exterior pathway, even with all that poison in his system? Anyone remember the pathway? I can't recall it."

Merry's features were scrunched behind her glasses. "I don't think we ever walked it. I need to go back to Seagrave, check it out for myself."

Frankie clapped her hands. "Brilliant idea! Your strength has always been location."

"Nope, not going to happen," said Earle. "The place is now a crime scene, and I can't see DI Morgan allowing you access."

"I could give you my trusty burglary tools," said Frankie, smiling mischievously.

"Or I could just get the codes from Verity," suggested Merry.

"Not happening," Earle repeated, flashing Frankie a frown because that was her modus operandi, not Merry's. Merry was supposed to be the sensible one. "Leave it with me please. I'll check with Odetta. She might know whether there were wheel marks found in the grass outside, what Morgan's theory is on all of that. Because, whether he was acting alone or was murdered, he had to get down there somehow. But yes, it does thicken the plot somewhat."

Martin rubbed his nose. "She's right though, Verity. It was so staged. Too staged. I don't like it. If it wasn't Sir George making a point, I think somebody else was. What do we know about his second wife, Pookie? She wasn't the mother of George's children,

Susan and Roman, was she?"

"No," said Frankie, the one who'd researched the family inside and out. "Their mother bailed when they were kids, married a shipping tycoon and moved to Greece, leaving George to bring them up on his own."

"Oh, how tragic!" said Merry.

"That's life," said Martin, and Merry gasped at her faux pas and mouthed the word "sorry". He shrugged like it didn't matter as Frankie continued.

"Pookie came along when the kids were still teenagers. She was barely out of her teens herself. They loathed her of course, especially Susan—cue the cliché stepdaughter theatrics—and the only time they ever seemed happy was when they all went up and stayed at the ski lodge, which they did, every single winter." She flashed Merry a look. "As you know. Anyway, despite its ancient facade, Seagrave is relatively new. Was built just twenty or so years ago. Pookie was forty by then, and rumour has it George built it to make her happy."

"I'm guessing it didn't if she threw herself off the cliff," said Merry.

"Allegedly," said Earle.

"Oh, it was suicide, no doubt about it," said Frankie. "Have you seen her book collection? Because it was all hers. George told me Pookie collected every single one. And you know what her favourite genre was? New Age and self-help crap. She was lost and searching for something."

"That's tragic too!" said Merry. "All the money in the world and yet George lost not one but two wives. Goes to show, money isn't everything."

"Ah but it helps," said Martin, his tone droll again.

"Anyway," said Frankie, "the official story, which Verity seems to want to stick to, is that Pookie slipped while walking near the cliff edge by the pool. The gossip is she was miserable and threw herself from a balcony one dark and stormy night. Which is why George could no longer stand the place and he handed it to his son, Roman, who was then almost forty himself and just married to his much-younger wife, Tawny. She adored Seagrave by all accounts. They had their two kids, Heath and Charlie, and lived happily there until, well, until her pesky sister-in-law Susan showed up and started shooting. The rest you know." She shook her head. "That house is cursed."

"Haunted, if you ask me," said Merry.

"Rubbish," said Martin, who might write fiction but didn't go in for supernatural nonsense.

"Does Pookie have any family or friends who might have resented George?" asked Merry. "Someone who wanted to wreak revenge perhaps?"

"After twenty years?" said Earle. "I think that's unlikely."

"*Family* I don't know," Frankie told Merry. "I wasn't reporting back then—I'm not as old as you lot! And George wouldn't speak of Pookie when I interviewed him for the *Herald*. But I do know one friend whose name has now popped up a few times. She's Pookie's oldest girlfriend and the one who's just inherited her lovely—*valuable*—book collection: Persephone Dupont."

"What is it with these names?" said Merry. "Persephone. Pookie. Tawny! Aren't rich people allowed to have boring, ordinary names anymore?"

"Susan did, and look how that turned out," said Martin just as Frankie's phone beeped.

She read the incoming text and smiled. "Looks like Verity has come through. I have a hot date with the PA's PA—Shannon Smith—first thing tomorrow, here at HQ."

Merry jumped up. "Speaking of hot dates, I'd best choof off or I'll be late for Dougie. So shall we all meet back here at nine?"

"Sure," said Martin, glancing at his phone again. "Unless this blasted CEO finally lowers himself to meet me. Maybe I'll switch my focus to Clem LeDoux. See what he's up to."

"Check out his socials," advised Frankie. "I bet he's all over it. I'm going to do the same with Persephone. Methinks there's nothing boring or ordinary about that woman..."

CHAPTER 13 ~

DIGGING AROUND AFTER DARK

"Persephone Dupont is anything but boring," said Dougie over dinner at Ballo's Café an hour later. "And you'd never call her ordinary. She'd chop your head off!"

He chuckled at that, a dimple appearing in one cheek, while Merry's eyes popped behind her cat's-eye glasses. "You *know* Persephone?"

The couple had just cracked open a bottle of shiraz they'd bought from the bottle shop next door and were awaiting their pasta orders when Merry began rambling on about the case and all the interesting, fascinating suspects. (Really she was just avoiding the topic of Archie, but he didn't need to know that!)

She'd just thrown Persephone's name into the mix when he'd dropped his bombshell. And she couldn't believe it! This was one of those things Earle loathed—a coincidence—but Dougie begged to differ.

"Persephone's an avid book collector, and I do own a collector's bookshop, Merry. There's not a lot of them in this city. It's not such a stretch that I would know her."

But it wasn't just that. "You never remember anyone," she said. "You have that face blindness disorder thingy."

He chuckled again, both cheeks now dimpling. "It's called prosopagnosia, Merry, and it is true that I don't remember people's faces very well, especially when they pop in and out. But she didn't pop in and out. Persephone's a regular, or at least she was until the pandemic. I guess she had to tighten her belt like the rest of us. But yes, I have to confess, if I saw her in gym wear on the esplanade, I'd probably walk straight past her. Context, remember?"

"Hmm...," said Merry, still trying to get a grasp on the strange memory condition her boyfriend had. (Hell, still trying to get a grasp on the fact she had a boyfriend. It felt so young and wild and wonderful!) She shook herself out and concentrated.

There was something he said…

"You think Persephone had to tighten her belt? How much do you sell your first edition books for, Dougie?"

"Oh, it all depends on the author and the condition of the work. Some for as little as sixty dollars, some for many thousands. I did sell a signed Ernest Hemingway once for twenty grand."

"Twenty thousand dollars!"

"I don't sell those every day, but yes, rare first editions can fetch a pretty price, as long as it's in decent shape and I have a client dedicated enough to the author—"

"And wealthy enough."

"That goes without saying."

"And Persephone was in both categories."

"Yes, but like I said, I haven't seen her lately, which is a pity because she loved the classics. As you know, I now have a very sweet boxed set of Jane Austens thanks to a certain tragedy that happened just down the road from here."

They both sighed thinking of Merry's last case.

Then Dougie added, "They're not first editions, despite what we assumed, but they are rare enough to keep the debt collectors at bay. But, as I say, perhaps Persephone is cutting back."

"Or perhaps she knew she was coming into her own fabulous collection and didn't need your bookstore anymore, Dougie." Merry was now thinking of Persephone's inheritance.

So was Dougie. He whistled. "That Seagrave collection was famous in collectors' circles. Very extensive I believe. I'd love to clap eyes on it."

"Would you now?" Merry grinned wickedly as the waitress strode up with two steaming plates of fettucine carbonara. She accepted the offer of cracked pepper and extra Parmesan, thanked her profusely, then said, "I know how you can check it out, Dougie. And help me in the process."

~

Just down the esplanade from Ballo's, Martin's stomach was growling as he completed his circuit of the oval and then cycled towards his building. There was a familiar figure standing just outside the art deco entrance, and his face lit up as he narrowed in.

"Hey Mum," he said, jumping off his bike and going in for a sweaty hug. "I wasn't expecting you."

"Sorry," Olivia said quickly, holding up a small bag of what looked like Indian takeaway. "My midwifery class finished early, and so I brought you some…"

"Come in," he said quickly. She didn't need food—or excuses—to visit him.

Not anymore.

As they made their way to the third floor, she said, "That woman you bought the place off, Rachelle is it? She tried to let me in, but I was happy enough to wait outside. She's quite lovely, isn't she, Martin? Certainly speaks highly of you."

He rolled his eyes—knew she was in matchmaker mode—and made no comment as they reached his apartment, except to tell her to mind the boxes he was still unpacking after all this time.

"What happened to the renovations they were going to do?" Olivia asked as they stepped inside.

"They start next month," he said, then stood back and watched as Olivia dumped the food on the coffee table, then made a beeline for the balcony as she always did.

"I never get tired of this view!" she said, unlocking the sliding doors and swooping straight out to stare at the moonlit bay beyond.

"Good, because it cost me a staggering fortune. So what's up?"

She turned back. He was leaning against one sliding door, arms crossed.

"Am I that transparent?"

He shrugged, smiled.

She smiled back. "Your father called."

Martin's smile vanished. He turned and headed for the living room. Or, more precisely, the mini-bar fridge and the bottle of shiraz that was corked on top.

She followed. "Glenn said he saw you at O'Reilly's the other day. You went all that way and didn't even speak to him?"

Martin's back stiffened as he reached for two enormous wineglasses. He filled them both to a third, then handed one over. What Olivia didn't know, Glenn either, was that Martin had driven all that way once before. Three months ago.

At least he'd entered the pub this time.

"He saw me? Really?"

She nodded, took the glass, gave him a sympathetic smile. "Said you were there five minutes, then just walked out."

"Must be in my genes then," Martin replied, watching as she now recoiled, wounded by the comment. He rubbed his nose and shook his head. "Sorry, that was low." Even for him. "But I couldn't do it. I... I just can't."

He gulped the wine down, then splashed some more in.

"There's no way I can sit down with him, Mum. No way I can pretend everything's rosy and ask him to give me his life story. I mean... I know what you're saying. I know it's important background for my story, but I don't think I can do it. I don't care how much you say he's changed or how much of a hero you think he was..."

She stepped forward then and took the glass from his hands, led him to the sofa and pulled him down into it.

"Martin...," she began, but he was shaking his head, appealing to her as he had appealed before.

"I don't understand why you can't just tell me everything," he said. "Why can't you and I just sit down and bang this story out? I'd have my book finished in six months."

"Because you need to hear it from Glenn first. I have no right to tell you."

"Rubbish! You were there too!"

"But only for five minutes, remember?" She shot him a pointed look. "When I walked out on you in that maternity ward..." She gulped, looked away, then back. "When I did that, Martin, I abandoned all my rights. *Glenn* is the one who stayed and brought you up. He is the one who gets to tell you the truth about what happened. You need to go back and talk to him."

"I can't! He won't speak to me anyway. He hates me."

"No, he doesn't and yes, he will! He told me he would. It's whether you're prepared to listen."

"What's the point? All he's going to do is bark about how tough he had it and what an ungrateful shithead I was and how he was a really good father even though that's not how I remembered it. That's the problem, Mum. Our two memories are so disconnected."

"That's not the problem," she said, rubbing a hand against the back of her neck and standing up. "The real problem, Martin, is that you don't know your father. You don't know him at all."

Then she reached in for a hug and left him all alone with the uneaten takeaway and his unopened boxes and an autobiography he could not bring himself to start, let alone complete.

~

Kila could not have been more disappointed. The address Lars had provided the police—a street number in Surry Hills—did not exist, and he wondered if it ever did.

After driving up and down Cleveland Street several times, he realised the relevant lot was just an empty pile of rubble. He pulled his car over and walked across to a chained gate with an old building permit on the front.

Had his old abode been pulled down for a new one? Or had Lars given the police a bum steer from the start? He growled, then got back into his car and put in a call to Trevor.

Lars would have given his employer his correct address, surely.

"How'd you go with those files, Trev?" said Kila when the barman picked up.

There was a lot of noise behind him. Taboo was clearly in full swing.

"Hello to you too, mate."

"Sorry. I'm desperate. I looked up the police file in the end, the one on Chili, and I noticed two of the names from Weaver's notebook are in there. Two staffers who worked Taboo that night."

"Yeah, Kiara and Jill," said Trevor, rushing in. "I got Antoine to cover for me while I had a look at the old shift sheets. They were both rostered on."

Kila was momentarily confused. "Kiara? No, her name wasn't in the report."

"Oh, okay. Maybe that's because she was rostered on later, so she wouldn't have been there at eight. You know, when your sister was outside, waiting for—"

"Yep, I get it now. Okay, but Kiara would have been there when Dragon dropped her off afterwards. Do you have a number for her?"

"I do. I can text it over, but you'll struggle. Last I heard she'd got some spiffy degree and moved to the US. And Jill—"

"Is backpacking through Europe," Kila said. *Was there a barwoman left in the country?* "I know. Her mother's not happy."

"Jesus, you're good. You should be a private dick."

"Hilarious. Go on."

There was a pause. "That's it," said Trevor. "Kiara and Jill. I can give you some landline numbers that might help."

"What about Lars?"

"Lars?"

"Yeah, Lars Karlsson was also questioned by the police. Was working Taboo that night." Or so he had said.

Another pause. A loud burst of noise. "Shit, Antoine's not coping. Okay, that's news to me. I must've missed that. Lars Karlsson... Okay, it's starting to ring a bell. If he was here, it wasn't for long." An exhale. "I'll look him up and get you his number too. Can I text it when I find it?"

"Sure," said Kila, about to ask another question when the sound of breaking glass made Trevor swear and hang up.

Kila dropped his phone to his lap and sat in his car for a few minutes, then turned back to the blue notebook and to a name that was beginning to get under his collar.

Lars Karlsson.

Who was this bloke? Why was he so elusive? And, more importantly, why didn't he last long at Taboo?

CHAPTER 14 ~

THE PA'S PA AND ZEUS'S DAUGHTER

Verity's assistant barely looked old enough to hold down a job, let alone take over from the beleaguered Verity who was now introducing Shannon Smith to Frankie and Martin, the only two sleuths who had shown up at the office that Wednesday morning.

Despite what they had agreed, Earle was meeting with Odetta first thing, and Merry had a date with Persephone.

Cherubic-faced and pretty, young Shannon shook first Frankie's then Martin's hands, and it was the latter who held hers just a fraction too long.

"Have we met before?" he said. "You look familiar."

She swished her plump ruby lips to one side. "You probably saw me at Mr Burlington's wake. I had to run the whole show after Verity..." She glanced at her boss. "Well, you know?"

Martin released her hand. "Ah, yes," he said, thinking of the flustered woman in the ill-fitting maroon suit. "That must be it."

But Shannon was already reaching for Verity, air-kissing her on both cheeks. "How are you, Ver'? It must have been just *awful!* I heard you spent the *whole weekend* in jail!"

"Just police remand," Verity said quickly. "Really, it wasn't that bad. How are *you?* This must be so unsettling for you."

"Yes, it has been stressful if you must know, but it's *you* I'm worried about."

"Which is why we've dragged you here," said Frankie, cutting through the chatter. "Hopefully you can help us get Verity off the hook."

"Oh absolutely!" Her eyes were back on her boss. "Anything I can do!"

"I'll leave you to it then," said Martin. "I have got to go and

101

find myself a sailor boy."

Shannon blushed a little at that. "I'm sorry?"

Frankie laughed. "Don't mind, Martin. For a straight man, he's extraordinarily camp. Come through. We'll grab a coffee, then chat out the back."

One of the selling points of their new office was the tiny terrace that hugged the back kitchen. Overgrown with ivy and furnished with an old, crackling wicker table set, Earle had assured them he'd tidy it all up when he got the chance. But Frankie thought it needed more than a tidy. When they finally got a decent revenue stream, she was going to give it the full Brazilian and start afresh. For now, it would do the job, which for Frankie was to afford them some privacy. The ex-reporter liked to do her interviews alone. In her experience, people spilled so much more without spectators listening in.

Verity had already set up camp at the central meeting table and was trawling through her online files again, awaiting a call from her solicitor, so they couldn't exactly speak in there. And the terrace clearly suited Shannon too, who began to gossip the moment Frankie handed her the coffee and shut the door behind them.

"How is she *really* coping?" Shannon asked. "Has she completely fallen apart? I mean, I can't even *imagine* Verity in prison!"

"She's coping," said Frankie, waving her into a seat. "You know how together Verity is."

"Yes, but that was *before* she was arrested for murder. I don't know how she gets through the night now. I would just *hate* it if someone thought I was capable of such a thing!"

Then she performed a dramatic shudder and sipped her coffee, staring over the top of the cup for a moment. "So you guys are *actually* going to try to help her dodge the charges?"

Dodge? That was an interesting term, thought Frankie. "We're investigating George's murder if that's what you mean. We're examining the case and seeing if there might be other suspects the police have neglected to examine."

"Right. Yes. Good. It's just... I'm not sure how helpful I can be. Verity was a very... How do I put this?" She glanced back towards the office. "*Hands-on*, I guess you would say. She liked to do *everything* herself. I'm not sure why she even hired me to be honest. She wasn't much of a delegator. Half the time she just wanted me to man the phones while she did all the work."

Frankie watched her for another moment. "Control freak was she?"

Shannon blinked rapidly. "I don't mean to sound ungrateful! Verity was *amazing* at her job. Like she was the gold standard, yeah? All the executives wished they had her as their P.A. But… Well, I can't help wondering if she had actually taken on a little less and handed over a little more, maybe she wouldn't have snapped."

There it was again. It was clear to Frankie whose side this woman was on. "You really think she did it? That she snapped?"

Shannon blushed bright crimson now, like she'd just been caught out. "Goodness, no!" Then lowered her voice. "At least I *hope* not. It's just that, like, the police came to talk to me and stuff, and from what they said, poor Mr Burlington was…" She lowered her voice further. "He was killed with *rat poison*. Did they tell you that?" Frankie nodded. "Right, well, they asked me how that could get into his food… and I kept thinking of Verity's stews. You know Verity liked to cook Mr B beef stews, and they reckon that's exactly how he must've been poisoned, and, like, how could anyone but Verity put it in there, right?"

"No one else had access to those stews?"

"I didn't if that's what you mean!"

Frankie sat back in her seat. "I'm not trying to pin it on you Shannon, but I do have to ask. Didn't you have access to the Seagrave kitchen, just like Verity?"

"Yes… but… but I was hardly ever there and certainly never at dinnertime and… I wouldn't do such a horrible thing! I wouldn't! The cops asked me that too, and I can tell you, no one touched the stew, no one but Verity. I'm sorry. I am." Another shifty look back towards the office. "She was nice enough. A good manager even if she didn't trust me with very much. But, like, you can't go around bumping off your boss so you can inherit his money now, can you?"

Frankie nodded. They were both on the same page with that one.

~

There was only one word for Persephone Dupont. Magnificent! From the moment she swept through the door in a waft of gardenia and rose, swathed in purple and velvet (and was that an *actual* peacock feather in her silvery hair?), she exuded a magnificence

Merry could never emulate. Rake thin with cheekbones that could cut the massive diamonds on her fingers, Persephone couldn't have been less than sixty-five, but she seemed ageless. Ethereal. And she exuded it from every pore.

When she spoke, it was like more than just a plum stuck in one cheek. It was like the whole tree had been wedged in there while her green eyes sparkled, which they were doing now as she pulled Dougie towards her and kissed him on both cheeks.

"So delightful to get your call, darling!" she said. "It's been far too long!"

Merry noticed Dougie blushed at all this, his cheeks deeply dimpled, and she didn't blame him. Not one bit. Merry was blushing too. Just at the magnificence of the woman!

"You look lovely as always Persephone," he said, then waved a palm towards Merry. "This is my partner Merry Kean."

Persephone swept her eyes to Merry and smiled. "Partner in crime, I hope, not just business."

"No... no, neither. We're, well, we're going out," Merry stammered, and Persephone clapped her gloved—yes, gloved!—hands together with delight.

"Oh, how tickety-boo!" She turned back to Dougie. "At last! My darling, I have long worried about you, all alone in your little shoppe."

Then she swept past them to the small leather sofa on one side of the store and threw herself upon it, tapping the seat beside her.

"Come, sit and tell me all about how you fell in love, Merry Kean." Then, "Oh! What a delightful name! Dougie, fetch us some tea while Merry and I get better acquainted."

Merry held up a finger. "Actually, sorry Persephone, I have some work to do. I'll fetch the teas, and you and Dougie can catch up."

Persephone's eyes narrowed. "Never stoop to becoming a man's tea lady darling, or he'll never see you as anything but."

Dougie's dimples had vanished. "Oh, I can assure you I don't see Merry like that at all."

"It's no trouble!" said Merry, scuttling away before the woman's magnificence hypnotised her. If needy women were Kila's kryptonite, bossy women were Merry's. She couldn't help but do exactly as they demanded.

Dougie watched as Merry disappeared out the back and wanted to apologise. Persephone was right. He really should be the one fetching tea, and not just on equality grounds. Merry was the expert in all this. *She* should be interrogating Persephone, but he'd made her a promise, so he'd stick to it even if it left him looking like a misogynist. His daughter, Pip, would be as horrified as Persephone.

"So, you're keen to build up your collection you tell me?" said the older woman. "That's wonderful, darling, because I have just come into a lovely collection of my own."

"Is that right?" he replied, feigning ignorance.

"Oh yes, indeed, and by little I mean massive!" She clapped her hands together again. "According to the inventory report, there's five hundred and thirty-three books in the mix! Can you imagine it? In my little library? Such a glorious surprise but I simply haven't the space. Of course I'm going to auction the lot—Sotheby's are gagging for it—but since you called, I'd be more than happy to give you first dibs. Although, just between you and me, the collector's taste wasn't quite as refined as ours."

"Oh? Who's the collector?" More feigning.

Persephone waved a hand in the air. "An old friend. She passed away long before this little shoppe was invented. Now, what did I do with my list..." She snatched up her bead handbag. "Settle in *mon sweet*, it runs to pages and pages..."

As she rifled through a delicate bead purse, Dougie glanced at Merry, who was just placing a tea set on the table in front of them. He offered her a resigned look, but she wasn't having any of it. Her eyes widened, then she subtly nodded her head towards Persephone. He knew what that look meant. He was to keep going.

"Ah, here it is," said Persephone. Then, "Thank you, Merry darling. You sure you can't join us?"

"No, no, must get on!" Merry vanished again.

As Persephone began reading through the list, Dougie pulled on his round spectacles and whistled, distracted by the impressive collection. "And you've been keeping this all to yourself for twenty years?" He added an innocent eye bat to the planted question, and she looked confused for a moment, then shook her head.

"No, no, her dreadful husband has. Or *had*. He's only just passed himself, hence the reason it's all passed to me." She chuckled at the play on words, then continued reading through the list.

He felt a moment of panic. Then Merry's eyes boring into his back from her agreed hidey-hole behind the Russian classics section, so he decided to be more forthright.

"You're not referring to Sir George Burlington, are you?"

Dougie was going off script now, but he'd been expecting Persephone to start babbling and she hadn't. She glanced up, squinting above her own chunky green eyeglasses.

"You knew George?"

"Um... sure! He... Well, he was a client," he lied. (Badly.)

"Really?" She dragged off her glasses. Eyeballed him. "I never saw him in here."

He shrugged nonchalantly. Or tried to. "Well... you know? He didn't come in often. We usually spoke by phone."

"Oh, right." She looked stumped—as well she might—and said, "Well, there's one of the books." Then she chuckled at another pun. "And now it's come to me. Ah, the synchronicity. Pookie would be delighted."

As she pushed her spectacles back on to continue reading, he tried one more time: "Sad about his stroke though, don't you think?"

She scoffed, not looking up. "Stroke? He was murdered, darling! By his secretary! Very grubby business, but then karma has a way of biting you on the tush."

"Karma?"

She pulled off her glasses again. Shrugged nonchalantly. Convincingly. "He wasn't the finest of husbands, old George. Pookie was his second wife, and she was simply miserable for most of the marriage. He worked far too hard, never gave her so much as a weekend of his time. That's why he built that monstrosity on the clifftop. You must have heard of it? Seagrave? He thought a towering mansion was going to make up for being missing in action. Like a pile of bricks can keep you warm at night! Me? Sure! It might have done the trick. I'm as shallow as a birdbath. A very pretty one, but shallow nonetheless. But darling Pookie was a sensitive soul—hence some of her books—" Persephone's nose looked like it was trying to crinkle. "She was always looking for true love, my Pooks. She simply should not have married that man."

"Why? What happened?"

"She threw herself from the nearest cliff! Surely I've told you that story, darling. Or do you struggle to remember stories too?"

"No, just faces. But never yours."

"You wouldn't dare! I spend far too much money in this little shop of yours." She glanced around. "How has it been going?" Her eyes narrowed.

Dougie could almost feel Merry's frown from behind him as he allowed the change of subject, rattling off about the horrors of COVID and the drop in customers. Then he knew she'd be smiling when he niftily segued into:

"How about you? You must be struggling too."

"Why must I?" She sounded offended.

"Well... it's just that I haven't seen you lately, so I just assumed..."

She exhaled dramatically. "Yes, my third husband took a large chunk out of me, and I'm not talking my heart, honey. That was never his to take. Still, it will teach me for hooking up with someone much younger, much poorer. I should've learnt from George, I suppose. At least mine didn't kill himself, although I could have killed him several times over."

She chuckled, oblivious to the thrill that was racing through both Dougie and the woman peeking from behind a leather-bound copy of *Anna Karenina*.

"Anyhoo," she continued, "I was afraid my days of collecting fabulous tomes was over, until old George came through. Quite a surprise, I can tell you, considering our mutual loathing for each other."

"So you weren't on friendly terms? After his wife died."

"That's one way of putting it. I gave him an earful at Pookie's funeral, then told him I never wanted to speak to him again. Although he got the last word in the end, the cheeky bugger!" She slapped her hand against the book list. "It was all so out of the blue. Although I *did* help Pookie collect some of the better books in this collection, so I guess it's not completely unexpected. Oh, we had some lovely trips to Paris, Pooks and I."

She sighed, lost in thought for a moment. Struggled to frown again. "There is a bit of new-age nonsense in the mix, I have to confess. She really was searching for something, the poor, misguided soul. And they were so out of place with the classics. Brought the whole collection down. But still, they're all early editions, even the bad ones, all collector's items, so I think you might be interested..."

Then she began to rattle off a list of book titles he was, indeed, interested in. As she did so, Dougie darted a glance to the back of the store, offering Merry a final look of resignation. He knew she'd be disappointed, but that was all he would get out of the chatty book collector today. Any more prompting and she would become suspicious.

From her secret post, Merry was not disappointed in the slightest. Dougie should join the Sleuths of Last Resort, she decided. He had got a lot more out of Persephone than she'd expected, including proof the woman had more than just murderous thoughts about the victim, she had five hundred and thirty-three reasons to act upon them.

CHAPTER 15 ~

MR SLEAZE AND THE LOST SOUL

Martin had not expected to track down Clem LeDoux so quickly. He already knew from Charlie (via Merry) that Susan's sleazy husband no longer resided at the house they once shared, and he suspected that after Susan was jailed and he lost his job at his father-in-law's company, he'd hardly fall back on his first job at George's sailing school, which he used to run before he married Susan.

But he *might* fall back on his old skill—teaching sailing.

And so Martin did the rounds of the sailing schools. And he stuck to Sydney because, while it seemed logical he'd leave town, tail between his legs, Susan's prison was in south-eastern Sydney and he knew from her (via Frankie this time) that Clem was a regular visitor.

He would have stayed close, Martin deduced. But not too close.

So Martin opened Google maps and found the sailing school the furthest from the Burly Sailing Club. Then worked his way inwards. He struck gold at a school in Manly, just on the other side of the harbour from Clem's old stomping ground but far enough away for his stench not to follow.

Because what school in their right mind would hire a known pervert to teach young children?

"I do not teach children!" Clem protested when Martin posed the same question soon after finding Clem scrubbing down a small sloop tied to the pontoon. "I only teach adults and only on weekday mornings, during school hours. But it does not matter because my boss knows of my background. He knows it was a simple case of— how do you say?"

"Perving?" suggested Martin, making the man bristle further.

"Misunderstanding!"

"Oh, sure, right." Martin let it go, not wanting to get into an

109

argument about semantics.

Sure, the slimeball might only have been accused of spying on his niece in the shower, but Martin knew as they all did, that one thing might very well lead to another. Why DI Morgan had never laid charges was beyond Martin, and beside the point today.

"Now please, you must leave," Clem implored. "My student will be here soon."

"Then you'll want to answer my questions quickly so I don't cause any—what's the word? Misunderstandings. Shall I launch in?"

Clem looked furious but nodded and turned the hose tap off.

Martin asked, "Where were you on the night Sir George died?"

"I was at home."

"Where's home? Because I know you're not at your old place."

"Of course I am not at my old place. You people made sure of that. Frankie Jo's stories, they destroyed my life!"

Martin cocked his head sideways. "You don't think you might've played a small part in that destruction?"

"I keep telling you, I never hurt a soul, never touched a hair on Charlie's body!"

Touching wasn't the only way of hurting, Martin knew, but he let it slide.

"My Susan, she knew this, she still does," Clem was saying.

"Yes, I was surprised to hear you two are still married."

"And why is this so surprising? I always told you, Martin, we are in love. I have eyes only for my elegant Susan."

Again, that wasn't strictly true, considering his eyes had strayed to Charlie. Again, he swallowed his bile and pushed on. "I recall you being very shocked when you learned what your wife had done to save your reputation, to keep you in the family."

Shocked was an understatement. The day the sleuths had announced that Susan was a killer, Clem had looked at her aghast, like she was vermin.

"But she did it for me, don't you see? It is the ultimate act of love, is it not? To go to such extremes for the man you adore. How can I turn my back on that? How can I abandon her? I will always be here for my Susan."

"How far will you go for your Susan?"

Clem scoffed. "I see through you, Martin. I know what you are trying to do. But I would not hurt my father-in-law! Never!

Why would I do such a thing? Why?"

Martin ignored that and asked, "So where do you live?"

He shook his head. "It is none of your business."

"Do you live alone?"

"Of course! What are you suggesting? That I have a lover? That I am cheating on my Susan?"

Martin took a step back. Actually he wasn't suggesting that at all, was just trying to firm up the man's alibi, but now that he mentioned it... "Twenty years is a long time to stay faithful, Clem. I know I couldn't do it."

Clem scoffed. "You Australians! You are so simple. It is all about the physical for you. For the French, it is also about *amoreaux*."

"But really?" said Martin. "Celibacy for the next fifteen to twenty years?"

"Of course!" He glanced up the walkway and lifted a hand to wave at a middle-aged man looking ridiculous in full nautical gear, then lowered his voice and hissed, "Please, Martin, you must go now! My client is coming."

Then he pulled a captain's hat from his trouser pocket and slipped it over his thick blond hair.

Martin stood back and watched as Clem greeted the student, not believing him for one moment. That French nonsense didn't add up. Besides, wasn't the cliché more to do with mistresses than soul mates? He didn't buy into clichés either, but he did know Clem. The guy was as fake and shallow as the cap he was now wearing. He might be saving his heart for Susan, but who was in his bed at night?

That posed a whole new set of questions, like was this secret lover (there just *had* to be a secret lover) an irrelevant side issue, or was it somehow connected to George's murder?

And if he really was faithful to Susan—utterly devoted as he seemed intent on showing—how far did that devotion extend? Would he murder for her if she asked him to?

Or would he do it to avenge his "elegant Susan" whether she asked him to or not?

~

Earle was almost at the pub near homicide headquarters where he'd arranged to meet Odetta for an early lunch when he got her text message. She would not be coming. No explanation, no apology and it left him worried. Was she caught up with a case? Or was she avoiding him?

Either way, he took the opportunity and turned his car towards Woolloomooloo and its homeless men's shelter.

Might as well do some sleuthing for his own family while he was out and about.

"Look out, here's trouble," bellowed a grizzly looking man at the front desk of the shelter when Earle walked in. "Haven't seen you for a while, DI Fitzgerald."

"It's just Earle now, thanks, Dave. I'm no longer in the game. Have retired."

"Lucky you. So what brings you in? Beryl finally had enough of you? Looking for a bed?"

Earle chuckled. "Not yet. But keep one on hold, just in case." He winked. "Listen, I want to ask you about someone. Neville Mottson is his name."

The man gave it some thought. "Mottson... Sounds a little familiar, but I don't believe he's one of ours. Got any other info?"

"Beds down near Wynyard station. Maybe as far afield as Town Hall?"

"In that case..." He turned and called out, "Hey, Jason! Jase!" A face looked up from behind a computer monitor. The manager waved him over.

"This is DI Earle Fitzgerald. Fitzy this is Jason." They swapped handshakes, Earle not bothering to correct Dave this time. "Listen, do you know a bloke by the name of Neville Mottson? Fitzy thinks he sleeps rough around Wynyard."

"Nev?" The young man frowned. "Oh shit, who found his body?"

Earle blinked. "He's not dead. I just have some questions about him."

"Oh, right. Sorry. Thought you were going to give me some bad news there."

"I'm not sure it gets too much worse than sleeping out in the elements."

"Could be sleeping six feet under," countered Jason.

Earle wasn't sure that was worse. "He was above ground and

breathing last time I looked. I just want some info on him if you don't mind. I have a concerned relative."

Jason looked even more surprised. "Okay, well, there's not much to say. He's a man of few words our Nev. Worked as a concreter in a past life, I think. At least that's what he used to mumble about."

"How long's he been on the streets?"

"No idea. I first met him about five, six years ago. Got him a home placement, but he's a chronic alcoholic and he was booted out. Usual cycle."

"Any other issues I should know about? Drugs? That kind of thing?"

"Nah, although he could do with some." Then, as Earle frowned, he added, "The bloke's health is nosediving. That's why I assumed he'd croaked it."

"What's he got?"

"What hasn't he got? Heart disease. Diabetes. High blood pressure. Dementia."

"Dementia? Really?"

"Well, brain damage of some sort. Doesn't recognise me half the time now. That could just be the alcoholism of course. Not that he cares. Refuses to see a doctor, certainly won't go to hospital. Sorry, that's why I thought his time was up."

"Not yet it's not," said Earle.

But it was running out fast for his daughter.

~

It was right on noon, and Trevor had been busy. He'd just called Kila to say he'd got up early and gone into Taboo, sifted through the old shift sheets again and struggled to find any signs of a Lars Karlsson working that fateful night.

"But I think I know why," he'd added quickly. "Lars must've been covering for me—I had that Thursday off, yeah? That's why he wasn't listed on the roster."

"Okay, that makes sense, but he was definitely working that night," said Kila. "His details are in the police file."

"So why do you need me then?"

"Because his details don't exist, at least not anymore."

"Really? What'd they have?"

"Landline and address, both defunct."

"That's dodgy."

"You're telling me. Now tell me you have something more. A mobile perhaps?"

"Maybe." Trevor hesitated on the other end. "What are you going to do, Kila?"

"What? Nothing. Just have a chat."

"A chat or—"

"Just give me the number, Trevor."

Another pause and then Trevor read out a mobile phone number slowly, giving Kila time to jot it down. He added, "You think he's involved in what happened to Chili? Really?"

"No idea."

"Exactly. You have no idea, so if you do find him, go easy, hey? Don't let Mad Dog Morea loose until you know what's what."

Kila scoffed like Trevor was talking nonsense.

CHAPTER 16 ~

ASSESSING THE SUSPECTS

By the time the sleuths gathered together later that afternoon—
sans Verity who was meeting with her legal team—their heads
were spinning and not in a good way. After sharing their recent
findings, the whiteboard now looked like a dog's breakfast,
all manner of names and motives scribbled across the front, Merry's
smiley faces long since wiped and covered over.

The "magnificent" Persephone Dupont had been added to the
suspect list, so too "Clem's mysterious lover", if indeed there was
one.

Earle looked especially grumpy.

"We're supposed to be tightening the suspect list, not expanding
it," he said. "I really need to speak to Odetta and see whose alibis
have been checked, which suspects we can tick off."

He stared at his silent phone, wondering again why she'd put him
off at the last minute and with no explanation. It wasn't like her.
Had Morgan got to her? He shook the worrying thought away.

"I don't *want* to tick Clem off," Martin was saying. "I think he's a
good lead. If he didn't kill George to avenge his wife, he might have
done it for his own purposes."

He sat forward, hands on the top of designer blue jeans.
"Think about it. What if Clem got tired of waiting for Susan? I mean,
even a saint would struggle to wait fifteen to twenty years. Maybe he's
fallen for someone new or maybe that's irrelevant. I wonder whether
he was considering divorce and wanted to take her for half of
everything she had. Except!" Martin raised a finger dramatically.
"If Sir George died first, then his half would be a lot more impressive
thanks to Susan's inheritance."

"I was thinking that too," said Merry. "Plus the longer George
lived, the more likely Susan would come to her senses and divorce

the weasel, especially if she did discover there was some lover on the side."

"But Susan must still be wealthy in her own right," said Earle. "Even before George left his legacy, Clem would get a pretty decent divorce settlement I'd suggest."

"Maybe, maybe not," said Martin. "And how much is she really sharing with her estranged husband? She already sold his house from under him, and he still has to work for a living, so he can't be getting that much off his wife. Visiting her every week must be a drag too. He's come right down a peg or two since his days swanning about pretending to be useful in George's cushy, air-conditioned office."

He stopped. That reminded him of something…

They were all staring, waiting, so he pushed the thought away and continued. "Now he can divorce Susan, get half her share of the inheritance, and be set up for life. He can now *buy* a sailing school if he likes. Plus—added bonus points—if there is some new *amoreaux*, that's another reason to act sooner rather than later, lest Susan find out. Like Merry said, he has a clear motive for speeding up George's death."

"And here's the other thing," said Merry, swapping a smile with Martin. "He might not have known that George was ailing. He's not in the loop anymore, yes? For all he knew the old guy could kick on for another decade. It's not like he ever saw him or had access to the house."

"Therein lies your first roadblock," said Earle. "If he couldn't access Seagrave, how did he administer the poison? You're forgetting the codes, folks, the dreaded access codes to the house. Verity told us herself, that only she, Charlie and her PA, Shannon, had them. And sure, Sir George still buzzed in business associates, but would he have buzzed in Clem? If he wasn't speaking to his daughter, he'd hardly be speaking to his son-in-law."

"He could have been disguised as a delivery man or followed one of the associates in," said Martin half-heartedly.

"Maybe…," said Earle, not really buying it. "But enough times to administer the poison over several weeks? And how would Verity not have noticed him?"

Martin shrugged like he'd plug the minor plot holes later.

As Martin leaned back in his seat, Earle sat forward.

"Look, Clem might have had a good motive, but I'm not sure he had means and opportunity, so let's move on, shall we? How are we all feeling about Charlie as a suspect?"

No one said anything as their eyes turned back to the whiteboard.

"If we think about it logically," Earle continued, "Charlie had means and opportunity—plenty of access to the house and stew— but her motive is not so sound. I'm not convinced she'd kill her grandfather prematurely to get a larger chunk of the inheritance. I mean, how much money does one young lady require?"

"I agree," said Merry, "about the money thing. She told me she was going to work for some animal shelter in South America. You don't do that if you care about money."

Martin scoffed. "You do if you know someone's paying the bills while you play the bleeding-heart animal rescuer."

Frankie snorted now. "So she murders her beloved Gramps so she can save a few critters? Do you know how absurd that sounds?"

"I'm just theorising."

"All right," said Earle. "Let's move on to the second wife's friend, Persephone Dupont. I'm not sure she had means, motive or opportunity. Merry, what's your vibe on her?"

Merry pulled out her notebook and opened it to a page of scribbles she'd made from behind the Russian classics. "Right, well, Persephone certainly had motive. She absolutely adores those books she just inherited, and they are a fabulous little nest egg. She was practically salivating talking about them—not that she'd ever do anything quite so uncouth as salivate!" She giggled. "You guys really must meet her! She was simply—"

"Magnificent, yes, you've already told us that, Merry," said Frankie. "But the question remains: Why jump the gun and kill George early? The collection was coming to her anyway."

"But I don't think she knew that," said Merry. "She told Dougie it was a 'glorious surprise'. And here's the thing—what if it had nothing to do with the books? That was just a fringe benefit. What if it was more about avenging her dear friend Pookie? Because the way she talked about George's second wife—they were close. Real close. And she definitely blamed George for her friend's suicide. Says Pookie was lonely and miserable and *that's* why she threw herself off the cliff at Seagrave."

"Hmmm," Frankie conceded, clearly warming to this new theory.

117

"That might also explain why George was wheeled down to the ballroom that final evening, with Pookie's music playing."

Merry nodded. "She was making a statement!"

"Could she pull it off though?" asked Martin. "How old and frail is she?"

"Late sixties."

"Spring chicken then," said Earle, giving them a wink.

Merry giggled. "And she has plenty of gumption, I can tell you that. She was so magnif—" She caught herself and darted a look at Frankie. "Any case, how hard could it be to wheel a sleepy old man down a pathway?" She stopped, groaned. "I really need to get back to Seagrave and check that out."

Earle cocked his head sideways at her, and her eyes slithered away.

Martin was also staring at her sideways. "I'm all for the revenge motive, as you know, Merry. I think I was the one who suggested it first." A smug smile that made Frankie look ready to smack him. "But revenge twenty years after the fact? Not even Flynn Bold could make that work. And how did she get into Seagrave several times to poison the stew without Verity finding out? If George did buzz her in on false pretences, surely he'd mention it to Verity at some stage. Otherwise, what's the big secret?"

Merry's eyes lit up. "What if there's a secret passage?"

Another snort, this one from Frankie.

"Think about it!" Merry pushed on. "Persephone knew Pookie back when they first built the house. Maybe there's a secret passage only they know about!"

"This is not a game of Cluedo, Merry," said Earle firmly.

She slumped in her seat as Earle pointed to the whiteboard again.

He said, "Which brings us finally to Verity's assistant Shannon. Ms Smith has means and opportunity—easy access to the house and stew—but so far no motive. What could she possibly gain by killing her boss? She didn't inherit anything from Sir George as far as we know, and if Verity goes to jail, she'll be out of a job. So if she did do it, there must be another reason. What do we know about her? Frankie?"

Frankie nudged a shoulder upwards. "I know she didn't like Verity. That much was obvious when I spoke to her. But she seemed such an airhead. I'm not sure she could pull off something quite so sophisticated." She glanced towards her phone. "According to her

Facebook status, Shannon's single, lives alone in some poky apartment in the inner West, but apart from lots of drunken nights out with girlfriends, I can't see any bitching about George, no griping about her job."

"So, means and opportunity but no motive," said Earle, pulling off his steel spectacles and rubbing his eyes. Bub had kept them all up again last night. Just wouldn't settle for poor Tess. "And we've officially run out of suspects. Which brings us back to the man himself."

"Sir George," said Martin as if that needed clarifying.

"Perhaps Ms Vine is spot on," said Earle. "Perhaps George did this all by himself. Talk about an oldie with gumption. I wouldn't put it past him. He was a proud man. Not the kind to just fade away. He does have the trifecta—means, motive and opportunity."

"He's not the only one though, is he?" said Frankie, dropping her phone into her lap and pulling her shoulders back as though preparing for some pushback. "There is one other suspect who has all three, in spades."

Then she turned defiant eyes to Merry and said, "It's time to consider the elephant in the room. And we need to do it while the elephant's busy with her lawyer."

CHAPTER 17 ~
FOCUSING ON JUST ONE

Verity Vine was the perfect suspect. Frankie was absolutely right; she ticked every box. She had the means—the ability to poison the food she was cooking for her boss. And the opportunity— ready access to the house, the kitchen, the stew pot.

And then there was the motive. All that glorious inheritance.

For all they knew, she might have coerced Sir George into giving her a third. Maybe Charlie's return had caused him to reconsider and he was about to change his will back. And the person who would have known that—arranged that—was Verity.

Had she acted before she called his lawyer?

That Verity had dissuaded them from contacting old Mr Fogerty just yesterday only strengthened the case against her. That Verity knew George was on blood-thinning medication, which made the rat poison even deadlier, was another stroke against her.

But not for Merry. "We're not putting Verity's name on the whiteboard, just so you can play devil's advocate, Frankie. It's rude. She's had a bad enough trot as it is."

"Oh for goodness' sake! I'll do it then!"

But Merry was scrambling now to remove the marker pens, which she held firmly behind her back while Frankie tried to reach behind her, grappling this way and that.

Martin started chuckling, and Earle smiled too. Merry was learning how to stand up to Frankie, and he liked it. But sadly he had to concede the latter was right. A frank and fearless investigation meant considering everyone, even the people you liked the most.

"Settle down, you two," he said. "We'll consider Verity, but leave her name off the board. She is a paying client, after all. Sit down Frankie, and tell us why you *still* harbour doubts."

Because he knew she had harboured doubts since the wake.

Frankie sneered jokingly at Merry and flung herself on the couch. "It all comes back to Occam's razor," she said.

"The simplest explanation is often the best one," said Martin.

Frankie pointed a finger at him. "Exactly. Or as Ms Rosey Glasses here would say, if it looks like a duck and quacks like a duck... The point is the person who has benefited the most from George's death is Verity. She's now a massively wealthy woman. I say she did it for the money."

"Yes, but she, more than anyone, knew how quickly George's health was declining," said Merry. "All she had to do was sit back and see the year out."

"Except," said Martin, his own forefinger now up, warming to this theory, "maybe his health *wasn't* declining. Maybe she made that up entirely. Maybe he was in top shape until she started slowly poisoning him. We do only have her word for that."

"Oh, you're good," said Frankie. "That is a very good plot twist!"

"But... but...," began Merry.

Now Frankie was sneering for real. "For the love of God, Merry! You really have to try to think objectively."

"No! I mean, yes, I get what Martin's saying, but by the same token, maybe Verity was being fooled too. She told us ages ago that George had given up on life after his daughter went to jail, but maybe that's when a third party started poisoning him. And that's why his health declined. It could have been anyone—Verity's assistant Shannon, George's new CEO..."

"Yes, except he's overwhelmed, according to Verity," said Frankie, "and Shannon hasn't benefited from George's death in the slightest. No motive, remember?"

"And so the circle continues," said Earle miserably.

"We need to find out more about Shannon," insisted Merry. "She's the biggest question mark that I can see. Pity we can't ask the missing elephant about her." She slapped Frankie with a scowl of her own.

Martin stood up and stretched as he read an incoming text on his mobile. "We might not need Verity. His Holiness the CEO can see me now. Or after work, this evening. He's now officially Shannon's boss, right? Perhaps he can enlighten us, point out a possible motive?"

"Good," said Earle. It felt to him like a circuit breaker. "Shall we finish up then, folks? Clear this mess up and get home to our families? Reunite first thing in the morning when we're feeling fresher." And less muddled.

They all agreed and began to clear their cups.

~

Kila filled his coffee cup with another shot of whisky and scowled at his mobile phone. Again. He'd tried the number Trevor had given him for Lars, with no luck. Like his landline before it, Lars's mobile number was now disconnected.

How convenient, thought Kila. How *suspicious*.

He'd then tried a bunch of other angles, contacts... Hell, he'd even looked him up on Facebook, Instagram, TikTok, Tinder... All to no avail. Just could not find a Lars Karlsson who fit the description.

Groaning, he opened his phone and called Trevor again, told him he needed Kiara's number this time.

"I thought I'd texted it to you."

"Nope."

"Shit, sorry. But I did tell you she left ages ago and is now State-side."

"Last I looked, they had mobile coverage in the US, Trev."

A small chuckle. "Fine. I'll get it to you when you come in. You are coming in, right?"

"Beats hanging out at the library."

Another chuckle. "What happened to the number I gave you for Lars?"

"Dead."

"That's weird. Wow. I mean, it's like he's dropped off the face of the earth."

"Yeah," Kila said.

And in his line of work there were only two reasons why people vanished without trace, and neither of them was good.

~

As Merry handed the dirty cups to Earle, who had his hands in soapy water, Frankie to his right, holding a tea towel, she asked, "Did you ever hear back from Odetta about the crime scene? They find wheelchair marks leading down to the ballroom?"

He couldn't say. "Odetta has gone suspiciously quiet. I hope all is well." He handed a dripping cup to Frankie. "But even if George didn't push himself, someone had to get him down that way, so I think that's a given. I'm not sure finding tracks will forward the case in any direction."

"Actually I beg to differ," said Merry. "If it's a muddy path and there *weren't* any wheelchair tracks, then that's very suspicious because we know he couldn't get himself down the stairs. So someone must have carried him down. Surely that would mean it's not suicide."

"Oh, it's rained since then; the evidence would have washed away," said Frankie, dismissing the whole suggestion.

"And carrying a man down steps is not as easy as it sounds, Merry," said Earle. "Despite what you see on TV, a corpse really is dead weight. George was a very large man even if he had wasted away of late. Would be difficult for the strongest of men, impossible for most of the suspects out there on the list."

Merry groaned. "I really need to get access to the house, see it all for myself." It was her strength, and she wanted to flex it.

Earle wasn't having it. "I told you before, it won't be happening."

Merry swallowed another groan and returned to the outer office, Frankie hot on her heels.

"Just text Verity," whispered Frankie. "Get her to sneak you in."

Merry glanced back towards the kitchen. "Earle will kill me."

"So? He's not the boss of us, you know. We're all equal partners here, but you're the expert in crime-scene layouts. Go, check the place out. Take one for the team. If there's nothing to report, he need never know."

Merry thought about it and grinned. She really did want to go back to Seagrave. "Okay then," she said, reaching for her smart phone, "I'll do it."

As she tapped out a message to Verity, Martin chuckled from the couch. "Somebody's a bad influence."

"Oh, shut up, smug author man!" Frankie shot back before flinging the tea towel in his lap. "What are you still doing sitting on your arse? This is an equal-opportunity workplace, you know."

"Hey, it's not *my* workplace. I'm just helping you guys out. You should be fanning me and feeding me grapes."

"Urgh, in your dreams," Frankie replied as Merry let out a loud whoop, then slapped a hand to her mouth.

She lowered her voice and said, "Verity says she can get me in tonight!" She continued reading. "Or at least Shannon can. Not sure what that's about but... yay. Just don't tell Earle."

Frankie gave Merry an "as if!" look as she snatched the towel back up and returned to the kitchen. Along the way she checked her own phone, fearful of finding another message from Jan. She'd been waiting days for one, and it filled her with dread.

It was all very well for Frankie to lecture Merry about who was bossing whom, but hadn't she been letting Jan boss her about for almost a decade? Perhaps it was time to swallow her fear and...

"Everything good?" asked Earle, making Frankie start a little.

She pocketed the phone and smiled. "Sure, everything's *great*."

He handed her a last wet teaspoon and watched her for a moment. "How are you going with that stalker of yours?"

Frankie looked up sharply. The man must have been a very good cop in his day. But she was once a very good journalist, so she lied easily as she said, "Oh, nothing to worry about now."

He watched her as she dried and put the spoon away. Then shrugged and turned back to the sink, pulling out the plug. "You don't have to put up with a stalker, you know? There are things you can do."

Then he gave her a pointed look, dried his hands with her towel and exited the kitchen. As she watched him go, Frankie realised she wasn't as good a liar as she thought. And it was time to find her backbone.

She pulled out her phone again and tapped a text of her own.

We need to talk. It's long overdue, she wrote, then pressed Send.

The response was instant: *You know where to find me*.

It was followed by a broken love heart.

CHAPTER 18 ~
CONVERSATIONS AFTER DARK

"Sorry about the late hour," said the elderly receptionist to Martin, who had just arrived at Burlington Holding's head office for their scheduled nine p.m. meeting and was now waving him into a plush armchair across from her desk.

"Not at all," said Martin. He was just glad to be there.

The last time he was in this building it was bustling. Today it was empty but for a bored-looking security man on the front door and a demurely dressed executive assistant who looked like she came from the same factory as Verity.

"Now," the woman said, her tone schoolmarmish, "unfortunately Mr Fergerson has one more conference call to tick off his list and then he'll be free. Are you able to wait? It might take a while."

Martin nodded. It's not like he had anyone to return home to. Unlike the others.

"Great. In the meantime, can I get you something? Coffee? Tea? A soft drink perhaps?"

He shook his head and reached for a magazine on the table in front of him. "All good," he said, then settled in.

~

It was a typically quiet, mid-week night at Taboo, and Kila was settled on his usual perch when Frankie strode in. He had a lager on one side and a soft drink on the other. Trevor was leaning across the bar smiling about something, but when he caught sight of Frankie, his smile vanished.

"Usual?" he muttered, then strode to the other end of the bar.

Frankie blinked blankly at Kila, swooped in to kiss his cheek, then followed Trevor across to where he was preparing her gin and tonic.

"That's not happy to see me, Trev," she said.

125

His scowl deepened as he stared at the glass. "You've done a number on my mate Kila, so no, I'm not happy."

"Sorry?"

He looked up. "The stupid Weaver case."

Oh, she'd almost forgotten about Phillip Weaver's murder and his very desperate sister.

"You're screwing with his head," said Trevor. "Kila doesn't need it. One day he was happy his sister's killer was locked up, now he thinks the killer's still out there, preying on young women."

Frankie blinked back at him now. "You think Kila was happy? Really?" She shook her glossy blond head Kila's way. "That's not the vibe I've been getting. I don't think knowing Dragon's locked up has made him any happier, has it?"

"What would you know? You met Kila five seconds ago. I've known the bloke for almost five years. Back when Chili was still around, ordering her own stupid bloody lemon squashes." His eyes welled up. "I'm telling you, you've done my mate no favours. Just let it go."

Then he slammed her drink on the bar, spilling a good part of it, and skulked off into the staff section at the back.

When Frankie returned to Kila, he was chuckling.

"Well, that's you told then," he said.

She scowled. "What's up his backside?"

"Don't mind Trev. He's just being protective."

"Being a prat is more like it." Frankie breathed in, then out. "Thanks for being here."

"Of course. Where else would I be?" Then, "So, I'm guessing this is about Jan? What's she done now? Scratched *your* car this time? Sent a letter bomb through the mail?"

"Worse. She dropped the bomb over in person. Monday night."

He turned to face her, eyes fiery. "You serious?"

She shrugged, sipped from her drink.

"Jesus, Frankie, why didn't you call me? That was days ago!"

"I can handle myself."

Except she couldn't. Not when it came to Jan. She'd been quivering every night since. Kept expecting to find Jan standing at her door, calico bag in hand, fresh bomb ready to detonate. Frankie had always considered herself a tough nut, yet Jan seemed able to turn her into a ball of jelly with a simple slice of carrot cake.

"What happened?" he asked.

Frankie sighed. "She wasn't there long, thank God. Just bailed me up outside the lift, handed me a cake, and left."

He blinked through his curls. "A cake?"

"Yes, a carrot-and-walnut one."

She gave him a pointed look, and he blinked again. Tried not to smile. "Shall we call the cake police? Get Sergeant Baker onto it pronto?"

Frankie slapped him across the arm. "It's not about the cake, you fool! It's what that cake represented."

"Crimes against gluten?"

She rolled her eyes and sipped her drink. "Be serious, Kila. It's my favourite cake. You'd know that too if you'd bothered to hang around and find out."

"Hey, you're the one who detonated this relationship."

"Really?" She glanced pointedly this time at his half-drunk lager. The full glass of lemon squash beside it. "Are we really going to blame me for our break-up?"

It was a break-up she hadn't revealed to anyone, least of all the other sleuths. Wasn't sure why. Perhaps because then it would make it real.

Kila shrugged like they were discussing the weather. "So what's the big deal with the cake then? What's she trying to say?"

"She's saying 'I know everything about you, Francesca Josephina—from your favourite cake to the lies you have told. I can deliver those lies as easily I can deliver a cake.'"

"That's a lot of words to ice on the top." He held up his palms. "Sorry. What do you want me to do? Kneecap her? Come stay with you for a bit?"

He nudged his eyebrows up and down, and she rolled her eyes back at him. "No chance." She sighed. "Nothing. I don't want you to do anything." She felt too weary, hadn't slept for nights. "I just need a distraction. How's your case going?"

"Hang on, yours first. How's Verity? You guys solved it yet?"

"We're good but not that good. This one… Well, there's more to it than we realise."

He leaned towards her. "How do you mean?"

"I don't know. Something's… *off*."

"You think Verity did it?"

She glanced at him. He was worse than Earle at reading her mind. "Don't let Merry hear you say that. She's as protective of Verity as Trevor is of you."

"Aw, I miss Festive. How is she? How are those kiddies of hers?"

"Who cares about her kids?" She jiggled her shoulders. "She's fine. Let's move it along. So, the Weaver case. How's it going?"

"It's not. I've come to a skidding halt. How'd you know I'd take the case by the way?"

She cocked her head to the side. "Damsel in distress? Mutual loathing of Dragon? Was a no-brainer. So what do you think of Tiffany's theory? Think there's a connection to Dragon—that he organised the hit on her brother? Or is she just barking up the wrong tree?"

"Woof," he said. "It's connected to Dragon, but it's not what she thinks." He produced the coaster from his shirt pocket. "I found this amongst Weaver's things. He came here to Taboo. Trevor doesn't remember him, but I reckon he was asking questions, questions that got him murdered."

Frankie frowned and turned the coaster over then back. "Yes, honey, I already established that months ago when I was reporting for the *Herald*. Remember? Why does this date sound familiar?"

"Chili," he said simply, and she nodded.

"Of course. Wow, okay, that's interesting. So we don't just have the connection to Dragon, we have the connection to Chili…"

As she stared hard at the coaster like it might reveal more clues, Kila's heart soared. We. She'd used the term *we*. Like they were working together again. Kila would have called Frankie himself, would have asked her more about Weaver, but she'd made it so clear they were done. He was not to call. He was to move on with his life.

But now…

He stashed the glorious feeling away and produced the notebook. "Weaver also left this. It contains a bunch of names, all of which mean nothing to Tiffany. Trevor's checked them out, and some were staff here four years ago. Problem is they've all vanished. Can't find a working number for any of them."

Earlier he'd tried the number Trevor had for Kiara, and that, too, was useless. A woman did pick up, but she was not Kiara and had never heard of Taboo.

"Interesting...," said Frankie, taking the book from him.

He nodded. "Especially one." He tapped on the name Lars. "He was the barman working the night my sister got taken. I'm focusing on him. He's the only bloke on the list other than this Jerry fellow, and he never worked Taboo. I think Lars either knows something about it or he's involved somehow."

Frankie's big almond eyes swept up at him. "Whoa! That's big. You think he was working with Dragon? Maybe they were preying on women together?"

Kila recoiled at that. Tiffany had come to the same conclusion. It was a conclusion he could not make space for in his head. Just could not.

Frankie, however, seemed delighted. "I *knew* there was more to Weaver's murder! I knew it! I told my editor that. I feel like ringing Ruffus right now and..." She stopped when she saw the hooded look that was coming into Kila's eyes. "Sorry." She took a sip of her drink. "So, what about the other names in the book?"

He slurped his own drink. "Not sure about them yet. It's Lars who's setting off alarm bells for me. Problem is, he's gone AWOL."

"Okay. Doesn't get more suspicious than that."

He nodded. She got it. That's what he loved about Frankie even if it did get her worryingly excited.

"Maybe Lars knows exactly what happened to my sister and he's the one who gave Weaver the cash to try to shut him up and/or killed him for it. Or not." He groaned, reached for his beer. "It's all too messy. I'm tying myself into knots, trying to make it fit. It could be as simple as a drug deal gone bad. I need to find out who Lars is. But like I said, he's vanished from the face of the earth."

"He's not an astronaut, Kila. Got to be here somewhere. Why don't you talk to the witnesses that Weaver was talking to? Maybe they pointed him in the direction of Lars."

"Hang on, what witnesses?"

Frankie sighed heavily. "You never listen to me, do you? I told you all this ages ago."

"You told me Weaver came in here asking questions. That's all you said."

"No, I told you he spoke to some girls." She blew a puff of air through her lips and pulled out her smartphone, began to scroll through it for the Notes app.

"So, three months back, when I was investigating Weaver's murder for the *Herald*—"

"Before Ruffus *sacked* you." He smiled but she did not smile back.

"Why can't you just let me live in La La Land about that?" Frankie's sacking was another thing she hated telling people.

"Hey, I'm all for La La Land." He nudged his eyebrows towards his sister's untouched drink. "But you're the stickler for the facts. So stick to them."

"Fine. Here are the facts as I uncovered them in the course of that investigation. Weaver's body was found a few blocks from here in Kings Cross, but his last known sighting that night, on CCTV at least, was on a street corner down from here. So I put two and two together and assumed he came in to Taboo. It was the only place open in the vicinity at that time of night. Sadly, I could never verify that, but I did learn that Weaver came in to Taboo a week or so *before* he was murdered. Which is just after he got out on parole. While you're right, Trevor doesn't remember him—and why would he? It was a bloody busy night by all accounts, there was a footy match on, a hen's party—a woman I spoke to says she did. She saw someone matching Weaver's description with a tall, skinny guy with skanky neck and face tattoos."

"That's JayJay. The one who got stitched up for his murder."

"The one who is currently awaiting trial for Weaver's murder. Whether he got stitched up is only conjecture. Facts, remember?"

"Jesus, Earle's been rubbing off on you. So tell me more about these girls, these so-called witnesses of yours."

"Ah, here it is!" She scanned her notes quickly. "There was one woman..." Frowned. "I can't believe I didn't take down her name and number. No wonder I'm not at the *Herald* anymore. Still, I did manage a description." She read from the note she typed into her smartphone three months ago: "Redhead with a dreamcatcher thigh tattoo, drinks tequila sunrises." She smiled. "That's right, textbook millennial." She read some more and said, "Ms Millennial said she spotted Weaver and his tattooed mate hassling some young girls by the bar. Apparently Trevor kicked them out, but don't check that with him, he's grumpy enough as it is. It makes sense though. Trev's as vigilant about sleazebags as you are." She smiled.

"Talk about rubbing off."

He frowned. "Okay, so now I have to find this redhead with the lame tattoo."

Frankie held up one finger. "No, you fool! She's a *second-hand* witness. You have to go straight to the source. You need to find those young girls Weaver was hassling. They might know more about Lars. I don't know. But they're definitely a direct link to Weaver. They spoke to him a week before he was murdered. What were they talking about? Find the answer to that, and I think you'll have the answer to everything."

"Sounds like a needle in a haystack, Frankie."

"Not at all. You just have to look for a fellow *wantok*." When he seemed baffled, she added, "Listen to this. This is what Ms Millennial said to me that night, and I quote: 'Two guys were hassling some Islander girls by the pool table. Trevor angry. Kicked them out.'"

"Islander girls?" Kila repeated. "What? Papuans like me?"

Frankie's smile widened. "I told you they were *wantoks*."

"Don't often see my kin in this bar." He glanced around, then back. "But I do know somewhere they might hang out." Then he tried his luck and added, "Fancy a change of scenery, Frankie?"

~

Seagrave didn't just look spooky, perched as it was on the top of a cliff with its ivy-clad sandstone turrets and shadowy stained-glass windows, but it felt haunted to Merry and with good reason. There were now six deaths associated with the place. Six *suspicious* deaths, in fact, but she tried not to think about that as she killed time outside the entrance gate with Verity, waiting for Shannon to show up.

"She's not as punctual as you," Merry said, checking her phone clock. It was 10:20 p.m. They'd been standing there since ten.

Verity sighed, pushing a wet red curl from her eyes. "She's nothing like me, in fact. I've been trying to train the girl up, but she's... well, lazy is a good word for it. Simply not up to the job."

"Tell me why you kept her on again?"

"I was doing a favour to George. He had a soft spot for Shannon, goodness knows why. I... Oh, quick duck."

They stepped back behind a bush as a car drove past. It was not the police, but Merry could see Verity was rattled.

"I'm in big trouble if I get caught here," she said. "It's against my bail conditions. My solicitor was using those exact words earlier this evening." She then ran a hand through her wet hair and added, "Hence the reason I'm fresh from a shower. For some reason, talking to Ginny—that's my solicitor—always leaves me feeling grubby."

Merry were barely listening. She was staring at her device. "We should switch off our phones so they can't ping us here later."

"Ping us here?" said Verity.

Merry giggled. "You know what I mean!" Then she pointed at the police tape dangling from one end of Seagrave's gate where it had snapped off. "I'm not allowed access either, so we're both in a pickle if we get caught."

Hence the reason they were waiting for Shannon. After Verity's arrest, the junior assistant was instructed by the police to change the access codes to Seagrave. And while she could have whispered them to Verity—had offered to do so, in fact—it felt slightly less illegal having her here, tapping them in herself.

That is if she ever arrived.

"Where is that silly girl!" said Merry, ducking as another car whooshed past. "Maybe we *should* have got the code from her first. Left her out of it."

"Mmm, pity she changed it…" Verity swished her lips to one side. Then swished them back. "Hang on a minute."

She stepped up to the intercom box and plugged in four numbers, then they both gasped as the gate creaked to life and slowly swung open.

Merry pumped a fist in the air. "How'd you guess?"

"I didn't. It's the *old* access code." Verity shook her head, laughing. "Good thing about a lazy assistant—she doesn't do her job properly. Shannon must've forgotten to change it. Come on, we don't want to get caught out here. I'll leave it open so she knows we're already inside."

CHAPTER 19 ~
GHOSTS FROM THE PAST

"Apologies, that took much longer than I was expecting," said Graham Fergerson as he waved Martin into a dimpled leather chair in front of an enormous glass desk. Not that you could see much of the glass—the entire surface was covered in papers and files and not one but three screens, each one blazing brightly, two with what looked like stock market reports. "It's a busy time, as you can imagine."

"It must be overwhelming," said Martin, "taking over the reins of a giant mining company."

"That's an understatement."

The CEO placed his hands on top of the clutter, snuck a look at the hefty watch on his wrist and said, "To ensure we get out of here before midnight, let's cut to the chase, shall we? How can I help Verity? What is it you need?"

"You think she's innocent?"

"Of course," he responded immediately. "It's preposterous what they're suggesting. Of Verity Vine? Not a chance! I've never met a more devoted assistant, and I mean *devoted*. Verity was so much more than George's assistant. She kept the cogs in place, the wheels turning. God knows it all would have gone off the rails towards the end there if it weren't for Verity. And since I took up this position, I've come to understand exactly how crucial she is." He paused. Smiled. "Ever watched that show *Mash*, Martin?"

Martin was surprised by the subject change. He shrugged. "The old army sitcom? Once or twice, why?"

Fergerson smiled. "We call Verity 'Radar' around here. She has an uncanny ability to know what you need long before you even know you need it." His smile faded, and his eyes darted out the glass door to where his own PA was still seated, merrily tapping away at her keyboard. "Helen is retiring this year, and I was hoping Verity would take her place now that George has passed, but... well..."

"She's not interested?"

"She's a little preoccupied, you might say."

Martin nodded. Yes, there was that.

"But it's not only her proficiency," he continued. "Verity's a good woman, salt of the earth. The idea that she would poison anybody, let alone old George, is *preposterous.*"

He'd used that adjective twice. Martin was buoyed by it. "So who then? Who could have done this?"

"I can't imagine anyone. I wonder whether they've got the story all wrong again. Isn't it the same detective who botched up the investigation last time? Why he's still in the job is beyond me. In the corporate world, he would've been shown the door without so much as a golden parachute. This amateur gets to stay and then investigate the family all over again. It's objectionable!"

"You think DI Morgan might be stitching the family up?" Was Fergerson suggesting a fresh suspect?

The CEO looked annoyed. "Of course not. It's not one of your books, Mr Chase." He smiled. "My wife is a fan."

Martin didn't return the smile. Fergerson was the one who'd brought fiction into it. He let it slide and said, "I agree with your summation of Morgan. I don't have a lot of faith in him, but the evidence does point to murder. Or perhaps suicide?"

"Not a chance," said the CEO.

"Verity suggested it."

Fergerson looked surprised. Then disappointed. "Perhaps Verity thinks that's the kindest solution, but I can't see that either. It wasn't George's way. He wasn't a quitter, not one to run from a challenge. So, while he didn't exactly look after himself or Seagrave in the final months, had certainly lost his raison d'être, I still can't believe he brought about his own demise. Not in his genes."

"So how did he end up poisoned?" Martin asked, circling back.

"It's a good question."

"Any business associates who might have held a grudge? Anybody ever threaten him?"

Fergerson went to answer, then exhaled and turned his palms over and appeared to be studying them. "Threats are par for the course in this industry, especially lately. Mining is now a dirty word, a scourge on the planet, apparently." He turned his palms back. "So yes, we do get messages of abuse from the lunatic green fringe from time to time, occasional pickets out the front. But I've never known anyone to cross the line, so to speak. It's never felt personal, at least not to me. Whether George got any individual threats, well, Verity would be better placed to answer that." His face clouded over. "How is she? Verity?"

"You haven't seen her since she got out?"

He shook his head. "I told her to take as much time as she needs. Whether she ever comes back to the team... Well, that's up to her. I do hope to absorb her into the business, just as we absorbed Shannon."

"Verity's assistant? Oh yes, I did want to ask about her. She's found another job here at HQ?"

"Not yet, no. I'm still trying to find her a placement." His brow furrowed like it was easier said than done, and Martin recalled how Verity wasn't exactly a glowing referee. "No, I was referring to last time. After all the drama with Susan. It was very unsettling for young Shannon—her first job no less. So for Verity to take her under her wing, well that was gracious."

Martin looked confused. "Sorry, just to clarify—are you saying Shannon worked for the company back then? When Susan went on her killing spree?"

"Yes, Verity didn't tell you?"

Not exactly, thought Martin as the CEO reached for a file on his desk. He opened it.

"Shannon started with us two years ago, straight out of business school, as a trainee receptionist. Human Resources don't normally place trainees in that position—working under a department head—but he wanted her, so he got her. Of course after the scandal, the young lass was floundering, which is why Verity stepped up."

"Sorry, who wanted her? Which department head did she work for?"

"Susan's husband," he said matter-of-factly. "Shannon worked for Clem LeDoux."

Martin sat back in his seat with a thud.

No wonder he'd recognised young Shannon when he met her this morning! It wasn't from George's funeral at all. It was because she was the cherub-faced receptionist who greeted him last year when he came here to interview Clem, back when Clem still worked for George. Before Susan was arrested and Clem was shown the door.

The plot had just got a lot thicker... and lot ickier too, perhaps.

~

The queue outside Bar Hola was ten people long and three people deep. They clearly hadn't got the memo about it being a quiet night, and Kila went to join the end when Frankie tsked, grabbed his arm and headed straight for the front.

When she got to the chiselled bouncer by the door, she flicked her blond hair about and said almost wearily, "Hey there, we're with the *Herald*. Doing a piece on the best nightspots in Sydney."

She didn't have to utter another word. He unlatched the velvet rope and in they went.

"Don't look so smug," Kila said. "They let me in last time without any tales."

"Must've been a slow night," she shot back, then allowed her eyes to adjust to the dark interior as they glanced around.

The place was bursting with people of colour, many of them from South Pacific nations, like Tonga, Samoa and, yes, Kila's homeland of Papua New Guinea.

"I've never been here before," Frankie said, and he snorted.

"What a shock, *Blondie*. Come on, I think I can see a friendly face in the corner."

They strode across to a leather booth where a thirty-something Papuan woman was mid-conversation with a younger woman of similar origin. Both looked up as they approached, and then the thirty-something's face lit up.

"Oh, hey! Kila! Long time, no see!"

"Hey, Violet," he said, leaning down to hug her. "Remember Frankie Jo? Can we have a quick word?"

"Sure, everything okay?"

Her smile dimmed and with good reason. This woman's best friend had been Lia Segeyaro, Susan's fourth victim. That's how Kila got to know her, but he held up a steady palm.

"All's fine. I just have another case I want to ask you about."

The other woman went to get up, but he waved her back. "You might be able to help too. I'm Kila, this is Frankie."

She introduced herself as Cherize and settled back into her seat.

"We usually hang at a bar called Taboo," said Frankie.

"Oh yeah, in Victoria Street?"

She nodded. "Do you ever go there?"

Cherize shook her head. "Not for years."

"You, Violet?" asked Kila.

Her head was also shaking, but her lips were smudging downwards. "Too young and too posh for me. Why? What's this about?"

"We're looking for some Islander girls who might go there or used to go there, at least a few months ago."

"Islander girls?" said Violet, lips smudging further.

He chuckled. "Yeah, apparently you all look the same to this white witness."

Violet and Cherize gave Frankie the once-over, then giggled.

"Got any more details than that?" asked Violet.

"Could've been there for a hen's party maybe?" said Kila.

"Or watching the footy," added Frankie. Ever the feminist.

Violet scratched her thick afro hair. "We can ask around for you, if you like. My cousins are younger. They might know."

"Do that," said Kila. "I'd be most grateful. And here." He handed them both his business card. "Call me if anyone comes to mind."

"Or maybe just call for some fun times?" said Violet, eyes flicking across to Frankie curiously. Wondering perhaps if they were together.

"I don't know about *fun*, but you should definitely call him," said Frankie, breaking Kila's heart all over again.

~

Merry's heart was in her throat as she followed Verity from the car to the mansion's front door, half expecting a police officer to jump out from the shadowy gardens and yell, "You're nicked!"

Yet the place was deadly quiet. Nothing but its old ghosts rattling about.

Or perhaps that was just the breeze swooping in from the neighbouring sea. Merry shuddered and wrapped her arms around herself. When they reached the door, a glaring sensor light came on and she almost ducked again, but Verity was unperturbed.

"Don't worry. No one can see this part of the house from the road." She reached towards the intercom box on the wall beside the large door and began plugging in four numbers. "If Shannon didn't bother changing the front gate," she said, "she'd hardly change the front door now would she?"

And she was right. The old code worked a treat and the door clicked open.

"Unbelievable," said Verity, sounding more disappointed than thrilled now.

But Merry was in the thrilled camp. This was going a lot easier than she expected!

Inside, they didn't muck about. They knew firsthand that there were no cameras on the property, despite its shocking history, but neither woman wanted to get busted there, nor did they want to leave too much of themselves behind. Merry shuddered again, this time at the thought of contaminating the crime scene.

Earle would never forgive her.

And so, after switching on the low lights along the skirting board—"Might as well play it safe," said Verity—they walked through the entrance atrium and across to the grand staircase that led down to the lower floor, which housed the ballroom and the pool deck. As they held on to the oak banister and stared downwards, Merry conceded that it would have been very difficult for anyone on their suspect list to carry a grown man down those steep marble steps.

Except perhaps for Clem.

Verity was too tiny, so too Shannon. Susan was locked up, and Charlie, while over six foot, looked like she struggled to hold her own skinny frame up.

Which left the exterior walkway. "Can we take a look at that?" Merry asked, and Verity began to lead the way down the stairs, but Merry held her back.

"No. Show me the path from up here please, Verity. I want to walk in the direction the killer might've walked. In fact, let's do it properly..."

Merry glanced down the low-lit hallway, then made the long trek to the kitchen, gasping as she walked in. She'd forgotten how large and well equipped it was! Not that there was anything of any substance in the pantry, which was wide open, its doors covered with smudged powder marks.

"Morgan's made a mess of everything with his fingerprinting," said Verity, her tone annoyed.

There were more smudge marks on the fridge, but that didn't stop Merry. She covered her hands with her sleeves and swept the door open, saying, "So the killer takes the stew from here..." The shelves were also virtually empty—just a few faded green apples and an unopened carton of long-life milk—but she imitated pulling out a pot, then pretended to place it on the kitchen bench as she closed the fridge again.

"...and then he adds the poison to George's final meal, leaving the poor man slumped in his wheelchair." A quick glance at Verity. "Sorry, I don't mean to be so insensitive."

"No, no, this is important. Go on."

Merry nodded. "Okay, so the killer wheels the chair out of the kitchen..." She retreated, pretending to push a wheelchair all the way back down the long hallway. "...then up to this front door."

The door had also been left open for Shannon, so Merry stepped out and onto the level driveway. "Which way would they go if they wanted to get down to the ballroom?"

"Take a hard right," said Verity, head nudging in the direction of a mossy pathway that skirted the exterior of the house and then disappeared down one side.

While the path was slippery and fringed with overgrown shrubs, it was wide enough for a chair to fit comfortably and had an easy decline. Even a child could have pushed a grown man down that slope, thought Merry as they traversed it.

Or an elderly man could have pushed himself.

Towards the bottom, the path split in three directions. One led towards the lower level of the house and an internal doorway, now firmly locked. One led away from the house and towards what looked like an unkempt garden and a fenced area. The tennis court, if Merry was not mistaken, and beyond that the old housekeeper's cottage. And the third path wound its way around to the other side of the house and out of view. Merry suspected that path ended at the swimming pool, which fronted the ballroom and the ominous cliff face. Merry began to walk it, but now Verity was pulling her back towards the internal doorway on the side.

"The pool doors were open that morning," she said, "but they can only be opened from the inside and I can't see why they would have been unlocked. So whoever came down here must have used this door to access them."

Verity shook her head again as she successfully opened the door with the code. "Once you have the front door code," she told Merry, "it's access all areas."

"Luckily for us," said Merry as they stepped inside.

The room was dark, and it took a moment for Verity to find the light switch, but when she did, Merry was back in full gasp mode.

"I'd forgotten all about this second kitchen!"

"It's the butler's pantry," explained Verity.

"Yeah, well, lucky butler," she shot back. "It's bigger and better than mine."

Glancing around at more unused, gleaming appliances, Merry slowly opened a few cupboards, then the fridge, finding nothing but an empty ice bucket inside.

"I don't think this kitchen has been used once since Tawny passed," said Verity. "Like I said, George never came down here."

"Except that final night of course," said Merry softly.

Now Verity was shuddering beside her, and Merry turned to give her a comforting hug when she spotted a contraption in the wall.

"Ha!" she said, opening the door and peering inside. Here was another thing she'd forgotten. Merry turned back to Verity, eyes wide. "I don't think it's suicide at all, Verity. And I think I know how the killer got him down here!"

CHAPTER 20 ~

THINGS THAT GO BUMP
IN THE NIGHT

Earle had only just put the young poppet down when the doorbell chimed through the house. He winced, glanced at the baby again, but she was soundly sleeping. For once! Still, he wasn't going to hedge his bets. He tiptoed as fast as his old legs could carry him and swiftly opened the front door.

"Crikey, Martin, what are you doing here at this hour?"

Martin charged straight in. "I need your help!"

Earle held a finger to his lips. "And I need you to keep your voice down, buddy. Bub's asleep."

"Sorry," he whispered. "But I'm worried. About Merry and Verity."

"Why? What's going on? Where are they?"

"They're at Seagrave, with a killer!"

"They're at Seagrave? After I specifically told Merry not to go there?"

"You've buried the lead, Earle. There could be a killer waiting for them."

"Everything okay?" came Beryl's voice from the hallway.

Earle shot Martin a grimace, then turned to face his wife. "All good, dear. It's just Martin from the agency. Go back to sleep."

Then he waved Martin into the kitchen and went to fill the kettle. "Take a breath, young man, and explain yourself. Who is this killer they went to meet?"

"Shannon! It's the PA's PA! I can't believe we didn't pick it earlier."

"Shannon? You think Shannon is the perp?"

"Yes! And there's no time for tea. Shannon is meeting with Merry and Verity right this minute, at Seagrave. We have to get over there!"

"Merry should not even be at Seagrave—"

"Earle! There's no time for this! I've tried calling them, but their phones are switched off. Come on, grab your jacket, I'll explain everything on the drive."

"But—"

"Come on! If I'm right about this, Merry and Verity could be walking into a trap this very minute!"

~

Merry walked towards the dumb waiter and swept the door open, revealing the small lift inside. She knew from the first case that it connected to the kitchen on the main level above and was large enough to hold a man in the hunched, seated position.

Especially one who was comatose.

"Maybe George didn't get wheeled down after all," Merry said, eyes wide. "Maybe someone just had to hoist him in here upstairs and press the lower floor button. Then carry the wheelchair down and pull his body back out again."

"I suppose," said Verity, shuddering again. "But oh, I hope not."

Now Merry did go in for the hug, holding Verity tight for a few moments before stepping back and then examining the dumb waiter properly. She hoped to find some evidence that George had been stuffed inside—a few grey hairs, a loose button from his dressing gown—but there was little more than a light coating of dust.

"Oh well, let's check out the ballroom."

Verity led the way through the internal kitchen door to the enormous dance floor beyond, and once again, Merry was goggle-eyed. She'd also been here before, but it still took her breath away, with its glossy parquetry flooring and gaudy chandeliers. They walked to the centre and admired the space for a few minutes, then Merry glanced around.

"Where's the record player?"

"It usually sits here," said Verity, striding to one end of the room to a small stage that had been built about a foot from the floor. She tapped a low table. "We stored it away after we found…"

She let it drop, and Merry gave her arm a rub.

"Okay, but where was it plugged in that night? Exactly?"

Verity pointed downwards to a power point hidden behind a velvet curtain. Low enough for anyone to use, including a suicidal man in a wheelchair.

"And the light switches? For the chandeliers?"

Verity turned and began pointing both hands, first towards the staircase entrance, then towards the kitchen, then at the sliding glass doors that Merry knew fronted the pool deck. "There're several ways to switch them on."

"But can you reach them in a wheelchair?" asked Merry, feeling more confident. She grabbed a lone chair and placed it beside the lowest of the light switches, the one by the kitchen, then extended her arm and groaned.

Yes, you can.

"So he could have made his own way down here," said Verity, "could have switched on the lights and then the music."

"Yeah, I guess so." Merry sounded disappointed. She shouldn't be. Suicide was the easiest—the kindest—option. Better to go out on your own terms, surely? And yet she had been convinced she'd find indisputable evidence to the contrary. All she'd found was a bunch of mixed messages.

Earle was right. She'd learned nothing of consequence.

"Okay, let's get out of here," she said, but Verity wasn't listening.

She had strolled across the dance floor to the sliding doors and was staring through them, out towards the shadowy pool beyond. She cupped her hands to the glass, then gasped and took a sudden step backwards.

"Everything okay?" Merry asked, heading towards her.

"We're... we're not alone," Verity said, her voice a hoarse whisper. "There's somebody out there."

Merry felt her blood run cold.

~

Martin was feeling hot under the collar. Wished he hadn't let Earle drive. The old copper stuck to the speed limit like he was sitting for his learner's licence. He'd only brought him in on it as Earle was ex-police and might know how to handle a homicidal maniac, because Martin sure didn't. He might have created a kick-arse hero in his books, but in real life Martin was a wimp.

Barely had the balls to confront his elderly father...

"Earle, come on, mate, we have to hurry."

"We also have to get there alive, Martin. Just settle down and tell me what the hell you're going on about. Why on earth would Shannon want to hurt George, let alone Verity and Merry?"

"I think she's in on it with Clem. I think she's doing it for him."

"Clem? How? Why?"

"She used to work for Clem as his receptionist. That's why she looked so familiar to me when she came to our office today. I'd already met her, back when I interviewed Clem at *his* office, the time he laughed in my face. The CEO has just confirmed it. He said Clem and Shannon were—and I quote—very close. He said she floundered after Clem was sacked, and that's why they moved her on to work for Verity."

"So what are you suggesting? An affair?"

"Yes! It probably started back then and has been ongoing. She's the only other person who could reasonably tamper with the stew on a regular basis. We're trying to make it complicated— a rookie error—but maybe it's very simple. Maybe she did it for Clem. Probably because she's in love with the guy and thinks he's in love with her, and maybe he is. Or maybe he's just using that to his advantage and has managed to manipulate her into poisoning his father-in-law. Either as revenge for how his life has turned out or to get at Susan's money."

"But why would Shannon do such a thing? It's one thing to be young and naive. It's quite another to agree to murder."

"Maybe she's as angry as Clem is. Think about it: life turned pretty shite for Shannon too after we busted Susan and Clem. Shannon had to work for Verity, someone she clearly doesn't like. Perhaps Clem told Shannon he'd divorce Susan, give her half and she'd never have to work again? I mean, I don't have all the answers, but I do think she's involved, and if I'm right, Verity and Merry could be in trouble because they're meeting her—maybe even *him*—right this second, so you need to put your foot on it."

"Okay, calm down, we're nearly there," Earle said, turning up the steep road towards Seagrave. "It's as good a theory as any, Martin, but that's all it is at this stage. Conjecture. You don't even know if Shannon and Clem are still together. Or even were together in the first place."

"Have you seen the woman? She looks about twelve. Definitely his type. I can assure you, they're together. They might not be when Susan gets out—Clem will have dumped her long before then—

but right now she's right up his alley. Either she did it with him or—"

He sat forward in his seat. "Look! That's Merry's car, and Verity's in front of it."

The two vehicles were parked on the side of the road, just beyond the front gate which, much to their surprise, was wide open.

Martin didn't know if that was a good sign or not, but he was grateful nonetheless. He'd forgotten all about the access codes. Earle let out a puff of air—he was grateful too—then swept his car through the entrance and down the long driveway to the front of the house.

There they both noticed a small white hatchback parked in one of the guest spots.

Martin's stomach dropped. "I think that might be Shannon's." He recalled seeing it on his way out of their office earlier that day.

"Hmmm," said Earle as he pulled the car to a stop just beside it and they both jumped out. "I hope you're wrong about this, Martin."

"Yeah, you and me—"

He didn't finish that sentence. They were just closing in on the open front door when they heard the first scream.

CHAPTER 21 ~
THE BODY BY THE WATER

Shannon Smith was sprawled on a banana lounge beside the pool at Seagrave, staring out at the view, but she couldn't see a thing and it had nothing to do with the dark purple sky and everything to do with the matching gash in one side of her head.

Leaning down beside her was a thirty-something in a white onesie, snapping away with a digital camera and beside her a surly looking Detective Inspector Morgan. He was talking with a uniformed officer, reading through notes on a pad and flicking furious scowls at Merry and Verity, who were both facing away from the pool, unable to look. They had seen enough for one night.

But Earle was looking, so too Martin. They were trying to soak everything up before Morgan booted them out.

When the men first arrived, Merry's screams had led them into the house, down the staircase, through the ballroom and out to the pool deck where they found Verity leaning over Shannon's body, Merry hovering nearby, one hand to her mouth like a muzzle.

"Step back!" Earle yelled when he realised what was going on. "Don't touch anything!"

"I was just checking for a pulse," said Verity, but he grabbed her arm, pulled her away.

"I think we can safely assume she's deceased."

He stared at Shannon's wide dead eyes, blood-splattered face. Shook his head sadly.

"What the hell happened?" asked Martin, almost breathless.

"We just found her like that!" Merry said, her voice going high-pitched again.

Earle turned to her. "Let's get you into a seat, Merry. And we'll call triple zero."

"No!" she screamed back. "We have to get Verity out of here first. She'll get in big trouble! She's not supposed to be here."

"And neither are you," Earle said, his tone low and calm. "I told you to stay away."

"Yeah well, she didn't," said Martin, the only one looking genuinely thrilled with this development. "So what are we going to do now?"

Earle was already reaching for his phone.

"But...," began Merry. "I... I can pretend it was just me who found her. Snooping about."

"You're in enough trouble as it is, missy, don't think you're going to get off lightly. Crossing police tape is a serious offence."

Now Merry was paling.

He breathed out heavily. "Truth is your best defence. The more lies you introduce, the more you have to lie, and you both have nothing to hide. Right?"

He waited for them to look him in the eye.

"We found her like that," Merry repeated as Verity nodded mutely beside her.

"Okay then," said Earle as he placed the call. "That's what we tell them."

And so there they were, scanning the deck, trying to find signs of something—anything—to show how Shannon ended up with a fatal gash in her skull. The first responders, two uniformed police officers from a nearby station, had turned the pool floodlights on, but beyond the bloody corpse and the puddle of red below her head, there was nothing more to see than stacked pool chairs and piles of dead leaves.

No bloody footprints leading in any direction, no dripping murder weapon, nothing.

The four intruders had already been questioned by both officers and again by a plainclothes detective who was now consulting with Morgan. But Earle knew there would be a lot more questions to come. It was only the beginning.

"What do you think happened?" asked Verity, who had finally found her voice again. "To poor Shannon?"

"Looks like she's been bludgeoned by something sharp and heavy," said Earle, "maybe an axe or a machete?"

"A machete?" said Verity. "Where would they get a machete

from? This isn't the wild yonder."

"Is there a garden shed somewhere?"

She nodded, then shook her head. "I got rid of most of the stuff in there. Was using contractors to tidy things up. When George let me."

Her eyes filled with tears while Earle shrugged. "Morgan will search the place thoroughly of course, but my guess is whatever weapon was used, it went over that cliff an hour ago."

They all turned to stare down at the crashing darkness below the pool fence when Martin said, "Uh-oh, incoming."

"Well, well, well, what a surprise to find you lot hindering another investigation," said Detective Inspector Morgan as he approached, his eyes resting on his one-time friend. "Are you stalking me, Earle, or is this just an unhappy coincidence?"

Before he could answer, Morgan turned his gaze to Verity and waved a hand in the air, bringing a uniformed officer scurrying. "Verity Vine, I'd like you to accompany my constable down to the station for questioning."

"Is she under arrest?" asked Earle.

He turned cold eyes to Earle again. "Did I say she was under arrest?" Eyes back on Verity. "We need to straighten out what happened here tonight. I'm sure you understand."

Verity nodded uncertainly and went to follow.

"Call your lawyer," said Earle. "Don't say a word until she gets there."

Morgan flashed him a frown. "Always good to know which side you're on, Fitzy." Then a look of contempt followed. "How about you pack up your fellow cartoon characters and get the fuck off my crime scene? You've done enough damage for one night."

"We weren't trying to—" began Martin, but Earle was already pulling them away, relieved they would not be kept there any longer.

The relief was short-lived.

"Except you, Mrs Kean," Morgan said, making them all swing back. "I want you to report to homicide headquarters first thing in the morning, do you understand?"

Merry blinked, looking horrified, but Earle just smiled assuredly back at her. She'd got off lightly. Morgan could have hauled her in now, alongside Verity.

She could have spent the night in the slammer.

~

Kila had just escorted Frankie home—lingering outside her building for a good ten minutes, looking for signs of her nutcase stalker—and was just about to pull his Toyota four-wheel drive away when he got the phone call. It was Violet's friend Cherize. Judging from the deep bass beat and violent shrieking in the background, he could tell she was still at Bar Hola. He half wondered if he should return and join her.

"I think I've found the girls you're looking for," she said, yelling into her phone. "Or one of them anyway."

"That was quick," he replied, reaching for a pad in the passenger-side glovebox.

"Yeah, I just asked around here. A guy I know says his little sister used to go to Taboo, was there on a bachelorette party about three months back. Reckons she might be the one you're looking for."

"Brilliant." He scrambled now for a pen. "What's her name?"

"Bertha. Bertha Thomas."

Kila smiled. Bertha! That was one of the names listed in Weaver's notebook. Things were finally starting to click into place. "Brilliant," he said again. "Got a number for her?"

There was a pause. He wondered if she'd been cut off. Then she said, "Sorry Kila, but Bertha drowned a few months ago."

Then, in case he didn't hear her, she yelled out, "Bertha is dead!"

CHAPTER 22 ~
FACING UP TO MORGAN

Thursday morning was bright and blue, Sydney back to a textbook spring day. The sun was shining, the birds were chirping, but Merry didn't notice any of it. And it had nothing to do with the drab interview room she was now seated in at homicide headquarters. All she could see was Shannon's dead eyes and that ugly bloody gash.

Oh, the poor, poor child! She was far too young to have met with such a fate!

"Your first corpse," said DI Morgan, not unsympathetically.

Merry nodded and sniffed and reached for a bedraggled tissue she'd tucked into her cardigan sleeve.

"It doesn't get any easier, in case you're wondering," he said. "And you should be if you want to keep interfering in police business."

"I wasn't—"

He held up a palm. No time for excuses. "Tell me again exactly how you came upon the deceased." His eyes shifted from the recorder on the desk and back to Merry.

She had already been over it with the first responders last night and then the plainclothes detective, then again with Morgan this morning. But had watched enough police dramas to know how this worked. The more times they asked the same question, the more chance they had of making her slip up. Except she had truth on her side—and Earle had reminded her of that when he met her at the station that morning, his lawyer friend beside him.

"Just speak calmly and slowly and stick to the facts, nothing but the facts. You can't slip up if there are no dodgy lies in front of you. And if you do start slipping, that's what Mr Lachlan here is for."

Then he handed over to the elderly lawyer who was now beside Merry in the interrogation room, looking oddly disinterested. And so she tried to stick to the facts as she knew them: she met up with

Verity at Seagrave's front gate at exactly ten o'clock last night. They had each driven there separately and were awaiting Shannon's arrival.

"Earle didn't know anything about it," she'd added, hoping that helped his already fractured relationship with Morgan.

"You met Miss Vine *at* the Seagrave premises? At *exactly* ten o'clock?" he asked like she hadn't just said that.

"Yes! Maybe five minutes past? But yes, we arrived at the same time. In fact, I saw her car when I turned up Seagrave's street, so I followed Verity up the hill and parked just behind her. Shannon was supposed to meet us there too, but she was a no-show... or at least that's what we thought."

Merry explained how they waited on the road for twenty minutes until Verity managed to open the gate. They had promptly made their own way inside—leaving the gate open, she quickly added—and had been in the house and its surrounds for less than forty minutes when Verity noticed someone lying on a banana lounge by the pool. That's when they stepped outside and found her body.

No, Merry did not realise that Shannon was already at the house and nor had she noticed Shannon's car parked in a guest car spot.

"It was dark," she said by way of explanation. Well, until the front light was triggered, but she didn't mention that, and he didn't ask. Yes, she wanted to stick to the facts, but she wasn't going to make it easy for Morgan either! Because the truth was she and Verity should have noticed Shannon's hatchback. She kicked herself that neither of them had.

"And you saw no one else in the vicinity of Seagrave?" asked Morgan. "Either out on the road or inside the premises?"

The inference being—you two were the only ones who could have done it—but she tried not to let that unsettle her as she shook her head. Then was prompted to answer aloud for the benefit of the recording device in the centre of the table.

"No," she squeaked, flashing her lawyer a worried grimace.

"Okay," said Morgan, leaning back in his chair. "And what exactly were you doing at Seagrave in the first place?"

The lawyer sat forward with a creak of his chair. "My client will not be answering that," he said. Perhaps he thought it was incriminating.

"But I want to answer!" Merry responded, and he shrugged and sat back. "Look, it's innocent enough," she told Morgan. "I was only helping Verity. We all are."

"By *all*, you mean…" Morgan hesitated, his voice dripping with mirth. "The Sleuths of Last Resort." He swapped a look with a detective sitting quietly to his right.

"Yes," Merry said, her tone defensive. "We're a legitimate detective agency. Earle has his licence, and I'm studying for mine now. So is Frankie. We believe Verity is innocent, and I was at Seagrave, trying to test the evidence for myself. You see, my superpower is layout."

"Your what?"

She blushed. "I'm a Cluedo champion, right? I know how to read a murder scene. It's… well, it's my skill set."

Her lawyer sighed softly beside her while Morgan swapped another glance with his lacky, then said, "So you just broke into the premises?"

The lawyer was moving forward again, but Merry was indignant. "It wasn't breaking in. We had the codes."

Morgan showed his first flicker of genuine annoyance. Someone was going to pay the price for not ensuring the entrance codes had been changed. He said, "Do you understand that crossing crime-scene barrier tape is a grave offence? You could be charged with criminal trespass."

"I'm so, so sorry, but…" Merry glanced at her lawyer, and he just shrugged, like he could no longer help her. She said, "But Verity's innocent, and I just wanted to see the place for myself and really you should be grateful because if we hadn't broken in"—a cough from the lawyer —"I mean *let ourselves in*, Shannon might not have been found for days! Weeks even!"

"Oh, so you were doing *us* a favour, were you?" said Morgan.

Merry glowered back at him. "No, actually, it was young Shannon I was thinking of."

~

Frankie paced the waiting room like a pit bull, swivelling at every sound, and Earle shook his head at her as he sat in a stiff plastic chair.

"Take a seat, Frankie," he said eventually. "You're making me nervous."

"Well, you should be nervous! Merry? Under police interrogation? She'll give up all her secrets in the first five seconds."

"Good, because honesty is the best answer."

"Humph!" she said and then threw herself into a neighbouring chair and reached for her handbag. "I blame myself entirely."

He turned to stare at her. That was uncharacteristically repentant. "You encouraged her to break into Seagrave, didn't you?"

"Not break in as such, but I did suggest she call Verity." She pulled out a packet of paracetamol and pushed two out. "I never suspected they'd find a dead body there. And Shannon. Wow, this case just gets more and more interesting."

"That's not the word I'd use," he muttered, although he knew what she meant. Watched as she reached for a water bottle and slugged the headache tablets back.

"Big night last night?"

She scowled. "Kila's a bad influence."

"You don't have to be here you know. I've already sent Dougie packing. He dropped Merry down first thing and was as good as useless in his distressed state. I'm thinking you're not much better."

"Oh, I'm fine. It's Merry I'm worried about. She's the softie in our group."

"She's harder than you and Martin give her credit for."

"Speaking of the man of the hour—where is Martin? I thought at least he'd be here."

Earle shrugged again. "Said he had some unfinished business to attend to. Whatever that entails."

~

Across town, Martin was sitting in his Aston Martin, in the car park outside the Manly sailing school, waiting for Clem to arrive. He wanted to find out what car George's son-in-law drove so he could tail him. Knew from their past conversation that the cretin worked school hours on weekdays, and it was just on nine now. Just hoped he hadn't missed him.

Martin spotted the gold Mercedes before he registered what he was looking at.

Sat up with a start.

Clem was driving his wife's old vehicle? The infamous gold Merc! They still owned that car even after it was impounded by the police during Susan's murder investigation?

Okay, that made things easier, as weird as it was.

He stayed low as he watched the man park, badly, and then get out. Watched again as Clem adjusted his hair and glasses in the side-view mirror, then strode breezily into the sailing school like he had nothing more to worry about than his appearance.

Was Clem truly so cold-blooded? Could he act so breezily after slaughtering a young woman?

Martin glowered just thinking about it.

~

Another hour of repetitive questioning and Merry was released with just a caution.

Verity was not so lucky.

"She's back in custody," Earle told Merry when she finally returned to the waiting room, her lawyer a step behind. "Nothing we can do to help her now," he added as he watched Merry's face crumple. "She broke the conditions of her bail. I can't believe you two were so foolish."

She whimpered and collapsed into a chair beside Frankie, who rubbed her back gently and gave Earle a glowering look of her own.

He creaked his neck and sat down on her other side. "I'm sorry to be harsh, but this has really put a spanner in the works and not just for Verity, who's now in serious strife. It's not going to help her case at all, but it also means we can't help her directly either."

"What? Why not? They can't forbid us from investigating, surely?"

"No, Merry, but they can forbid us from contacting her now that she's back in prison. And I've just had a word with her solicitor. She's livid. I don't think she's going to be much use as an intermediary."

"Oh God," said Merry, dropping her head into her lap.

"I'll leave you to it," said Mr Lachlan, looking from Earle to Merry again. He placed a reassuring hand on her shoulder and added, "I'll be in touch."

As he walked away, Frankie mumbled, "Yeah, with a nice hefty bill, thanks very much."

"*Oh God!*" Merry whimpered again.

"You can charge it to the agency," Earle told her. "You were on agency business after all. Although you shouldn't have been."

"I think she gets the picture, thanks, Earle," said Frankie. "The I-told-you-so routine is getting stale."

Earle didn't like chastising Merry, but he was the lawman in the group and he just wished they would respect that and listen to him for once!

"Shall we go to your favourite café?" said Frankie, giving Merry a shoulder bump. "Get ourselves some breaky and you can tell us how it all went?"

Merry looked up, a small smile on her lips, but Earle was looking elsewhere. He'd just spotted Morgan coming out of the interview room.

"You folks go ahead. I'll meet you there."

Just as Earle had berated Merry, he was now expecting the same treatment from Morgan, and he steeled himself as the detective approached.

"You're lucky I didn't slap her with charges," Morgan said, nodding towards Merry, who was now exiting the building with Frankie.

"I appreciate it," Earle replied.

"I wasn't doing you a favour, Fitzy. I've got enough on my plate right now. I don't need the headache."

"Okay, but this has got to help Verity's case. Proof that there's another party involved in all this. And they're covering their tracks."

Morgan looked at him like he was demented. "The only tracks I can see lead straight back to your client."

"Verity? But she couldn't have killed Ms Smith. She was with Merry the whole time."

"Is that right?"

Earle frowned, not sure what that was about. "Look, I have another suspect I think you should explore." Morgan snorted but let him continue. "Last night my team discovered the victim has an affiliation with Clem LeDoux, Susan Burlington's hus—"

"I don't need a has-been to tell me who Clem LeDoux is, thanks, Earle."

"Fair enough. But did you also know that Ms Smith was Clem's receptionist back when Susan went on her killing spree? The CEO has already confirmed that the two were very close. We suspect Shannon and Clem entered into some kind of relationship—"

most likely an affair—and she may have been the person responsible for poisoning Mr Burlington."

"Really? That's your angle, is it?"

Earle held up a palm. "I realise it's speculation at this point, but it's an angle you really should investigate. Shannon had access to Seagrave and to the stew. And if she was, as we suspect, in a relationship with Clem, she also had a motive. In any case, I think you ought to bring Mr LeDoux in, check his alibi for last night and the night of George's murder. Did you ever speak to him?"

"He's not involved," Morgan said sharply.

"How do you know that? Have you questioned him? He's a viable suspect, Morgan."

"I have my suspect, thanks, Fitzy, a very good one."

"But if Shannon—"

"Oh Fitzy, you drive me berserk!" Morgan barked back. "Look, mate, I'm trying to help you here. You're making a fool of yourself. Shannon Smith is not a suspect. She's a *victim*. And how do I know this, other than the bloody great hole in her head? I know because it's Miss Smith who first called in the tip-off."

"Tip-off?" Earle looked confused. "I don't follow."

"No, you don't Earle, because you're old and past it. How do you think this all blew up in the first place? It was *Shannon* who rang the station the night before George's funeral to alert us to the poisoning. She suspected Verity had been tampering with George's meals for some time. It was *Shannon* who came in to tell us about her suspicions that Mr Burlington had been murdered."

Earle's jaw had dropped. Okay. That he had not been expecting. "So that's why you put a stop to the burial and arrested Verity."

"Bingo. Two questions for you, Earle: If Shannon was the one poisoning the old man, why would she alert us to the fact on the eve of his burial? He was about to be concealed, six feet under, and she was about to get away with murder. Oh, and question number two. How does that figure into the aforementioned hole in the head? Can you and your super team explain that?"

Earle rubbed a hand across his beard and didn't bother to answer. There were no words. It was all a muddle.

"Didn't think so," said Morgan. "But I can. Shannon had agreed to be a police witness. She was going to testify against Verity. Did Miss Vine ever mention that? No, of course she didn't.

She's been pulling your strings from the start, and all you are is a pathetic, outdated puppet. Shannon was about to turn state's witness and suddenly she shows up dead. How bloody convenient for Verity. Now, if you don't mind, I'd like to get on with the business of convicting that woman before anyone else gets hurt."

CHAPTER 23 ~

FACING MORE UGLY FACTS

Kila stared at the tombstone, a thick lump lodged in his throat.
"She was twenty-five going on fifteen," came a deep voice
behind him, and he didn't look around, didn't trust himself to speak.
"Bertha was a free spirit, a party girl. Too much of a party girl as it
turns out." A small, sad chuckle.

Waiting a beat, Kila turned to face the man behind him, a fellow
Papuan by the look of him, same unruly black curls as Kila. Shorter,
stockier, but the haunted look in his eyes was familiar.

"Thanks for agreeing to meet me," Kila said, offering him a hand
to shake. "I'm sorry about your sister."

Eddie Thomas shook it and said, "Yeah, so am I." Then he pulled
a small photo from his back pocket, handed it to Kila.

It showed Eddie with his arm around a woman who made Eddie
look tall and lean. She was tiny, on the chubby side, but it suited her.
Her thick lips were coated in something glossy, her twinkling eyes
lined in black, and her dark curls were flying wildly around a bright
pink faux-fur jacket. She was yelling something at the photographer,
something cheeky judging by the glint in her eyes, and it thickened
the lump in Kila's throat again.

Bertha looked like someone he would've partied hard with in
his day.

He handed the photo back. "So what happened to her? D'ya mind
me asking?"

"Booze. Too much of it." Another sad chuckle. "That's what
happens when you mix water and spirits. She went swimming after a
big night out. Rock fisherman found Bertha's body the next morning.
Probably got caught in a rip. Didn't stand a chance."

"So, a drowning accident?"

Eddie nodded, then knelt down at her headstone, plucking away some frangipani flowers that were browning at the edges.

"We're not great swimmers us *wantoks*, hey?" he said. "Funny considering the water's so beautiful in PNG."

"Didn't grow up with private pools and pricey swimming lessons," offered Kila.

The man nodded again. "But she loved it, swimming, the beach. Paid too much for a shitty little rental not far from Bondi."

"That's where she was found?" He nodded. "Anyone with her? When she drowned."

He shook his head. "Wasn't the first time she went swimming at night alone—her rental's just a quick stroll up the hill. I warned her about sharks, not drowning. Her mates said she often skinny-dipped late. Loved the freedom, felt like she was back home."

"And you're sure it was an accident?" Kila had to ask.

He looked almost annoyed now. "She wasn't suicidal. No way, brother."

"No, I didn't mean—"

"It was the grog. She was loaded. Had been at a local pub, the Bondi Brewers. Mates say she was pissed as a newt. Cops said her stomach was full of grog and not much else. Would've just slipped under."

There were worse ways to go, Kila knew, but he didn't say as much because he was wondering whether that was how she went. Really.

Another death associated with Taboo. It had to be connected.

He watched for a moment longer while the devastated brother continued clearing around the grave, then said, "So you told me on the phone that Bertha might've been at the Taboo Bar in Victoria Street three months ago?"

"Yeah, maybe. Can't be certain, but it fits the timeline you were asking about. She used to hang at Taboo fairly religiously but got jack of it a few years back. Was only there that night for a girlfriend's hen's party. And I know because I was at the buck's party just down the road in Kings Cross, same night."

Kila produced his phone. Looked at the note Frankie had forwarded on and showed him the relevant date.

He nodded. "Wedding was two days later, so that sounds about right. I spoke to Bertha at the reception—before she got so tanked I had to pour her into a cab." Another sad smile. "She told me the hen's party was fun, but some creep was annoying them, asking weird questions."

Okay, this was promising. "She mention anything else?"

He shook his head.

"Didn't describe the creep to you, mention the name Phillip? Maybe another man with face tattoos?"

Another head shake. "Sorry. That's all I remember. It's the last time I saw her. Two weeks later..." His eyes drifted down to the tombstone. His jaw tightened. "I want to help. Cherize mentioned something about your own sister? You lost her too, hey?"

Kila took a step backwards. They were part of a unique club, Eddie and him, but it's one he didn't want to belong to, let alone acknowledge. They weren't going to bond over that.

"Actually, I'm investigating for a client," he said instead. "I think her brother was the creep your sister was talking to."

Now Eddie looked confused. Wary. So Kila explained: "His name was Phillip Weaver and he was murdered about a week after that hen's night. Last person he was seen talking to, I think, was Bertha."

They both turned back to her headstone now.

Eddie sounded defensive suddenly. "So? What's Bertha got to do with it?"

"Good question, brother. I'm just trying to fill in the blanks."

The man shrugged and started weeding around the plot like he really didn't care, and Kila didn't blame him. Ignorance was bliss, he suspected, so he thanked him for his time and went to leave, when something occurred to him.

"Just one more question, if you don't mind. You said Bertha stopped going to Taboo a few years back. Do you know why?"

Eddie shrugged again, not looking around. "I think it had something to do with a sleazy barman, something like that."

Kila's eyes widened. "Guy called Lars? Lars Karlsson?"

He looked back. "Lars Karlsson? Yeah... that name does ring a bell. Why? Who is he?"

"It's complicated," said Kila, although it was starting to feel very simple.

All roads led back to Taboo, and now they were detouring towards Lars. He needed to find where that guy was hiding away, because Frankie was right, he had to be somewhere, couldn't stay hidden forever.

"Sorry I'm not more use," Eddie added.

"Nah man, I'm sorry for your loss."

Then Kila left him leaning over his sister, stroking her marble headstone like it would grant him a wish. But Kila had already tried that.

Knew it didn't work.

~

The sleuths sat around the conference table, their expressions as pale and flat as the whiteboard in front of them, their respective lunches barely eaten. Things did not look good for their client.

Martin could not get past the fact that Shannon had placed the call to the police the evening before George's funeral. "She dobbed her own boss in. Wow, I mean, it's horrible what's happened to her, but she's one cool cucumber. She was here just yesterday, sucking up to Verity like they were old pals. Meanwhile, she was about to turn state's witness."

"I should've picked it," said Frankie, plucking up her sushi roll, then dropping it again. "She was so passive-aggressive about Verity when I got her alone. Clearly blamed her and I didn't push her on it. Damn it, I'm losing my edge!" A tiny crinkle crossed her brow. "You think Shannon might've been wearing a recording device? For Morgan?"

Earle shrugged like it didn't matter anymore. He dusted sandwich crumbs from his hands and looked at Martin. "Still think Shannon was in it with Clem?"

"Yep," he replied. "More so now that she's dead."

"Then talk us through it."

Martin's theory was that Shannon had fallen head over heels for Clem when he was her boss. Whether it was blind loyalty or they'd had an affair almost didn't matter. "He's older, savvier, more sophisticated. Would've been easy to twist her around his finger. I bet she was beholden to Clem, adored him, would do anything he asked."

"Like poison her boss's stew," said Merry, and he nodded.

"She had the means, she had the opportunity, and now we know she had the motive. A connection to Clem, a man who must hate George with every cell in his body."

"So explain to me why *she's* now in the morgue," said Earle.

"I told you last night, Clem was probably just using Shannon. Maybe he was acting for his real love, Susan. He might have told Shannon he would leave Susan when the inheritance came through but never intended to. So he arranged to meet her at Seagrave earlier, then took her out of the equation. While stitching up Verity even further."

"And me," said Merry. "I was there as well. I could've been blamed too! At least now I'm her witness and her alibi."

"About that—" said Frankie.

Martin cut her off. "Clem might not have been expecting you, Merry. He might have thought Verity was showing up alone. We need to find out where Clem was last night. What's his alibi?" He checked his watch. "I know he still drives Susan's Merc, so he'll be easy to follow."

"He still drives—"

"Yep," he said. "But he no longer lives in their house. Maybe he lives with Shannon? I'm going to follow him, after work, see where that leads, see if there're signs they were living together."

"What, you're going to force your way in and check for happysnaps of Clem with Shannon on the mantlepiece?" asked Frankie.

"Something like that."

"Be careful," said Earle. "If Clem is behind all this..."

"Oh, he's behind it all right," said Martin. "I'm sure of it."

"Okay," said Earle, trying to keep things clear in his head. "If that's true, Martin, if Shannon and Clem really were working together, why tip off the police just before the burial? They had succeeded."

"Regrets?" said Merry, ever the kind one.

"Because it was never about killing George," said Martin. "I've said this all along. This was about vengeance—upon both George and Verity. One had been ticked off—George was gone— but it looked like Verity was going to get off without even being questioned. Their great plan to plant it in her stew did not work. No one got suspicious; worse, Verity was being rewarded with a third of George's estate! That must have infuriated the exiled son-in-law, so he got Shannon to make the call. Point the finger at Verity. That way she gets punished too. It's a win-win."

"It's a risky game is what it is," said Earle, "because it also points the finger back at Shannon. She had equal access to the stew."

"Maybe *she* realised that in retrospect," said Martin, thinking on his feet. "For all we know, she caught a case of the guilts and began to have second thoughts. Maybe she was about to double-cross Clem and strike a plea deal with Morgan? Point the finger at the real mastermind of it all, and so Clem had to act, and fast. Got lucky when Shannon told him she was helping Verity break into Seagrave last night. Knew it was his chance to kill two birds with one stone— if you'll excuse my utterly brilliant pun."

Frankie groaned as Martin continued: "Clem got to silence his accomplice and throw more guilt Verity's way. He just didn't factor on Merry being there, providing Verity's alibi."

"About that," said Frankie again, her tone more forceful. "I'm not sure Merry is Verity's alibi."

"Of course I am," said Merry. "They can't possibly think I had anything to do with it, and Verity was with me from the minute we got into Seagrave until we found Shannon."

"I'm talking about before then," said Frankie. "You both arrived separately, to Seagrave, correct?"

"Yes, just after ten. Like I told Morgan, I followed her car up the hill. Then we both parked out of sight and stayed together until we went inside."

"Okay, so where had she been beforehand?"

Merry looked confused. "Home. I mean, her hair was wet and she said she always showered after meeting with her lawyers, so I just…"

"Assumed?" said Frankie, an eyebrow raised. "So was it the lawyer Verity was washing away? Or Shannon?"

Merry humphed loudly. Looked to Earle. "I thought we had agreed we were working for Verity, we're on her side."

He rubbed his beard. "I'll check her alibi again with Odetta. If she ever calls me back." He pulled his phone from his top pocket, just in case. "Let's put our suspicions about her aside for now and—"

"Not *our* suspicions," said Merry. "Just Frankie's. There are still other suspects, you know."

He exhaled loudly. "Okay, Merry, which suspect would you prefer?"

Merry frowned uncertainly, not sure if she was being mocked. She pushed her plastic container of leftover fried rice aside and stood up, reading through the names on the board.

"What about Susan?" said Merry, reaching for a suspect, any suspect that wasn't Verity. "We've let the ball slip a bit there. But like Martin said, Clem could have been working for her. Didn't you say, Frankie, that she could have made some dodgy contacts in jail? Might have been able to pay someone to kill her."

"Shannon, sure, but not George," said Frankie. "Remember, he was slowly poisoned. Not exactly a hitman's modus operandi."

"Maybe Susan got *Shannon* to do the poisoning, then paid a hitman to take out Shannon. Or got Clem to do it. That would work!"

Earle frowned. "Too many players, too convoluted."

"And easily checked," said Frankie. "I'll give my warden friend another call."

Merry nodded. Turned back to the board.

"And we still need to cross Persephone off the suspect list. For all we know, she could be Shannon's grandmother or godmother or something."

Frankie looked up from her phone, eyebrows high, and Martin, too, looked delighted.

"Wouldn't that be a shocking twist!" he said. "Oh, I do hope so." Then, "Has she got any French in her? Persephone Dupont sounds French. What if she was in it with Clem? Maybe Clem's her son or something?"

Now Merry looked delighted. "She did say she accompanied Pookie to Paris a few times to collect books!" She sat forward. "And she does do that double-kissing thing! You know?"

Merry kissed the air twice, just as the French did.

"Oh, case closed then," said Frankie. "That's all the evidence we need! Let's pack up our trench coats and go home."

"It does feel like a bit of a stretch," said Earle.

"But again, *easily checked*," said Merry, echoing Frankie's words. "It just so happens that Dougie's going to Persephone's place this arvo to inspect her book collection. I could go with?"

"Do it!" said Martin. "You can also check her mantelpiece for happysnaps. Look for photos of her with Shannon and Clem while you're at it."

Martin winked at Merry, and she gave him two thumbs up. They were really bonding these days! She loved it!

"Who else do we— Oops, that's me," said Earle, leaping on his beeping phone. "Excuse me, folks." He clumsily opened the incoming text and smiled as he read. "Looks like Odetta's talking to me again. She wants to meet in an hour at our usual spot. She better not bail on me this time."

He began to reply—even more clumsily—so the others took a moment to check their own phones for messages although Martin was checking the time and doing some calculations.

"Okay, so leave here at two? That works well for me. I'm going to sit on Clem's tail and see where it leads. What about you, Frankie? You still gunning for Verity?"

Frankie was tapping her chin with her mobile. "Yes, I am." A quick flash at Merry. "And I know how I can settle the question of exactly where Verity was before you met her at Seagrave. I'm going to talk to her flatmate or houseguest or whatever he was. Another person we keep forgetting. What was that guy's name again? The one who bowled me over when we went to see Verity. You know? With the giant SUV?"

They all stared at each other. No one could recall.

"I never even met him," said Merry. "I didn't go to her house that day, remember?"

"Was it Grant?" said Frankie, wrinkling her nose.

"Ross maybe?" said Martin.

Merry shook her head at them. "You guys are as bad as Dougie."

"No one's as bad as Dougie," said Earle, pocketing his phone. "I swear your man had no clue who I was when he shook my hand at the station this morning. Bet he thought I was the victim liaison officer not the bloke who's been spending every day with his girlfriend."

"Be nice!" said Merry. "He does have that condition, you know? The one I can never remember the name of."

"Must be catching then," said Earle, chuckling as they gathered their things to head off in various directions.

CHAPTER 24 ~

CHASING DOWN LEADS

Martin picked up a newspaper on his way to Clem's sailing school in Manly. It was currently 2:25 p.m. on Thursday. Not quite knock-off time, but he'd park in a shadowy spot and read his paper until then.

He didn't get a chance to park, let alone catch up on the news.

Martin had only just pulled into the sailing school when Clem appeared from the back of the building, a carryall over one shoulder, phone at his ear. The author quickly pulled his car over and slid down his car seat lest he be spotted, but Clem was clearly distracted, talking into his phone, one hand gesturing wildly as he did so. When he stopped at the gold Mercedes, he started yelling into the phone, then opened his car door and flung it onto the passenger seat like he was furious with it. He then glanced around surreptitiously, so Martin slid even further under his steering wheel.

By the time he looked back up, Clem's Mercedes was roaring past and on to the main street. Martin smiled to himself as he turned his own car around and followed.

Something had changed in the past five hours. Clem was under pressure, immense pressure, that much was obvious.

And he had a hunch it had everything to do with young Shannon.

~

Frankie banged and banged on the front door of Verity's house, jabbed at the doorbell, then banged again.

No reply.

She looked around, noticing that the large SUV that had been parked in the driveway a few days ago was gone, and she wondered about that. Was Verity's houseguest at work? Would he be back later? Had he left for good?

166

She pulled out a card with the Sleuths of Last Resort logo on the front, then jotted a quick note: *We're assisting Verity with her case. Please call us as soon as you get this. Any time.*

Then she circled her mobile number and slipped it under the door, just as someone began singing out from the front of the house.

Frankie stepped back and saw an elderly woman with lurid magenta hair, watering some azaleas.

"What are you after?" the woman called out.

"Oh, hello there!" said Frankie, putting on her professional reporter voice. "I was looking for Verity Vine and her flatmate, what was his name again?"

The woman shrugged. "Haven't seen Verity for days sorry. Don't know about any flatmate."

"Really? Man with reddish beard, about yay high?" She held a hand just above her head. The woman was smudging her lips downwards, so she added, "Drives a big white SUV."

"Gus? Oh, he was just staying over for a few weeks, but he's gone now." The woman stopped her watering. Frowned. "What are you *really* after?"

She was no idiot then, thought Frankie, wondering if she should even try asking her about Verity's movements last night, when her phone began to buzz. It was her warden buddy, Rosetta, from Long Bay jail.

"All good!" she called out as she turned away to take the call.

~

Persephone's house wasn't nearly as magnificent as Persephone. At least, not the exterior. Merry had been expecting a Seagrave-style mansion, but it was much, much smaller, just a two-bedroom red-brick townhouse tucked away in the well-heeled eastern suburb of Woollahra. The interior, however, did not disappoint!

As Persephone showed them in, double-kissing them both as they went, Merry saw that every space was painted a bright shade of something and cluttered with antique furnishings. There were artworks on the walls that would suit the Louvre and a chaise lounge that looked like it'd been swiped from the Palace of Versailles.

Or maybe she was just reading into it all now?

Any case, the furnishings were luxuriant and cluttered and suited the elegant lady to the ground. But there wasn't so much as a tacky framed happysnap in sight. Certainly nothing to indicate a connection to Shannon Smith or Clem LeDoux. Not even a picture of Pookie.

"So lovely to see you again, Merry," Persephone said, eyes boring into hers. "Perhaps this time you can interrogate me directly, not through your lover."

Merry blushed and Dougie chuckled.

"I knew I was being indiscreet," he said.

"Oh, you did a fabulous job, darling! I only discovered your ruse when I started gossiping about George with my icebergers the next day—that's my swim group, down at Bondi. They reminded me of the 'supersleuths' as the papers had dubbed you, the fabulous five who investigated the Burlington murders and helped find poor Prue's missing daughter."

"You know Prue?" said Merry, thinking of the distraught mother who'd turned to them to help find young Chanel.

"We're not bosom buddies, she's far too uptight for me, but we were all once friends of Pookie's. Anyhoo, your name came up and the penny dropped. Now, if you were called Mary, I might not have twigged."

"I'm so sorry," Merry said. "I didn't want to deceive you—"

"Oh yes, you did, you naughty thing! And I must confess I'm delighted! I've never been suspected of murder in my life! It's rather exciting." Then she chuckled again at Merry's obvious discomfort. "Come, let's point Dougie in the direction of my collection, and you and I can have a proper chinwag this time. You can come right out with all your accusations and see how well I elude you."

Thirty minutes later, the two women were out on the balcony, sipping iced tea and gossiping like old friends. They hadn't got on to George's murder yet, were too busy chatting about Merry's children and Persephone's three husbands.

"Number one was for love. That didn't last long. Love doesn't keep you in diamonds, my dear. Number two was for money. Much smarter, lots more diamonds, pity he was such a beast."

"And number three?" asked Merry.

"Lust. The biggest mistake of all, I'm sad to report. Hence the reason I've been reduced to this." Persephone flung a hand back towards the tiny interior. "Turns out he was reading from the same playbook as me, except he was in it for the money, the young scamp.

Took off with an even younger woman and took half of everything while he was at it." Then she chuckled like it was nothing.

"I must say you have a very healthy state of mind," said Merry. "I was a mess after my hubby ditched me for someone else."

"Waste of energy. He did you a favour and not just because it's brought you to our Dougie. Just make sure you remember where you true heart lies—"

"Yes, I know, with Dougie."

"No, you silly girl! I'm talking about your lovely children."

"Oh, right!" Merry blushed. "Of course!"

"I never had children—would have been a dreadful mother, let's face it—but it is a regret. I must confess." She sighed, glancing back into her cluttered yet surprisingly empty apartment. "Don't ever take family for granted, Merry. Now, shall we get on with your interrogation before Dougie finishes up?"

Merry nodded. She'd forgotten all about that. "It's just a few follow-up questions really."

"Delightful! What do you need to know? Was I baying for blood? Did I avenge my Pookie?"

"That's a good start," said Merry, smiling apologetically.

"No interest in revenge, Merry. As I think I've just proven, I don't hold grudges, not when it comes to the weaker sex. Now if *Pookie* had betrayed me—which she sort of did, let's face it—I'd never speak to her again. But since I can't speak to her again anyway, it's a moot point. At least I now have her lovely books."

"See that's why you made it to the suspect list," said Merry. "We wondered whether, well, the books…"

"The *books!*" Persephone barked with laughter. "That's supposed to be my motive? For killing a man? Honey, that's positively humdrum. I thought perhaps you suspected we were having an affair or something."

"Oh… well, no… I mean… were you?"

There was more uproarious laughter, and Dougie appeared at the doorway.

"Everything all right?"

Persephone waved him away. "She's a hoot this new woman of yours, Dougie. You simply must keep her!"

By the end of the hour, Dougie had handed over a cheque for

forty of Persephone's books—a whopping $37,000 no less—while Merry was mulling over what she had learned from Madam Magnificent. Between bursts of laughter and snippets of gossip, Persephone had revealed that she couldn't possibly have poisoned old George, she hadn't been near Seagrave in twenty years, nor did she know anyone who could have helped her sneak in, let alone poison the stew. That included some woman by the name of Shannon Smith—"sounds too common for me"—and a Frenchman called Clem LeDoux. He sounded more her style, but she insisted she'd never met him. *Heard* of him, sure, but had never come face-to-face. In fact, according to Persephone, the first she heard the name Verity Vine was when she got a copy of George's will.

Persephone reiterated that she had never had children of her own, nor had she ever been a godmother—"Who would be foolish enough to subject a poor child to my whims?" She also confessed, quite happily, that she had "absolutely no alibi" for either murder—"I live alone, mon sweet, gathering dust with all my fabulous things!" And despite her loathing of George as a husband—"I really did not wish him ill. But I guess you only have my word for that."

And with those words Merry had slumped a little in her seat. Because it was true, as magnificent as Persephone was, she was still very much a live suspect.

~

The dead bodies at the door of Taboo were beginning to pile up, at least that's how it felt to Kila, who was back in his office, scribbling down names in a notebook of his own, trying to sort through the Weaver case.

There was Kila's sister, Chili, slain after being picked up outside Taboo (dropped off there later if Dragon was to be believed).

Then Phillip Weaver himself, also murdered a week or so after being spotted at the bar.

And now Bertha. A woman who mysteriously drowned just a few weeks after talking to Weaver inside Taboo.

Of course that death had been ruled misadventure, but Kila wasn't buying it.

He pulled out the beer coaster and stared hard at the image on the front for a few minutes, then flipped it over and reread the date on the back. It still sent shivers down his spine, even after all this time.

Then he opened Weaver's blue notebook and read the name Lars. Over and over. He needed to find Lars, but with Bertha gone, his chances, too, were gone.

Or were they?

Kila sat forward suddenly, rubbing a hand at his stubble. Frankie had mentioned that Weaver was seen speaking to some "Islander girls". *Plural*. Bertha was gone. What about the others?

He reached for his phone, looked up Eddie Thomas's number again and dialled. But this time he didn't want to talk about Bertha. He wanted to talk about her friends, her "Islander" friends—the ones she partied with at Taboo, both recently at the hen's night and four years earlier when she was a regular. Before a sleazy barman scared her away.

Eddie couldn't be sure which of Bertha's friends frequented Taboo four years ago, although he was happy to hazard a guess, but he did know who was there the night of the hen's party. "You might want to start with the Hen," he told Kila. "She's from the Highlands."

"Sounds perfect," said Kila. "Now please tell me she's still breathing."

CHAPTER 25 ~
CHASING THEIR TALES

Martin kept Clem LeDoux within range, trying hard not to be spotted as he carefully followed in his Aston Martin. They were heading through town towards the outer eastern suburb of Maroubra. He frowned at the direction as he tuned the car radio to Classic FM. Frankie said Shannon lived in an apartment in the inner West, on the other side of the city. He wasn't sure where "magnificent Persephone" lived, but he doubted it was in the ugly "wog palace" Clem was now parking in front of.

He watched as the other man alighted his vehicle, fixed his hair again, then headed for the front door of the brick monstrosity with the tacky faux pillars out the front. He was just reaching it when the front door swung open and a short, full-figured woman with equally voluminous black hair appeared. She looked around furtively, and so Martin continued driving straight past, hoping he hadn't been spotted.

By the time he'd circled back and parked across the road, both had disappeared behind the closed front door.

Martin was just about to get out and start snooping around—see if he could catch a glimpse of what they were up to behind the curtains—when he saw a police car pull up, then another two slide in behind it.

"Ooh, this is exciting," he said, turning Vivaldi down and slinking back under the steering wheel.

~

Across town, it was now Earle batting Odetta's apologies away. "No need to explain, Detective. I know you're a busy woman. I don't expect you to be at my beck and call."

"It's not just that, Earle. Morgan's staying very tight-lipped on this one. I probably don't have any answers for you. But let's see how we go."

They were back at the Wobbler's Arms near homicide headquarters, and he glanced around as they spoke, thinking he should really find a nicer meeting place. The place stunk of stale beer and greasy chips. Odetta was too good for this dive. She'd ordered nachos for a late lunch—or was it an early dinner?—and he waited until she'd got some into her stomach before launching in.

"Our first concern is our client. We need to check Verity's alibi for the time Shannon was murdered last night."

Odetta formed a perfect O with her lips. "Trouble in paradise? Turning on the good secretary?"

"Just ticking boxes."

"Can't help you there then. Other than to say that if she's being held for Shannon Smith's murder, you can only assume she hasn't got an alibi to speak of."

He frowned. "I thought she was being held for breaking her bail conditions. Has she been formally charged for Ms Smith's murder? Do you know?"

Odetta chewed for a bit. "I might have that wrong." Then she grimaced. "I told you, I'm not getting a lot of *intel*. Especially after the latest homicide."

He nodded, didn't waste time with apologies. "What about Clem LeDoux? George's son-in-law. We know he had a prior relationship with Ms Smith. We wonder whether he had something to do with both murders."

Odetta finished a mouthful of corn chips and said, "Right, well, I'm not sure if this is good news or bad, but he has an alibi."

"For which murder?"

"Shannon's. Does he need an alibi for Mr Burlington's? Didn't he die from the long-term effects of rodenticide poisoning?"

"Yes, but the way the victim was found—in the ballroom, a room he never entered, and down a flight of stairs that his wheelchair would not have got down…"

"Ah, I see. That does sound suspicious. Well, I have no info on that situation, as odd as it is, but I do know that Mr LeDoux has an alibi for last night."

He groaned.

She gave him a sympathetic look. "Turns out, Clem has been very wicked. He was hanging out with… Well, let's just call her an *associate*. She's just vouched for his whereabouts."

"Mistress, I'm guessing."

"Don't know about that. She was dragged into HQ just before lunchtime—that's how I'm privy to all this. Woman by the name of Maria Montenetti. She's known to us already. Has confirmed that Mr LeDoux was with her from the time he left work about four p.m. until two a.m. this morning. Or so my only friend in Homicide tells me."

Earle thought about that, felt almost buoyed. Morgan must have followed his tip-off and checked on Clem's whereabouts last night. That means he was taking Earle seriously. For once.

"Okay," he said, "but can Miss Montenetti be believed? Can Clem? He could have snuck out while she was sleeping, even drugged her to make sure she didn't notice."

"Oh, there were drugs all right, but it's not what you think. That's his alibi. They were both doing lines of coke at her gaudy Maroubra mansion, apparently, until the wee hours."

Earle felt deflated but did not give up. "They could *both* be lying."

"Why admit to a misdemeanour if it's not true?"

"Because it gets you off a felony charge. Clem knows the score. Better to 'fess up to a smaller charge than be lumped with murder. That worked for him last time."

"Sure, but what's in it for Montenetti? She's on thin ice as it is. Morgan's got his goons raiding her premises as we speak." She grinned. "He doesn't know I know that. Two can play his game!" Then she dropped the smile. "Sorry, Earle. From what I know of the family, Clem LeDoux would have made a terrific suspect. Who else are you looking at? What about the granddaughter? She's still viable. More so now, I'd suggest."

"Charlotte? Yeah…" He rubbed his beard. They had dropped the ball on Charlie lately. "I can see her poisoning her grandfather, the inheritance and all that. But why kill Ms Smith? That bit isn't so clear."

"Maybe they had a tiff over a hair straightener." She chuckled as she plunged a cheesy fork into her mouth.

Earle went to smile, but he didn't really get the joke. "So any pathology back yet? Can we nail down Shannon's time of death?"

"Bit early for that, but it had to be sometime between eight p.m.

and ten thirty, right, when your lot found her?"

"Why eight?"

"That's when Charlie saw Shannon leaving the house."

"Hang on, what house? How did Charlie see Shannon?"

"George's granddaughter has been staying with Shannon, you didn't know? Verity didn't mention it?"

No, he thought, grumpy again. So *that's* why Odetta said they were squabbling over hair thing-a-me-bobs. He got the joke now.

"Where do you think young Charlie has been staying since all this blew up?" Odetta asked. "She can't get back into Seagrave."

"There is her grandfather's apartment. She does have friends. In fact, we were informed she was residing at a girlfriend's place."

Odetta nodded her arctic-white head. "Yes, that friend's name was Shannon. They've been thick for a while, apparently. Funny that Verity didn't mention it."

"Yes," said Earle. Except he couldn't see this punchline either. It was one more thing Verity had neglected to tell them.

CHAPTER 26 ~

BIG NEWS AND A BULGING BELLY

The team were back at Sleuth Central, teacups in hand now, each one bursting with news.

Earle had some news of his own, of course, but he wasn't sure how well it would be received, so he let them babble away first.

Frankie explained that she'd tried to interview Verity's house guest—"Gus! His name is Gus!"—but he'd already flown the coop.

"Gus?" said Merry. "Do you mean Angus? George's old ski lodge manager? Could he be the guy you ran into at Verity's house the other day?"

Frankie just shrugged. "No idea. We never met Angus, remember? You interviewed him on your own last time."

"Yes, but... didn't you see him at the wake?"

"If I did, I didn't know him to recognise him, Mez. Doesn't matter anyway. Whoever Gus is, he's no use now—he's flown off, according to the neighbour. And my warden friend Rosetta wasn't much use in pinning it on Susan either. Says if she did organise it from her jail cell, it wasn't through contacts she made in Long Bay. Rosetta reckons Susan keeps herself to herself. Says Miss—and I quote—High and Bloody Mighty refuses to mingle with the riffraff. Very unpopular, as a result. Rosetta checked for me and says Susan's never had a visit from a Shannon Smith—so there's no clear link there—and insists even her beloved Clem hasn't visited in weeks. So if Susan is pulling the strings from inside, I'm struggling to see how."

"I don't reckon Susan's involved either," said Martin, who was practically bouncing in his seat. "I just followed Clem to a strange woman's house. If he did do it, he's in on it with someone else entirely. I think they're lovers, and I think the police think so too."

He almost shimmered as he added, "A crew of cops suddenly

swarmed the place! We're close now, people! It could all be over any minute."

Earle cleared his throat. Almost didn't have the heart to break it to him.

"Was it a big white house in Maroubra?" he asked, and Martin's shimmer began to dim. "That's Clem's dealer, Maria Montenetti. She's confessed to supplying Mr LeDoux with cocaine last night and says he was with her from four yesterday until two this morning. Whatever else they were up to, sorry, Martin, but Clem has an alibi. I think we can wipe him off the list."

"Unless they're lying or working with someone else..." Martin's voice dropped away as the others looked less convinced.

"How'd you go with Persephone?" Earle asked Merry, moving things along. She didn't seem as excitable as the others.

"Okay, I suppose," she replied before describing her visit to Persephone's house.

It was a long-winded account, and Frankie had to hurry her up several times—"We really don't need to know what her marriages were like, Merry!"—and it left them none the wiser. Her alibi was wide open and yet...

"What's your gut instinct?" Earle asked.

Merry chewed maniacally at her thumbnail. "I don't think Persephone did it. I mean, if her lousy ex-husbands are all still walking this earth, I can't see why she'd kill somebody else's hubby. As for Shannon? Persephone did say she doesn't forgive female friends as easily, so if they were working together and Shannon double-crossed her, then I could see her bumping her over the head. But she insists she's never met the girl, and I couldn't see any signs to contradict that..." She let that drift as no one seemed especially interested. "So who's left? Shannon's off the list, Clem's off the list, if we believe his dealer, which effectively clears Susan, if we believe the warden, which you clearly do, Frankie."

She nodded. "Rosetta doesn't miss a trick. If she's not suspicious, neither am I. There is one suspect remaining..."

"It's *not* Verity!" wailed Merry.

Earle sat forward and cleared his throat, getting their attention before they started bickering again. "Verity's not the only remaining suspect. I have a dreadful feeling it might be Charlie."

Because it did feel dreadful to Earle. He wasn't as sentimental

177

about young people as Merry, had seen enough to know that the sweetest angels could be devils in disguise, but he didn't like the idea of George's granddaughter being a suspect either.

They all listened intently as he revealed Odetta's second piece of news.

Then Frankie began to growl. "Charlie and Shannon are old friends? And they've been *living* together? Why are we only just learning this?"

But it wasn't Verity she was angry with. Her eyes were firmly on Merry, who was shrinking under her gaze.

"Sorry, but Charlie told me she'd been staying with someone called Penelope!"

"And did you check with this Penelope person?"

Merry shrank even further.

"Don't start laying into Merry," said Martin. "Charlie's a consummate liar, remember? Even the great Frankie Jo was blindsided by her last time."

Frankie scowled at him, not quite ready to concede the point, while Merry looked gratefully towards Martin.

Earle said, "The fact is Verity should have told us all that, if indeed she knew. And we've always been distracted by the young woman's history; we've let our sympathy for Charlie cloud our judgement."

"So let's remove the fog lights and look at her properly," said Martin. "What do we all think?"

They considered her quietly for a few minutes, most of them half-heartedly. None of them could see her doing such a thing to her grandfather, let alone Shannon, and yet she did have means and opportunity. Spookily so. She had come back from London two weeks before her grandfather died—just in time to start poisoning him. She did have easy access to both the stew and the victim. And it was in her interest to shuffle Gramps off this mortal coil before he started giving more of her precious inheritance away.

"Maybe Shannon is totally innocent but was starting to suspect Charlie," said Frankie. "They were hanging together, right? Charlie might have let something slip, and Shannon suddenly realised it wasn't Verity doing the poisoning after all but her BFF, Charlie."

"What?" said Merry, sitting forward. "Can you repeat that please, Frankie?"

Frankie gave her a smirk. "I'm just hypothesising, don't get excited. But it could all work. Charlie feared Shannon was about to blow the whistle, so she had to silence her."

Earle mumbled under his breath. It still felt too complicated for his liking.

"Once again we have an alibi to check," he said. "According to Odetta, Charlie says she saw Shannon leave her house at eight last night. But did she? Really? And what did Charlie do after that time? Did she stay there? Go out? Follow Shannon to Seagrave?" He looked at Merry. "These are questions that need to be presented to Charlie, and she needs to give us some straight answers this time. And quickly."

"Hang on, you're going to let Merry question her again?" said Frankie. "No offence but—"

"I'll do it here!" said Merry. "You can be in on it, Frankie. But I need to do this. Please. I want Charlie to explain why she lied to me about where she was staying. I want to get the truth out of that little scamp, once and for all!"

Frankie's eyes narrowed. "Fine, but I am going to be present, making sure she doesn't play any more of her games with you."

"Oh, there won't be games," said Merry.

The time for playing games was over.

~

The new bride was halfway through a jigsaw puzzle—and a pregnancy by the look of her enormous belly—when she answered the door to Kila. Mary Paul rubbed her stomach gently as she led the way into a living room beautifully decorated with a combination of Aboriginal and Papua New Guinean artefacts.

"Todd's from the north coast, a Bundjalung man," she said as Kila inspected the puzzle and its swirling, brightly coloured dot pattern that had taken over the coffee table. "Met on an indigenous-rights march."

"Cute," he said.

"Corny!" she shot back, laughing as she dropped heavily into the sofa. "You're from Moresby, I hear?"

Eddie Thomas had already filled them both in on the situation, and each other, and so the two Papuans sat and swapped small talk about their homeland for a while.

Then Kila said, "How'd your folks react, knowing you were pregnant?"

He meant out of wedlock—that belly predated the hen's night—and she smiled.

"Why do you think we got married?" Laughed again. Then her laugh fizzled out. "Poor Bertha though. I'm *so* relieved she didn't go swimming after the wedding. I know it's selfish to say it, but, *man*, that would've cursed the whole thing! If she had, she would've drowned then for sure. Bertha was smashed! Then again, I was the only one sober. Just like my bachelorette party."

Mary stroked her stomach again, almost sadly, but Kila was pleased. That meant her memory would be more reliable.

"Do you recall two blokes coming up to you and Bertha that night?"

"Oh, loads of guys tried their luck that night. Even with me up the duff and a veil on!" More laughter.

"Okay, but these two would have stood out. They were older, mid-thirties, and one of them was covered in ink. They would have been asking some odd questions about the past maybe?"

Her head was nodding. "Okay, yeah, I do vaguely remember one older guy. Not sure about the tatts, but he had toxic aftershave." She wiggled her nose. "The slightest smell makes me nauseous. He was clearly on the prowl though. He opened with 'Do you come here often?' I just laughed and left him to Bertha."

Kila thought about that. Unlike Mary here, he suspected it wasn't a cheesy pickup line at all, that Weaver genuinely wanted to know because he was trying to find a witness who was at Taboo four years earlier—on September 20.

"How long did they talk for?" he asked.

"Not that long but I figured he must have improved his act because I could see him taking down her number. God knows why. Wasn't Bertha's type at all. And that aftershave reeked!"

Then she smiled sadly at the memory of her friend.

Kila was frowning. That didn't add up. He produced Weaver's notebook. "Did he write Bertha's number in here? Did you see?"

She waggled a hand. "Maybe. It looks familiar."

Kila flicked through the pages. Weaver had written down the name Bertha, but there was no phone number next to it, no number anywhere inside. This proved it for Kila. Weaver wasn't looking to pick her up, he was looking for a murderer. And Bertha must have helped him find one.

He showed Mary the page with the names and said, "Do you recognise any of these?"

She took the book and read through them. Then tapped a manicured nail on one name.

Lars Karlsson.

"You know him?" said Kila, trying not to sound too excited.

"I know a Lars. Not sure it's the same one."

"He used to pour drinks at Taboo. Was real sleazy, we think."

"Okay, not sure about sleazy either, but yeah, that's the one. Worked at Taboo for a short while, back when I used to hang there with the girls. With Bertha."

Her expression saddened again, but Kila could have done a silly Merry dance.

Mary added, "We hadn't been there for ages, and I only chose the venue because it was close to where Todd was holding his bachelor party." She giggled. "*Not* that I was keeping an eye on him or anything!"

He smiled. "What do you remember about Lars?"

"Not much. Tall, blond, not bad-looking. Much more Bertha's type. She had a bit of a crush on him. Barmen were always Bertha's weak spot, bless her. If you poured drinks, Bertha was your bestie. If you were tall and blond, even better."

"Okay." Bloody brilliant. "Any idea where he is now? Where I might find him?"

He crossed his fingers as her lips swished to one side. "I think he went to work at some posh bar in the middle of the city somewhere. I only know because she wanted to start hanging there, and I was like, way too pricey for me, girl! That place was for stockbrokers on a million bucks a minute! Bertha went off him pretty soon after that anyway, started crushing on some new barman at the Bondi Brewers, just near hers."

That was the last place Bertha was seen alive.

Kila took the book back and smiled at the names this time. Felt like he had the case almost sewn up. Was certain now that Bertha was the one who'd given Weaver those names—that's what he was jotting into his book that night.

One week later, Weaver was dead.

A week or so after that, so too was Bertha.

Did one of these people kill them both? Was it Lars?

"You didn't happen to be out with Bertha the night she drowned?" he asked. "At this Brewers place?"

The woman shook her head firmly and glanced down at her ample belly, then across to the jigsaw. "My partying days are over in case you hadn't noticed."

Then she smiled like she couldn't be happier.

CHAPTER 27 ~
GETTING TO THE TRUTH?

It took forty minutes, five texts and the promise of a "free ride and sugar hit" to finally get Charlie to agree to meet with Merry *again* (Charlie's emphasis) but at the sleuths' office this time. While Merry scurried off to raid the corner store of its chocolate supply, Frankie organised the Uber and some "decent bloody questions", and the two men made themselves scarce. Martin was heading to the NSW Registry of Births, Deaths and Marriages to research his latest book while Earle muttered something about family dramas.

When she finally got to Sleuth Central, Charlie did not look happy to be meeting with Merry again, and it didn't help that Merry wasn't making life fun or comfortable for her this time. Other than the sugary treats, there was nothing to put the young woman at ease. She was shown straight to the meeting table, offered the stiffest chair and handed a cup of tea and two Mars bars before Merry took a seat across from her.

Frankie was listening in from her desk a few short metres away. She still believed that interviews were best done *tete-to-tete*, but she also wanted to keep an eye on proceedings.

"You're the one who's bonded with her, so you need to take charge," she told Merry. "But I'll be here for backup if she starts getting slippery again."

For her part, Charlie looked worried. Kept flashing glances back towards Frankie as Merry began to speak.

Unable to help herself, Merry started with commiserations. "I'm sorry about Shannon. I heard you two were close."

Charlie blinked back at her, looked ready to cry. "It's messed up! It's like no one can get too close to me."

"Oh, honey." Merry held a hand out to stroke hers and was rewarded with a discreet cough from Frankie. She pulled back.

"Why didn't you tell me you were friends? You and Shannon. You never mentioned it."

Charlie looked bewildered. "So? Am I supposed to make a list of all my friends in case one of them gets *murdered*?" Then, before Merry could respond, she said, "So that's why you're interrogating me again is it? You've run out of suspects, so you're trying to plant *Shannon's* death on me now?"

Merry sat back. "No... I mean... not really." She clasped her hands together on the table. "What I'm trying to do, Charlie, is make sure you are well and truly off the hook. So help me out. No more games. No more lies. Because, well, you know Frankie Jo over there." She nodded her head to where Frankie was pretending to be engrossed in her screen. "She'll uncover them all anyway."

"And then embarrass me in front of everyone?" This was loud, directed straight at Frankie, who just shrugged and did not bother to look around.

Merry smiled. "Not if you tell me the truth."

"I have been!"

"No, honey, you have not. For starters, you told me you've been staying with a friend called Penelope, when I've just learned you've been at Shannon's the whole time."

"No... I mean, yes, but I've been staying with lots of different friends since I got back. I only stayed at Shannon's for two nights!"

"Okay so let me ask you again. Where were you on the night your grandfather died?"

Charlie went to say something, then must have thought better of it. She blew air up into her bangs. "Fine, whatever. If you must know, I was with a guy I met on Tinder."

Her face crumpled as Merry shot a glance towards Frankie. She was looking back towards them, surprised. Gave Merry a visual nudge and turned back to her computer.

Merry said, "A Tinder date? Why didn't you say that?"

"Because I know what you *boomers* are like—you think women who use Tinder are skanks even though guys are allowed to use it all they like."

"Hey, I'm not a boomer," Merry shot back. "And you're the only one here using those words. I think what's good for the goose is good for the gander." Even though, just quietly, she was horrified at the thought of her Lola meeting up with some online stranger.

She knew how that had ended for Kila's baby sister. Shook it away. Tried to refocus as Charlie began to wail.

"What is it with my shitty timing? The night Gramps dies, I'm out hooking up."

"Once again, honey, that might have saved you. If you'd had some of that poisoned stew, you could have been very sick."

"Oh, I wouldn't have eaten the stew. I'm veggo. Thinking of going vegan." She swivelled to face Frankie. "You're vegan, right, Frankie?"

The other woman ignored her, and Merry said, "I'm going to need some proof of that please."

Charlie turned back and frowned and Merry suddenly giggled.

"Not the veggo part! I don't need you to eat vegetables in front of me. I mean, I need proof of the Tinder date." Then Merry swallowed down another giggle, knowing Frankie's eyes were rolling in her head.

Charlie reached for her iPhone and produced the date's profile. "Whatever. He was a flop. Fit though."

He *was* fit, thought Merry, glancing at the phone, very handsome despite the tattoos. Clearly Charlie had a type. She jotted down his number. "So, are you saying you stayed at this fellow's place all night? I will be calling him, so you sure you want to stick to this new alibi?"

"No, I don't. Once again I look like a sex addict. But it's the truth."

"Good. So let's establish your alibi for Shannon's murder now. Where were you last night?"

Merry already knew but wanted to hear it from the horse's mouth.

"*Last* night I was at Shannon's place," said Charlie. "Like I said, I'd been staying with her for a few nights."

Good. "Can I ask you this—do you think she and Clem were... well, in a relationship?"

"Shannon and *Clem*? Ew! No way. Why would you think that? She was into guys her own age. Puke!"

So much for Martin's theory, Merry thought, as Frankie could now be heard snickering. "I never realised you and Shannon were so close."

"She was cool. I got to know her back when she worked for Clem. He was her boss, not her... *ewww!*" She shuddered again. "Anyway, she used to collect me from boarding school when Clem and Susan were busy. We hung out a bit. I wasn't *going* to stay with her after

Gramps died, but the cops kicked me out of Seagrave and I didn't want to stay at that hideous penthouse by myself. I was actually going to stay with Verity. But then Shan said—"

Charlie stopped abruptly and her eyes darted away.

Merry sat forward. "What were you going to say?"

"Nothing." Charlie shook hair from her face.

"Shannon put you off, didn't she?" said Merry. "She told you she thought Verity had poisoned your grandfather."

Charlie's eyes returned to Merry's. They were fiery. "I was fuming! Couldn't believe Verity would do that!"

"But you must know it's not true."

"Why? Why must I know that? Shannon said she and Verity were the only ones who could have done it and it certainly wasn't Shan, so it had to be Verity, the lying snake! That's why Shan went over to Verity's last night. To set her straight."

"Hang on," said Merry just as Frankie's chair swivelled around. "Shannon went to *Verity's house* last night?"

"Yaha!" Charlie glanced across to Frankie who was now openly watching.

"Don't you mean Seagrave?" said Merry, feeling her stomach tighten. "She was meeting Verity and me at *Seagrave*."

Charlie shrugged. "She never mentioned Seagrave to me. Just said she was heading to Verity's house and—"

"At what time?" This was Frankie. No more pretending then.

Charlie shrugged. "I don't know, around eight-ish. I told the police all this, this morning."

Frankie rolled her chair across to the table. "Why would Shannon leave at eight? She wasn't due to meet her boss until ten?"

"How would I know?" Charlie peeled the wrapping from a Mars bar while the two sleuths swapped a look.

Merry's bones were tingling and not in a good way. Verity had never mentioned meeting with Shannon earlier that night. For twenty long minutes they had stood outside Seagrave, making small talk and wondering where Shannon was, and Verity didn't think to mention seeing the woman earlier? Was it an oversight, or deliberate?

Frankie went to speak, but Merry held a hand up. She wasn't giggling anymore.

Pushing her glasses into position on her face, Merry said, "Let's just back up a bit please, Charlie. Talk me through last night.

Hour by hour. So, you were staying over, and she was telling you her suspicions about Verity. Then what happened? Tell me exactly."

"Nothing. I mean, we'd ordered some Uber Eats, right? And Shan started bitching about Verity again. Got really angry and said we both needed to confront her about the poisoning and stuff. I told her to calm it, that's what the police were for, but she said, 'Nope, I'm going to her house right now. It's long overdue.' Or something like that."

Charlie blushed suddenly, like it was only just occurring to her she might have played a part in Shannon's murder. Her doe eyes turned teary. "I did tell her not to go! I did tell her to be careful! I never expected..."

"What did you do then?" said Merry, no time for sympathy now.

"What did I *do*? Nothing! I mean, I had some dessert and crashed early, watched a show in bed. Why?" Like she was beyond reproof.

"Did you talk to anyone? Meet up with anyone yourself? Go anywhere that night?"

"No! I stayed at Shannon's apartment. But who cares what I was doing? It's *Verity* you need to talk to. Verity was the last person to see Shannon alive. I told you this before, Merry! Verity has been calling the shots from the start."

Then she offered them a smarmy look as she ate her chocolate.

~

Kila stood at the entrance to Tudor's Wine Bar in the heart of the city, collecting his thoughts. Bertha's married friend had been a fount of knowledge, and her tip had brought him here. To Lars.

At least, indirectly.

He'd spent the better part of the afternoon checking out all the posh bars in the city and struck gold at this lavishly decorated, dimly lit venue on the top of a high-rise tower. Wasn't his scene; he wouldn't have left Taboo to work in this dump. But Lars clearly had—Kila could see him across the room. The so-called sleazy barman had his name on a small badge on his shirt and a bored look below a mop of blond curls as he scrolled through his mobile phone behind the bar. It was just after five p.m., the joint half-empty. A good time to approach and yet Kila didn't want to, not yet.

Trevor was right. Mad Dog Morea could not be trusted.

He turned to his own mobile, pressed a familiar number, and mentally crossed his fingers.

~

Dr Fiona Mottson was just leaving St Vincent's Hospital when a familiar sedan pulled in beside her, and she went to smile when she realised who it was.

"Jump in, if you don't mind," the man called out. "I want to take you for a spin."

She leaned down and gave him a look. "I don't normally get into cars with strangers."

"I'm glad to hear it. Now hop in. Please."

Sighing dramatically, Fiona did as he asked and then turned to face the driver. "If you are trying to get me to kiss and make up with your daughter, Mr Fitzgerald—"

"Call me Earle," he said, like he hadn't told her dozens of times before. "And it has nothing to do with Tess. At least not directly. Now buckle up please. This is not a joyride."

She rolled her eyes as she reached for the seat belt.

It was only as they turned in to Wynyard Street that Fiona finally got it. Her eyes were now narrow slits.

"You really think it's as simple as this?" she said to Earle as he pulled into a bus zone. "You can just drop me off on the corner and my dad will come running into my arms?"

"It can't hurt to talk to him." He nodded towards a man huddled inside a doorway just outside the train station.

She looked across, then back at Earle. "No offence, *Earle*, but I'm not sure this is any of your business."

"I'm trying to help."

"Then stay out of it please. I'm not your daughter. It's *my* choice whether I talk to that... person. It's *my choice* whether I accept him into my life."

"I'm just suggesting—"

"You're just meddling!" And she was yelling now. "You have no idea what it's like. Neither does Tess. To have the man you once adored, the man who was supposed to protect you, now living like... like *that*."

Her head nodded towards the derelict.

"Neither do you," Earle shot back. "Did you ever stop to ask him what it's like? Why he's there? How it's come to that?"

She frowned. "No... I mean I—"

"I know it's not easy, but you have to find the courage, Fiona.

You have to go up and you have to face him."

"I did!"

He blinked. "What's that now?"

"I tried six months ago, and it was an unmitigated disaster. Didn't Tess tell you? I'm not completely heartless you know. I bought him a cup of coffee and a sandwich, I put on my bravest smile and I said, 'Hey Dad, it's been a while.'"

"What happened?"

"Nothing. He stared straight through me and just shuffled off." She mock laughed. "I think I would have preferred if he'd growled at me, cursed or something. But to be stared through like I was nothing! So I'm sorry if I'm not giving that man the kind of attention you and Tess think he deserves, but I tried, and it was too damn painful. I sobbed for weeks afterwards. Tess didn't mention that either? It broke my friggin' heart, and I'm not putting myself through that again."

"He didn't recognise you, Fiona."

"Oh, that's okay then!" More mock laughter. "He didn't recognise his only daughter. That's just fine and dandy!"

Earle shook his head sadly at her. "He didn't recognise you because he has brain damage, probably alcoholic dementia."

"What?"

"Brain damage, diabetes, heart disease… a whole bunch of other chronic conditions that you're probably treating complete strangers for, and happily. Graciously. The point is, Fiona, your father does not have much time left. But you do. So if you decide not to talk to him, I won't mention it again. Because you're right. It is your choice. But if you don't choose soon, the choice will be taken from you."

Then he carefully pulled back into the traffic while she turned to stare, gobsmacked, at the old man in the doorway.

CHAPTER 28 ~
MORE THEORIES TO MULL OVER

Frankie was trying very hard not to say "I told you so" to Merry. But boy it was tempting! Things sure looked bad for Verity. And all four sleuths knew it.

It was now six o'clock Thursday evening, and Earle and Martin had returned, both looking glum but keen to hear how the interview had gone. They were as surprised by the revelations as Merry.

"So let's think about this logically, shall we?" said Frankie. "Shannon went to Verity's house two hours before she was found murdered, yet Verity never bothered to mention it."

She produced a hand, raised a finger at Merry. "Not when you were killing time outside the mansion—*pun intended.* Not when you discovered her dead body lying by the pool or later when Earle and Martin showed up. Never did Verity bother to mention the teeny-weeny fact that she was the last person to see the victim alive."

"Well, she—"

"The same victim, I might add," Frankie continued, "who was going to turn state's witness against Verity."

"In all fairness, Charlie could be lying," said Martin, coming to Merry's aid. Again.

Frankie stared at him. Hard. Why was he sucking up to Merry these days?

"We've long established that Charlie's a chronic liar," Martin was saying, "and yet, once again, we believe everything she tells us. Why do we keep doing that?" A glance at Earle. "Can we try to make peace with Verity's legal team? Be really helpful if we can get some questions across to our client, give her a chance to answer to this claim."

"Verity's had more than enough chances," said Frankie.

"Still," said Earle, "Martin's right. Charlie has always been loose with the truth. Let's consider, for a moment, that she is lying. She says she waved Shannon off at eight that night, then sat all alone, watching a show. It's not much of an alibi. Did you ask her about the first murder, Merry? Where she was when her grandfather died?"

"Says she was on a Tinder date all night, and we can definitely believe this one." Merry offered her first small smile. "I called the date while we were waiting for you guys to return."

"Oh, give the girl a medal," said Frankie. "And?"

"His name's Dillon Szeto, and he confirms it. He was a bit confused hearing from me! But he says yep, she stayed the night. Said she hasn't replied to a single text since. Asked if I could put in a good word for him. I felt sorry for the lad."

"Well, don't," said Frankie. "He got his leg over, didn't he?"

Merry looked appalled by that comment, but Martin was shaking his head. "You know, once again, it's all sounding a little too convenient to me. Charlie seems to have an answer for everything, an alibi that puts her far, far away from the murders. It's very suspect."

"Go on," said Earle.

Martin jumped up and turned to face them. "Let's start with Gramps. Charlie is supposed to be staying with him but just *happens* to be having a one-night stand on the very night he takes his final breath. Maybe she was giving herself an alibi. I've got another theory if you want to hear it."

"Yes please," said Merry.

"Not really," mumbled Frankie.

"If it explains why Shannon is deceased, then go ahead," was Earle's comment.

"Okay, well, bear with me, this might get confusing. What if I got it wrong about Clem, and it was *Charlie* who was in it all along with Shannon? They're besties from way back, right? Maybe it was for the inheritance—and Charlie promised her bestie a big cut—or maybe it was for revenge. They were both once big fans of Clem. Maybe, like George, they hated the way our first case ended up, and they blamed both George and Verity for all of it. Charlie has already admitted they sat around eating home delivery and bitching about Verity, so they clearly didn't like her. Maybe it was those two—not Clem and Shannon—who plotted the whole thing."

"Go on," said Earle, trying not to look befuddled.

"Okay, so Charlie gets back from London and starts bitching with

Shannon, and that's when they plot to poison George—a very female thing to do I might add."

"What? The bitching or the poisoning?" said Frankie, one manicured eyebrow hitched high.

He knew better than to answer that. "So they poison George and implicate his personal assistant. They're young. They would have known how to access banned rat poison on the internet. They were both in a position to pop it in the Irish stew any old time they liked, then point the finger at Verity after the fact. However!"

He produced his own finger now. "Being the primary heir, Charlie knew she would be a suspect, so she had to be absent on the final night of the poisoning and they needed to position Gramps in a way that made it look like murder. That's why she organised a Tinder date with a man she clearly has no interest in seeing again, then she got Shannon to sneak in, using her codes to administer the final lethal dose to old George's stew, then wheel him down to the ballroom—"

"Actually, I think she used the dumb waiter!" said Merry.

"Even better." He high-fived her like they were co-writing his latest crime novel. "She positions George in the middle of the room, music playing, chandeliers burning, to make a statement. Expecting it to reflect back on Verity. Except, as we know, it did not. Nobody thought to suspect poisoning, and Verity was getting away with everything, including a third of the inheritance. So that's why Shannon had to tip off the police—to ensure Verity got arrested."

"Okay, this is sounding promising," said Earle, sitting forward. "So talk us through Shannon's murder then."

"Same logic I was using with Clem. Shannon was always just a means to an end. Or maybe she was a loose cannon. Again, maybe she felt remorse and was going over to Verity's house that night— not to confront her—but to confess all, and Charlie knew it. Or maybe Shannon was *never* going to Verity's house but was going to 'fess up when she met you guys at Seagrave, and that's why Verity didn't mention seeing her earlier. Because Charlie made that bit up."

He let that sink in for a moment. Was back to his shimmery self. "Either way, the only one who really knew where Shannon was going and at what time that night was Charlie. She's admitted that. Maybe she convinced her friend to go to Seagrave earlier and killed her there to shut her up and/or plant it on Verity. But here's the thing."

He placed his hands on his hips, his smug smile now in full throttle. "Verity might not have an alibi, but *neither does Charlie*. Because we only have *her* word for it that Shannon left the apartment at eight on her own and was heading to Verity's. She could be lying about both. Like I said, wouldn't be the first time."

Merry's bones were tingling so much she was almost dancing. They were close, real close. She just knew it. And she much preferred Martin's theory even if it did put Charlie back in the hot seat.

As much as she loathed the idea of blaming the young woman for anything, better her than Verity. Besides, the more she got to know Charlie, the more she had to concede she was one cold fish. Had bounced back suspiciously quickly from the death of her grandfather (and her own parents and brother before that, if she was being honest) and barely spilled a tear today over the sudden slaughter of a woman who was supposed to be her friend.

Perhaps there was more of Aunty Susan in Charlie than anyone would have liked.

"So how do we prove all this?" asked Merry.

"I know a way," said Frankie. "Can't we check the street camera outside the girls' school down the road from Seagrave? Like you did last time, Earle? See if we can place Charlie driving past there last night, earlier than ten o'clock? Or Verity for that matter, because I haven't given up on her yet."

Merry ignored that and said, "But Charlie doesn't drive, so if she was there, she must have got a lift with Shannon."

"Either way," said Earle, "the camera is not ideal. It's several blocks from Seagrave and pretty hazy vision. It can make out a vehicle passing by but not much else. Certainly not passengers or number plates. Martin's right. Charlie might be a liar, but she's also no fool. She's seen us operate before and would know we'd check the cameras. I'd say she got a lift with Shannon and then hopped it on foot after the killing."

"Oh, that girl hasn't done a day of exercise in her life!" said Frankie. "There's no way she walked the ten kilometres or so from Seagrave back to Shannon's place afterwards."

"You think she caught a cab down the road, once she cleared the cameras?" said Earle. "We could call the taxi companies, but it'll take a long time and I'm not sure they'll—"

"*Taxi?* You're so circa 1990, Earle. Charlie's a modern woman. There's no way she used a *taxi*." She smiled and looked at Merry. "We need to get access to her phone. That will tell us everything."

"Oh God," said Merry. "Not more chocolate! I'm not sure I can bear it." Then she glanced at her watch. Jumped up like she'd been bitten. "Darn it, I have to get home. Archie's due back from soccer training any minute now!"

"You go for it, Mother Hen," said Martin.

Frankie frowned at both of them, then realised she, too, was running late. "Okay, fine, we'll do it first thing tomorrow then. But we must check Charlie's phone, Mez. It's crucial!"

Merry nodded vigorously as she grabbed her bag and scrambled for the door. What she didn't tell them was there was another phone she wanted to check, and she had to do it soon—while her son was in the shower.

~

The sleazy barman wasn't being very sleazy, and it was pissing Kila off. He'd lured Frankie out of her office and to Tudors Wine Bar with the promise of overpriced cocktails and undersized bar meals, then they'd sat at a side table and watched Lars Karlsson as he tended the well-dressed crowd.

Yet as he poured designer beers and mixed elaborate cocktails, he didn't so much as smile at anyone, let alone young women.

So Kila sent in the big guns.

"Okay, Sexy Reporter Girl, choose the most complicated cocktail so it takes ages, then bat your eyelashes and get him talking, see if you can slip in the name Taboo."

"Subtle," she said, snatching the Visa card from his hands and heading across.

Ten minutes later, Frankie was back with a strawberry cilantro margarita, a tall glass of staggeringly expensive lager, and a sad shake of her blond locks. Lars had barely looked at Frankie as he prepared her drinks, just dumped them on the bar, processed the card, and almost flung it back at her as he rushed on to the next customer.

"He seemed completely uninterested, and everybody's interested in me," said Frankie, sipping the frosty red drink. "Oooh that's quite lovely." Took another sip. "Sorry, Kila, but I don't think he's our man. Maybe you've got the wrong Lars."

"Or maybe you're not as cute as you think you are."

"No chance," she replied, winking. "Might be time to face this head-on. Just ask him about Chili and be done with it."

"Now who's being subtle? 'Oh, hey, are you the sleazy barman who might have killed three people?' Don't think so. Besides, we've missed our opportunity. Look at that queue of suits. Settle in, we'll accost him when things go quiet."

But it was Thursday night and quiet was not on the after-work crowd's agenda. While Frankie looked annoyed and turned back to her cocktail, Kila couldn't help smiling.

There were worse ways to spend an evening.

CHAPTER 29 ~

SOME TELLING CONVERSATIONS

Soccer training was long over by the time Merry got home, and she dashed straight for Archie's bedroom. Felt a flood of relief when she spotted him sprawled on his duvet, footy boots still on, flicking through his phone.

"How was training, honey?" she said, glancing at the boots.

He dropped them to the floor, then grunted and returned to his phone.

"Right, well, how about you take a good, long shower and I'll get some dinner going?"

That got his attention.

"Lasagne?" he asked, his big eyes hopeful, and she felt her heart plummet.

"Well, no, I mean I can't make it *now*. Lasagne takes ages. I was thinking green chicken curry. I can whip that up in ten minutes. You like that too, right?" He shrugged, looked back at his device. "I tell you what. I'll make lasagne this weekend. How does that sound, munchkin?"

"You're never here long enough to make it," he muttered, and she blinked back at him.

"Well, I'll make sure I am."

He shrugged again, eyes back on his device. Then said, "Okay, sounds G."

She knew that meant "good," and she'd take it. "So while I get the curry going, how about you jump on in the shower?"

Merry suspected she was pushing it, but she needed to get her son off that device and her own beady eyes upon it.

"Okaaaay," she sang, "I'll just head to the kitchen now..."

Merry slowly made her way down the hallway while keeping one ear out.

The second she heard the bathroom door close she bolted back into Archie's bedroom, scooping up the phone he had tossed on his bed before the screen locked her out. Merry knew what kids were like. There was no way she was going to crack his password and get access herself. They should all be working in cybersecurity, this sneaky generation.

Luckily, it was still open and accessible, so she started frantically scrolling.

"What are you doing?" came a voice from the doorway, and Merry jumped as she looked up and around. It was Lola.

Merry exhaled. "You scared me, honey! Nothing."

"Doesn't look like nothing. You spying on Archie?"

"What? No..." Merry had the good grace to blush. "I'm just checking on him. I'm worried, that's all."

Lola stepped in and sat down beside Merry on Archie's crumpled bed. Then waved a hand at her nose and said, "Urgh, when did he last wash his sheets? That's rank!"

Merry sniffed. Yes, they did smell a bit, mostly of bad body odour and something that didn't bear thinking about. But she had bigger fish to fry. The shower was now running, but who knows how long he would take? Sometimes Archie was in there for an eternity, other times he wasn't in long enough to get wet.

That thought made her stop and think of Verity suddenly...

She shook it away. *No time, Merry! Focus!* She kept scrolling, clicking first on Snapchat, then on Instagram.

"Don't know why you bother," said Lola, looking over her shoulder. "Just videos of useless sports stars and sexist rappers but not much else. No shots of him snorting lines or whatever it is you're worried about."

She sniggered at that, and Merry looked up. "How do you know what's on here? Are you his friend? On Insta?"

"Aren't you?"

"I... Well, I didn't think he'd want me to be his friend. I mean, I'm his mother."

"Yeah, but he's a total mummy's boy. Wouldn't put it past him."

"Not lately he's not," said Merry glumly.

"With good reason," said Lola, getting to her feet again.

Before Merry could ask her what that meant, Lola said, "Shower's stopped running, by the way. You're gonna get busted!"

Then she laughed as Merry dropped the phone like it was a burning coal and bolted back to the kitchen.

~

Back at his own house, Earle was having a heated conversation with his only child.

"I cannot believe you did that to Fiona!" Tess said, her voice one octave away from screaming. "So embarrassing, Dad! You can't meddle in her life. You have no right!"

He glanced worriedly at Beryl, who was at the ironing board in front of the telly. "I was just trying to help," he said.

"Who? Who were you helping exactly? Fiona? Me? *Yourself?*"

"Huh?"

"You just want us to get back together so you can have your house back. Your life back. Your *sleep* back!"

He blinked at her and then across to Beryl again. She was shaking her head, at both of them by the look of her. Sighed heavily as she switched the iron off.

"Bub's gonna stir if you two keep this up," she said as she made her way through the lounge room. "I'm going to check on the casserole."

Then she shuffled off to the kitchen while Earle and Tess eyeballed each other across the room.

"I'm sorry," said Earle, deflating first.

"No, I'm sorry," said Tess, dropping down on the couch beside him. "That wasn't fair. You and Mum have been amazing."

Earle swallowed hard, cleared his throat. "I love having you here, Tess. You know that. I'd die for you and your little girl. I've told you that. This is not about me."

She nodded. Nodded again. "It's not about me and my little girl either. It's about Fiona and her dad. I can barely get her to talk to me about him. She's hardly going to sit down on the pavement and start chatting to him now, is she?"

"Probably not," he said, squeezing his daughter's hand. "But she's going to have to come to terms with it all at some point because her dad's dying, Tess, and this might be her last chance."

Last chance for you too, he thought, and young Saffron. Because if Fiona didn't reconcile with her father, Earle wasn't sure his daughter would ever reconcile with Fiona.

And that would mean a lifetime of sleepless nights for *their* daughter. He was sure of it.

~

It was not until well after eleven that Kila finally pounced. Not until most of the revellers at Tudor's Wine Bar had moved on to local night clubs or cigar bars or wherever else this stuck-up crowd went that Lars finally took a break.

They spotted him out on the gusty roof bar that looked down over the sparkly skyline, puffing on a vape. Kila nodded to Frankie, and they made their way out but not before Frankie had rattled off a similar speech to Trevor's.

"Be calm, be professional. This guy could be innocent, make no assumptions."

And so he politely introduced himself as a private detective and said, "I'm working for a woman whose brother was killed about three months back. Guy called Phillip Weaver."

Kila waited, expecting a reaction—fear, worry, a fist to the face. The barman just blinked casually as he blew a stream of strawberry-smelling vapour towards them, then said, "Oh yeah? How can I help?"

Frankie swapped a look with Kila. "You know Weaver?"

"Don't think so. Is he a regular?"

Kila frowned and produced Tiffany's smudged photo. "So this bloke never came in here asking you questions?"

Lars blinked more rapidly this time and shook his head firmly. Glanced at Frankie, then back. "No, he did not. What's this about? Really?"

Kila pocketed the photo. "You ever work at Taboo?"

The change of subject *was* like a fist to the face. "What?"

"You heard me."

Lars glanced between them again. "Why would you think I worked that bar?"

"I remember seeing you there that's all."

"Bullshit. I was there for three weeks. What's this about? You guys reporters? I knew you looked familiar!" He was pointing his vape at Frankie now, and she held a palm up.

"Hey, I'm not a reporter anymore, I'm working with Kila. We're trying to help a dead man's sister."

"Bullshit," he said again, eyes back on Kila. "This has something to do with that young chick, doesn't it? The one who got killed on a night out, a couple of years ago?"

"Why would you think that?"

He ignored the question. "I had nothing to do with it. I already told the pigs when they showed up with her picture. I'd never seen that scrag before in my life."

"That scrag was my sister," said Kila, his voice hard.

The barman took a step back. "Shit, sorry." A quick look at Frankie, like she was going to save him. "No offence or anything. It's just—I lost my job over that."

"You got sacked?" said Kila. Trevor never mentioned that. Barely remembered the bloke.

Lars sucked on his vape again. Exhaled. "Not exactly but they cut all my shifts back. After two weeks of no work, I told them where they could stick their job and came here." He looked inside. "They appreciate me here. Better tips too."

"Maybe there was a good reason they cut your shifts," said Kila. "Maybe you're sleazy."

Lars scoffed and Frankie almost scoffed along. She knew sleaze and this man didn't fit the template. More's the pity. He was cute. Tall, blond...

"I didn't do anything wrong," he said.

"So why'd you suddenly move house? Change all your numbers?" said Kila.

"Move house?" He blinked rapidly, then put his vape away. "Landlord kicked us out. They were pulling the building down. It had nothing to do with your sister."

"Okay, what about Bertha?" said Kila, and he looked confused again by the subject change.

"Who?"

"Bertha Thomas. Another *scrag*, looked a bit like my sister."

"*Bertha?*" Then he squinted at Kila like he was only just seeing him for the first time. "So *that's* what this is about! Is she family too? Did she send you? Tell you I had something to do with it?"

Kila swapped another look with Frankie as Lars charged on: "If Bertha said that, it's also bullshit. Just because I'm not into her, doesn't make me a killer. You tell her I don't appreciate this crap. I was always polite to Bertha. I let her down gently."

Now Kila was the one looking confused.

The way Lars was talking, it was as though he assumed Bertha was still alive.

"Bertha's dead," he said bluntly. "Probably murdered too."

Lars's jaw dropped and he reached for the guardrail. Leaned against it. "Shit." Then, "How? What happened?"

"What do you care? I didn't think you were interested."

"No… not like that, but…"

"She drowned," said Frankie gently, flashing Kila a frown. "So you never saw Chili, you didn't hear about Bertha, and you don't know any Phillip Weaver, is that what you're saying?"

He nodded, still looking stunned. "I promise you guys, I had nothing to do with all this…" A glance at Kila. "Nothing to do with your sister. I never saw her come in. Honest."

"Bullshit," said Kila now, fists clenched by his side. "You must have seen her."

"No, no way, man." He was madly shaking his head, eyes back at Frankie. "And I would've noticed; the bar was pretty empty at that time."

"I'm not talking about eight o'clock. This would've been closer to midnight. And you would have noticed her—she would have been half-dressed and fucking distressed."

Frankie placed a hand on Kila's arm while Lars kept shaking his head.

"They were all half-dressed, the chicks at Taboo, but no one was distressed. I promise you, man. I would've noticed. It was quiet all night, I remember that. In fact…" He gave it some thought. "That's right. It was so dead I closed up early and we went straight home."

"Who's we?" asked Frankie. Always on the beat.

"Hang on, you closed early?" said Kila. "You weren't open until one?"

"Not that night. It was bucketing down, no one about, so we shut the doors just after eleven. We were allowed to close early if there were no paying customers."

Kila felt his heart deflate. God bloody damn it. If this fucknuckle was telling the truth, it cracked the case wide open again, because Dragon said he'd dropped Chili on the street outside Taboo around midnight.

So if it wasn't open, where the hell did Chili go?

"Who's we?" said Frankie for the second time.

Lars went to dismiss that, then seemed buoyed again. "That's right! Gerry, my flatmate. Check with her. She'll tell you. She was with me the whole time."

"Jerry's a *chick*?" said Kila.

"Gerry with a G," Lars explained. "It's short for Geraldine."

Kila exhaled again. Okay, that must be the "Jerry" from Weaver's notes. But there was something else about that name... couldn't stop to consider it now.

"You still know Gerry?" Kila asked. "Is she okay?"

"She was fine this morning. We're now renting a place in Rozelle. Why?"

"No reason." Relief washed through Kila like a cool breeze. "All right, give me your new address." Then he gave him a growly look and added, "And it better not be an empty block, Lars, or I'll be back here to shove that vape right up your—"

"Okay, that's all for now!" said Frankie, pulling Kila away.

CHAPTER 30 ~

FOOD FOR THOUGHT

As Merry waved her kids off to school on Friday morning, she didn't head into HQ as promised but returned to her kitchen and reached for a large cooking pot. She was determined to make Archie's lasagne and get back in his good books.

Merry's social media search of Archie's phone last night had proved fruitless, and she couldn't get a word out of him over dinner other than the usual grunting. Lola had just snickered like this was situation normal, but Merry was beginning to fret. What was she missing? What was making her once vibrant boy so... *odd?*

Was it typical teenage angst? Or was there something else going on?

Humming to herself, she fossicked through her pantry for some onions and tinned tomatoes. Perhaps the lasagne would open his heart and mouth—in more ways than one.

Back at the kitchen bench she began chopping the onions when her phone sang out. A glance at the screen brought a smile to her face. It was Dougie.

They exchanged some pleasantries, a little gossip about the case, and then he asked, "Would you like to pop over after work tonight? There's something... well, something I'd like to talk to you about." Then, quickly, "I'm making my famous pot roast."

She smiled wider, thinking about the meal that first brought them together. Then sighed. "Sorry, not tonight, Dougie. I'm having some problems with Archie."

"Oh dear, that's no good. Well, he's very welcome to come along, and lovely Lola of course. My daughter's at her mum's this weekend. Plenty of room. In fact, you could all stay the night if you like."

Merry baulked at that. Wasn't sure the kids were ready for sleepovers. And now with Archie acting out...

"Thanks, Dougie, but I promised Archie his favourite dish."
Or his new favourite dish, at least. *When had he gone off her spaghetti bolognaise?* "I'm going to woo him back to his old self using my delicious homemade lasagne."

"Homemade lasagne hey? What a very lucky lad."

She laughed. "Very subtle, Dougie! How about this then? I'll make extra and bring some to you tomorrow night. Archie's got a sleepover then anyway."

"To quote Persephone, that sounds ticketyboo!"

They both laughed as he hung up, and Merry laughed some more as she dribbled olive oil into the pot, the sound echoing around her kitchen. Dougie made her so happy. He always had from the first moment they met. Her laughter stopped. Her smile turned wistful. It felt like a long time since she'd heard laughter coming from Archie. *Why had her darling boy stopped laughing?*

~

Lars's flatmate Gerry did not return Kila's smile when she opened the door to him. Lars was nowhere to be seen, but he'd clearly given her the heads-up and she looked ready for battle.

Kila didn't care. The way people associated with Taboo were dropping dead, he was just glad she was alive and kicking. And boy was she kicking.

"I think it's criminal what you guys are doing to Lars!" she declared, holding the door fast, refusing him entry. "He's a good guy, and he doesn't deserve all these outrageous accusations!"

"All? Who else is accusing him?"

She huffed and straightened down the front of the navy-blue scrubs she was wearing. "I have to get to work. What do you want?"

"I'm just checking his alibi for the night my sister was taken. It was—"

"A Thursday. September 20. I know. I remember it very well. I graduated from college that day. Was at Taboo celebrating with Lars. We stayed there all night, never saw anyone that looked anything like your poor sister—as if I would have ignored a distressed woman if she had walked in!—then Lars shut up early and we went home together. No way he could've done it. No way in hell. I'll tell you what I told that other guy—"

"Hang on, what other guy?"

An impatient shrug this time. "Can't remember his name. Was here a few months ago. Mid-thirties, heavy on the Old Spice aftershave. Half my male residents wear it. Cannot persuade them otherwise." She smiled to herself then.

Kila grabbed his phone and produced the picture of Weaver. "This him?"

She looked, nodded.

"What did he want?"

"Same as you—lots of shifty questions about Taboo and your sister and did I think Lars had anything to do with it. Just because he worked at that blasted bar for all of a month. Look…" Her voice softened, and she opened the door wider. "I'm really sorry about your sis. Horrendous way to go. But I'm confused by all this. I thought they caught the bastard who did it."

Kila exhaled. Rubbed a hand over his stubbled jaw. "Yeah, so did I. Maybe not."

She offered him a sympathetic smile. "So you want to find answers, I get that. But you're looking in the wrong place. I might be stupid, but I'm not a fool. I'm not flatting with a psychopath. Lars is a good guy. I've known him for years. Wouldn't hurt a fly."

"Is he ever sleazy?"

"Sleazy? I wish!" She winked. Looked cute with it. "And he's certainly not a killer."

Kila nodded but it was not what he wanted to hear. He thanked her for her time and was just turning away when something she said made him turn back. Something she was wearing…

"Hang on, sorry, Gerry. Are you a nurse?"

She looked back from behind her door, like he was now the fool. "Yeah. A geriatric nurse. Why?"

You could have bowled Kila over with a feather.

~

Merry was slowly stirring the bechamel sauce, trying not to look at the clock for the tenth time that morning—gee this dish took ages, the sleuths would be getting antsy!—when something occurred to her.

It made her stop stirring.

Flicking off the gas flame, she pulled her mobile phone from its charger and put in a call to Frankie.

"Where are you, woman?" Frankie demanded. "We're all at the office, and there's no one here for me to bicker with."

"Sorry, I'm still at home making lasagne, and that's got me thinking about Verity's house guest, Gus. I know you only met him once, but do you have any idea how long he was staying with Verity? Are we talking days or...?"

"A few weeks, according to the neighbour, why?"

Merry gasped, speechless for a moment. Brain in overdrive.

"You still there?" said Frankie. "Merry?"

Then: "Oh my God, oh my God, oh my God! We've been looking in completely the wrong direction! If only Verity had told us, and maybe she did, but I don't remember... I mean, I'm not sure we ever really checked. And we should have *checked*—"

"Merry. Stop. You're rambling. What's going on? What are you trying to say?"

Merry took a deep breath and stared back at the lasagne. "I think I know a way to solve this whole thing once and for all. Where does Verity live again?"

"Why?"

"Just text me the address *please*, and meet me there in ten minutes!" Then she glanced at the half-made dish and said, "Make that thirty."

"Okay, but again, *why*? What's going on?"

"Not sure yet, but don't say a word to Earle."

"Not even if I wanted to," said Frankie. "You're not making any sense, honey."

"Sorry!" She giggled now, her nervous, hysterical giggle, and said, "I'll explain everything better when I see you. But Frankie?"

"Mmmm?"

"Bring that trusty burglary kit you were boasting about. I'm going to perform another break-in, and this time you're going to help me."

~

By the time Kila left Gerry's house, his mood had dramatically soured. There was only one thing left to do. He had to head to Bondi, to the brewery where Bertha was last seen drinking.

There was one more barman he needed to talk to.

One more person with answers he was convinced he no longer wanted to hear...

~

Forty minutes later, two women were standing behind a large poinciana, scoping out Verity's house.

"Just give it five," said Frankie. "There's a very nosey neighbour with a really bad dye job. We need to make sure she's not out pretending to water her garden again."

Merry laughed. "While we wait, tell me more about this house guest of Verity's. Gus."

Frankie turned back. "Why are you interested in him suddenly? He might have been around at the time of the murders but he wouldn't have had access to Seagrave. Only three people had that, according to Verity."

"Just humour me please."

"Okay, but gee you're being annoyingly elusive! So he was fairly short, well built, red beard. Actually, he looked a little like—"

"Dougie? Did he look like Dougie? But older, straighter, fitter?"

"Yes, why?"

Merry almost started dancing on the spot. It was all starting to slip into place. "Come on," she said, "we've waited long enough. Let's get inside."

It was easier said than done and not just because they had to be subtle with the neighbour about. The front was clearly impenetrable with its security grill door, so they strolled nonchalantly down the side, sneakily trying every window along the way. All were firmly secured. The back door, too, was locked, and Merry glanced around.

"What's that?" She was pointing at what looked like a small outhouse attached to the back.

"Spare loo? Laundry maybe."

Merry pushed at the door and smiled when it swung open. Inside, they saw it was once an outhouse but had been renovated and now featured a small washing machine/dryer set as well as a toilet/sink combo and a shower. As well as another door that led inwards.

Merry gave that a push too. It was flimsy but locked fast.

"Out of the way, softie," said Frankie, pulling out her tool kit and bending down to crack the lock.

It took some doing, but she was soon smiling, too, as the lock unclicked and the door swung wide. Merry almost danced again as they made their way into what turned out to be Verity's kitchen. Frankie looked around.

"So what are we doing here?" she asked. "You want to get an idea of the floorplan or something?"

"Not the floorplan this time. Just the contents of the pantry."

Merry didn't explain further, just headed first to the fridge, sweeping it open, then to the pantry where she did start to dance. A little jig that made her look ridiculous.

"Sorry!" she said as Frankie frowned at her. "It's just as I thought. This proves it."

"It does?" said Frankie, following Merry's gaze.

"Yes! The evidence is right there!"

Frankie looked again. All she could see were a few onions, a parsnip, a large bag of potatoes, lots of tinned tomatoes and a container of powdered beef stock. She picked up the stock. "You think maybe the poison's in this?"

Merry giggled. "You wish! Okay, so as far as I can see we have a few more jobs to tick off and then it might all be over. Where are the guys?"

"Back at HQ."

"Goodoh. Let's get over there and delegate tasks—we need to check Charlie's phone, get hold of that CCTV footage, get some questions to Verity if we can manage it, and then fill up my car with petrol."

"Huh?" Frankie said as Merry just laughed, letting the sound echo through the old house, not caring if the neighbour heard them now.

"It's time to pay an old friend a visit. But first we have a long, hard road ahead of us."

CHAPTER 31 ~
TICKING FINAL BOXES

It took some doing, but finally Earle was seated in front of Verity's stern solicitor, Ginny, in her plush, downtown office. She had her arms crossed over a wad of files and a scowl behind thick black spectacles.

"I can't believe my client is still talking to you lot after everything you did."

Everything we've done, we've done for Verity, Earle thought, but didn't want to argue the point. Not at her hourly rates. And not after everything Merry had just told them at the office earlier that day.

They now had a pretty good idea who had killed Sir George and then Shannon, but first they needed some answers from the woman accused of both murders. And the afternoon was ticking on...

"Did you present the questions I emailed you?" he asked.

Ginny nodded. "They were rather *odd*, to say the least."

"Trust me, this whole case is odd. It will all make sense soon."

She stared at him for a moment longer, then uncrossed her arms, opened a file, and produced a typed piece of paper, which she pushed across her desk towards him.

"Why you needed to know how long my client spends in the shower sounds, frankly, *inappropriate*."

Earle shrugged nonchalantly as he read through the answers Verity had dictated over the phone to Ginny. He didn't care what the woman thought of his questions. Or of him for that matter.

This was one situation where niceties were irrelevant.

~

Frankie smiled as Charlie scowled back at her. She'd tracked her down to Sir George's city penthouse, the one he'd lived in before his daughter went psycho.

209

"Running out of friends to bunk with?" said Frankie, giving her a smug look.

Charlie smooched her ruby lips together. "I'm keeping my distance, actually. In case somebody else drops dead."

"Nobody's dropping dead, honey," said Frankie. "They're being murdered."

Charlie's lips went wide. "I keep telling you guys! It has nothing to do with me!"

Frankie smiled and held out her palm. "Hand over your phone then, and let's prove it."

~

Martin smiled politely as the principal of Trinity Ladies College approached. She was younger than he was expecting, a lay teacher, with a warm smile on a very pretty face.

"Thanks for seeing me," he said. "I'm an associate of Earle Fitzgerald's, and I believe he's phoned ahead?"

The woman's smile widened. "Such a lovely man, Mr Fitzgerald. He dropped in last month and gave the girls a wonderful presentation on personal safety. It was very empowering."

Martin blinked back at her. *Okay, that he did not know.*

"How is he going?" she asked. "And how's that delightful granddaughter of his?"

Martin went to block the questions, then remembered what Earle had said about making time for niceties. "She's great I believe. So is Earle. He speaks very highly of you."

The principal looked chuffed. "That's so lovely to hear! And once again, we're more than happy to help."

Then finally she produced a small thumb drive and handed it to Martin.

~

The third thumbs-up emoji came through just as Merry was paying the hefty petrol bill. She apologised to the sweet young man behind the cash register and grabbed a couple of extra bottles of water and a large bag of lollies, then added them to the order. When he'd rung them up, she paid, grabbed a receipt, thanked him, then returned to her bright yellow hatchback.

There she popped the snacks to one side and sent an apologetic text to Lola and Archie with instructions on cooking her pre-made lasagne, then switched on her vehicle's GPS. She tapped in the quickest route to the snow fields, then looked at herself in the rear-view mirror and said, "Okay, Mrs White, let's bring this baby home!"

~

The burly detective cut a lonely figure as he strode into the Bondi Brewers Bar. It was early afternoon on Friday, but the place was packed and pumping—like no one had work or worries of any kind. But Kila did. And he wasn't going to wait for calm this time, or Frankie for that matter. Nor was he using her tricks to get to the front of the swirling queue of patrons that crowded the central bar.

He had tricks of his own.

Looking around, it didn't take long to find a door marked MANAGER, poorly concealed behind a bamboo partition. He headed straight for it, giving it a firm knock. There was no answer, so he opened it and walked straight in, knowing he'd be attended to in minutes.

And he was.

"You can't be in there!" came a flustered voice from the doorway. A server by the look of the empty plates in her hands.

"Get your manager please," was Kila's reply.

Ten minutes later Bertha's last crush was seated across from him in the manager's office. His name was Kash, he was tall and blond like Lars, and he looked delighted.

"Don't know how you managed that, but I'm glad of the break. It's mental out there today."

Kila nodded back. He had his ways. He had his means. And they had a lot to do with his thorough knowledge of the state's liquor laws. According to the Independent Liquor and Gaming Authority, it was an offence to sell and supply alcohol to an intoxicated person, and yet here he was investigating a person who had left this premises so intoxicated she drowned. So intoxicated the pub could lose its licence if anyone wanted to make a fuss. Turns out the manager did *not* want to make a fuss, and so he was swiftly granted ten minutes with the barman of his choice.

But there was no time to tell Kash all of that. So he launched straight in.

"Your manager tells me you were pretty friendly with a patron who used to come here, a Papua New Guinean woman called Bertha Thomas?"

The barman blinked. "Bertha? Sure, we were friendly. But... but nothing happened between us. I mean, it was just the one time and—"

"I'm not interested in your sex life."

"Good, good, so what's this about? You know she drowned, right?"

"I do. After she came here drinking one night."

Now he had his palms up, mirroring the manager from earlier. "Whoa! Dude! Nothing to do with me! I told her, her limit was up. Didn't serve her any more alcohol after that."

"You didn't need to. I think she had a friend who was buying drinks for her."

His expression turned sour. "I knew it! They moved from the bar to a back table, but I had a hunch those shots were for her."

"Vodka shots?"

"Yeah, that's right. Top-shelf stuff too." His frown settled. "She loved her spirits."

"So I hear." Kila leaned forward. "I don't really care about the vodka either. I care about the friends. Tell me about them."

"What do you want to know? It was her usual crew from what I could see, lots of chicks, a few young guys, all pretty harmless."

"Anyone unusual that night? Anyone in particular stand out?"

Kash shook his head. "Like I said, she was amongst friends, they were having fun." He went to sip from the water bottle he'd brought in when something occurred to him. "Except there was that one dude."

"What dude?"

He waved it off, sipped his drink. "But she already knew him, told me they went way back. Were old friends." He smiled. "Like I was going to be jealous or something." Another sad shake of the head.

Kila felt his skin crawl. "You get a name? For this bloke?

"Nope."

"Tell me about him."

And so he did. Kash described how the large group had been drinking for several hours, propped up close to the bar—"that's where Bertha liked to be, close to the action"—when a man approached. Kash didn't recognise him, but Bertha sure did. At first she seemed worried.

"She said to me, 'I'm in the shit now' or something like that," said Kash.

"She say why?"

He shook his head. "I had to keep pouring drinks, but when I looked again, they'd scarpered. Thought she'd scored with this dude, yeah? But then they came back and they were both laughing and stuff. Bertha looked…"

He smudged his lips to one side, giving it some thought. "*Relieved*, I guess. Like she'd missed a bullet."

That made Kila's heart spike.

Kash then explained how the two old mates started doing vodka shots together at the bar until he told Bertha he was cutting her off. "She could put 'em away with the best of them, old Bertha, but I could tell she was close to hammered."

"So what happened then?"

"They told me I was a buzzkill, promised to switch to soda and moved to a table at the back. I couldn't see them from there." Then, defensive again, "I didn't know she was drinking all those shots. He kept buying them, said they were for her girlfriends. They were over there too. I—"

"Told you, Kash. Don't give a shit about the booze. Then what happened?"

He shrugged. "Nothin'. I mean… I felt kind've sorry for her to be honest, 'cause the guy bailed on her."

"He *left*?"

"Yeah, which was odd. He'd shouted her top-shelf vodka like he was hoping to get lucky. I see that all the time."

"I bet you do," said Kila, his own tone now sour. "So how'd you know he took off? If you were busy at the bar?"

Kash thought about that. "That's right, he waved goodbye to me like we were old mates or something. Weirdo. Then I saw Bertha still at the back table with her crew."

"When did Bertha leave? How soon after?"

"It's all a bit dusty… maybe thirty minutes? An hour? Most of her mates had bailed by then too, and she came up to say goodbye. She always said goodbye, kind've wistful like she wished I was coming with her."

"She was alone by then?"

He nodded. Sadly. "I told her to go straight home. I knew she had a thing for skinny-dipping; her friends used to rib her about it. I told her, you're smashed, get some sleep. Something like that. If I'd known she was going to head to the beach, I would've walked her home myself. Maybe she was feeling bummed after lucking out with that dude. Maybe that's why she went swimming alone."

Oh, she wasn't alone, thought Kila, but he kept that to himself too. Kash didn't need any more guilt than he was already carrying.

The guilt all rested with this so-called friend who'd been first a source of anxiety, then of relief, a friend who had plied her with vodka, then waited in the shadows until she staggered out of the pub before following her to the beach and then into the water.

But now he had to ask the question he had been avoiding from the start. The manager was back at the office door, glaring at Kila. He held up a finger and turned back to Kash.

"Just one more question and then I'll let you get back to it."

Kash nodded eagerly and the manager turned away.

"Describe him to me," Kila said. "This old friend who was buying Bertha shots all night. Tell me exactly what he looked like."

And as he did so, everything Kila thought he knew was thrown in the air, then smashed to smithereens as it landed. And that's how he felt as he stumbled back to his car soon after, like a million splintered pieces that would never be whole again.

CHAPTER 32 ~
THE (FIRST) GRAND REVEAL

"Hello, Angus, thought I might find you here," said Merry, stepping into Sir George Burlington's old winter ski lodge. She'd forgotten how drab it was, with its outdated '70's hues— all *Brady Bunch* shades of greens and oranges and browns.

The red-bearded lodge manager was strolling out of the kitchen and nearly dropped his mug. "Wha—?"

Merry waved a set of fingers at him. "Sorry to scare you Angus. Or would you rather I called you Gus? Like Verity does."

It was fairly dark in the lodge, just the kitchen light on, and he squinted across at her. "Is that...? Mary is it?"

"*Merry* actually, but don't worry. Everybody muddles it up."

"What are you doing here?" he asked, his face a mess of wrinkled confusion. "How... How did you get in?"

"Door was unlocked, soz. Should I have knocked? It's just, well, I was passing and saw the light."

It was a lie, of sorts, but there would be plenty of lies tonight, no doubt. She smiled sweetly as he continued to frown and added, "It's odd to find you here, Angus. I thought George had sold this place a few months back and you had a new posting."

His jaw hardened. "No, the job fell through. And the new owners haven't moved in here yet. Are going to renovate, so..."

"So you thought you'd help yourself until then?"

He frowned now. "I'm helping them actually. It's always better to have a place occupied. Keep the home fires burning, the firewood piled up, the *rodents* out."

The way he said *rodents*, the way he was glancing towards the wood-fire burner in the living room and the axe that was leaning up against it, gave Merry her first shiver of trepidation.

215

She shook it off and reminded herself why she was there. What exactly she was doing.

Took a few steadying breaths. "Mind if I get a cuppa too?" Dropped her handbag by the front door, then slowly pushed it closed with the back of one leg. "That's a very long drive."

Angus stared at her, bemused. Then said, "Help yourself."

He didn't move though, so she had to brush past him—another quick shiver—as she walked to the kitchen and looked around for a cup. There was one drying on the sink, and she grabbed it, then glanced about for some teabags.

"Above your head," he said, adding, "Milk's in the fridge."

Merry thanked him as she set about making a cup and could feel his eyes on her as he leant against the kitchen door now, slurping his own tea. He didn't ask what on earth she was doing all the way out here—a six-hour drive from Sydney no less—and she didn't volunteer anything. Needed to make a fortifying drink first.

"I still have my set of keys," he said eventually, determined to explain his own presence. "I didn't break in. I would never do that."

"Of course not."

"And where else am I supposed to live now? Since George sold the place from under me."

Merry glanced back at him as she dangled the teabag into some boiling water. "Actually, we thought you were living with Verity. In Sydney. My colleagues saw you."

"What? No, I was just there briefly."

He watched her for a little longer and, tea now steeped, allowed her to lead the way back to the living room where Merry had sat with him nine months earlier, where Merry had asked him a dozen questions about the Burlington family and gotten almost nowhere.

"Shall we?" she said, pointing at two large, mismatched armchairs that were between the front door and the floor-to-ceiling windows that looked out to the dark beech forest beyond.

He nodded and then switched on a lamp, and so they sat in strained silence as they quietly sipped their teas. Then he said, almost casually, "So how's the case going?" like she'd just popped round to chew the fat. "I see you haven't managed to help Verity. She's back behind bars I hear."

"Yes, terrible isn't it?" said Merry. "You heard about Shannon Smith too, I'm guessing?"

He looked away, towards a small TV against one wall. "Just through the news."

She took a tentative sip of her tea. "We can't believe they're trying to pin both murders on poor Verity. Especially when there are so many other suspects, so many *better* suspects they should be looking at."

His eyes swept back. "Is that right?"

She tried for her bravest smile. "Shall I talk you through them?"

"I don't think that's necessary. I—"

"Our first suspect was Susan!" Merry wouldn't be put off, not after that drive. Not while her nerves were still working. "We really wished we could have pinned it on her. She does, after all, fit the description of a cold-blooded killer."

Merry let those words linger in the room. Then she sighed. "Such a pity she's got such a good alibi. All locked away safely in jail."

"That is a pity," he said, and she nodded, vigorously.

"That's when we learned that poor George had been poisoned and over a period of time. As horrendous as it was, it sort of narrowed down the suspects because, well, it had to be—"

"Someone with access to Seagrave," he said, leaning back in his chair.

"That's what we thought! So, of course we had to look at who could waltz in and out of the Seagrave kitchen at will. Other than Verity of course."

"Of course."

"Our first thought was Shannon, it has to be said."

"Oh yeah?"

"Yeah. We linked her with Clem. Did you know they used to work together? We were quite excited about that—or at least Martin was—but then she went and got herself murdered. Boy that was a shock. And I was there when Verity found her. Did you know that?"

He shook his head, eyes slithering away.

"It was horrible," Merry said, her tone less chipper now. "Horrendous what happened to that poor young woman."

She let that sit in the room for a bit too, then took a deep, steadying breath. Blew some of it out onto her hot tea. "Then we learned Clem had a pretty good alibi for that night, which was also a shame because he would have made a terrific suspect. But no luck there, sadly."

"Hmmm," said Angus.

"So then we moved on to Charlie…"

"Charlotte?" He looked surprised by this.

"Don't worry, I wasn't gunning for her either. She's so sweet—albeit a little narcissistic. But I really didn't want it to be the granddaughter. I think she's suffered enough, don't you? But we couldn't get past the fact that she'd returned from London at the opportune time, that she had access to the Seagrave kitchen and the stew. Could easily have poisoned old Gramps, maybe with help from Shannon, and then killed Shannon to shut her up."

His eyes narrowed. "That makes some kind of sense, you know."

"I know!" Merry sat forward. Then let her lips droop southward. "But like I said, I really didn't want to see Charlie locked away." Her eyes lit up. "Needn't have worried though. The good thing about this generation is they leave digital fingerprints everywhere. Digital alibis. And you know what's even more amazing? Sometimes it's what's *missing* that's as telling as what's there."

He looked confused, and she held up a hand. "Sorry! I can waffle a bit. Let me explain. See, even if Charlie had been involved in Sir George's murder, she had a very good alibi for Shannon's. My friend Frankie—you remember Frankie? You saw her at Verity's house earlier this week?" He shrugged. "Anyway, Frankie's just gone through Charlie's phone with a fine-tooth comb—and it's all there in black and white. Or not, as the case may be."

She placed her cup on the table between them and turned to face him. "There I go, waffling again. Suffice to say, everything Charlie told us pans out. Thanks to her smartphone, we know for a fact that Charlie ordered Uber Eats around seven o'clock the night Shannon died—two lots of tofu ramen and bubble tea, as disgusting as that sounds! The delivery guy showed up at Shannon's apartment at 7:33 to hand the order over. That was poor Shannon's final meal as it turns out." Again she paused to let that sink in. "Charlie says that Shannon left straight after the meal. Went to Verity's house at eight that night." She pointed at Angus. "You didn't happen to see Shannon there, did you?"

"No, no," he said quickly. "I'd left for here by then. I've been here for days."

"That's unlucky. You could have been Verity's alibi. Charlie insists *she* never left Shannon's place after eight that night, and we could find no evidence to the contrary. No ride-share booking—either going to or from Shannon's apartment or Seagrave. There's no public transport close by, so if she was going anywhere, she was going to have to use something like an Uber. But her Uber account was untouched."

"She could have flagged a taxi down," said Angus.

"That's what Earle thought," said Merry. "But here's the other wonderful thing! Charlie is a sweet tooth. Ridiculously so! She's going to have to get on top of that, or she'll be the size of a house by the time she gets to my age!"

She giggled, knew it sounded nervous. "Anyhoo," she continued, swallowing the giggle as he frowned back at her. "Just her luck, Charlie placed a *second* Uber Eats order that night—a really disgusting-sounding chocolate-and-almond gelato—and that order was placed at nine and arrived at Shannon's address at 9:25 p.m. Perfect timing, hey? We can't imagine that Charlie managed to kill Shannon at Seagrave and get back to her house—ten kilometres away—in time to do all that. I mean, she could have, but well, it's very unlikely, right?"

He didn't say anything, so she added, "Which got us thinking about Verity."

"Verity?" He seemed surprised, emboldened too. "Wow," he said. "You think she could have been behind this all along?"

Merry smiled. "I didn't, no. I'm a bit of a softie like that. But Frankie did. And it does all point to her, when you really think about it. I mean, she did have a very good motive to bop old George off early."

"The inheritance," he said, his tone matter-of-fact, and she nodded.

"We only really had her word that George was unwell and ailing. For all we knew he was fighting fit, had years to live, until she started feeding him that infamous Irish stew."

"She was poisoning him all along." Another comment. Like it was fact.

"Indeed! At least, that's what Frankie thought, and I had to wonder. I mean Verity did do an awful lot for Sir George. Maybe she got sick of it! Maybe he told her he was rewarding her with a third of his estate, and maybe that was the catalyst. Maybe she wanted to get on with her life now—not nurse an old, grumpy, cantankerous…"

"Ungrateful!" he added, and she gulped.

"Yes, *ungrateful* man like George." She blinked. "You think she had a valid reason to do it? Verity?"

He cleared his throat. "I'm not saying that. But you're right. She did a lot for that old bugger. I'm not sure he appreciated it, that's all. I… Well, I couldn't blame her if she had done it."

Merry nodded vigorously. "That's what the police thought too. And it helped that Shannon was pointing the finger at Verity, accusing her of poisoning George with the stews. So when Shannon got murdered, it seemed to solidify the case against Verity, and then Charlie made it even worse when she said that Verity was the last person to see Shannon alive."

"The visit to the house."

"Exactly! Pity you weren't still at Verity's house then. You might have been able to help her. Could have been her alibi. But we only have her word for it. You see, Verity insists she never got a visit from Shannon that night. The first she saw her was lying dead by George's pool, with me. At ten forty. But maybe she's lying! She could have been home when Shannon visited. It would have been around eight thirty that night. She could have fought with her and then followed her to Seagrave and slaughtered her by the pool. Then cleaned herself up—Verity's hair was wet that night. She could've showered to remove the blood and evidence. In any case, she could have then tacked back and pretended to meet me outside Seagrave half an hour later. I wouldn't have known. She knew the back roads around that house better than any of us and which cameras to avoid, including the one outside the girls' school."

Angus's eyes slapped across at Merry then. His jaw tightened, but he said nothing.

"It could easily have been her," Merry continued. "Such a pity you weren't still at Verity's house to help her disprove it."

"Hmm."

Merry sat forward. "You know, I keep thinking about that, about you at Verity's house." She giggled. Nervously again. "I didn't go to Verity's that day the team went, the day they met a guy called Gus that they barely remembered. Didn't think he was consequential—

no offence or anything. But I would have recognised you, Angus. We go way back, right?"

He shrugged.

"And, well, if I had known you were in the picture, maybe—just maybe—I might have popped *your* name on the suspect list. Again, no offence."

"Oh, none taken." Angus half chuckled. It sounded strained, muffled. "But why, pray tell, would I be a suspect? I had no reason to harm George. I never inherited anything."

"Oh, I would have come up with something," said Merry before taking a deep breath. "Like that very fact, for starters. I mean, after all your years of loyalty, George goes and sells the lodge from under you! Turfs you out with just a thank-you! That must have made you mad."

He shook his head. "Not really."

"Surely! I mean, it's like you said, a place like this doesn't just look after itself. You keep the home fires burning, the firewood piled up, the rodents at bay…"

"And the rest," he said, glancing around. "Gotta maintain the property, clear all the snow in winter and the mould when it's humid, make sure the pipes don't freeze over, keep the pantry stocked and the equipment in good nick."

"Sure, sure," she said. "And you must have been a bit of a help when they came and stayed every winter."

"Help?" He gave another strained chuckle. "I did more than *help*. I was the one who taught George's grandkids to ski, did you know that? Tawny too. She'd never skied a day in her life when she married into that posh family. And Pookie before her. George used to just ski off without a care in the world." He made a *pft!* sound. "He's the one who insisted everybody ski every day, but he wasn't around to make that happen. That was me! It was *me* who took them up the slopes every morning and brought them back down safe and sound. Me who cooked their meals and washed out their sweaty socks while they sat about drinking their Penfolds red." He stopped, his cheeks suddenly matching the Penfolds. "Not that I'm complaining…"

"No, no," said Merry. "But you had every right. I mean, no one would blame you if you started to get grumpy, maybe even a little bitter. Maybe thought about popping a bit of that rodent poison in the old guy's stew."

Angus sat forward suddenly, eyes fiery, matching his skin tone.

Merry sat back. Shit. She'd gone too far!

"What are you on about?" he demanded. "What are you trying to say?"

"Nothing..."

He dropped his cup to the coffee table with a clunk. "You're not *accusing* me are you, Merry? You're not suggesting that I would do such a thing?"

Now Merry was the one blushing. "No... I mean, I'm just saying you would be a pretty good suspect."

"*Suspect?*" He stood up. "You serious?" He took a step towards her.

"Well, no, I was just—"

Shit, shit, shit!

"You were just accusing me of killing my old boss. That's a pretty big call coming from a little lady all alone out here in the mountains." He leaned forward then as she leaned back even further. "What are you really doing here, *Merry?*"

Merry gawked back at him as he placed his hands on both sides of her chair, effectively locking her into place.

"I mean, you *are* all alone, right?"

Then he smiled an ugly, garish grin as Merry felt her stomach drop into her feet.

~

Five hundred kilometres away, Kila crossed his boots together under the bar stool at Taboo.

"You look beat," said Trevor as he placed Kila's usual order on the bar coasters in front of him.

Kila stared at the drinks, unable to meet Trevor's eyes. Tried to pull himself together and calm his ragged breathing. This was no time for Mad Dog Morea. Not yet. He still had so much to uncover...

He picked up the lager and polished it off in two gulps, then he turned to the soft drink and sculled that down too. Finally he looked up at Trevor, whose eyes were now saucer wide.

"Jesus, man," Trevor said. "I've never seen you drink Chili's lemon squash before."

"Yeah, well, maybe it's time to swallow the truth, hey Trev? Stop ignoring what's been right beside me all this time."

The barman looked baffled and then concerned. "Everything cool?"

"No, it's not." Kila's voice was low and shaky. "And it never will be again. But I'm going to need another beer for this. Maybe three or four. If you're not too busy?"

"Of course not, mate. Anything for you. Do you want another lemon squash too?"

He was frowning towards Chili's empty glass.

Kila stared at it a long while, then back at Trevor and said, "Sure, why not? But maybe this time, put some vodka in it. Top shelf, thanks Trev. Like you always do."

The barman was as pale as the upturned beer coaster when he stepped away.

CHAPTER 33 ~
THE (FIRST) GRAND REVEAL, CONTINUED

For what felt like an eternity, Merry sat in the lodge armchair staring up at Angus, speechless, her heart stuck firmly in her throat, her stomach still in her shoes. She knew what she had to do, but for a terrifying moment she could not find her voice, let alone her breath.

She was frozen in place.

Then it came to her in a whoosh, and she gulped in a deep lungful of air as she said, "No, Angus. I am not alone." Another breath. "I... I've got Thelma with me."

He leaned back slightly then. "Who?"

She took another deep breath then yelled, "Thelma! *Thelma!* You can come in now!"

And with that, the front door to the ski lodge flew open and Angus reeled back and around just in time to see Frankie stride through.

"Hey, Louise!" she called out breezily, then stood to one side as Martin and Earle walked in behind her.

Angus had now paled. "W-what is this?" he said, staring between them.

"Oh, that's just an old joke between two road-trippers," said Frankie. "Don't mind us."

"What are you doing here?"

"We're here for the grand denouement of course. Can't let Merry have all the fun."

"The... the *what?*" He edged away from Merry as Martin slammed the front door behind them.

"That's just fancy speak for *the big reveal*," said Earle, his voice low and gravelly as he strode straight to Merry's side, leaned down in front of her and said, "You okay?"

She nodded, offering a weak smile. Tapped a hand to her chest to try to calm her pounding heartbeat.

Earle looked back at Angus. "I hope you weren't threatening Merry just now."

"What? No!" He continued to back away.

"Sounded very much like a threat to me. What do you folks think?"

Frankie and Martin were also at Merry's side, perched on each arm of her chair.

"Definitely a threat," said Martin.

"Oh yeah," said Frankie. "A pretty sinister one actually."

Angus had now backed himself up against the large glass window. "No, I was just hearing Merry out, telling her how crazy it all is. I mean, she was accusing me of something terrible! I... It's not true. I would never hurt George."

"Really?" said Frankie. "'Cause that's not how we see it."

"But..." He glanced furtively between the three newcomers. "Who *are* you people?"

"Oops, we did it again," said Frankie, an apologetic look at Earle. "Forgetting all the niceties. I'm Frankie Jo, this is Martin Chase and the old-timer is Earle Fitzgerald." Then she placed a hand at her lips as though whispering an aside as she added, "He looks like Santa, but I can assure you he's anything but."

Then she said, almost breezily, "We're the Sleuths of Last Resort, and we're here to prove that Verity Vine is innocent."

He blinked rapidly. "Okay." He gulped. "I mean... that's good." But he didn't look like it was good. He looked like he was going to pass out. "I... I hope you have some decent evidence and stuff like that."

"*Evidence?*" said Frankie, shifting her eyes from Angus to Earle. "He's like you, hey Earle? Wanting it all to be neatly proven."

"Good thing we can do that then," said Earle, his eyes firmly on Angus.

"Mind if I make some more tea first?" said Martin. "It was cold out there. You sure took your time, Merry."

She laughed then, a girlish, gigglish laugh, and Frankie knew it was all nerves, a little hysteria in the mix. Leaned across and gave her back a rub. "I was just relieved you wedged the door open with your handbag so we could listen in. I was so terrified you'd forget that step in all the excitement."

After they'd run around earlier that day, performing the final tasks, the four sleuths had piled into Merry's car and driven to the Snowy Mountains together, chewing Merry's lollies and plotting the whole denouement—and they had six long hours to plot it. It was Merry who guessed first that Angus had been Verity's mysterious houseguest—the red-bearded SUV driver with ski racks on the roof and the nickname Gus—and that the likeliest place to find him was hiding in plain sight at his former workplace, George's old ski lodge.

Verity told them he had a new job at Jindabyne, but Merry wasn't so sure.

What she did know, what Verity had recently confirmed, was that the new owners of the lodge were not moving in until after renovations, and those weren't happening for several months. It was unlikely the locks had been changed because there was nothing worth stealing inside and they were planning on ripping half the front wall out anyway.

It had been one of the many questions Earle had asked Verity via her surly solicitor.

Of course the sleuths took a gamble, driving all the way to Jindabyne, but if Merry was wrong about where Angus was hiding, chances were they would still find him somewhere in the small township—at the aforementioned new job, a friend's house perhaps?

But they struck gold at their first stop. It was only faint, but they could see a light coming from inside the lodge, and so they had parked up the road and then traipsed down the long driveway on foot. Merry was all prepared to knock on the front door if she had to, but it was already unlocked, and so she had left it slightly ajar so the others could loiter close by and eavesdrop.

They didn't want to confront him as a group, suspected they'd get nowhere and he'd clamp right up. But he already knew Merry, was comfortable with Merry, and if he thought she was alone, vulnerable, he might be more likely to confess to something. It had been another gamble, a more dangerous one this time and one that Earle had not wanted Merry to take. But six hours is a long time cooped up in a vehicle, and by the time they got to Jindabyne, the others had convinced him otherwise.

And so Merry had gone in alone, and it had all gone to plan. Except the confession part. Merry still hadn't got to that, but Earle didn't care. He was relieved they were doing this together. They always worked better as a team.

Now he just had to get the show back on track.

So, once they all had hearty cups of tea in hand, Earle nodded at Angus, who was still wedged up against the window, and said, "You might want to take a seat for this part."

The lodge manager didn't have to be asked twice. He dropped back into his armchair and glanced between them, eyes furtive, cheeks back to crimson red.

"Now, where were we again?" Earle asked, joining Frankie and Martin on an enormous old couch.

"I think Angus here was demanding some evidence," said Frankie, blowing on her tea.

"Ah yes, and fair enough too," said Earle. "Let's start with Sir George's death, shall we? Because that's the first murder we believe you committed, Angus. The one you nearly got away with."

"I had nothing—"

"Let... me... finish," said Earle, his voice slow, deep, authoritative, making the other man clamp his lips shut. "This is going to go a lot more smoothly, buddy, if you let me finish at least one sentence before you jump in, okay?"

Angus's eyes were gleaming now, with fear and fury. He looked like a trapped rat. But he managed to nod somehow.

Earle cleared his throat and continued. "So, Sir George. He was elderly, sickly, so when he dropped dead one night, nobody thought twice about it. Except a young assistant called Shannon Smith, a woman nobody took very seriously—except Detective Inspector Morgan that is."

Earle thought now of how at least Morgan's hunch was half correct; that was something he could take to his retirement. He said, "Morgan got the tip-off that George was poisoned, learned it was via his meals. The obvious suspect, the one who prepared his meals, was Verity. Ergo she must have done it."

Angus was now madly nodding, and when Earle began to sip his tea he said, "Exactly! I... I couldn't have done it! I never went to Seagrave. I didn't have the codes."

"Ah, yes, but you didn't need them, Angus," said Earle. "Because that was our first big mistake. We all assumed that the stew was cooked at Seagrave."

Angus frowned. His jaw tightened as Earle turned to Merry.

"You up for this bit, Mez? This was your discovery. You should be the one to explain it."

Merry swallowed hard and nodded. She felt stronger now with the supersleuths around her. Turned her eyes to Angus.

"Earle's right," she said, "you didn't need access to Seagrave to poison the stew. You just needed access to the stew, and that's where we've all been so misguided, assuming that the stew was cooked at Seagrave. I worked it out while I was cooking lasagne to take to my boyfriend's place. You see, most people prepare meals in their own kitchens before they take them elsewhere, especially when the meal is one that takes ages to cook, such as lasagne."

"Or Irish stew," said Martin, and she smiled back at him.

"Exactly! That really is something we should have double-checked with Verity but didn't think to, and she never mentioned it because, frankly, the poor woman has not been herself—stressed to her eyeballs by the charges." A glower at Angus. "But I started to wonder—what if she prepared the stew at her *own home*, not at *Seagrave* as we all assumed? That would change the case considerably!"

"Especially if she lived with someone else," said Frankie. "Someone who could tamper with it while it was stewing."

Angus wasn't stupid. He was fired up again. "I never saw Verity make so much as a toasted sandwich at her place. You've got that wrong. She cooked it at Seagrave."

"That's odd," said Merry, "because I was at Seagrave the night Shannon was killed. I happened to go into the kitchen that night, and there were no stew ingredients to be seen. Fridge was empty, so too the pantry. Not a single shrivelled-up onion, no potatoes or half-used tomato paste, barely any salt and pepper."

"Verity must have chucked them after he died."

"You could be right, Angus. But here's the interesting thing—I did see all those items in the kitchen at *Verity's* house earlier today. Her kitchen was a smorgasbord of stew ingredients. But, any case, Earle was able to check with Verity's lawyer, and she's confirmed what Verity should have clarified right from the start—she made the blasted stew at *her house*, not at Seagrave. Like I said, she's been in a muddle, so we have to forgive her for not steering us straight, there."

She took a breath and asked, "Was that when you added the poison, Angus? Back in her kitchen while she was cooking?"

"I don't know what you mean."

Merry glanced at Earle. He urged her onwards with one of his warm, fuzzy smiles.

She took another breath and said, "It won't be hard to check all this with Verity. You must have seen her cooking those stews."

"Sure, maybe I did. But I didn't add poison to them. That's absurd. Ask her *that!* Did she ever see me even touch one?"

"That must have annoyed you though," Merry continued. "The way she came home late and cooked all night for Sir George."

He stared at her blankly, not taking the bait.

"I mean, did she ever cook *you* any?" Merry persisted. "Or did it all go to a rich old man who clearly didn't deserve it?"

"He barely even ate them!" he spat back now, bait in his mouth. "I told her she was wasting her time. With the stews, with all of it! I saw how hard she worked and realised she would always be beholden to that bastard. She wouldn't agree with me, said he was a good boss. She was as delusional as I was. But my blinkers were finally off. I knew he'd toss her aside as quickly as he'd tossed me, once he'd used her up. So I..."

He stopped short, clamped his lips shut.

"So you grabbed a bit of rat poison you have around here for your little rodent problem, yes?" said Merry. "And you started adding some to the stew."

"Nope, no way."

"No one would blame you, Angus, at least for being disgruntled. George did treat you like a common servant. Then selling this lovely lodge with barely a thank-you—"

"A thank-you? Huh!" he said. "Wouldn't even give me a bloody reference. Said I'd had a good ride for decades, like I'd been sitting on my arse the whole time, sipping wine with them! I begged George when he kicked me out, so did Verity. All I wanted was a decent reference, that's all I asked for. Just wanted him to put in a good word with the new owners. But he refused! Blamed me for what happened to his family. Can you believe it? You... you know, Merry! You came here that time. You tried to ask me questions! I wouldn't tell you anything!"

"I know," Merry agreed. "You were very loyal." *Too loyal, she thought, but let it go.*

He'd already read her mind. "It wasn't *my* fault! That was part of the job. I'd signed a nondisclosure agreement. Was *obliged* to keep the family's secrets. But he blamed me, George. Said if I had spoken up sooner about Clem, about the spying in the bathroom, then none of it would have happened. Like it was *my* fault that *his* daughter went berserk! But I only stayed quiet for him, don't you see? I did it for George's reputation, and that's how he treated me?"

"So you got your revenge," she said softly. "You poisoned his stew."

He went to speak, then somehow stopped himself. Began to chuckle. It was ugly. "Good try, woman, but I'm not admitting to that. You can get rat poison from anywhere. This is all circumstantial. I'm still not hearing any evidence."

Frankie sat forward now and tutt-tutted. "There's that pesky word again—evidence." She smiled at Merry and then glanced back at Earle. "Shall we move on to Shannon's murder? Maybe we'll fare better there, what do you think?"

Earle nodded, taking over from Merry. Eyes firmly on Angus. "Actually, we probably should have started with Shannon's murder because that's where I think you really slipped up. You might've got away with poisoning George if you hadn't panicked. Because we think you did panic, Angus, when Shannon came to your door that night. Or Verity's door we should say, because you were just a guest, right? Just staying until you could sort your life out. Verity told us as much, and well, we didn't connect the dots."

Earle flashed a look at Merry. "Such a pity you weren't with us when we first met 'Gus', hey? Might have wrapped this all up long before Shannon was murdered. But we didn't." A frown now, eyes back on Angus. "More's the pity."

"But I—"

"What did I tell you about interrupting?" Earle said, voice still eerily calm. "Turns out Charlie was telling the truth for once. Shannon did show up at Verity's house at around eight thirty that night, but that's also the time that Verity happened to be having a nice, long shower. Twenty minutes long, in fact, as she admitted to her solicitor. What she didn't tell her but what she'd already told Merry was that she always took a long shower after meeting with her lawyers, said the whole business left her feeling grubby."

He waved a hand in the air. "That's neither here nor there. The fact remains, Verity was otherwise occupied when Shannon showed up at her door. We've seen the house for ourselves. The doorbell doesn't work, so Shannon had to knock. The bathroom is way up the back of the property, in a renovated outhouse, so chances are Verity did not hear Shannon knock. But we think you did, Angus."

The lodge manager was shaking his head as though ready for this. Earle had paused, so he quickly said, "I'd left by then. Just ask Verity. We said our goodbyes just after she got back from her meeting. She waved me off at the door; saw me drive away. Then I came straight here."

Earle shrugged. "It's a good story, but it's not what we think happened. We think you were still home when Verity was in the shower. Perhaps you'd forgotten something and had returned? We think you opened the door when Shannon knocked, but what happened next we can only guess. Did Shannon realise you'd been staying with Verity all along and piece it all together like Merry did? Did she realise that *you* could have been involved? Or were you just worried she would implicate you inadvertently down the track? In any case, you jumped in your SUV and you followed her to Seagrave to shut her up."

"Rubbish," he said, shaking his head.

Martin stood up then and reached for something deep in his jeans pocket. They were good at sharing denouements, and he had a vital piece of the evidence. He held up the thumb drive.

"Got this from the girls' school down the road from Seagrave. Looks like they've come through again. Your white Nissan Patrol slid past their cameras just before nine that night. It was just behind Shannon's small hatchback."

"It's a common vehicle," he muttered.

"You're right. Except this one has ski racks on the top, just like yours. Not so common. Either way, it's all part of the circumstantial evidence we're building up. We think you followed fast on Shannon's heels. When she unlocked Seagrave's front gate, you could easily have slipped your SUV in behind her before it closed again. Then tracked her down to the pool, smacked her over the head when she wasn't looking."

"Rubbish, rubbish, rubbish," he said again. "I'm hearing lots of— what did you call it? *Circumstantial evidence?* I'm still not seeing any actual proof."

"How about a smoking gun then?" said Martin, stepping towards the wood-fire burner. "Or better yet, a bloody axe?"

Then he pointed towards the weapon that was propped up against some logs.

"Careful," said Earle as Angus suddenly paled.

"Don't worry," said Martin. "I won't touch it. But the police will, followed by forensics. You see, they say Shannon was killed by something heavy and sharp. A machete, they said, maybe an axe." He pointed again. "Did you use this axe, Angus? Or is it the one I saw earlier in the back of your vehicle?"

Angus was also on his feet now, his eyes ablaze. "This is rubbish! If there's blood on that axe, you can't prove it was me. Someone planted it there to make it look like me."

"No, Angus," said Martin, standing his ground. "The only one doing the planting around here is you."

"Rubb—"

"*Sit down!*" Earle roared now, his patience over.

And Angus gulped back at him before slowly dropping into his seat. Then Earle looked back at the sleuths, and Merry held a hand up. He gave her the nod.

She was feeling angry, Merry, angrier than she thought possible. Shannon's blood-soaked skull kept flashing before her eyes. The deep purple gash messing up her beautiful thick hair. Her life taken with one simple smash.

"You killed that poor child," she said, her voice quivering. "She was barely a woman, Shannon. So much life ahead of her. And her only fault was her loyalty to Sir George."

"Then she deserved it too!" he roared back, making her gasp and shake her head.

Angus didn't seem to care what he was saying. Not anymore. "None of them could see the writing on the wall, even after what had happened to me," he said. "Like they were immune. They'd all seen how poorly he'd treated me—selling the lodge without a second thought—and yet they kept working for him! Cooking for him! Cleaning and typing and fussing over him, like he was King bloody George! Then that silly girl goes and tells the police about the poison! Why? Why did she do that? George was already dead! He couldn't reward her anyway."

"Maybe she did it because it was the right thing to do," said Merry softly.

"More fool her then," he spat back before exhaling loudly and staring out the window, like he was lost in thought.

The sleuths all swapped looks that weren't quite victorious. Not yet. Earle gave a subtle shake of his head, urging them to stay quiet.

Eventually, after many minutes, Angus spoke again. He was calmer, but his anger was still palpable. "She did come to Verity's house that night, that stupid girl. And yes, I hadn't quite left. My load wasn't secure. I'd stopped down the street a bit to fix it, and then I'd seen her drive up. Knocking on Verity's door. Verity didn't answer, so I went to see what she wanted. She recognised me. I don't know how. I knew of her, but we'd never met. She looked weird when she realised who I was, and I knew she was putting it all together. I think maybe she thought Verity and I were in it together. I don't know. But she looked real nervous suddenly and said she needed to go, and that made *me* real nervous, see? Knew I didn't have any choice then. I had to follow. She drove to Seagrave. I switched off my car lights and followed her in… You know the rest."

He shrugged at his own reflection, like it wasn't important. Said nothing more but Merry was ropable. Killing an old and ailing man was one thing, a terrible thing, but killing a young, vibrant woman? On a *whim*? For all he knew Shannon hadn't suspected a thing! Perhaps he was just being neurotic.

It made her feel so angry and so, so sad.

She glanced at Earle again, and he nodded now, so she tried to calm herself as she said, "I get that you needed to silence Shannon," even though she didn't, not at all. "What I don't get, Angus, is why you had to plant it all on Verity. I thought she was your *friend*."

"She is my friend!" he bellowed, turning back to face them. "At least... she was. Once."

"You were jealous of her, weren't you?" said Frankie, taking over now. "Jealous of her massive inheritance, of how *her* loyalty got rewarded by Sir George, but *yours* did not. Perhaps, in the end, you thought she had it coming."

"No, it was George I hated. He's the only one..." His voice croaked as he slumped back into his seat. "I was just doing her a favour at first. That's all I was doing. Saw her cooking those stupid stews. Every week, another bloody stew! She never even kept any for herself, or *me*! Insisted His Royal Highness get the lot while she ate crappy takeaway. I... I always took care of the vermin around here. I just thought I'd add a little to the mix to kick the old bastard along. I wanted to free Verity. That's all I was doing. I never imagined she'd be accused..."

"Of course she was going to be accused!" said Frankie. "It was *her* stew."

"But he was dying anyway. She told me that. So I just brought it all forward."

"Why'd you wheel him down to the ballroom then?" asked Merry. "What was that about?"

He smiled suddenly. It looked strange under the circumstances. He said, "I didn't! That was all him. He must've known what was coming. Must've sensed it. Ha! It was like poetry, wasn't it? So poignant. So perfect." His smile deflated. "It all would have stayed perfect if it wasn't for that stupid, bloody girl..."

He looked up at them all, and his eyes were now red and frantic. "I wouldn't have hurt her. Shannon. And I would have got away with it. If only she'd shut her mouth, if only she hadn't been so damn..."

"Loyal?" said Merry sadly, finishing the sentence for him.

It took a good hour for Earle to get through to Morgan back in Sydney and explain where they were and what they'd just heard and another ten minutes of Morgan barking down the phone, bellowing obscenities, before agreeing to rally the local police at Jindabyne.

They'd arrived relatively slowly—pulled from their beds no doubt—and so the team had secured Angus in a locked bedroom until they'd come to officially arrest him and haul him away, both his axes also bagged and secured as evidence.

It was almost midnight by then, and all they could find in the kitchen was sliced bread and cheese, so Earle had whipped up cheese toasties and Martin had made another pot of tea, and then they'd all collapsed into the various rooms—Merry and Frankie taking the two double bedrooms, the two men sharing a bunk in what was once the grandkids' quarters. Back when the lodge was a place of laughter and happiness.

Before one man's wickedness and another's resentment put an end to all of that.

CHAPTER 34 ~

THE (SECOND) GRAND REVEAL

Kila tried to enjoy his beer—his seventh lager for the night—but it tasted as bitter as he felt and he couldn't keep his eyes off Trevor, whose own eyes kept flitting between Kila and his customers, worriedly. It was getting late, and Trevor told them this.

"Last drinks!" he called out before his eyes turned back to Kila.

"I'm gonna have to boot you out soon too, mate," he said, but the PI was shaking his head.

"No, Trev, I'm not going anywhere. Not tonight and neither are you. But I'm not sure I can wait much longer, so you'd better clear them out now. And Antoine. Before it all gets ugly."

"Ugly?" Trevor half laughed, but Kila did not smile back, so he gave the assistant bartender an early mark, then told the small group still lingering by the bar that their time was up.

"Everybody out, I'm closing shop."

"What? No! You said last drinks," grumbled one.

"I lied. Sorry, let's go."

There was more grumbling, some cursing, but they all did as they were asked, and then it was just Trevor and Kila, alone at Taboo.

Trevor avoided Kila for some minutes, pretending to clear glasses and wipe the surrounding tables, but Kila knew what he was doing. Didn't mind. He needed the time, too, to calm his breathing.

To quell his fury.

Eventually, finally, he said, "Okay, Trevor, time to talk."

Trevor stopped mid-wipe, closed his eyes briefly, then opened them and turned them to Kila. He attempted a smile. It was very lopsided. "What's going on, mate? What is it with you tonight?"

"Got some more questions. If you don't mind."

"What about?"

236

Kila stared hard at him. "I think you know what this is about." When Trevor didn't say anything, he said, "Where were you that night again? Tell me one more time."

Trevor didn't need to ask what night. They both knew he was talking about the night Chili was murdered.

"Told you before, many times," said Trevor, acting annoyed although his voice was wobbly as he marched back towards the bar. "I was with my girlfriend. We were up the coast. I feel so bad—"

"Yeah, yeah, yada yada. What was her name again? This *girlfriend* of yours?"

"Why are you asking—"

"Just answer the bloody question."

Trevor turned. "Okay, take a chill pill. Jesus, you're in a mood tonight. Um. Geraldine. Her name was Geraldine."

"Gerry," Kila said, and Trevor frowned.

He secured the latch door to the bar and stood behind the beer taps. "I called her Geraldine."

"Yeah, but her flatmate didn't."

"What?"

Kila crossed his arms and leaned back on his stool. "See, it's another one of those weird coincidences around this case. I tracked down Lars, did I tell you that?"

Trevor shook his head, was beginning to pale again.

"Wasn't easy." Kila gave him a loaded look. "But I did find him. Had a nice long chat. He says he had nothing to do with my sister's death. Or Bertha for that matter."

"Well, he would say that, wouldn't he?"

"That is true, Trev. Some arseholes will lie through their teeth, even to their best mates." He stared hard again. "Turns out this arsehole happens to have a flatmate called Gerry. They lived together back then."

"Really? I don't remember that."

"Yeah, but he does, and he reckons Gerry was with *him* the entire night—first here, keeping him company, then back at their share house. Turns out she was *his* alibi."

Trevor crossed his own arms over his chest. "He's lying, I'd say."

"Sure, sure," said Kila. "Lars had to be lying, that was the only thing that made sense. I wanted to give you the benefit of the doubt. Not him."

"That's what mates are for." The words were barely audible.

"Exactly. But then I thought I'd better do what Frankie always nags me to do—double-check the facts, go straight to the source." Kila smiled. "I dropped in on Gerry this morning. I can see why you wanted to go out with her. She's a feisty one, but I liked her."

Trevor's cheeks were back to coaster pale.

Kila said, "She remembers you, Trev. Problem is, she doesn't remember ever going out with you as such. Certainly doesn't remember any dirty holiday away."

"Must be a different Geraldine then."

"Must be, right? But then I realised she was wearing a nurse's uniform. So I asked her what type of nursing she did, and you wouldn't believe it! She works in aged care, Trevor." Then, in case he wasn't following, Kila added, "There she was, Geraldine the geriatric nurse—in the flesh!"

Trevor was shaking his head, not quite meeting Kila's eyes.

Kila said, "We had a good chat, Geraldine and I. She tells me you *tried* to go out with her—many times, in fact. Says the only reason she was here at Taboo that night, hanging with Lars, was because you weren't rostered on."

"I was away."

"Not with Geraldine you weren't. Sorry, mate, but how many geriatric nurses called Geraldine hung around here in those days? Can't be more than one." When Trevor didn't answer, Kila said, "Still, I gave you the benefit of the doubt. Had to be some confusion. Like I said, maybe it was just another of those strange coincidences that Earle doesn't like."

Trevor's chin had jutted out. "Yep, that's what it was. Is. Must be a whole different Gerry. I'm telling you, mine went out west, ages ago. I can give you her mobile num—"

"If it's anything like the numbers you gave me for Lars and Kiara, don't fucking bother."

Trevor blinked, looked away.

"Another thing Gerry told me, Trev. Got me a bit hot under the collar." The eyes slithered back. "She said it wasn't Lars who was the sleazy barman back then. Reckons it was you."

"What?" Trevor stepped back, slamming into the enormous glass fridge behind him. "Bullshit, nah. You've seen me. I'm not a sleaze."

"Not anymore, you're not. At least not around me. You wouldn't dare. But she reckons you were back then. And I reckon you were the sleazy barman who scared Bertha and her friends away as well. That's why they stopped coming here, because you kept hitting on them."

"In their dreams, mate. They're all lying. They're all liars."

"Right. What about Kash then? The barman at the Bondi brewery. Is he a liar too?"

Trevor looked confused for a moment. "Who?" Then it must have hit him because he reached a hand to one cheek, like he'd just been smacked.

Kila was shaking his head, his throat constricting, his heart heavy. "He saw you, Trevor. He identified you."

"No."

"Yes. You were the old friend buying Bertha shots of vodka at a bar in Bondi the night she died."

"Nope, no, I haven't been to Bondi in ages, don't know what you're talking about."

"You got her drunk and then waited until she staggered out of that pub. You followed her to the beach, and you drowned her."

"What? Bullshit! This is crazy talk. You know me, Kila! You know I wouldn't—"

"Did she see you that September night? Bertha? Did she see you with Chili, after Dragon dropped her off? Or were you just worried she did? Worried that's what she told Weaver?"

"Don't know what you're talking about."

"*I'm talking about the night my sister was murdered!*" Kila roared now, making Trevor jump. Kila kicked his stool back and it smashed loudly across the wooden floor. "I want to know why you lied to me about that night! And I want to know what else you've been lying about!"

Trevor flattened himself against the glass doors, like he was hoping they might open and swallow him whole.

"Kila, please," he said, head madly shaking. "Please, it's Lars who is lying, and Gerry and Weaver and... and Dragon! He's been lying from the start! You're going to believe *them*—people you don't even know! One a blackmailer! One a rapist! You're going to believe them over your best mate? Your buddy?"

239

Kila shook his head at Trevor, quivering now against the fridge, and felt his heart go into free fall. He placed his hands upon the bar to steady himself. He whispered, "Just tell me it was an accident. Please, Trevor. Just tell me you were walking her home and she fell and hit her head. Tell me anything but what's going through my brain right about now."

"Oh, Kila... I... I..."

"*Tell me!*" Kila roared again, and Trevor suddenly roared back:

"I didn't mean to hurt her!"

Then he gasped as the truth hit Kila smack between the eyes. Watched as Kila slumped across the bar, head down, hands over his ears like he didn't really want to hear.

Trevor stepped forward, reached out a palm, pulled it back. "You have to remember, Kila..." Trevor's voice was croaky; tears were now streaming down his cheeks. "I... I was *helping* her. I was only trying to *help*."

Kila moaned beneath his hands, his eyes closed, his tears also flowing. "Just... tell... me."

Trevor sniffed, nodded, looked across at the front door, which was still ajar, pedestrians strolling by happily, oblivious to the tempest brewing inside.

"I was just passing," Trevor said. "That's all I was doing. I had a few days off and I was bored. It was pouring and I thought I'd drop in for a freebie. Then I saw her. Chili."

Another moan from Kila, but he didn't look up and so Trevor forged on. "She was standing out on the street, banging on the door. I... I stopped. I asked if she was okay. She was distraught, man, she was screaming and crying and trying to get into Taboo, but the bar was locked. They must've closed early. So I told her this, but she wasn't hearing sense. She was looking for you, desperate for you. But you weren't answering your phone, remember?"

His tone was accusatory, and again Kila moaned, now sounding like a wounded animal.

Again, Trevor rattled on: "I couldn't calm her, man, she was hysterical. So I made her come into the bar. I had the keys, yeah? I got her to sit down, and I made her a strong drink—just to stop her from shaking—that's all I was doing. But it seemed to knock her out. Like straight away she just flopped. I... Well, I took her into the back, just to put her on the staff couch, right? But she woke up, see?

I was taking off her shoes, making her comfortable, but she got the wrong idea, man! She totally flipped! Turned hysterical again. Started accusing *me* of hurting her! Like I was Dragon! She was delirious... confused. Started looking for her phone, screaming that she was going to tell you and you were going to kill me, and I was just trying to shut her up. That's all. Just needed her to stop screaming..."

"So you killed her?" This was Kila, barely audible now.

"*No*! I mean, I didn't *mean to*! I... I just had one hand over her mouth, just trying to make her shoosh but then... but then..." He gulped, slid down the fridge door onto the floor. "It's like in one split second all the life went out of her. I thought at first she was sleeping again but then... Then I could see she was gone."

Kila looked down at him through his fingers. Blinked through wet eyes. "Why didn't you call for help? Dial triple zero? Why didn't you call *me*!"

"It was too late! She was gone. And... like she said, if you found out, you would have killed me."

Kila stood straight, his face ashen. "So you just took her and dumped her like a piece of garbage in an *alleyway*?"

"No, it wasn't like that! I put her down gently. I put the blanket on her, I..."

Kila swiped at his tears. Swiped again. "You left her there, then lied to me all these years; acted like nothing had happened."

"No, that's bullshit too! Why do you think I've been chained to this dump all this time? I've been here, helping you! Helping you get through, helping you rescue girls like Chili. I've been making up for it, see?"

"Nothing makes up for that! Nothing!"

"You think I like being here, Kila?" Trevor was back on his feet again. "You think I want to stay at this shithole? I could've left years ago, but I stayed for you, holding your hand as you sit here sobbing every night over Chili, like she was a virgin fucking princess."

Kila stepped back, emitted a low growl, but Trevor didn't seem to notice.

"She wasn't perfect, Kila. I'm sorry, but it has to be said. She was a lot like Geraldine and Bertha and all the rest of them. All the ones you think are worth saving. They act like they're special, like they're better than me—"

"They are better than you!" cried Kila, but still Trevor did not hear the tension, kept rambling on, like he'd had this in his head for years and needed to spit it out.

"You ever stop to wonder, mate? If Chili had not been on Tinder?" His eyes were now boring into Kila's. "I mean, it might help you work through it, right? Chili wasn't perfect. I'm sorry but she wasn't! She was the one trawling for blokes! You can't ignore that! *She* went looking for Dragon. *She* has to take some of the blame for what happened that—"

But he never got to finish that sentence because Kila was now launching himself across the bar and on to Trevor. Was now pulling him up from the ground where he'd fallen, was now hammering his fist into his face.

Over and over and over again.

He was doing it for Chili and he was doing it for Bertha, and he was doing it for all the years this turd stood across from him and served him lie upon lie with every lemon squash and lager, never once admitting that he was the last person to give Chili her favourite drink. He was the one who had laced it with vodka.

And he was the *only* one to blame for the fact that Chili was now *dead, dead, dead…*

CHAPTER 35 ~
TYING UP LOOSE ENDS

Eddie Thomas placed a fresh bouquet of frangipanis in front of Bertha's gravestone, and Kila watched from a distance, giving him a moment before he approached.

The young man heard him though and turned abruptly, fiercely, his hands two fists at his sides, before his expression lightened and the fists relaxed. "Hey."

"Hey," Kila replied. "How're you holding up?"

Because the police had already spoken to him about Bertha, and he knew the truth now. But Kila was not sure learning your sister was murdered by a friendly barman was any better than thinking she had accidentally drowned.

It had taken four passers-by to pull Kila from Trevor the night he confessed to killing Chili. Then forty-eight hours in a police cell before the Sleuths of Last Resort had posted his bail.

It was a group effort, really.

Earle first heard about Kila's arrest, via Odetta, when they were driving back from Jindabyne the morning after their own shocking revelations. Merry had then rung Earle's old lawyer friend to represent him at the bail hearing that Monday, and Martin had organised quick cash for his bail.

But it was Frankie who had collected him and driven him home, asking him the same question he'd asked Bertha's brother just now.

"How are you holding up?"

Because *she* was not sure that learning your sister was murdered by your best mate was any better than thinking she was murdered by a fire-breathing dragon.

"Earle says they'll throw the book at Trevor," Frankie told Kila when he didn't reply. "Not just for your sister. Even if he convinces them it was an accident, what he did to Bertha was premeditated murder. You were right. He plied her with spirits, then waited for her to leave the pub alone. Got lucky when she went swimming. Joined her and that's as far as his confessions go. Insists he left her swimming alone. She drowned herself."

"Bullshit," he'd said. "He's just scared to face Bertha's brother. Eddie's anger is still fresh. Rawer than mine."

She nodded, glancing down at his bandaged fists as she drove. "Trevor's still under police guard in hospital, you know? You really worked him over."

"You feel sorry for him?"

"God no. But I do for Bertha. And Chili."

He nodded, sniffed, looked away. "Chili would have gone into Taboo with Trevor, thinking I was in there, thinking she was *safe*." He sniffed again, looked out the window, wiped away a tear. "Instead, he spiked her drink with vodka and took advantage. I don't believe for a second it was all innocent. Or an accident of any kind. I think he tried his luck. He was the sleazy barman."

He was also the reason Phillip Weaver was dead.

Detective Odetta Soderbergh was now reviewing the Weaver case, Frankie told Kila. She was running cold cases after all. "They'll have to release JayJay, once she gets her facts lined up."

But Kila didn't need Odetta's facts. He already had a hunch he knew how it all went down.

He suspected Weaver went to Taboo and began asking dangerous questions. Thanks to Dragon, he knew the date Chili was killed but not the culprit. Thought there was an easy buck in it, so he started looking around for customers who were at Taboo back then. That's when he ran into Bertha at a hen's party. She must have given him the names of past patrons and barmen. He must have tracked down Gerry and then put it all together as Kila had.

Trevor was the sleazy barman.

Trevor was the likely suspect.

Weaver knew it was Trevor, and Trevor knew he knew it. Must have paid him $5,000 to shut up. Then promised more but double-crossed him instead. Lured him to a dark alley in neighbouring Kings Cross and stabbed him to death.

Then Trevor got lucky all over again when the police nabbed the most likely suspect—a lowlife called JayJay, who was holding Weaver's money.

But Trevor wasn't taking anything for granted, not this time. He'd seen Bertha talking to Weaver that night at the bachelorette party. Thought she was the one who'd given him up—and yet Trevor's name was never written into Weaver's little blue book.

She might not have even mentioned him.

Frankie had her own ideas about that. She suspected Bertha did finger Trevor, just not inside the pub with Trevor watching. Frankie remembered CCTV footage the police had released back when she was working the Weaver story for the *Herald*. One of Weaver's last sightings was on a Kings Cross street, deep in conversation with a short woman with black curls and a faux-fur winter jacket. Frankie suspected that was Bertha and perhaps Trevor did too.

Perhaps he'd been following them, or perhaps he'd seen the footage that was flashed across every news bulletin that night.

Either way, he knew he had some unfinished business.

So he dropped in on Bertha at her new Bondi hang, pretending to bump into her, then got her nicely drunk before making a big show of leaving—waving to the barman, securing his alibi. An hour later, he followed Bertha from the pub, got lucky again when she went for a swim, was easy to drown with such a high blood-alcohol level.

Meantime JayJay got charged with Weaver's murder and nobody cared whether he really did it, because he was as big a scumbag as the victim, his best friend. No one, that is, except Tiffany Weaver who knew what true mateship was and didn't believe any of it.

Trevor must have been worried when first Frankie and then Kila started poking holes in the investigation. He must have worked hard to steer Kila in the wrong direction—first pretending not to remember Weaver or Lars. Then feeding Kila a fake mobile number when he tried to call Lars, another fake number for Kiara.

Hoping that would be the end of it.

But he didn't factor in Kila's determination or his sleuthing skills. Didn't realise Kila would hunt down Lars. Then make his way to Geraldine the geriatric nurse—Trevor's alibi for Chili's murder. An alibi as fake as the tears he'd shed with Kila the days and weeks and months after they'd found Chili's broken body.

Trevor must've plucked Gerry's name out of the air the day the police asked for his alibi, and they never stopped to check with her because, well, they didn't have to. They had the perfect suspect, a monster called Dragon Malone.

Turns out he wasn't quite as monstrous as they thought.
Turns out the monster was pouring drinks at a bar called Taboo.
Turns out he was Kila's best friend.

Kila didn't say any of this to Eddie Thomas now as he hovered over Bertha's grave. It was too convoluted, too ugly. Too hard to articulate.

So, instead, he just offered his condolences and added, "I wish I could have given you better news."

"There was never any good news," said Eddie. "Not with Bertha. Like I said to you before, she was a free spirit. Never wanted to take life seriously. And I guess life repaid the favour."

Kila nodded at that but felt a sudden stab of fury. Because Chili *did* take her life seriously, and life had chewed her up and spat her out anyway.

These women should have been allowed to live their lives exactly as they pleased.

Life could take a flying bloody leap…

He cleared the lump in his throat, nodded again, then left Eddie sobbing softly over his sister's grave. And he tried to remember what Frankie had told him, her perfect brow furrowed, her almond eyes boring into his own: "Now you know the truth about Chili, it's time to let it go."

There was just one problem with that. By proving Trevor was a killer, Kila had now proven that Dragon was not. The bastard was probably organising an appeal of his murder conviction that very minute.

By locking away one monster, he'd just released another.

Kila's days of vigilantism were far from over…

~

Earle stood at the door to the palliative care ward, watching quietly.

A man who looked decades older than his sixty-nine years lay sleeping in one bed, tucked up tightly under crisp clean sheets, lost to the world but no longer lost to his daughter.

Fiona was seated on a chair beside him, holding his hand awkwardly. Probably relieved he was no longer cognisant. Probably whispering things to him anyway, all the things she wished he'd stuck around to find out—her brilliant career and beautiful partner and the adorable child they shared together.

Because they were back together, that much Earle knew.

His eyes slid across to his daughter, who was seated by the window, also watching. Tess looked over at him and smiled.

And once again he knew it had all been worth it, and he felt tremendous pity for this man who had missed so much. Earle knew it would soon be over for Fiona's father, but not for Fiona and Tess and young Saffie, fast asleep in the pram between them.

They would forge new memories together, these three, and Earle would be a part of it. A willing and active part.

He offered one more smile, then he closed the door gently behind them.

~

Merry pushed her dirty plate away and nodded back at the half-demolished pan of lasagne.

"One more slice?"

Archie thought about it for all of half a second, then nodded gleefully as she loaded his plate up for the third time.

"You're such a *pig*," said Lola, but there was no grunt in it.

"He's a growing lad," said Merry. "Leave him alone."

Except she wasn't going to, not anymore. Not for a long time to come.

Merry had finally realised on that long drive back from Jindabyne—with help from a wise elder—what it was that was eating at her youngest, causing him to implode.

Archie was hungry! Starving, in fact, for his mother and her cooking, and the life they used to share.

"Parents often step back when kids become adolescents," Earle had told her. "You ask me, that's a big mistake. Fourteen-year-olds need as much love and attention as four-year-olds, maybe even more."

And yet Merry had given Archie so little of both lately.

She'd been so keen to move on with her own life she'd forgotten all about the life she was leaving behind. Had been so determined to give herself permission to let go—of her ex-husband and this house and her eldest son who had left home and broken her heart in the process—and all the while Archie felt like she was letting *him* go.

And who could blame him? They'd barely spent an hour together since she'd met the sleuths, and then Dougie, since she'd started the agency and then been working to save Verity. She hadn't even asked Archie for help with that case, just put him off with excuses and reheated leftovers, when all he wanted—all he really needed— was some quality face-to-face time with his mother.

That, and some good old-fashioned home cooking.

And she'd told Dougie all of this only that morning when he'd popped around with a bouquet of flowers and a tiny velvet box and asked if she would marry him.

"I know it's fast," he said, his voice beautifully jittery! "I know we haven't been together long, but I also know that I love you, Merry. I want you and the kids to move in with me above the book shop. Or we can move in here. Whatever suits!"

She'd already suspected this was on the cards; Merry was a super sleuth after all. So she took a deep breath, then his hands in hers, and said, "I love you too, Dougie, but I can't marry you, and we can't move in together. Not yet. Right now, Archie has to be my focus."

The poor man's face had gone from dimpled hope to flat dejection with just a few words, and she went to apologise when she stopped herself.

"I've spent my whole adult life apologising for my choices," she told him gently, "but I won't apologise for choosing to put Archie first. The others got to come first, and now it's his turn."

"Of course," he said quickly. "I shouldn't have been so gung-ho—"

"I *love* that you're gung-ho! And I love the idea of living with you, marrying you, just not yet. But maybe in a few years, if you'll still have me."

Dougie whipped off his glasses and pulled her into a hug and declared that he'd wait as long as she needed. "Just don't give up on us," he added.

"Not a chance," she'd replied.

"Can we see the new Marvel movie this weekend?" asked Archie, breaking through her thoughts now, his mouth bulging with pasta.

Merry nodded but Lola looked disgusted.

"You're gross! Don't talk with your mouth full! Urgh!"

"What… like this…," he replied, spluttering food everywhere while Lola screamed and Merry laughed, her heart exploding, just like the lasagne.

~

Frankie didn't feel a single flutter of fear as she stood in front of Jan. And it had everything to do with the A4 envelope she was holding out as they eyeballed each other on the street down from Frankie's apartment.

The only good thing about having a stalker—you can always find them close to home.

"What's this, honeybun?" asked Jan, taking the envelope with a confident smile. "I hope it's not another pathetic legal attempt to keep me at a distance. You know I'm the legal expert here, hmm? Your last AVO was such a waste of everybody's time."

"No, Jan, I won't be needing those anymore," Frankie replied. "Actually, it's a gift, a way to repay you for the cake you baked the other day."

"Oh, that's not—"

"*And* for all the threats you made and the cars you destroyed and the *Herald* job you sabotaged."

"Aww," said Jan, tsking loudly. "Is someone feeling a little *grumpy?*"

Frankie held her ground and smiled back. It felt genuine for once. Must have looked it too because Jan's own smile began to splinter.

"Just read it in your own time," Frankie told her. "It's the story of my brilliant career. A sorry tale of how one woman overstepped, badly, and how another woman used it to blackmail her for years."

There was more tsking, but it felt like bluff this time. Jan said, "Frankie, darling, let's not get hysterical. Let's just sit down and—"

Frankie held a hand up like a stop sign. "Just open it, Jan. Read it from beginning to end. Then do me a favour? Leave me the fuck alone!"

And with that, Frankie turned and walked away.

As she did so, Jan called out to her over and over, as Frankie knew she would, but she didn't turn back. There was no turning back now.

Frankie had just opened a can of worms and was staring the little blighters in the face. The story of her career was all there in black and white. Jan had an early copy; the edited version would appear in the *Herald* tomorrow. A book version might come later.

It was really the story of a corrupt politician and Frankie's part in his downfall. Over two thousand words, Frankie explained to the world exactly what happened that night in Canberra when she was finishing her journalism degree. How she sat in a boozy bar and flirted her way into the politician's confidence, urging him to reveal his secrets and promising never to utter a word. How she'd left his bed and headed straight to her computer. Typed out an award-winning article that shattered his government and pushed the man to suicide. Leaving a wife and two children behind.

Frankie's story was a sage warning to other young, ambitious journalists. Ambition has consequences, and she'd lived with them long enough. Sure, the pollie was corrupt, but she should have uncovered his story honestly, with integrity.

Not with booze and sleaze.

And she should not have let her best friend hold it over her for the following decade. Because Jan was the only one who knew the true story—had used it to cement their relationship.

Well, not anymore! Frankie was finally smashing through the concrete, and it was an utterly liberating feeling. Her whole identity was no longer bonded to her journalistic career, and she revelled in the freedom for a few minutes as she sat in her car, staring across at Jan.

The other woman was still standing on the street, calico bag sprawled at her feet, envelope ripped open, frantically reading through the pages. Her head was shaking, her frizzy hair flying about, one finger following every sentence. Then she stopped dead and looked up blinking, eyes searching for Frankie.

When she found her, Jan just stared, gobsmacked, like she didn't know what to say. And Frankie shook her head at her, because there was nothing left. Their relationship was over.

And so Frankie drove away.

~

Martin, too, had been trying to make sense of his life, trying to understand a relationship that never felt right. Had wasted hours letting it eat him up inside and then more hours recently, trawling through library archives and Ancestry.com to fill in the missing pieces.

But he didn't really need any of it to understand his father. Had a hunch he'd known the truth all along.

"He's not my dad, is he?" he said to his mother as they sat, sharing steaks and salad out on his sun-drenched balcony. "Glenn Wicks is not my real father."

Olivia looked across at him, completely unsurprised, shook her head, offered a sympathetic smile. Probably wanted to know what took him so long. She had been hinting at it for months, then told him outright just the other night, and he'd chosen not to hear her words: *The real problem, Martin, is that you don't know your father. You don't know him at all.*"

Those words had echoed through his living room long after she'd left, yet it had taken a few days for them to sink in. Olivia wasn't being philosophical or theoretical or any of that authorly nonsense. She meant it *literally*. He did not know his father because he had never actually met the man.

Martin's biological father was a teenage bully who had got young Olivia pregnant, then fled at the first red line on the pregnancy test. She'd fled not long after, leaving baby Braxton with the only decent human who had bothered to hang around, her family having long given up on her. She left him with Glenn Wicks, her legal guardian at the time. Glenn was also her godfather, but Martin did not know that. He just thought Glenn was the high school janitor who got Olivia knocked up, and nobody had ever set him straight.

To young Martin—Braxton back then—Glenn was also a cold, hard father, as unsuited to parenting as bookish Braxton was to the shabby fishing village in which he'd grown up. So he fled the town and changed his name to Martin Chase the first chance he got.

"Are you going to go back and talk to Glenn properly this time?" asked his mum. "Or maybe try to find your real father? Write your real story this time?"

Martin shook his head on both counts. "I've started too many books lately, and all of them have gone nowhere. I think it's time to stop trying to write life stories and start living my own, hey?" He plucked at some marinated goat's cheese, popped some in his mouth. "It's time to find out who I am, Mum, regardless of my history. So I'm swearing off books. Not writing another one. At least not for a while."

"Good for you. Maybe now you can focus on love." Then she wriggled her feathery eyebrows and nudged her head downwards. "I can tell that woman who owns half this building has a bit of a crush."

He laughed. It felt good to laugh. "Yeah, Rachelle. She's an interesting one. Not my usual type but she's… Well, she's fascinating, Mum. Did you know she's a literary professor? At Sydney University? Did her thesis on true crimes carried out during the Tudor Dynasty of all things!" He smiled. "We have more in common than I realised."

"Good to see you going for brains this time," Olivia said, also smiling, "but what about *your* brain, Martin? You're a very smart lad. Won't you be bored if you don't write books? I mean, what are you going to do with yourself?"

Martin's smile turned mischievous. "Oh, I have a plan, Mother dearest. A very good plan indeed. In fact, it's already happening…"

EPILOGUE

Seagrave looked like a fairy-tale castle, all lit up with lights. The overgrown gardens had been tidied up and trimmed to perfection, and the front gate was now wide open as Kila's scratched-up four-wheel drive approached. He'd never seen Fort Knox look so welcoming.

Verity had invited all five sleuths to meet her at Seagrave for a celebratory dinner, and while Kila wasn't sure why *he* was being asked—he'd been as good as useless to her case—he was looking forward to seeing the others, and not just Frankie. He loved Merry like a sister now and had a soft spot for Earle too. Could even tolerate Martin these days, and that was saying something.

So he tried to push his recent woes from his mind as he drove down the steep driveway, then parked beside four familiar vehicles, each one as unique as its driver.

Inside the Yellow Room the gang were all gathered. Everyone except Verity, that is.

"Late as always," said Earle, getting up to shake Kila's hand.

"Kila!" squealed Merry, pushing Earle out of the way so she could smother him with one of her bear hugs.

"Hey, Festive, you look well," he replied, then he waved at Martin and Frankie before turning back to Merry's hand and pointing at one finger. "What's going on here?"

Merry giggled as she wriggled her fingers and flashed the sparkly diamond. "Don't get excited! It's just a commitment ring from Dougie. We're keeping things casual for now until my youngest is a bit older."

"Good for you," said Earle, who hadn't even noticed.

"*Commitment ring?*" said Frankie, jumping up to grab Merry's hand and inspect the bling. "What is this? The 1950s?"

"I think it's sweet," said Martin, and now Frankie was squinting at him.

"What's going on with you, smug author man? Why are you being so nice to Merry these days?"

"I'm always nice to Merry." Then, when her squint deepened, he added, "I just think she's a decent person and a really devoted parent, and it's only recently that I've realised how precious those things are."

"Awww, thank you, Martin," said Merry, tearing up.

"Speaking of commitment," said Earle. "I've got a wedding to go to next month. An odd one but I'll get used to it."

"Tess and Fiona are getting hitched?" squealed Merry, and he nodded.

Then he too was looking teary. He cleared his throat and glanced at Kila and then Frankie. "When are you two going to tie the knot?"

"*Earle!*" said Merry.

"It's okay, Festive," chuckled Kila. "I've proposed, she won't have me."

"We've only just got back together!" said Frankie, falling into his embrace. "Give us a minute. Besides, I am letting Kila move in. That's something."

"It's as good a start as any," said Earle.

Then all eyes turned to Martin.

He blinked back at them. "What? I'm married to this agency now, remember?"

"And we're glad to have you on board," said Merry. "And you too, Mad Dog."

Now all eyes were on Kila. He smiled. It was true, like Martin, he had agreed to officially join the sleuths and not just because he liked them. There was the minor matter of losing his own operating licence. Turns out smashing people's heads in—even confessed killer's heads—was a step too far even for his dynamo lawyer Sheila. She hadn't managed to save his bacon this time, but he was allowed to work under supervision from Earle. And if he behaved himself for a bit, he might eventually get his own licence back.

It suited them all just fine because the clients were now banging on their door. Finally! They had four clients lined up, and all of them were needy enough for Merry, with sufficient funds to keep Frankie in designer clothes.

"We really need to toast all of this," said Merry, glancing around. "Where did Verity get to?"

"In the kitchen, checking on dinner," said Earle.

"Hope it's not Irish stew," Frankie murmured below her breath, making the men chuckle and Merry look scandalised.

Verity was standing behind them in the doorway to the Yellow Room, tray of champagne in hand, watching the sleuths. Mesmerised. She didn't mind the joke, envied them their bond, but knew it was also the thing that had saved her, would save countless other clients too.

"I'm here!" she sang out as she stepped in. "And don't panic, Frankie, I'm not going to poison you, not tonight! I've brought in caterers. I think we could all do with the break."

Frankie had the decency to blush, and Verity laughed now as she handed out the champagne. When she got to Kila, she leaned in for a welcoming kiss, then looked surprised as he waved his glass away.

"I'm giving my liver a break for a bit," he told her, flashing Frankie a smile.

"Good for you," Verity said now.

Merry's eyes were two wet puddles again. "Oh Kila, honey! I heard about your *poor, poor sister*—"

"Nope, no time for that, Festive," Kila broke in. "I'm not bringing the mood down; we're here to celebrate Verity's release. Right, Verity?"

Verity passed him a soft drink from the mini-bar and shook her head. "Actually this is more of a housewarming."

Then she plonked in George's favourite armchair and gave them a knowing smile.

"*Housewarming?*" said Martin. "You're living here now?"

"I am." Now she was beaming.

"I thought Clem and Susan want to sell this place and start divvying up the loot," said Merry. "At least, that's what Charlie said."

"They did, until I came back with a better offer. I've waived my right to the bulk of the estate—all those other properties and shares and the company income—in exchange for just one thing."

Her eyes danced around the room again, and Frankie gasped. "You're seriously going to choose Seagrave over all of that?"

Verity laughed. "It's a staggering property in its own right, but sure, it's just a fraction of what George left me. Still it's all I want, it's all I need. I've loved this house from the moment I clapped eyes on it. I think part of the attraction of working with George was spending time in this extraordinary pile of bricks. It's always reminded me of the grand old homes of Ireland, and it's where I've always felt happiest, working beside George. And I think he would hate to see it sold off to strangers. So I'm keeping it."

"But then you'll have to keep working," said Frankie, and she laughed.

"I love working! I couldn't bear to wake up every day without purpose. Just look at how well that worked out for Susan! No, no, I've accepted a new position with Mr Fergerson. Not his PA— I won't ever work that hard again—but I will be working in the HR department, training up future assistants."

"Perfect job for you," said Martin.

"I know! And I get to come home every evening to this place."

"Aren't you worried about the ghosts?" whispered Merry.

She laughed again. "I think the ghosts should be worried about me!" Then her eyes saddened. "I want to create new memories here, happier memories..."

"You won't be lonely?" asked Earle.

"Perhaps, at the start. But I think it *will* be a start—the start of something new and exciting, and I'm hoping, if I'm lucky, I might be able to turn it back into the family home it was intended to be."

"Is there a fella on the scene we don't know about?" asked Kila, wriggling his bushy eyebrows.

"Or a woman!" said Frankie.

Verity smiled. "Not yet, but a girl can dream, can't she?"

"Oooh yes," said Merry, "especially one who lives in such a pretty castle." She raised her glass. "Here's to Verity building her own happy family!"

"No," said Verity, shaking her head firmly. "Here's to the Sleuths of Last Resort for making it all possible."

~~ *the end* ~~

ACKNOWLEDGEMENTS

A big thank-you to my readers, Michelle and Elaine, for taking the time to review my manuscript and provide such wonderful feedback. And it *does* take time, I understand that, so thanks for giving yours with such good humour and generosity.

Another clap on the back to Nimo for the stunning cover, and to Christian and Felix for allowing me to slip into my own La La Land without so much as a complaint. Thanks also to Annie at the Editing Pen for bringing me back out and getting this book fit to print. Love your work, Annie!

But to you, my devoted readers, I offer my warmest thanks. I've been self-publishing now for more than a decade, and you have been a constant source of inspiration and support. I could not have done it without you, and I don't say that lightly. Indie authors rely solely on readers and their reviews. We don't have a giant machine behind us, so it's all up to *you*. Every single time you select my book from the millions of wonderful books out there, you're giving me the income and impetus I need to keep going.

For that I am eternally grateful.

If you'd like to receive news, views and the odd free e-book, just sign up to my author newsletter: **calarmer.com**.

Lightning Source UK Ltd.
Milton Keynes UK
UKHW040627170223
417118UK00004B/207